THE FUTURE MAY BE— AND THEN AGAIN, IT MAY NOT. . . .

But it's possible to have a lot of fun looking at the possibilities . . .

At least if we do so through the cynical eye and skillful talents of the writers in this sparkling collection of stories that take a well-informed look at what might happen if technology continues unchecked and affluence progresses unabated. And people, of course.

That's really where it all starts—with *homo sapiens*, the most successful predator this planet has ever seen. Successful because, not being physically all that strong, he had to become smart to survive.

But that was in an earlier and simpler time. Lately, life has gotten pretty complicated; in fact, it's a moot point whether we aren't in the process of complicating ourselves out of existence. After all, what happens when the world's most savage predator has nothing left to prey on but himself?

Science Fiction by Frederik Pohl:

Short Stories

ALTERNATING CURRENTS
THE CASE AGAINST TOMORROW
TOMORROW TIMES SEVEN
THE MAN WHO ATE THE WORLD
TURN LEFT AT THURSDAY
THE ABOMINABLE EARTHMAN
DIGITS AND DASTARDS
DAY MILLION

Novels

SLAVE SHIP
EDGE OF THE CITY
DRUNKARD'S WALK
A PLAGUE OF PYTHONS

In collaboration with C. M. Kornbluth

THE SPACE MERCHANTS
SEARCH THE SKY
GLADIATOR-AT-LAW
PRESIDENTIAL YEAR
WOLFBANE
THE WONDER EFFECT

In collaboration with Jack Williamson

THE REEFS OF SPACE
STARCHILD

Anthologies

THE STAR series (No. 1 through No. 6)
STAR OF STARS

All published by Ballantine Books, Inc.

This is an original publication—not a reprint.

NIGHTMARE AGE

Edited by

FREDERIK POHL

BALLANTINE BOOKS • NEW YORK
An Intext Publisher

CONTENTS

How we are destroying our world—
Eco-Catastrophe! by Paul R. Ehrlich   3

—and will destroy it faster—
Uncalculated Risk, by Christopher Anvil   19

—by pollution, especially people pollution—
The Census Takers, by Frederik Pohl   39

—bringing disasters not only of scale but of quality—
The Marching Morons, by C. M. Kornbluth . . .   47

—until somehow we wipe ourselves out—
A Bad Day for Sales, by Fritz Leiber   83

—by war, famine, or the automobile—
Station HR972, by Kenneth Bulmer   91

—leading to a fragmented society—
X Marks the Pedwalk, by Fritz Leiber 105

—a long, hot lifetime of urban conflict—
Day of Truce, by Clifford D. Simak 111

—and in fact, separate nations—
Among the Bad Baboons, by Mack Reynolds . . 135

—over that or other issues—
The Luckiest Man in Denv, by C. M. Kornbluth 179

—until the curse of want gives way to the curse of plenty—
The Midas Plague, by Frederik Pohl 195

—and everything hits the fan at once—
New Apples in the Garden, by Kris Neville 259

—probably a lot sooner than you think!
The Year of the Jackpot, by Robert A. Heinlein 273

NIGHTMARE AGE

One of the things wrong with science-fiction writers is that they don't go far enough. When Cyril Kornbluth and I were writing *The Space Merchants* we put it in a world that was overpopulated, overpolluted and, our own inner hearts told us, over-exaggerated. We talked about people needing "soot extractor plugs" to walk in the city streets; we didn't think it would really happen, but since then, in the streets of New York and Los Angeles, I've seen people wearing absorbent masks for the same purpose. We talked about a world with too many people—the one we lived in had not much over two billion then—and now it's headed fast for four. And I remember that while we were kidding the advertising agencies we thought of writing in a sort of latter-day equivalent of the Boy Scouts, called the "Boy Advertisers" or something like that. We dismissed the idea as too silly. Shows what kind of prophets we were, because—not two centuries later, in fact not even two months later, but while the book was still on press one of the cereal companies came out with a "Junior Copywriter" boxtop offer.

So perhaps science-fiction writers should have a little more confidence in their predictions. If so, I urge upon everyone the gravest caution in making any long-term plans, because as the thirteen stories in this book show, there are nightmare episodes in the science-fiction writers' dreams of tomorrow.

Of course, the stories aren't meant to be taken as literal predictions. That, after all, is not the business of science fiction; what we are up to when we write S.F. is not telling you what *will* happen, but giving you a sort of shopping list of possible futures that *may* happen. There are many differences between these two kinds of crystal-gazing, and peculiarly enough, the second kind of glimpse at the future is far more valuable than the first. (After all, what's the use of a prediction that can't be made to fail to come true? The only reason for wanting to know what's ahead is to steer away from the events you don't like and toward the ones you do.)

Each of these stories, to put it as simply as possible, is one man's vision of some possible Apocalypse, and how likely it is that any or all of them will come true does not so much depend on how good the writer is as

1

a prophet as on how resolutely we human beings take the reins in our hands and start restoring this rather pleasant little planet we live on to something like the shape it was in when we moved in.

Since you are reading this book, it is likely that the hard-headed will chide you with being the kind of visionary who wastes his time on made-up stories about futures that haven't happened. Since you are a rational human being (at least, I think you are), it is probable that you are also deeply concerned about the mess *Homo Sap* is making of things, and so those same hard-heads are likely to scoff at you as an impractical soul who panics at the sight of a cast off gum wrapper and trembles at the thought of war.

Speaking personally, I have had about a bellyful of those hard-heads. I know them well. I've seen them hoarse with passion at a $500 sewer charge, but uncaring at a five million gallon dump of oil onto beaches. How wonderful it must be to be so hard-headed and unafraid! . . . Wonderful, that is, if you are, say, a chimpanzee, or better still, a gorilla; not so wonderful if you think you are a man, with a man's time-binding sense of cause and effect, of crime and punishment. Indeed, it is as gorillas that I think of some of my hard-headed friends. That sturdy, paranoid monster of the bush is so hard-headed and uncaring that he is alone among mammals in that he soils his own nest, excretes into his bower in his sleep, and wakes to a squinting ferocity a lot like a commuter's on Monday morning with his pelt filthy, his disposition atrocious, and his whole being consecrated to the philosophy of "I'm all right, Jack, and the hell with you." And what's more, as a species, he's on his way out. . . .

Well. They are not afraid, these gorillas and gorilloid men; they face the future with as little terror as they have understanding. I have a tagline I sometimes use when I'm lecturing; that applies to them. With apologies to that celebrated S.F. writer (As Easy as ABC, With the Night Mail, etc.) Rudyard Kipling, it goes like this:

If you can keep your head when all about you
Are losing theirs—
Then you really ought to consider the possibility that you just haven't understood what the problem is.

Paul Ehrlich is not a science-fiction writer, but it happens I met him first at a science-fiction convention, which reveals him to be at least a person of reasonable open-mindedness on the subject. What he is is a scientist. More than that, he is a prophet. A couple thousand years ago he would have been thundering imprecations at the Moabites from the branches of a shittah tree. Today he tells the world that it is destroying itself from the studio of the Johnny Carson show.

But if he is not a science-fiction writer, he is *like* a science-fiction writer in that his warnings are cast in the form of something as much like a science-fiction story as—.

ECO-CATASTROPHE!

Paul R. Ehrlich

The end of the ocean came late in the summer of 1979, and it came even more rapidly than the biologists had expected. There had been signs for more than a decade, commencing with the discovery in 1968 that DDT slows down photosynthesis in marine plant life. It was announced in a short paper in the technical journal *Science,* but to ecologists it smacked of doomsday. They knew that all life in the sea depends on photosynthesis, the chemical process by which green plants bind the sun's energy and make it available to living things. And they knew that DDT and similar chlorinated hydrocarbons had polluted the entire surface of the earth, including the sea.

But that was only the first of many signs. There had been the final gasp of the whaling industry in 1973, and the end of the Peruvian anchovy fishery in 1975. Indeed, a score of other fisheries had disappeared quietly from overexploitation and various eco-catastrophes by 1977. The term "eco-catastrophe" was coined by a California ecologist in 1969 to describe the most spectacular of man's attacks on the systems which sustain his life. He drew his

3

inspiration from the Santa Barbara offshore oil disaster of that year, and from the news which spread among naturalists that virtually all of the Golden State's seashore bird life was doomed because of chlorinated hydrocarbon interference with its reproduction. Eco-catastrophes in the sea became increasingly common in the early 1970's. Mysterious "blooms" of previously rare microorganisms began to appear in offshore waters. Red tides—killer outbreaks of a minute single-celled plant—returned to the Florida Gulf coast and were sometimes accompanied by tides of other exotic hues.

It was clear by 1975 that the entire ecology of the ocean was changing. A few types of phytoplankton were becoming resistant to chlorinated hydrocarbons and were gaining the upper hand. Changes in the phytoplankton community led inevitably to changes in the community of zooplankton, the tiny animals which eat the phytoplankton. These changes were passed on up the chains of life in the ocean to the herring, plaice, cod, and tuna. As the diversity of life in the ocean diminished, its stability also decreased.

Other changes had taken place by 1975. Most ocean fishes that returned to freshwater to breed, like the salmon, had become extinct, their breeding streams so dammed up and polluted that their powerful homing instinct only resulted in suicide. Many fishes and shellfishes that bred in restricted areas along the coasts followed them as onshore pollution escalated.

By 1977 the annual yield of fish from the sea was down to 30 million metric tons, less than one-half the per capita catch of a decade earlier. This helped malnutrition to escalate sharply in a world where an estimated 50 million people per year were already dying of starvation. The United Nations attempted to get all chlorinated hydrocarbon insecticides banned on a worldwide basis, but the move was defeated by the United States. This opposition was generated primarily by the American petrochemical industry, operating hand in glove with its subsidiary, the United States Department of Agriculture. Together they persuaded the government to oppose the U.N. move—which was not difficult since most Americans believed that Russia and China were more in need of fish products than was the United States. The United Nations also attempted to get fishing nations to adopt strict and enforced catch limits to preserve dwindling stocks. This move was blocked by Russia, who, with the most modern electronic equipment, was in the best position to glean what was left in the sea. It was, curiously, on the very day in 1977 when the Soviet Union announced its refusal that another ominous article appeared in *Science*. It announced that incident solar radiation had been so reduced by worldwide air pollution that serious effects on the world's vegetation could be expected.

Apparently it was a combination of ecosystem destabilization, sunlight reduction, and a rapid escalation in chlorinated hydrocarbon pollution from massive Thanodrin applications which triggered the ultimate catastrophe. Seventeen huge Soviet-financed Thanodrin plants were operating in underdeveloped countries by 1978. They had been part of a massive Russian "aid offensive" designed to fill the gap caused by the collapse of America's ballyhooed "Green Revolution."

It became apparent in the early '70s that the "Green Revolution" was more talk than substance. Distribution of high yield "miracle" grain seeds had caused temporary local spurts in agricultural production. Simultaneously, excellent weather had produced record harvests. The combination permitted bureaucrats, especially in the United States Department of Agriculture and the Agency for International Development (AID), to reverse their previous pessimism and indulge in an outburst of optimistic propaganda about staving off famine. They raved about the approaching transformation of agriculture in the underdeveloped countries (UDCs). The reason for the propaganda reversal was never made clear. Most historians agree that a combination of utter ignorance of ecology, a desire to justify past errors, and pressure from agro-industry (which was eager to sell pesticides, fertilizers, and farm machinery to the UDCs and agencies helping the UDCs) was behind the campaign. Whatever the motivation, the results were clear. Many concerned people, lacking the expertise to see through the Green Revolution drivel, relaxed. The population-food crisis was "solved."

But reality was not long in showing itself. Local famine persisted in northern India even after good weather brought an end to the ghastly Bihar famine of the mid-'60s. East Pakistan was next, followed by a resurgence of general famine in northern India. Other foci of famine rapidly developed in Indonesia, the Philippines, Malawi, the Congo, Egypt, Colombia, Ecuador, Honduras, the Dominican Republic, and Mexico.

Everywhere hard realities destroyed the illusion of the Green Revolution. Yields dropped as the progressive farmers who had first accepted the new seeds found that their higher yields brought lower prices—effective demand (hunger plus cash) was not sufficient in poor countries to keep prices up. Less progressive farmers, observing this, refused to make the extra effort required to cultivate the "miracle" grains. Transport systems proved inadequate to bring the necessary fertilizer to the fields where the new and extremely fertilizer-sensitive grains were being grown. The same systems were also inadequate to move produce to markets. Fertilizer plants were not built fast enough, and most of the underdeveloped countries could not scrape together funds to purchase supplies, even on concessional terms. Finally, the inevitable happened, and pests began to reduce yields in even the most carefully cultivated fields. Among the first were the famous "miracle rats" which invaded Philippine "miracle rice" fields early in 1969. They were quickly followed by many insects and viruses, thriving on the relatively pest-susceptible new grains, encouraged by the vast and dense plantings, and rapidly acquiring resistance to the chemicals used against them. As chaos spread until even the most obtuse agriculturists and economists realized that the Green Revolution had turned brown, the Russians stepped in.

In retrospect it seems incredible that the Russians, with the American mistakes known to them, could launch an even more incompetent program of aid to the underdeveloped world. Indeed, in the early 1970's there were cynics in the United States who claimed that outdoing the stupidity of American foreign aid would be physically impossible. Those critics were, however, obviously unaware that the Russians had been busily destroying their own environment for many years. The virtual disappearance of sturgeon from Russian rivers caused a great shortage of caviar by 1970. A standard joke among Russian scientists at that time was that they had created an artificial caviar which was indistinguishable from the real thing—except by taste. At any rate the Soviet Union, observing with interest the progressive deterioration of relations between the UDCs and the United States, came up with a solution. It had recently developed what it claimed was the ideal insecticide, a highly lethal chlorinated hydrocarbon complexed with a special agent for penetrating the external skeletal armor of insects. Announcing that the new pesticide, called Thanodrin, would truly produce a Green Revolution, the Soviets entered into negotiations with various UDCs for the construction of massive Thanodrin factories. The USSR would bear all the costs; all it wanted in return were certain trade and military concessions.

It is interesting now, with the perspective of years, to examine in some detail the reasons why the UDCs welcomed the Thanodrin plan with such open arms. Government officials in these countries ignored the protests of their own scientists that Thanodrin would not solve the problems which plagued them. The governments now knew that the basic cause of their problems was overpopulation, and that these problems had been exacerbated by the dullness, daydreaming, and cupidity endemic to all governments. They knew that only population control and limited development aimed primarily at agriculture could have spared them the horrors they now faced. They knew it, but they were not about to admit it. How much easier it was simply to accuse the Americans of failing to give them proper aid; how much simpler to accept the Russian panacea.

And then there was the general worsening of relations between the United States and the UDCs. Many things had contributed to this. The situation in America in the first half of the 1970's deserves our close scrutiny. Being more dependent on imports for raw materials than the Soviet Union, the United States had, in the early 1970's, adopted more and more heavy-handed policies in order to insure continuing supplies. Military adventures in Asia and Latin America had further lessened the international credibility of the United States as a great defender of freedom—an image which had begun to deteriorate rapidly during the pointless and fruitless Viet Nam conflict. At home, acceptance of the carefully manufactured image lessened dramatically, as even the more romantic and chauvinistic citizens began to understand the role of the military and the industrial system in what John Kenneth Galbraith had aptly named "The New Industrial State."

At home in the USA the early '70s were traumatic times. Racial violence grew and the habitability of the cities diminished, as nothing substantial was done to ameliorate either racial inequities or urban blight. Welfare rolls grew as automation and general technological progress forced more and more people into the category of "unemployable." Simultaneously a taxpayers' revolt occurred. Although there was not enough money to build the schools, roads, water systems, sewage systems, jails, hospitals, urban transit lines, and all the other amenities needed to support a burgeoning population, Americans refused to tax themselves more heavily. Starting in Youngstown, Ohio, in 1969 and followed closely by Richmond, California, community after community was forced to close its schools or curtail educational operations for lack of funds. Water supplies, already marginal in quality and quantity in many places by 1970, deteriorated quickly. Water rationing occurred in 1,723 municipalities in the summer of 1974, and hepatitis and epidemic dysentery rates climbed about 500 percent between 1970 and 1974.

Air pollution continued to be the most obvious manifestation of environmental deterioration. It was, by 1972, quite literally in the eyes of all Americans. The year 1973 saw not only the New York and Los Angeles smog disasters, but also the publication of the surgeon general's massive report on air pollution and health. The public had been partially prepared for the worst by the publicity given to the U.N. pollution conference held in 1972. Deaths in the late '60s caused by smog were well known to scientists, but the public had ignored them because they mostly involved the early demise of the old and sick rather than people dropping dead on the freeways. But suddenly our citizens were faced with nearly 200,000 corpses and massive documentation that they could be the next to die from respiratory disease. They were not ready for that scale of disaster. After all, the U.N. conference had not predicted that accumulated air pollution would make the planet uninhabitable until almost 1990. The population was terrorized as TV screens became filled with scenes of horror from the disaster areas. Especially vivid was NBC's coverage of hundreds of unattended people choking out their lives outside of New York's hospitals. Terms like nitrogen oxide, acute bronchitis and cardiac arrest began to have real meaning for most Americans.

The ultimate horror was the announcement that chlorinated hydrocarbons were now a major constituent of air pollution in all American cities. Autopsies of smog disaster victims revealed an average chlorinated hydrocarbon load in fatty tissue equivalent to 26 parts per million of DDT. In October, 1973, the Department of Health, Education and Welfare announced studies which showed unequivocally that increasing death rates from hypertension, cirrhosis of the liver, liver cancer, and a series of other diseases had resulted from the chlorinated hydrocarbon load. They estimated that Americans born since 1964 (when DDT usage began) now had a life expectancy of only 49 years, and predicted that if current patterns continued, this expectancy would reach 42 years by 1980, when it might level out. Plunging insurance stocks triggered a stock market panic. The president of a major pesticide went on television to "publicly eat a teaspoonful of DDT" (it was really powdered milk) and announce that HEW had been infiltrated by Communists. Other giants of the petro-chemical industry, attempting to dispute the indisputable evidence, launched a massive pressure campaign on Congress to force HEW to "get out of agriculture's business." They were aided by the agrochemical journals, which had decades of experience in misleading the public about the benefits and dangers of pesticides. But by now the public realized that it had been duped. The Nobel Prize for medicine and physiology was given to Drs. J. L. Radomski and W. B. Deichmann, who in the late 1960's had pioneered in the documentation of the long-term lethal effects of chlorinated hydrocarbons. A presidential commission with unimpeachable credentials directly accused the agro-chemical complex of "condemning many millions of Americans to an early death." The year 1973 was the year in which Americans finally came to understand the direct threat to their existence posed by environmental deterioration.

And 1973 was also the year in which most people finally comprehended the indirect threat. Even the president of Union Oil Company and several other industrialists publicly stated their concern over the reduction of bird populations which had resulted from pollution by DDT and other chlorinated hydrocarbons. Insect populations boomed because they were resistant to most pesticides and had been freed, by the incompetent use of those pesticides, from most of their natural enemies. Rodents swarmed over crops, multiplying rapidly in the absence of predatory birds. The effect of pests on the wheat crop was especially disastrous in the summer of 1973, since that was also the year of the great drought. Most of us can remember the shock which greeted the announcement by atmospheric physicists that the shift of the jet stream which had caused the drought was probably permanent. It signalled the birth of the Midwestern desert. Man's air-polluting activities had by then caused gross changes in climatic patterns. The news, of course, played hell with commodity and stock markets. Food prices skyrocketed, as savings were poured into hoarded canned goods. Official assurances that food supplies would remain ample fell on deaf ears, and even the government showed signs of nervousness when California migrant field workers went out on strike again in protest against the continued use of pesticides by growers. The strike burgeoned into farm burning and riots. The workers, calling themselves "The Walking Dead," demanded immediate compensation for their shortened lives, and crash research programs to attempt to lengthen them.

It was in the same speech in which President Edward Kennedy, after much delay, finally declared a national emergency and called out the National Guard to harvest California's crops that the first mention of population control was made. Kennedy pointed out that the United States would no longer be able to offer any food aid to other nations and was likely to suffer food shortages herself. He suggested that, in view of the manifest failure of the Green Revolution, the only hope of the UDCs lay in population control. His statement, you will recall, created an uproar in the underdeveloped countries. Newspaper editorials accused the United States of wishing to prevent small countries from becoming large nations and thus threatening American hegemony. Politicians asserted that President Kennedy was a "creature of the giant drug combine" that wished to shove its pills down every woman's throat.

Among Americans, religious opposition to population control was very slight. Industry in general also backed the idea. Increasing poverty in the UDCs was both destroying markets and threatening supplies of raw materials. The seriousness of the raw material situation had been brought home during the congressional hard re-

sources hearings in 1971. The exposure of the ignorance
of the cornucopian economists had been quite a spectacle
—a spectacle brought into virtually every American's
home in living color. Few would forget the distinguished
geologist from the University of California who suggested
that economists be legally required to learn at least the
most elementary facts of geology. Fewer still would forget
that an equally distinguished Harvard economist added
that they might be required to learn some economics too.
The overall message was clear: America's resource situation was bad and bound to get worse. The hearings had
led to a bill requiring the Departments of State, Interior,
and Commerce to set up a joint resource procurement
council with the express purpose of "insuring that proper
consideration of American resource needs be an integral
part of American foreign policy."

Suddenly the United States discovered that it had a
national consensus: population control was the only possible salvation of the underdeveloped world. But that same
consensus led to heated debate. How could the UDCs be
persuaded to limit their populations, and should not the
United States lead the way by limiting its own? Members
of the intellectual community wanted America to set an
example. They pointed out that the United States was in
the midst of a new baby boom: her birth rate, well over
20 per thousand per year, and her growth rate of over
one percent per annum were among the very highest of
the developed countries. They detailed the deterioration
of the American physical and psychic environments, the
growing health threats, the impending food shortages, and
the insufficiency of funds for desperately needed public
works. They contended that the nation was clearly unable
or unwilling to properly care for the people it already
had. What possible reason could there be, they queried,
for adding any more? Besides, who would listen to requests by the United States for population control when
that nation did not control her own profligate reproduction?

Those who opposed population controls for the U.S. were equally vociferous. The military-industrial complex, with its all-too-human mixture of ignorance and avarice, still saw strength and prosperity in numbers. Baby food magnates, already worried by the growing nitrate pollution of their products, saw their market disappearing. Steel manufacturers saw a decrease in aggregate demand and slippage for that holy of holies, the Gross National Product. And military men saw, in the growing population-food-environment crisis, a serious threat to their carefully nurtured cold war. In the end, of course, economic arguments held sway, and the "inalienable right of every American couple to determine the size of its family," a freedom invented for the occasion in the early '70s, was not compromised.

The population control bill, which was passed by Congress early in 1974 was quite a document, nevertheless. On the domestic front, it authorized an increase from 100 to 150 million dollars in funds for "family planning" activities. This was made possible by a general feeling in the country that the growing army on welfare needed family planning. But the gist of the bill was a series of measures designed to impress the need for population control on the UDCs. All American aid to countries with overpopulation problems was required by law to consist in part of population control assistance. In order to receive any assistance each nation was required not only to accept the population control aid, but also to match it according to a complex formula. "Overpopulation" itself was defined by a formula based on U.N. statistics, and the UDCs were required not only to accept aid, but also to show progress in reducing birth rates. Every five years the status of the aid program for each nation was to be re-evaluated.

The reaction to the announcement of this program dwarfed the response to President Kennedy's speech. A coalition of UDCs attempted to get the U.N. General Assembly to condemn the United States as a "genetic aggressor." Most damaging of all to the American cause was the famous "25 Indians and a dog" speech by Mr.

Shankarnarayan, Indian Ambassador to the U.N. Shankarnarayan pointed out that for several decades the United States, with less than six percent of the people of the world, had consumed roughly 50 percent of the raw materials used every year. He described vividly America's contribution to worldwide environmental deterioration, and he scathingly denounced the miserly record of United States foreign aid as "unworthy of a fourth-rate power, let alone the most powerful nation on earth."

It was the climax of his speech, however, which most historians claim once and for all destroyed the image of the United States. Shankarnarayan informed the assembly that the average American family dog was fed more animal protein per week than the average Indian got in a month. "How do you justify taking fish from protein-starved Peruvians and feeding them to your animals?" he asked. "I contend," he concluded, "that the birth of an American baby is a greater disaster for the world than that of 25 Indian babies." When the applause had died away, Mr. Sorensen, the American representative, made a speech which said essentially that "other countries look after their own self-interest, too." When the vote came, the United States was condemned.

This condemnation set the tone of U.S.-UDC relations at the time the Russian Thanodrin proposal was made. The proposal seemed to offer the masses in the UDCs an opportunity to save themselves and humiliate the United States at the same time; and in human affairs, as we all know, biological realities could never interfere with such an opportunity. The scientists were silenced, the politicians said yes; the Thanodrin plants were built, and the results were what any beginning ecology student could have predicted. At first Thanodrin seemed to offer excellent control of many pests. True, there was a rash of human fatalities from improper use of the lethal chemical, but, as Russian technical advisors were prone to note, these were more than compensated for by increased yields. Thanodrin use skyrocketed throughout the underdeveloped world. The Mikoyan design group developed a dependable, cheap agricultural aircraft which the Soviets donated to the effort in large numbers. MIG sprayers became even more common in UDCs than MIG interceptors.

Then the troubles began. Insect strains with cuticles resistant to Thanodrin penetration began to appear. And as streams, rivers, fish culture ponds and onshore waters became rich in Thanodrin, more fisheries began to disappear. Bird populations were decimated. The sequence of events was standard for broadcast use of a synthetic pesticide: great success at first, followed by removal of natural enemies and development of resistance by the pest. Populations of crop-eating insects in areas treated with Thanodrin made steady comebacks and soon became more abundant than ever. Yields plunged, while farmers in their desperation increased the Thanodrin dose and shortened the time between treatments. Death from Thanodrin poisoning became common. The first violent incident occurred in the Canete Valley of Peru, where farmers had suffered a similar chlorinated hydrocarbon disaster in the mid-'50s. A Russian advisor serving as an agricultural pilot was assaulted and killed by a mob of enraged farmers in January, 1978. Trouble spread rapidly during 1978, especially after the word got out that two years earlier Russia herself had banned the use of Thanodrin at home because of its serious effects on ecological systems. Suddenly Russia, and not the United States, was the *bête noir* in the UDCs. "Thanodrin parties" became epidemic, with farmers, in their ignorance, dumping carloads of Thanodrin concentrate into the sea. Russian advisors fled, and four of the Thanodrin plants were leveled to the ground. Destruction of the plants in Rio and Calcutta led to hundreds of thousands of gallons of Thanodrin concentrate being dumped directly into the sea.

Mr. Shankarnarayan again rose to address the U.N., but this time it was Mr. Potemkin, representative of the Soviet Union, who was on the hot seat. Mr. Potemkin heard his nation described as the greatest mass killer of all time as Shankarnarayan predicted at least 30 million deaths from crop failures due to overdependence on Thanodrin. Russia was accused of "chemical aggression," and the General Assembly, after a weak reply by Potemkin, passed a vote of censure.

It was in January, 1979, that huge blooms of a previously unknown variety of diatom were reported off the coast of Peru. The blooms were accompanied by a massive die-off of sea life and of the pathetic remainder of the birds which had once feasted on the anchovies of the area. Almost immediately, another huge bloom was reported in the Indian Ocean, centering around the Seychelles, and then a third in the South Atlantic off the African coast. Both of these were accompanied by spectacular die-offs of marine animals. Even more ominous were growing reports of fish and bird kills at oceanic points where there were no spectacular blooms. Biologists were soon able to explain the phenomenon: the diatom had evolved an enzyme which broke down Thanodrin; that enzyme also produced a breakdown product which interfered with the transmission of nerve impulses, and was therefore lethal to animals. Unfortunately, the biologists could suggest no way of repressing the poisonous diatom bloom in time. By September, 1979, all important animal life in the sea was extinct. Large areas of coastline had to be evacuated, as windrows of dead fish created a monumental stench.

But stench was the least of man's problems. Japan and China were faced with almost instant starvation from a total loss of the seafood on which they were so dependent. Both blamed Russia for their situation and demanded immediate mass shipments of food. Russia had none to send. On October 13, Chinese armies attacked Russia on a broad front. . . .

A pretty grim scenario. Unfortunately, we're a long way into it already. Everything mentioned as happening before 1970 has actually occurred; much of the rest is based on projections of trends already appearing. Evidence that pesticides have long-term lethal effects on human beings has started to accumulate, and recently

Robert Finch, Secretary of the Department of Health, Education and Welfare, expressed his extreme apprehension about the pesticide situation. Simultaneously the petrochemical industry continues its unconscionable poison-peddling. For instance, Shell Chemical has been carrying on a high-pressure campaign to sell the insecticide Azodrin to farmers as a killer of cotton pests. They continue their program even though they know that Azodrin is not only ineffective, but often *increases* the pest density. They've covered themselves nicely in an advertisement which states, "Even if an overpowering migration [*sic*] develops, the flexibility of Azodrin lets you regain control fast. Just increase the dosage according to label recommendations." It's a great game—get people to apply the poison and kill the natural enemies of the pests. Then blame the increased pests on "migration" and sell even more pesticide!

Right now fisheries are being wiped out by overexploitation, made easy by modern electronic equipment. The companies producing the equipment know this. They even boast in advertising that only their equipment will keep fishermen in business until the final kill. Profits must obviously be maximized in the short run. Indeed, Western society is in the process of completing the rape and murder of the planet for economic gain. And, sadly, most of the rest of the world is eager for the opportunity to emulate our behavior. But the underdeveloped peoples will be denied that opportunity—the days of plunder are drawing inexorably to a close.

Most of the people who are going to die in the greatest cataclysm in the history of man have already been born. More than three and a half billion people already populate our moribund globe, and about half of them are hungry. Some 10 to 20 million will starve to death *this year*. In spite of this, the population of the earth will have increased by 70 million in 1969. For mankind has artificially lowered the death rate of the human population, while in general, birth rates have remained high. With the input side of the population system in high gear and the output side slowed down, our fragile planet has filled with people at an incredible rate. It took several million years for the population to reach a total of two billion people in 1930, while a *second two billion will have been added by 1975!* By that time some experts feel that food shortages will have escalated the present level of world hunger and starvation in famines of unbelievable proportions. Other experts, more optimistic, think the ultimate food-population collision will not occur until the decade of the 1980's. Of course more massive famine may be avoided if other events cause a prior rise in the human death rate.

Both worldwide plague and thermonuclear war are made more probable as population growth continues. These, along with famine, make up the trio of potential "death rate solutions" to the population problem—solutions in which the birth rate-death rate imbalance is redressed by a rise in the death rate rather than by a lowering of the birth rate. Make no mistake about it, *the imbalance will be redressed.* The shape of the population-growth curve is one familiar to the biologist. It is the outbreak part of an outbreak-crash sequence. A population grows rapidly in the presence of abundant resources, finally runs out of food or some other necessity and crashes to a low level or extinction. Man is not only running out of food, he is also destroying the life support systems of the Spaceship Earth. The situation was recently summarized very succinctly: "It is the top of the ninth inning. Man, always a threat at the plate, has been hitting Nature hard. It is important to remember, however, that NATURE BATS LAST."

If Paul Ehrlich's scenario is somehow averted and we manage to stop all the *known* destruction that the human race is carrying on, are we safe for all time? Not exactly. Not as long as a clerk's blunder drops one chunk of plutonium into our atmosphere and a blown oxygen tank and an aborted Apollo 13 mission drops another. Not as long as thalidomide can come on the market as it did in Europe, or the SST can destroy our eardrums here. We will always have the unexpected. Sometimes the unexpected may take trivial forms (those walking catfish aren't all *that* bad). But once in a while it will be serious, and very likely now and then it may be catastrophic. That's the price we pay for an occasional—

UNCALCULATED RISK

Christopher Anvil

Lieutenant general Lyell Berenger held to the opinion that life would have been much simpler if the human race had never invented Science. General Berenger occasionally tried, as he was trying tonight, to prove this proposition to a friend or acquaintance. Berenger was vaguely aware, as he talked, of the high-pitched laughter in the room, the occasional clink of glasses, and the surflike murmuring of voices around him. In his hand he absently held a glass, two-thirds of the contents of which he had tossed into the fireplace at the first opportunity, and which he had now forgotten. His attention was concentrated on his friend, Senator Vail, who was trying inconspicuously to unload his own glass into a pot holding a kind of lacy fernlike plant.

"In the old days," Berenger said, noting with suspicion the tolerant smile on the senator's face, "back, say, in the time of the early Romans, a soldier's job was difficult and demanding. The army had to be well equipped, strong, and well-trained. The general commanding needed to be

19

alert, and to know his job thoroughly. The same holds true today. The difference is this: in those days virtue was rewarded. If a soldier did what he was supposed to, the odds were very great that he would win. In modern times, it's all a hodgepodge. The cause, as the cause of a lot of our troubles, is this pet of yours, Science."

Vail smiled. "Come on, now, Lyell, don't tell me you aren't happy whenever one of our technical teams beats the Russians to the punch."

Berenger nodded. "Yes, and I'm grateful that we were the first to get nuclear fission. But think back a while. How did it seem when the Germans came out with rocket-planes, flying bombs, and V-2s? The trouble is that you can't predict who is going to get what, or when. Military calculations can be completely unhinged by some mild individual who hardly knows one end of a gun from the other, and cares less."

"True," said Vail, who had now succeeded in transferring half his drink to the hapless plant, "but what is going on is doing more than merely upset your plans. Each scientific advance increases the power and well-being of the race as a whole."

"I don't object to Science, within bounds," said Berenger. "But I have reservations as to its violent, uncontrolled, headlong nature. Look, Vail, you speak of 'beating the Russians to the punch.' Doubtless they think of it the same way. It's a race. But where *to?*"

"To greater power and well-being. Obviously, the greater our capabilities, the more we can do. If we race someone, that means we both get there faster. You want to work it all out before we take a step. At that rate, we'd still be figuring out the implications of gunpowder, and wild-eyed theorists would be making radical predictions to the effect that some day in the next two thousand years steam engines would begin to replace the horse—in certain applications."

Berenger nodded. "It would probably be just that bad. But now consider one aspect of this 'race' you like so much. It is *uncontrollable*. Because it is a competition, neither side can stop. The side that stops, loses. Therefore each side *must* go on. Isn't that so?"

"Right. And a good thing."

O.K. But when you speak of winning an ordinary race, you have in mind a definite physical goal. Suppose, instead, you took a group of men out into the wilderness and told them simply to run, and if any one got ten yards ahead of his nearest opponent, that one would instantly win, and could impose his will, if he so desired, on the other runners. That is more what this race is like, isn't it?"

Vail scowled. "Yes. Go on."

"Ten yards," said Berenger, "is no great distance. In the race we're in, a small definite lead can be conclusive. Now, if either side takes the lead, the other must run faster. Running faster, it is likely to cut down the lead the other side has, which will in turn force the other side to run faster. So it goes."

Vail nodded. "There's something to what you say. It could, in theory, get out of control. But actually, of course, both sides are pretty hard-headed, and this, combined with the natural inertia of human beings, keeps the process from running out of control."

Berenger said, "It may be that the *process* isn't running out of control. But in any race where you are not running on a beaten track, there is the possibility of a sharp surprise to the individual runners. The runners may go very fast, but they take as their standard of performance their position relative to the other runners. None of the runners knows the territory ahead. Now, what happens if, during some desperate spurt, the leader suddenly arrives at the edge of a ravine? *Then* what?"

"A purely rhetorical question," said Vail, smiling. "The scientists are often afraid the military men will do something irresponsible, so I shouldn't be surprised to find a military man afraid the scientists will do something irresponsible. Meanwhile, both sides think politicians are irresponsible. Nobody thinks the other man knows his business. But he does."

"You've missed the point," said Berenger. "It isn't irresponsible for a scientist to make discoveries. That's his business. But making discoveries is like running through unknown territory. Do it too fast and sooner or later, you're likely to get a severe fall."

Vail nodded, grinning. "We politicians learn to use words, but to look to reality. The situation you describe *sounds* convincing, but it doesn't fit in with reality. Tell you what. If you're free next weekend, why don't you come on out to Iowa with me and see a scientist in action on a real project. It's part of the race between us and the Soviets. Nothing spectacular, but pretty effective all the same. It'll get your head down out of the clouds and onto solid ground. What do you say?"

Berenger smiled. "I don't think I want my head on 'solid ground,' Vail, but, yes, I can get away next weekend. I'll take you up on that."

That was how, the next weekend, Lyell Berenger came to find himself on the edge of a flat windy field with Senator Vail and a short, broad man who'd been introduced as Dr. Franklin Green. The college tower was visible in the distance, but Dr. Green had eyes only for the field, where a tractor was churning methodically back and forth.

"Soil texture," said Dr. Green, stopping to pick up a handful of the rich-looking soil and crumbling it in his fingers, "soil texture is an important matter to the farmer. If the texture is right, rainfall is absorbed, the working of the soil is easy, and plant development takes place naturally. With the wrong texture, everything goes wrong. Now, you've seen this. Let me show you the control plot."

They plodded across the yielding, somewhat spongy soil to a strip of arid ground with a surface like cracked cement. Dr. Green looked at them significantly. "*This* plot wasn't treated. The one you've just seen was. Suppose you gentlemen were farmers. Which plot would you rather farm?"

Berenger glanced from the soft, yielding, even-textured

plot to the hard-surfaced plot. Something began vaguely to disturb him. He heard Vail say, "Well, I have no doubt which *I* would rather work, doctor. Is your texturing agent so effective on *all* soils?"

"Not entirely, I'm sorry to say. But we are working at it steadily. We expect to have it ready for commercial use by early next year. First we have to make further tests on a variety of soil types."

Vail said, "What do you expect will be the effect on farming in general?"

Dr. Green said, with a hard effort at modesty, "It should increase the yield, in some cases very considerably."

Berenger and Vail were on the plane the next day before Vail got around to saying triumphantly, "What did you think of *that?*"

Berenger said, "I thought we already had surpluses."

"Yes," said Vail, "and there you hit the sore point on the head." He lowered his voice, "But, you see, some of our allies and a considerable number of the neutrals don't share that problem. They desperately need food. It takes a long time to increase yield by conventional methods. You have irrigation projects, huge quantities of farm machinery to ship overseas, and all kinds of technical training programs to carry out. It's a slow process; it may go head-on against local prejudices; and while you're carrying it out, people are starving. But this new process holds out the possibility of increasing yields by, say, fifteen percent the first year. It will fit right in with local customs, since nearly everyone is used to adding manure to soil. It isn't expensive; it won't use much shipping space; and it is *immediate*. Now what do you have to say?"

Berenger was silent for a while. Finally he said, "I'll be frank with you. There's something about it I don't like."

"Too big an advance?" Vail looked at him curiously.

Berenger shook his head. "I don't know what it is. I just have an uneasy feeling about it."

Vail smiled, and settled back on his seat. "Not I," he said. "It makes *me* very happy."

Berenger was back at work the next day, and the incident soon slipped into the back of his mind. As the months rolled by, with shifts and changes in foreign affairs, new surprises in technology, and the continuing need to fit these variables into the overall picture, he in time forgot the incident entirely. He was reminded of it by a newspaper article, which first discussed the development in general, then went on:

> "Thus Dr. Green's development of the Catalytic Texturing Agent will largely do away with problems caused by too-heavy soils. Best of all, from the point of expense, the effect is permanent. The texturing agent, operating on an entirely new principle of ionic interchange, actually generates more of itself over the course of time from the chemicals of the surrounding soil. The proper 'dosage' is scientifically determined by soil analysis, to assure that regeneration of the catalyst proceeds at a rate just sufficient to restore that used up in the course of the soil-conditioning operation. In explaining this, Dr. Green, winner of the McGinnis Medal for Agricultural Chemistry, remarked . . ."

Berenger read back carefully over the article, then, frowning, read on:

> ". . . Winner of the McGinnis Medal for Agricultural Chemistry, remarked, 'Any catalyst is theoretically capable of handling an unlimited quantity of material. But in practice, the catalyst usually becomes 'poisoned' and ceases to operate. In this instance, the poisoning is offset by the generation of new catalyst. This effect must not, of course, be allowed to proceed too rapidly, or it could have most disagreeable consequences. That is easily avoided by

the use of proper initial testing procedures, as has been demonstrated repeatedly in field tests in all types of soil . . ."

Berenger looked up from the paper, sat back, and thought it over. Scowling, he glanced at his watch, picked up a phone, and tried to call Vail. Vail, it developed, was away on a trip, but would be back by early next week. Berenger put the phone down again, thought some more, then picked the phone up and called long-distance for Dr. Franklin Green. In due time, Green came on the line. Berenger first reminded Green of his previous visit, then said guardedly, "I don't ask you to reveal anything that might be classified, doctor. You understand that?"

"Of course," came Green's voice. "There isn't much that *is* classified about this project, general. It's all perfectly straight agricultural chemistry. We've evolved a new twist that should be useful, that's all."

"Yes," said Berenger, "but I notice that you say the generation of new catalyst mustn't be allowed to proceed too rapidly. Can you tell me, without revealing classified information, what happens when catalytic regeneration *does* proceed too rapidly?"

Green was silent a moment, then said, "Well, you understand, that is amply guarded against by proper preliminary tests."

"Yes," said Berenger, and waited.

Green said, "There's really no need of any such eventuality *ever* arising in practice."

"I see."

"Newspaper reports tend to be somewhat sensational. Actually, we've never had that happen in the field."

"I see," said Berenger. "But—if this information isn't classified—what takes place when it *does* happen?"

There was a considerable silence. Berenger could hear faint voices in the background. Then Green said, "General, I wonder if you could come down here for a few hours this week end?"

Berenger was silent a moment.

Green said, "I can *show* you, much better than I can tell you. If this seems important to you, I hope you can come down here."

"Yes," said Berenger. "Thank you for the invitation, doctor. I'll be there."

The college looked about the same as when Berenger had been there last, but Dr. Green seemed preoccupied. He opened the door to the darkened laboratory, snapped on the lights, stood aside for Berenger, then locked the door behind them. He led Berenger the length of the room, and up several steps to a smaller laboratory. Inside, on a soapstone-topped bench, sat a very large brown-enameled earthenware crock. Green locked the door behind them, and lifted off the lid of the crock. "Here it is. See for yourself."

Berenger glanced in at a gray-brown glop that looked about the thickness of molasses.

"This is what happens if you add too much of the catalyst?"

"A great deal too much," said Green. "That was made by adding, originally, one liter of conditioner to one liter of untreated soil."

Berenger glanced into the mammoth crock again. Green, he noticed, seemed willing to give him information on request, but he certainly wasn't volunteering it. "So," said Berenger, "you had two liters to start with?"

"That's right."

"You've got a lot more than two liters here now. What did you do then?"

"We were disturbed at the results of the experiment. Naturally, we had to allow for a possible malfunction of the equipment used to spread the texturing agent. We also had to consider the possibility that a quantity of the agent might be spilled accidentally. If this caused a breakdown of the soil at the spot where the accident happened, it could result in a . . . a mudhole. We wanted to avoid that."

"Yes," said Berenger patiently, "but where did the rest of this stuff come from? You say you started out with a liter of dirt and a liter of catalytic agent. A liter is roughly a quart. This is a lot of more than two quarts."

Green nodded sourly. "We added a large quantity of untreated soil."

"And the soil did what?"

"There you see it."

Berenger looked in at the glop. "You mean the original muck transformed the untreated soil into more of itself?"

"As far as we can tell, something like that happened."

"What would happen if we added some more dirt to this?"

"I'd have to try it to know."

"Does this look any different from the stuff you had when you added one liter of texturing agent to one liter of soil?"

"There's more of it, that's all."

Berenger thought this over, and fought off the urge to profanity. Carefully, he said, "Let's say, as a hypothetical case, that a farmer had a container of this texturing agent and dropped it. Would he get a mudhole?"

"Apparently."

"Then what would he do?"

"He would have a serious problem."

"Could he collect the muck in . . . say . . . an empty oil drum, and then put it in his spreader and spread it over the same number of acres he'd originally planned to treat?"

"No," said Dr. Green uncomfortably, "I'm afraid that wouldn't be the thing to do."

"Why not?"

Green hesitated, then said, "The reaction is so complex that, frankly, I don't know how to explain what happens. Normally, the agent is vastly diluted by the soil. When it is used in so large a concentration, the agent itself seems to undergo a change. The result is this—substance. If this were spread over a field, I hate to think what it might produce."

"Suppose it were worked into the soil finely?"

"If the ionic complex itself were broken up, that of

course would stop it. If not, each small particle would still be of the same substance. Not the texturing agent, but the substance the concentrated texturing agent and the soil had reacted to form. As far as I can see, the process would not be stopped. It would be accelerated."

"There would be more of this stuff, then? A whole field of it?"

Green hesitated. "I'm afraid so."

"And this would then spread to adjacent fields?"

Green shrugged helplessly. "All I can say is, we added the dirt, and there you see the result. We didn't mix it. We just added it."

"How long did it take?"

"About forty minutes before the reaction was complete."

"So it *would* spread?"

"Apparently."

"Where would it stop?"

"I don't know."

Berenger drew a deep breath, and let it out slowly. In the back of his mind was the awareness that the texturing agent was even now being manufactured. No doubt, it was being loaded onto trucks, transported, unloaded, transferred to ships tied up at docks, perhaps even already being unloaded at foreign ports. His natural instinct was to do something fast. Get on the telephone, bulldoze his way to the highest available authority. Every second might count.

With an effort, he pulled out a laboratory stool and sat down. He glanced at Green, who now looked very pale. Berenger said, "What have you done about it?"

Green shook his head. "The possibility of something like this never occurred to me. It was one of my graduate students who thought of this experiment. It seems an obvious thing to try, now; but to begin with we had only small amounts of the texturing agent to work with. Later, I supposed as you did, that if the agent were mixed with too little soil, it would merely be a diluting of the agent. I was very angry when I learned of this crude experiment, which was only carried out *after* the agent was in commercial production. Before, it was too expensive. When I finally did realize what this might mean, I tried to explain the situation to the president."

"The President?"

Green shook his head. "The president of the college. He decided I was suffering from overstrain, and refused to take the matter seriously. I wrote a letter to the head of the corporation producing the agent, and got a letter back assuring me that they were using proper safeguards in shipping the agent, and congratulating me again on its discovery. Several days later, I received a whole drum of the texturing agent, compliments of the company. Gradually I began to think perhaps I *was* suffering from overstrain. I locked up the laboratory here, and tried not to think of it."

Berenger noted that his own hammering pulse was beginning to quiet down again. He could now see clearly what he had only sensed before: Any effort on his part to get this picture across would have to be done carefully, or he, Berenger, would also get sent off for a rest cure.

But to do it carefully would take time. While he was doing it carefully, trucks, trains, and ships would be in motion, increasing the likelihood of spillage.

Green said shakily, "It looks bad to you, too, doesn't it?"

Berenger said, "Suppose spillage makes just one mudhole? Small animals will track it around locally. Bits of muck stuck to men's shoes can easily end up forty miles away in an hour. And you said it only took forty minutes for a batch of fresh dirt to get converted to muck?"

Green nodded.

"How long would it take you to carry out complete laboratory tests, check your results, find out how this stuff reacts when finely divided in a comparatively large quantity of earth, how it reacts when treated with various chemicals, what effect heat and cold have on it, and anything else that seems useful?"

Green shook his head, "General, it would take several

years to do a thorough job. But I can get my best graduate students and have a rough idea in the next eight or ten hours."

Berenger got up. "Good. I'll get to work right away and see what I can find out."

The next eight hours Berenger spent in long-distance phone calls, and in some nerve-wracking calculations. He discovered that the soil texturing agent was already well-dispersed in stores and warehouses across the United States. Eight ships carrying sizable quantities of the agent in drums were at sea, destined for ports in Europe, Asia, Africa, and South America. The first of these cargo ships was due to dock in London in twelve hours, and others now in American ports were regularly taking on the texturing agent as part of their regular cargoes. There seemed to be no existing legal machinery that Berenger could put in motion to stop the shipment or sale of the substance.

Senator Vail, Berenger discovered, was on a hunting trip in the Canadian woods, and to get in touch with him would be no easy matter.

The president of the chemicals corporation manufacturing the agent was on a cabin cruiser fishing in Long Island Sound—no one knew exactly where—and the cabin cruiser was not equipped with a ship-to-shore radio.

Berenger paused to think things over. He was accumulating information rapidly, but he had yet to discover any way he could do anything about it. Fortunately, since it was the weekend, it was unlikely that any of the texturing agent would be sold. But for the same reason, it was hard to get hold of anyone who might know what to do about the situation.

Berenger paused to think what he could do himself. No doubt, he had enough rank so that he could create a stir in the effort to stop the shipments. He could probably even stop, or delay, *some* of the shipments. But, he thought, if a pile of dynamite has twenty lighted fuses eating their way toward it, it isn't enough to put out even nineteen of the twenty fuses. They *all* have to be put out, or the end result will be just the same as if none at all had been put out. And he did not by any means have the authority to stop all the shipments.

Next, Berenger tried to consider who he might reach who would have the authority to stop the shipments.

To begin with, many of the consignments of texturing agent must by now have changed ownership, so that the actual owners would be citizens of various foreign nations. These nations would have different regulations, and to stop all the shipments by any legal procedure would almost certainly be too complicated. After thinking this over it was clear to Berenger that there was probably no individual on the face of the earth with the legal authority to stop all the shipments.

Berenger then tried to think who might have the practical physical power to stop the shipments. This quickly narrowed down to one person. The eight ships at sea could almost certainly be stopped, and most of the sales in the United States in some way blocked, by only one man: the President. But he would never do it without being convinced.

Berenger thought the thing over and could see that it would take more than the assurances of Dr. Franklin Green to convince the President that drastic action was needed. Berenger's own word would mean nothing. A colleague need only say, "I didn't realize you were a soil chemist, Lyell."

Berenger looked at it objectively and saw how it would work out. He could hear a voice saying to the President, "There's a general out here, sir, who claims that the world's about to be eaten up by some kind of fertilizer. Shall I . . . ah, get the M.P.'s, sir?"

If it turned out that Green was mistaken, Berenger would never live this down if he lived to be two hundred years old.

Frowning, Berenger sat back to consider Green. Maybe Green *was* in need of a rest cure.

At that thought, Berenger felt both a sense of exasperation over wasted effort, and a sudden relief from tension that he hadn't realized was growing unbearably tight.

And the more he thought of it, the more likely it seemed that Green *was* unbalanced.

And in that case, there was no need to do anything. Just then, the phone rang.

Berenger warily lifted the phone from its cradle. "Hello?"

"General Berenger?"

"Right here."

"This is Franklin Green. I think you ought to come down to the lab right away."

Berenger frowned. "I'll be right there." He hung up, thinking that now at least he should find out definitely whether the man was right or wrong.

Green met Berenger at the door to the laboratory; drew him inside, and locked the door. Inside, three pale young men in lab coats stood at one of the long benches. They looked up nervously as Berenger came in, and Green made hurried introductions.

Berenger interrupted to say sharply, "What did you find out?"

Green said, "Let me show you." He pointed to several bucketfuls of dirt at the far end of the bench. "We put samples of that in these glass dishes, and added small quantities of the transformed texturing agent to each dish. Some we put in in lumps, others we worked carefully into the soil. There you see the result."

Each of a line of the glass dishes contained the same kind of brown-gray glop that Berenger had seen earlier.

"Worse yet," said Green, "we put a little of this transformed agent into a flask, poured in ordinary tap water, decanted the water over the soil, and look here, the soil is changed just as in the other cases. It was a little slower, that's all."

Berenger felt as if an iron band were tightening around his chest. "What about the effects of chemicals?"

Green shrugged. He removed the top of a bottle of sulfuric acid, and carefully poured it over one of the dishes of glop. The substance swelled up, and gave a faint hissing sound as the acid poured into it. Next, he poured a sodium hydroxide solution over one of the dishes. The gray-brown glop shrank slightly, and cracked, leaving the solution in a pool on top of it.

"Now," said Green, "we have found one hopeful thing. We tried ordinary tap water, as I mentioned. We also tried to obtain a solution, or dispersion, in a saline solution." Green pointed to a dish of damp, but unchanged dirt. "Nothing happened." He glanced around. "Jerry. Show the general what you discovered."

One of the graduate students took a paper heaped with tiny white crystals, shook it over a dish of gray glop, and stirred methodically. The grayish color vanished; the texture changed; and then Berenger was looking at ordinary dirt.

"So," said Green. "The process can be reversed. But you have then sowed the soil with salt."

Berenger shook his head. "Can you show me the actual change, from dirt to glop."

Green glanced at one of his graduate students. "Arthur."

The student spoken to put some dirt from a bucket into a clean dish, took a small lump of glop from one of the other dishes, and began working it carefully and methodically into the dirt.

Berenger watched tensely. After a considerable time had passed, his attention began to waver. With an effort, he held his gaze on the dish, and shifted it from one part to another to try to avoid the hypnotic affect of Arthur's ceaselessly-working hand.

Just when it began to happen, Berenger could not say, but suddenly the dirt was no longer dirt, but the gray-brown stuff that looked and acted like a kind of thick muck.

Berenger drew a deep breath, and straightened up. "Did you duplicate the experiment that started all this?"

Green nodded. "The same result."

"Did you use a different batch of the texturing agent?"

"Yes, we used some from the complimentary drum the manufacturer sent us. So it isn't just a freak side-effect from one batch of the agent."

Berenger said, "What about heat and cold? What effect do they have?"

"Cold seems to have no effect whatever, except that the substance becomes somewhat more stiff. Intense heat, however, reverses the reaction."

Berenger said tensely, "You're sure of that? Heat reverses it?"

In answer, Green lit a burner, and held it so that the flame played on the surface of one of the samples. Where the flame heated it, the gray color was gradually replaced by the look of ordinary dirt. Green took the burner away. The gray coloration gradually returned.

"The heat," said Green, "only penetrated a thin layer. But we heated one sample in an oven. That sample didn't change back, though it became extremely crumbly."

"Did you try adding water?"

"Yes. The soil absorbed it quite well. But it didn't change . . . or hasn't yet, at least."

Berenger looked around at all the samples. The graduate students were standing around looking at the floor, as if they thought they had committed some criminal act.

Green said tensely, "You've got to stop the shipments."

Berenger shook his head, "I don't have the authority."

"Take it to someone who has the authority. Why can't you take it right to the President?"

"For the same reason that you can't simply walk over there and convince the president of your own college. To function at all, the head of an organization has to recognize and weed out crackpots and alarmists. Anyone who walks in and tries to get action on this will get automatically hustled right out again. To convince the President, I'd have to build up a case first."

"Can you do that?"

"It would take too long." Berenger glanced at his watch.

"Four hours from now, the first cargo ship will reach Britain. While I'm building my case, shipments will be going over the Canadian and Mexican borders. Stores will be selling the stuff, and farmers using it. Ships will dock in Africa and South America. While I convince the men who will have to convince the President, this stuff will spread out over the globe. By the time they have him convinced, it will be too late for him to do anything."

Green said, "But there's *got* to be something we can do."

"How is this stuff manufactured? Under a patent?"

"No. The company decided the process was sufficiently unusual to justify trying to keep it a trade secret."

"Did you publish any account of the process?"

"No, I wanted to be sure what I had first. Then I was persuaded not to publish." Green's voice climbed. "But the important thing is, *how can we stop the shipments?*"

Berenger said, "Let me take another look at that stuff that formed first."

"But what does that—" Green saw Berenger's expression, hesitated, then led him down to the little laboratory. He locked the door behind them. "This was just so we could talk alone, wasn't it? What are you thinking?"

"What will happen if we take that stuff out onto the campus and plant it?"

Green swallowed. "It will start the reaction. In time, the whole campus will be affected."

"How fast will it happen?"

"It will depend on how finely we divide it. But what good will that do?"

"Can we make a horrible example? Can we have the grounds one sea of spreading muck?"

"Yes," said Green. "But general, we *can't* do that."

"All right," said Berenger. He sat on the edge of a stool and glanced at his watch. "The first ship docks in London in about three hours and fifty-four minutes. We can go at the problem in slow stages and gamble the whole world. Or we can run the risk here that we will have to run anyway as soon as the stores open on Monday."

Green looked down. In a low voice, he said, "How will we stop it?"

Berenger said grimly, "If heat will stop it, we can stop it all right."

Green nodded slowly. "Yes, I see." He hesitated, then said, "All right."

It was about 4:00 in the morning when Berenger sent for the paratroops. At 5:00 he got through to the Army Chief of Staff, who listened, and then exploded, then listened again.

By 5:30, the college buildings were evacuated, and the headlights of cars competed with the gray light of dawn as excited reporters were held back by police from the expanding edge of the slop. By 6:30 the paratroops had blocked the roads, and the sound of crashing bricks told of buildings toppling as the soil at their foundations softened. By 7:00 the word had gotten to the President, who rejected the whole idea angrily, and sent singed aides scurrying to unload their own wrath at the "hoax." By this time, the Pentagon was receiving direct reports from the paratroops.

At 8:00, a new set of envoys reached the President, bringing photographs, statements of witnesses, and a statement by Dr. Green. The paratroops reported that the perimeter now appeared to be moving out at the steady rate of about one-and-one-half feet per hour. A penciled notation added the calculation that this would amount to an increase in the diameter of the affected area of seventy-two feet every twenty-four hours, with no end in sight. A brief analysis of the situation by Lieutenant general Lyell Berenger, fortunately on the scene, pointed out the impossibility of transport through such muck as this, the danger of it being seeded in new localities, the dangers of hysteria as the muck spread, the political effects of shipments of similar materials being sent overseas, and the desirability from every viewpoint, of immediate drastic action to end the trouble before it had time to gather any more momentum.

The President looked over the photographs and the reports, glanced at an appended list of ship sailings, read Berenger's recommendations through again, and looked at the Army Chief of Staff.

."Is Berenger reliable?"

"He always has been, sir."

"I want to talk to some of these people on the scene. And I want to be very sure they are the people they represent themselves to be."

"Yes, sir."

At 8:35, the urgent message went out to the British Prime Minister.

At 8:55, British troops were racing the police for the docks.

By 9:00 all the ships still at sea were notified, and the United States Navy was in hot pursuit of one that refused to change its course.

By 9:25, the FBI was at work tracing down all the smaller shipments of the texturing agent.

By 9:40 there was a panic in Chicago as an excited newscaster announced that a "wall of annihilation is approaching at supersonic speed from the state of Iowa."

By 9:55 the college and its surroundings had been forcibly evacuated by troops and police. By this time, also, the warning messages had been received in the capitals of the NATO nations, the Soviet Union and Japan.

By 10:00, the President was speaking to the nation, and as he spoke, the first jet bomber was already on its way. At the conclusion of his speech, he was handed a slip of paper, and announced that a hydrogen explosion had destroyed the college and surroundings, and was believed to have burned out, by its intense heat, the action of the catalyst.

By 10:55 the Premier of the Soviet Union was receiving Intelligence reports on the situation, and looking it over from a variety of unpleasant angles.

By 11:00 the Pentagon was beginning to subside toward normal, and the Army Chief of Staff was pouring questions at Berenger, at the end of which he gazed off into the distance and remarked, "So, now if we want to we could drop one drop of this stuff anywhere we want to, and eight hours later have a pool of glop twenty-four feet across. It would be tough on people who depend on stretched-out rail and road communications, wouldn't it?"

"Yes, sir," said Berenger. "But I'd hate to start it. They could do it back."

"Oh, but I was just looking at it from their point of view, to see how it strikes them. Besides, they don't yet *know* they could do it back."

And several weeks later, Berenger was talking to his friend, Senator Vail.

"You know, Lyell," said Senator Vail, "that experience kind of knocks the spots off your argument. There's been no activity from the Crater, and the whole business seems to have faded away to nothing. We're still competing with the Russians, and I believe we are all running just as fast as ever. I thought that fall was supposed to finish us."

Berenger smiled and shook his head. "I don't expect to convince you that Science is, inherently, unavoidably, and of its own nature, deadly dangerous. But there's one thing you ought to recognize."

"What's that?"

"When you think it's necessary, you run a risk. But you have to use the right names when you label things."

"What of it?"

"You haven't used the right name for that experience."

Vail frowned. "What do you mean?"

"That wasn't a fall," said Berenger. "Far from it."

He thought a moment, then added, *"That* was only a stumble."

It's a poor editor who can't print a story of his own now and then. It isn't that my story is the only one which deals with that most basic of all forms of pollution, people pollution, the insane overbreeding which puts Levittowns on potato farms on Long Island and sleeping beggars on the sidewalks of Calcutta. The reason I offer you my own story instead of one of the many others is that most of them deal with rather peaceful and ingenious solutions to the population problem, when they see any solution at all. I don't believe in that. I wish I did, but all history makes me suspect that the most tempting simple way to deal with surplus population, if ever we reach the point when it is clear that some way to deal with it must be found, will be the way of—

THE CENSUS TAKERS

Frederik Pohl

It gets to be a madhouse around here along about the end of the first week. Thank heaven we only do this once a year, that's what I say! Six weeks on, and forty-six weeks off—that's pretty good hours, most people think. But they don't know what those six weeks are like.

It's bad enough for the field crews, but when you get to be an Area Boss like me it's frantic. You work your way up through the ranks, and then they give you a whole C.A. of your own; and you think you've got it made. Fifty three-man crews go out, covering the whole Census Area; a hundred and fifty men in the field, and twenty or thirty more in Area Command—and you boss them all. And everything looks great, until Census Period starts and you've got to work those hundred and fifty men; and six weeks is too unbearably long to live through, and too impossibly short to get the work done; and you begin living on black coffee and thiamin shots and dreaming about the vacation hostel on Point Loma.

Anybody can panic, when the pressure is on like that. Your best field men begin to crack up. But you can't afford to, because you're the Area Boss. . . .

Take Witeck. We were Enumerators together, and he was as good a man as you ever saw, absolutely nerveless when it came to processing the Overs. I counted on that man the way I counted on my own right arm; I always bracketed him with the greenest, shakiest new cadet Enumerators, and he never gave me a moment's trouble for years. Maybe it was too good to last; maybe I should have figured he would crack.

I set up my Area Command in a plush penthouse apartment. The people who lived there were pretty well off, you know, and they naturally raised the dickens about being shoved out. "Blow it," I told them. "Get out of here in five minutes, and we'll count you first." Well, that took care of *that;* they were practically kissing my feet on the way out. Of course, it wasn't strictly by the book, but you have to be a little flexible; that's why some men become Area Bosses, and others stay Enumerators.

Like Witeck.

Along about Day Eight things were really hotting up. I was up to my neck in hurry-ups from Regional Control— we were running a little slow—when Witeck called up. "Chief," he said, "I've got an In."

I grabbed the rotary file with one hand and a pencil with the other. "Blue-card number?" I asked.

Witeck sounded funny over the phone. "Well, Chief," he said, "he doesn't have a blue card. He says—"

"No blue card?" I couldn't believe it. Come in to a strange C.A. without a card from your own Area Boss, and you're one In that's a cinch to be an Over. "What kind of a crazy C.A. does he come from, without a blue card?"

Witeck said, "He don't come from any C.A., Chief. He says—"

"You mean he isn't from this country?"

"That's right, Chief. He—"

"Hold it!" I pushed away the rotary file and grabbed

the immigration roster. There were only a couple of dozen names on it, of course—we have enough trouble with our own Overs, without taking on a lot of foreigners, but still there were a handful every year who managed to get on the quotas. "I.D. number?" I demanded.

"Well, Chief," Witeck began, "he doesn't have an I.D. number. The way it looks to me—"

Well, you can fool around with these irregulars for a month, if you want to, but it's no way to get the work done. I said, "Over him!" and hung up. I was a little surprised, though; Witeck knew the ropes, and it wasn't like him to buck an irregular onto me. In the old days, when we were both starting out, I'd seen him Over a whole family just because the spelling of their names on their registry cards was different from the spelling on the checklist.

But we get older. I made a note to talk to Witeck as soon as the rush was past. We were old friends; I wouldn't have to threaten him with being Overed himself, or anything like that. He'd know, and maybe that would be all he would need to snap him back. I certainly would talk to him, I promised myself, as soon as the rush was over, or anyway as soon as I got back from Point Loma.

I had to run up to Regional Control to take a little talking-to myself just then, but I proved to them that we were catching up and they were only medium nasty. When I got back Witeck was on the phone again. "Chief," he said, real unhappy, "this In is giving me a headache. I—"

"Witeck," I snapped at him, "are you bothering me with another In? Can't you handle anything by yourself?"

He said, "It's the same one, Chief. He says he's a kind of ambassador, and—"

"Oh," I said. "Well, why the devil don't you get your facts straight in the first place? Give me his name and I'll check his legation."

"Well, Chief," he began again, "he, uh, doesn't have any legation. He says he's from the"— he swallowed— "from the middle of the earth."

"You're crazy." I'd seen it happen before, good men

breaking under the strain of census taking. They say in cadets that by the time you process your first five hundred Overs you've had it; either you take a voluntary Over yourself, or you split wide open and they carry you off to a giggle farm. And Witeck was past the five hundred mark, way past.

There was a lot of yelling and crying from the filter center, which I'd put out by the elevators, and it looked like Jumpers. I stabbed the transfer button on the phone and called to Carias, my number-two man: "Witeck's flipped or something. Handle it!"

And then I forgot about it, while Carias talked to Witeck on the phone; because it was Jumpers, all right, a whole family of them.

There was a father and a mother and five kids—*five* of them. Aren't some people disgusting? The field Enumerator turned them over to the guards—they were moaning and crying—and came up and gave me the story. It was bad.

"You're the head of the household?" I demanded of the man.

He nodded, looking at me like a sick dog. "We—we weren't Jumping," he whined. "Honest to heaven, mister —you've got to believe me. We were—"

I cut in, "You were packed and on the doorstep when the field crew came by. Right?" He started to say something, but I had him dead to rights. "That's plenty, friend," I told him. "That's Jumping, under the law: Packing, with intent to move, while a census Enumeration crew is operating in your locale. Got anything to say?"

Well, he had plenty to say, but none of it made any sense. He turned my stomach, listening to him. I tried to keep my temper—you're not supposed to think of individuals, no matter how worthless and useless and generally unfit they are; that's against the whole principle of the Census—but I couldn't help telling him: "I've met your kind before, mister. Five kids! If it wasn't for people like you we wouldn't *have* any Overs, did you ever think of that? Sure you didn't—you people never think of anything but yourself! Five kids, and then when Census comes around you think you can get smart and Jump." I tell you, I was shaking. "You keep your little beady eyes peeled, sneaking around, watching the Enumerators, trying to count how many it takes to make an Over; and then you wait until they get close to you, so you can Jump. Ever stop to think what trouble that makes for us?" I demanded. "Census is supposed to be fair and square, everybody an even chance—and how can we make it that way unless everybody stands still to be counted?" I patted Old Betsy, on my hip. "I haven't Overed anybody myself in five years," I told him, "but I swear, I'd like to handle you personally!"

He didn't say a word once I got started on him. He just stood there, taking it. I had to force myself to stop, finally; I could have gone on for a long time, because if there's one thing I hate it's these lousy, stinking breeders who try to Jump when they think one of them is going to be an Over in the count-off. Regular Jumpers are bad enough, but when it's the people who make the mess in the first place—

Anyway, time was wasting. I took a deep breath and thought things over. Actually, we weren't too badly off; we'd started off Overing every two-hundred-and-fiftieth person, and it was beginning to look as though our preliminary estimate was high; we'd just cut back to Overing every three-hundredth. So we had a little margin to play with.

I told the man, dead serious; "You know I could Over the lot of you on charges, don't you?" He nodded sickly. "All right, I'll give you a chance. I don't want to bother with the red tape; if you'll take a voluntary Over for yourself, we'll start the new count with your wife."

Call me soft, if you want to; but I still say that it was a lot better than fussing around with charges and a hearing. You get into a hearing like that and it can drag on for half an hour or more; and then Regional Control is on your tail because you're falling behind.

It never hurts to give a man a break, even a Jumper, I always say—as long as it doesn't slow down your Census.

Carias was waiting at my desk when I got back; he looked worried about something, but I brushed him off while I initialed the Overage report on the man we'd just processed. He'd been an In, I found out when I canceled his blue card. I can't say I was surprised. He'd come from Denver, and you know how they keep exceeding their Census figures; no doubt he thought he'd have a better chance in my C.A. than anywhere else. And no doubt he was right, because we certainly don't encourage breeders like him—actually, if he hadn't tried to Jump it was odds-on that the whole damned family would get by without an Over for years.

Carias was hovering right behind me as I finished. "I hate these voluntaries," I told him, basketing the canceled card. "I'm going to talk to Regional Control about it; there's no reason why they can't be processed like any other Over, instead of making me okay each one individually. Now, what's the matter?"

He rubbed his jaw. "Chief," he said, "it's Witeck."

"Now what? Another In?"

Carias glanced at me, then away. "Uh, no, Chief. It's the same one. He claims he comes from, uh, the center of the earth."

I swore out loud. "So he has to turn up in my C.A.!" I complained bitterly. "He gets out of the nuthouse, and right away—"

Carias said, "Chief, he might not be crazy. He makes it sound pretty real."

I said: "Hold it, Carias. Nobody can live in the center of the earth. It's solid, like a potato."

"Sure, Chief," Carias nodded earnestly. "But he says it isn't. He says there's a what he calls neutronium shell, whatever that is, with dirt and rocks on both sides of it. We live on the outside. He lives on the inside. His people—"

"Carias!" I yelled. "You're as bad as Witeck. This guy

turns up, no blue card, no I.D. number, no credentials of any kind. What's he going to say, 'Please sir, I'm an Over, please process me'? Naturally not! So he makes up a crazy story, and you fall for it!"

"I know, Chief," Carias said humbly.

"Neutronium shell!" I would have laughed out loud, if I'd had the time. "Neutronium my foot! Don't you know it's *hot* down there?"

"He says it's hot neutronium," Carias said eagerly. "I asked him that myself, Chief. He said it's just the shell that—"

"Get back to work!" I yelled at him. I picked up the phone and got Witeck on his wristphone. I tell you, I was boiling. As soon as Witeck answered I lit into him; I didn't give him a chance to get a word in. I gave it to him up and down and sidewise; and I finished off by giving him a direct order. "You Over that man," I told him, "or I'll personally Over you! You hear me?"

There was a pause. Then Witeck said, "Jerry? Will you listen to me?"

That stopped me. It was the first time in ten years, since I'd been promoted above him, that Witeck had dared call me by my first name. He said, "Jerry, listen. This is something big. This guy is really from the center of the earth, no kidding. He—"

"Witeck," I said, "you've cracked."

"No, Jerry, honest! And it worries me. He's right there in the next room, waiting for me. He says he had no idea things were like this on the surface; he's talking wild about cleaning us off and starting all over again; he says—"

"*I* say he's an Over!" I yelled. "No more talk, Witeck. You've got a direct order—now carry it out!"

So that was that.

We got through the Census Period after all, but we had to do it shorthanded; and Witeck was hard to replace. I'm a sentimentalist, I guess, but I couldn't help remembering old times. We started even; he might have risen as far as I—but of course he made his choice when he got married and had a kid; you can't be a breeder and an officer of the Census both. If it hadn't been for his record he couldn't even have stayed on as an Enumerator.

I never said a word to anyone about his crackup. Carias might have talked, but after we found Witeck's body I took him aside. "Carias," I said reasonably, "we don't want any scandal, do we? Here's Witeck, with an honorable record; he cracks, and kills himself, and that's bad enough. We won't let loose talk make it worse, will we?"

Carias said uneasily, "Chief, where's the gun he killed himself with? His own processor wasn't even fired."

You can let a helper go just so far. I said sharply, "Carias, we still have at least a hundred Overs to process. You can be on one end of the processing—or you can be on the other. You understand me?"

He coughed. "Sure, Chief. I understand. We don't want any loose talk."

And that's how it is when you're an Area Boss. But I didn't ever get my vacation at Point Loma; the tsunami there washed out the whole town the last week of the Census. And when I tried Baja California, they were having that crazy volcanic business; and the Yellowstone Park bureau wouldn't even accept my reservation because of some trouble with the geysers, so I just stayed home. But the best vacation of all was just knowing that the Census was done for another year.

Carias was all for looking for this In that Witeck was talking about, but I turned him down. "Waste of time," I told him. "By now he's a dozen C.A.'s away. We'll never see him again, him or anybody like him—I'll bet my life on that."

The worst thing about overbreeding might not be sheer numbers; it might be the deterioration of humanity to below-human standards. This is not fantasy, you ought to know. It appears to be happening right now. Overpopulation produces inadequate diet. In many parts of the world—some in Africa and Asia, some in South America, possibly a few nearer home—these diets are markedly deficient in protein; and when a very young child's diet lacks proper minimal protein his brain fails to develop properly. He doesn't die, or at least not physically. All that dies is his humanity, so that he grows up physically and mentally stunted.

Or it might happen the way Cyril Kornbluth suggested. It doesn't make much difference. Either way we wind up with—

THE MARCHING MORONS

C. M. Kornbluth

Some things had not changed. A potter's wheel was still a potter's wheel and clay was still clay. Efim Hawkins had built his shop near Goose Lake, which had a narrow band of good fat clay and a narrow beach of white sand. He fired three bottle-nosed kilns with willow charcoal from the wood lot. The wood lot was also useful for long walks while the kilns were cooling; if he let himself stay within sight of them, he would open them prematurely, impatient to see how some new shape or glaze had come through the fire, and—*ping!*—the new shape or glaze would be good for nothing but the shard pile back of his slip tanks.

A business conference was in full swing in his shop, a modest cube of brick, tile-roofed, as the Chicago–Los Angeles "rocket" thundered overhead—very noisy, very swept-back, very fiery jets, shaped as sleekly swift-looking as an airborne barracuda.

The buyer from Marshall Fields was turning over a

47

black-glazed one liter carafe, nodding approval with his massive, handsome head. "This is real pretty," he told Hawkins and his own secretary, Gomez-Laplace. "This has got lots of what ya call real est'etic principles. Yeah, it is real pretty."

"How much?" the secretary asked the potter.

"Seven-fifty each in dozen lots," said Hawkins. "I ran up fifteen dozen last month."

"They are real est'etic," repeated the buyer from Fields. "I will take them all."

"I don't think we can do that, doctor," said the secretary. "They'd cost us $1,350. That would leave only $532 in our quarter's budget. And we still have to run down to East Liverpool to pick up some cheap dinner sets."

"Dinner sets?" asked the buyer, his big face full of wonder.

"Dinner sets. The department's been out of them for two months now. Mr. Garvy-Seabright got pretty nasty about it yesterday. Remember?"

"Garvy-Seabright, that meat-headed bluenose," the buyer said contemptuously. "He don't know nothin' about est'etics. Why for don't he lemme run my own department?" His eye fell on a stray copy of *Whambozambo Comix* and he sat down with it. An occasional deep chuckle or grunt of surprise escaped him as he turned the pages.

Uninterrupted, the potter and the buyer's secretary quickly closed a deal for two dozen of the liter carafes. "I wish we could take more," said the secretary, "but you heard what I told him. We've had to turn away customers for ordinary dinnerware because he shot the last quarter's budget on some Mexican piggy banks some equally enthusiastic importer stuck him with. The fifth floor is packed solid with them."

"I'll bet they look mighty est'etic."

"They're painted with purple cacti."

The potter shuddered and caressed the glaze of the sample carafe.

The buyer looked up and rumbled, "Ain't you dummies through yakkin' yet? What good's a seckertary for if'n he don't take the burden of *de*-tail off'n my back, harh?"

"We're all through, doctor. Are you ready to go?"

The buyer grunted peevishly, dropped *Whambozambo Comix* on the floor and led the way out of the building and down the log corduroy road to the highway. His car was waiting on the concrete. It was, like all contemporary cars, too low-slung to get over the logs. He climbed down into the car and started the motor with a tremendous sparkle and roar.

"Gomez-Laplace," called out the potter under cover of the noise, "did anything come of the radiation program they were working on the last time I was on duty at the Pole?"

"The same old fallacy," said the secretary gloomily. "It stopped us on mutation, it stopped us on culling, it stopped us on segregation, and now it's stopped us on hypnosis."

"Well, I'm scheduled back to the grind in nine days. Time for another firing right now. I've got a new luster to try . . ."

"I'll miss you. I shall be 'vacationing'—running the drafting room of the New Century Engineering Corporation in Denver. They're going to put up a two hundred-story office building, and naturally somebody's got to be on hand."

"Naturally," said Hawkins with a sour smile.

There was an ear-piercingly sweet blast as the buyer leaned on the horn button. Also, a yard-tall yet of what looked like flame spurted up from the car's radiator cap; the car's power plant was a gas turbine, and had no radiator.

"I'm coming, doctor," said the secretary dispiritedly. He climbed down into the car and it whooshed off with much flame and noise.

The potter, depressed, wandered back up the corduroy road and contemplated his cooling kilns. The rustling wind in the boughs was obscuring the creak and mutter of the shrinking refractory brick. Hawkins wondered about the number two kiln—a reduction fire on a load of lusterware mugs. Had the clay chinking excluded the air? Had it been a properly smoky blaze? Would it do any harm if he just took one close—?

Common sense took Hawkins by the scruff of the neck and yanked him over to the tool shed. He got out his pick and resolutely set off on a prospecting jaunt to a hummocky field that might yield some oxides. He was especially low on coppers.

The long walk left him sweating hard, with his lust for a peek into the kiln quiet in his breast. He swung his pick almost at random into one of the hummocks; it clanged on a stone, which he excavated. A largely obliterated inscription said:

ERSITY OF CHIC
OGICAL LABO
ELOVED MEMORY OF
KILLED IN ACT

The potter swore mildly. He had hoped the field would turn out to be a cemetery, preferably a once-fashionable cemetery full of once-massive bronze caskets moldered into oxides of tin and copper.

Well, hell, maybe there was some around anyway.

He headed lackadaisically for the second largest hillock and sliced into it with his pick. There was a stone to undercut and topple into a trench, and then the potter was very glad he'd stuck at it. His nostrils were filled with the bitter smell, and the dirt was tinged with the exciting blue of copper salts. The pick went *clang!*

Hawkins, puffing, pried up a stainless steel plate that was quite badly stained and was also marked with incised letters. It seemed to have pulled loose from rotting bronze; there were rivets on the back that brought up flakes of green patina. The potter wiped off the surface dirt with his sleeve, turned it to catch the sunlight obliquely, and read:

"HONEST JOHN BARLOW"

"Honest John," famed in university annuals represents a challenge which medical science has not yet answered: revival of a human being accidentally thrown into a state of suspended animation.

In 1988 Mr. Barlow, a leading Evanston real estate dealer, visited his dentist for treatment of an impacted wisdom tooth. His dentist requested and received permission to use the experimental anesthetic Cycloparadimethanol-B-7, developed at the University.

After administration of the anesthetic, the dentist resorted to his drill. By freakish mischance, a short circuit in his machine delivered 220 volts of 60-cycle current into the patient. (In a damage suit instituted by Mrs. Barlow against the dentist, the University and the makers of the drill, a jury found for the defendants.) Mr. Barlow never got up from the dentist's chair and was assumed to have died of poisoning, electrocution or both.

Morticians preparing him for embalming discovered, however, that their subject was—though certainly not living—just as certainly not dead. The University was notified and a series of exhaustive tests was begun, including attempts to duplicate the trance state on volunteers. After a bad run of seven cases which ended fatally, the attempts were abandoned.

Honest John was long an exhibit at the University museum, and livened many a football game as mascot of the University's Blue Crushers. The bounds of taste were overstepped, however, when a pledge to Sigma Delta Chi was ordered in '03 to "kidnap" Honest John from his loosely guarded glass museum case and introduce him into the Rachel Swanson Memorial Girls' Gymnasium shower room.

On May 22nd, 2003, the University Board of Regents issued the following order: "By unanimous vote, it is directed that the remains of Honest John Barlow be removed from the University museum and conveyed to the University's Lieutenant James Scott III Memorial Biological Laboratories and there be securely locked in a specially prepared vault. It is further directed that all possible measures for the preservation of these remains be taken by the Laboratory administration and that access to these remains be denied to all persons except qualified scholars authorized in writing by the Board. The Board reluctantly takes this action in view of recent notices and photographs in the nation's press which, to say the least, reflect but small credit upon the University."

It was far from his field, but Hawkins understood what had happened—an early and accidental blundering onto the bare bones of the Levantman shock anesthesia, which had since been replaced by other methods. To bring subjects out of Levantman shock, you let them have a squirt of simple saline in the trigeminal nerve. Interesting. And now about that bronze—

He heaved the pick into the rotting green salts, expecting no resistence, and almost fractured his wrist. *Something* down there was *solid*. He began to flake off the oxides.

A half hour of work brought him down to phosphor bronze, a huge casting of the almost incorruptible metal. It had weakened structurally over the centuries; he could fit the point of his pick under a corroded boss and pry off great creaking and grumbling striae of the stuff.

Hawkins wished he had an archeologist with him, but didn't dream of returning to his shop and calling one to take over the find. He was an all-around man: by choice and in his free time, an artist in clay and glaze; by necessity, an automotive, electronics, and atomic engineer who could also swing a project in traffic control, individual and group psychology, architecture, or tool design. He didn't yell for a specialist every time something out of his line came up; there were so few, with so much to do . . .

He trenched around his find, discovering that it was a great brick-shaped bronze mass with an excitingly hollow sound. A long strip of moldering metal from one of the long vertical faces pulled away, exposing red rust that went *whoosh* and was sucked into the interior of the mass.

It had been de-aired, thought Hawkins, and there must have been an inner jacket of glass which had crystallized through the centuries and quietly crumbled at the first clang of his pick. He didn't know what a vacuum would do to a subject of Levantman shock, but he had hopes; nor did he quite understand what a real estate dealer was, but it might have something to do with pottery. And *anything* might have a bearing on Topic Number One.

He flung his pick out of the trench, climbed out and set off at a dog-trot for his shop. A little rummaging turned up a hypo, and there was a plasticontainer of salt in the kitchen.

Back at his dig, he chipped for another half hour to expose the juncture of lid and body. The hinges were hopeless; he smashed them off.

Hawkins extended the telescopic handle of the pick for the best leverage, fitted its point into a deep pit, set its built-in fulcrum, and heaved. Five more heaves and he could see, inside the vault, what looked like a dusty marble statue. Ten more and he could see that it was the naked body of Honest John Barlow, Evanston real estate dealer, uncorrupted by time.

The potter found the apex of the trigeminal nerve with his needle's point and gave him 60 cc.

In an hour Barlow's chest began to pump.

In another hour, he rasped, "Did it work?"

"*Did* it!" muttered Hawkins.

Barlow opened his eyes and stirred, looked down, turned his hands before his eyes—

"I'll sue!" he screamed. "My clothes! My fingernails!"

A horrid suspicion came over his face and he clapped his hands to his hairless scalp. "My hair!" he wailed. "I'll sue you for every penny you've got! That release won't mean a damned thing in court—I didn't sign away my hair and clothes and fingernails!"

"They'll grow back," said Hawkins casually. "Also your epidermis. Those parts of you weren't alive, you know, so they weren't preserved like the rest of you. I'm afraid the clothes are gone though."

"What is this—the University hospital?" demanded Barlow. "I want a phone. No, you phone. Tell my wife I'm all right, and tell Sam Immerman—he's my lawyer— to get over here right away. Greenleaf 7-4022. Ow!" He had tried to sit up, and a portion of his pink skin rubbed against the inner surface of the casket, which was powdered by the ancient crystallized glass. "What the hell did you guys do, boil me alive? Oh, you're going to pay for this!"

"You're all right," said Hawkins, wishing now he had a reference book to clear up several obscure terms. "Your epidermis will start growing immediately. You're not in the hospital. Look here."

He handed Barlow the stainless steel plate that had labeled the casket. After a suspicious glance, the man started to read. Finishing, he laid the plate carefully on the edge of the vault and was silent for a spell.

"Poor Verna," he said at last. "It doesn't say whether she was stuck with the court costs. Do you happen to know—"

"No," said the potter. "All I know is what was on the plate, and how to revive you. The dentist accidentally gave you a dose of what we call Levantman shock anesthesia. We haven't used it for centuries; it was powerful, but too dangerous."

"Centuries . . ." brooded the man. "Centuries . . . I'll bet Sam swindled her out of her eyeteeth. Poor Verna. How long ago was it? What year is this?"

Hawkins shrugged. "We call it 7-B-936. That's no help to you. It takes a long time for these metals to oxidize."

"Like that movie," Barlow muttered. "Who would have thought it? Poor Verna!" He blubbered and sniffled, reminding Hawkins powerfully of the fact that he had been found under a flat rock.

Almost angrily, the potter demanded, "How many children did you have?"

"None yet," sniffed Barlow. "My first wife didn't want them. But Verna wants one—wanted one—but we're going to wait until—we *were* going to wait until—"

"Of course," said the potter, feeling a savage desire to tell him off, blast him to hell and gone for his work. But he choked it down. There was The Problem to think of; there was always The Problem to think of, and this poor blubberer might unexpectedly supply a clue. Hawkins would have to pass him on.

"Come along," Hawkins said. "My time is short."

Barlow looked up, outraged. "How can you be so unfeeling? I'm a human being like—"

The Los Angeles–Chicago "rocket" thundered overhead and Barlow broke off in mid-complaint. "Beautiful!" he breathed, following it with his eyes. "Beautiful!"

He climbed out of the vault, too interested to be pained by its roughness against his infantile skin. "After all," he said briskly, "this should have its sunny side. I never was much for reading, but this is just like one of those stories. And I ought to make some money out of it, shouldn't I?" He gave Hawkins a shrewd glance.

"You want money?" asked the potter. "Here." He handed over a fistful of change and bills. "You'd better put my shoes on. It'll be about a quarter mile. Oh, and you're—uh, modest?"—yes, that was the word. "Here." Hawkins gave him his pants, but Barlow was excitedly counting the money.

"Eighty-five, eighty-six—and it's dollars, too! I thought it'd be credits or whatever they call them. 'E Pluribus Unum' and 'Liberty'—just different faces. Say, is there a catch to this? Are these real, genuine, honest twenty-two-cent dollars like we had or just wallpaper?"

"They're quite all right, I assure you," said the potter. "I wish you'd come along. I'm in a hurry."

The man babbled as they stumped toward the shop. "Where are we going—The Council of Scientists, the World Coordinator or something like that?"

"Who? Oh, no. We call them 'President' and 'Congress.' No, that wouldn't do any good at all. I'm just taking you to see some people."

"I ought to make plenty out of this. *Plenty!* I could write books. Get some smart young fellow to put it into words for me and I'll bet I could turn out a best-seller. What's the setup on things like that?"

"It's about like that. Smart young fellows. But there aren't any best-sellers any more. People don't read much nowadays. We'll find something equally profitable for you to do."

Back in the shop, Hawkins gave Barlow a suit of clothes, deposited him in the waiting room, and called Central in Chicago. "Take him away," he pleaded. "I have time for one more firing, and he blathers and blathers. I haven't told him anything. Perhaps we should just turn him loose and let him find his own level, but there's a chance—"

"The Problem," agreed Central. "Yes, there's a chance."

The potter delighted Barlow by making him a cup of coffee with a cube that not only dissolved in cold water but heated the water to boiling point. Killing time, Hawkins chatted about the "rocket" Barlow had admired, and had to haul himself up short; he had almost told the real estate man what its top speed really was—almost, indeed, revealed that it was not a rocket.

He regretted, too, that he had so casually handed Barlow a couple of hundred dollars. The man seemed obsessed with fear that they were worthless, since Hawkins refused to take a note or I.O.U. or even a definite promise of repayment. But Hawkins couldn't go into details, and was very glad when a stranger arrived from Central.

"Tinny-Peete, from Algeciras," the stranger told him swiftly as the two of them met at the door. "Psychist for Poprob. Polasigned special overtake Barlow."

"Thank Heaven," said Hawkins. "Barlow," he told the man from the past, "this is Tinny-Peete. He's going to take care of you and help you make lots of money."

The psychist stayed for a cup of the coffee whose preparation had delighted Barlow, and then conducted the real estate man down the corduroy road to his car, leaving the potter to speculate on whether he could at last crack his kilns.

Hawkins, abruptly dismissing Barlow and The Problem, happily picked the chinking from around the door of the number two kiln, prying it open a trifle. A blast of heat and the heady, smoky scent of the reduction fire delighted him. He peered and saw a corner of a shelf glowing cherry-red, becoming obscured by wavering black areas as it lost heat through the opened door. He slipped a charred wood paddle under a mug on the shelf and pulled it out as a sample, the hairs on the back of his hand curling and scorching. The mug crackled and pinged, and Hawkins sighed happily.

The bismuth resinate luster had fired to perfection, a haunting film of silvery-black metal with strange bluish lights in it as it turned before the eyes, and the Problem of Population seemed very far away to Hawkins then.

Barlow and Tinny-Peete arrived at the concrete highway where the psychist's car was parked in a safety bay.

"What—a—*boat!*" gasped the man from the past.

"Boat? No, that's my car."

Barlow surveyed it with awe. Swept-back lines, deep-drawn compound curves, kilograms of chrome. He ran his hands futilely over the door—or was it the door?—in a futile search for a handle, and asked respectfully, "How fast does it go?"

The psychist gave him a keen look and said slowly, "Two hundred and fifty. You can tell by the speedometer."

"Wow! My old Chevy could hit a hundred on a straight-away, but you're out of my class, mister!"

Tinny-Peete somehow got a huge low door open and Barlow descended three steps into immense cushions, floundering over to the right. He was too fascinated to pay serious attention to his flayed dermis. The dashboard was a lovely wilderness of dials, plugs, indicators, lights, scales and switches.

The psychist climbed down into the driver's seat and did something with his feet. The motor started like lighting a blowtorch as big as a silo. Wallowing around in the cushions, Barlow saw through a rear-view mirror a tremendous exhaust filled with brilliant white sparkles.

"Do you like it?" yelled the psychist.

"It's terrific!" Barlow yelled back. "It's—"

He was shut up as the car pulled out from the bay into the road with a great *voo-ooo-ooom!* A gale roared past Barlow's head, though the windows seemed to be closed; the impression of speed was terrific. He located the speed-ometer on the dashboard and saw it climb past 90, 100, 150, 200.

"Fast enough for me," yelled the psychist, noting that Barlow's face fell in response. "Radio?"

He passed over a surprisingly light object, like a foot-ball helmet, with no trailing wires, and pointed to a row of buttons. Barlow put on the helmet, glad to have the roar of air stilled, and pushed a pushbutton. It lit up satisfy-ingly and Barlow settled back even farther for a sample of the brave new world's super-modern taste in ingenious entertainment.

"TAKE IT AND STICK IT!" a voice roared in his ears.

He snatched off the helmet and gave the psychist an injured look. Tinny-Peete grinned and turned a dial associated with the pushbutton layout. The man from the past donned the helmet again and found the voice had lowered to normal.

"The show of shows! The supershow! The super-duper show! The quiz of quizzes! *Take it and stick it!*"

There were shrieks of laughter in the background.

"Here we got the contes-tants all ready to go. You know how we work it. I hand a contes-tant a triangle-shaped cutout and like that down the line. Now we got these here boards, they got cut-out places the same shape as the triangles and things, only they're all different shapes, and the first contes-tant that sticks the cutouts into the board, he wins.

"Now I'm gonna innaview the first contes-tant. Right here, honey. What's your name?"

"Name? Uh—"

"Hoddaya like that, folks? She don't remember her name! Hah? *Would you buy that for a quarter?*" The question was spoken with arch significance, and the audience shrieked, howled and whistled its appreciation.

It was dull listening when you didn't know the punch lines and catch lines. Barlow pushed another button, with his free hand ready at the volume control.

"—latest from Washington. It's about Senator Hull-Mendoza. He is still attacking the Bureau of Fisheries. The North California Syndicalist says he got affidavits that John Kingsley-Schultz is a bluenose from way back. He didn't publistat the affydavits, but he says they say that Kingsley-Schultz was saw at bluenose meetings in Oregon State College and later at Florida University. Kingsley-Schultz says he gotta confess he did major in fly-casting at Oregon and got his Ph.D. in gamefish at Florida.

"And here is a quote from Kingsley-Schultz: 'Hull-Mendoza don't know what he's talking about. He should drop dead.' Unquote. Hull-Mendoza says he won't publistat the affydavits, to pertect his sources. He says they was sworn by three former employees of the Bureau which was fired for in-competence and in-com-pat-ibility by Kingsley-Schultz.

"Elsewhere they was the usual run of traffic accidents. A three-way pileup of cars on Route 66 going outta Chicago took twelve lives. The Chicago–Los Angeles morning rocket crashed and exploded in the Mo-have—Mo-javvy—what-ever-you-call-it Desert. All the 94 people aboard got killed. A Civil Aeronautics Authority investigator on the scene says that the pilot was buzzing herds of sheep and didn't pull out in time.

"Hey! Here's a hot one from New York! A Diesel tug run wild in the harbor while the crew was below and shoved in the port bow of the luck-shury liner *S. S. Placentia*. It says the ship filled and sank taking the lives of an es-ti-mated 180 passengers and 50 crew members. Six divers was sent down to study the wreckage, but they died, too, when their suits turned out to be fulla little holes.

"And here is a bulletin I just got from Denver. It seems—"

Barlow took off the headset umcomprehendingly. "He seemed so callous," he yelled at the driver. "I was listening to a newscast—"

Tinny-Peete shook his head and pointed at his ears. The roar of air was deafening. Barlow frowned baffledly and stared out of the window.

A glowing sign said:

MOOGS!
WOULD YOU BUY IT
FOR A QUARTER?

He didn't know what Moogs was or were; the illustration showed an incredibly proportioned girl, 99.9 per cent naked, writhing passionately in animated full color.

The roadside jingle was still with him, but with a new feature. Radar or something spotted the car and alerted the lines of the jingle. Each in turn sped along a roadside track, even with the car, so it could be read before the next line was alerted.

IF THERE'S A GIRL
YOU WANT TO GET
DEFLOCCULIZE
UNROMANTIC SWEAT.
"A*R*M*P*I*T*T*O"

Another animated job, in two panels, the familiar "Before and After." The first said, "Just Any Cigar?" and was illustrated with a two-person domestic tragedy of a wife holding her nose while her coarse and red-faced husband puffed a slimy-looking rope. The second panel glowed, "Or a VUELTA ABAJO?" and was illustrated with—

Barlow blushed and looked at his feet until they had passed the sign.

"Coming into Chicago!" bawled Tinny-Peete.

Other cars were showing up, all of them dreamboats. Watching them, Barlow began to wonder if he knew what a kilometer was, exactly. They seemed to be traveling so slowly, if you ignored the roaring air past your ears and didn't let the speedy lines of the dreamboats fool you. He would have sworn they were really crawling along at twenty-five, with occasional spurts up to thirty. How much was a kilometer anyway?

The city loomed ahead, and it was just what it ought to be: towering skyscrapers, overhead ramps, landing platforms for helicopters—

He clutched at the cushions. Those two 'copters. They were going to—they were going to—they—

He didn't see what happened, because their apparent collision courses took them behind a giant building.

Screamingly sweet blasts of sound surrounded them as they stopped for a red light. "What the hell is going on here?" said Barlow in a shrill, frightened voice; because the braking time was just about zero, he wasn't hurled against the dashboard. "Who's kidding who?"

"Why, what's the matter?" demanded the driver. The light changed to green and he started the pickup. Barlow stiffened as he realized that the rush of air past his ears began just a brief, unreal split-second before the car was actually moving. He grabbed for the door handle on his side.

The city grew on them slowly: scattered buildings, denser buildings, taller buildings, and a red light ahead. The car rolled to a stop in zero braking time, the rush of air cut off an instant after it stopped; and Barlow was out of the car and running frenziedly down a sidewalk one instant after that.

They'll track me down, he thought, panting. *It's a secret police thing. They'll get you—mind-reading machines, television eyes everywhere, afraid you'll tell their slaves about freedom and stuff. They don't let anybody cross them, like that story I once read.*

Winded, he slowed to a walk and congratulated himself that he had guts enough not to turn around. That was what they always watched for. Walking, he was just another business-suited back among hundreds. He would be safe, he would be safe—

A hand tumbled from a large, coarse, handsome face thrust close to his: "Wassamatta bumpinninna people likeya owna sidewalk gotta miner slamya inna mushya bassar!" It was neither the mad potter nor the mad driver.

"Excuse me," said Barlow. "What did you say?"

"Oh, yeah?" yelled the stranger dangerously, and waited for an answer.

Barlow with the feeling that he had somehow been suckered into the short end of an intricate land-title deal, heard himself reply belligerently, "Yeah!"

The stranger let go of his shoulder and snarled, "Oh, yeah?"

"Yeah!" said Barlow, yanking his jacket back into shape.

"Aaah!" snarled the stranger, with more contempt and disgust than ferocity. He added an obscenity current in Barlow's time, a standard but physiologically impossible directive, and strutted off hulking his shoulders and balling his fists.

Barlow walked on, trembling. Evidently he had handled it well enough. He stopped at a red light while the long, low dreamboats roared before him and pedestrians in the sidewalk flow with him threaded their ways through the stream of cars. Brakes screamed; fenders clanged and dented; hoarse cries flew back and forth between drivers and walkers. He leaped backward frantically as one car swerved over an arc of sidewalk to miss another.

The signal changed to green; the cars kept on coming for about thirty seconds and then dwindled to an occasional light-runner. Barlow crossed warily and leaned against a vending machine, blowing big breaths.

Look natural, he told himself. *Do something normal. Buy something from the machine.*

He fumbled out some change, got a newspaper for a dime, a handkerchief for a quarter and a candy bar for another quarter.

The faint chocolate smell made him ravenous suddenly. He clawed at the glassy wrapper printed "CRIGGLIES" quite futilely for a few seconds, and then it divided neatly by itself. The bar made three good bites, and he bought two more and gobbled them down.

Thirsty, he drew a carbonated orange drink in another one of the glassy wrappers from the machine for another dime. When he fumbled with it, it divided neatly and spilled all over his knees. Barlow decided he had been there long enough and walked on.

The shop windows were—shop windows. People still wore and bought clothes, still smoked and bought tobacco, still ate and bought food. And they still went to the movies, he saw with pleased surprise as he passed and then returned to a glittering place whose sign said it was THE BIJOU.

The place seemed to be showing a triple feature, *Babies Are Terrible, Don't Have Children,* and *The Canali Kid.*

It was irresistible; he paid a dollar and went in.

He caught the tail-end of *The Canali Kid* in three-dimensional, full-color, full-scent production. It appeared to be an interplanetary saga winding up with a chase scene and a reconciliation between estranged hero and heroine. *Babies Are Terrible* and *Don't Have Children* were fantastic arguments against parenthood—the grotesquely exaggerated dangers of painfully graphic childbirth, vicious children, old parents beaten and starved by their sadistic offspring. The audience, Barlow astoundedly noted, was placidly champing sweets and showing no particular signs of revulsion.

The *Coming Attractions* drove him into the lobby. The fanfares were shattering, the blazing colors blinding, and the added scents stomach-heaving.

When his eyes again became accustomed to the moderate lighting of the lobby, he groped his way to a bench and opened the newspaper he had bought. It turned out to be *The Racing Sheet,* which afflicted him with a crushing sense of loss. The familiar boxed index in the lower left hand corner of the front page showed almost unbearably that Churchill Downs and Empire City were still in business—

Blinking back tears, he turned to the Past Performances at Churchill. They weren't using abbreviations any more, and the pages because of that were single-column instead of double. But it was all the same—or was it?

He squinted at the first race, a three-quarter-mile maiden claimer for thirteen hundred dollars. Incredibly, the track record was two minutes, ten and three-fifths seconds. Any beetle in his time could have knocked off the three-quarter in one-fifteen. It was the same for the other distances, much worse for route events.

What the hell had happened to everything?

He studied the form of a five-year-old brown mare in the second and couldn't make head or tail of it. She'd won and lost and placed and showed and lost and placed without rhyme or reason. She looked like a front-runner for a couple of races and then she looked like a no-good pig and then she looked like a mudder but the next time it rained she wasn't and then she was a stayer and then she was a pig again. In a good five-thousand-dollar allowances event, too!

Barlow looked at the other entries and it slowly dawned on him that they were all like the five-year-old brown mare. Not a single damned horse running had the slightest trace of class.

Somebody sat down beside him and said, "That's the story."

Barlow whirled to his feet and saw it was Tinny-Peete, his driver.

"I was in doubts about telling you," said the psychist, "but I see you have some growing suspicions of the truth. Please don't get excited. It's all right, I tell you."

"So you've got me," said Barlow.

"*Got* you?"

"Don't pretend. I can put two and two together. You're the secret police. You and the rest of the aristocrats live in luxury on the sweat of these oppressed slaves. You're afraid of me because you have to keep them ignorant."

There was a bellow of bright laughter from the psychist that got them blank looks from other patrons of the lobby. The laughter didn't sound at all sinister.

"Let's get out of here," said Tinny-Peete, still chuckling. "You couldn't possibly have it more wrong." He engaged Barlow's arm and led him to the street. "The actual truth is that the millions of workers live in luxury on the sweat of the handful of aristocrats. I shall probably die before my time of overwork unless—" He gave Barlow a speculative look. "You may be able to help us."

"I know that gag," sneered Barlow. "I made money in my time and to make money you have to get people on your side. Go ahead and shoot me if you want, but you're not going to make a fool out of me."

"You nasty little ingrate!" snapped the psychist, with a kaleidoscopic change of mood. "This damned mess is all your fault and the fault of people like you! Now come along and no more of your nonsense."

He yanked Barlow into an office building lobby and an elevator that, disconcertingly, went *whoost* loudly as it rose. The real estate man's knees were wobbly as the psychist pushed him from the elevator, down a corridor and into an office.

A hawk-faced man rose from a plain chair as the door closed behind them. After an angry look at Barlow, he asked the psychist, "Was I called from the Pole to inspect this—this—?"

"Unget updandered. I've deeprobed etfind quasichance exhim Poprobattackline," said the psychist soothingly.

"Doubt," grunted the hawk-faced man.

"Try," suggested Tinny-Peete.

"Very well. Mr. Barlow, I understand you and your lamented had no children."

"What of it?"

"This of it. You were a blind, selfish stupid ass to tolerate economic and social conditions which penalized child-bearing by the prudent and foresighted. You made us what we are today, and I want you to know that we are far from satisfied. Damn-fool rockets! Damn-fool automobiles! Damn-fool cities with overhead ramps!"

"As far as I can see," said Barlow, "you're running down the best features of time. Are you crazy?"

"The rockets aren't rockets. They're turbo-jets—good turbo-jets, but the fancy shell around them makes for a bad drag. The automobiles have a top speed of one hundred kilometers per hour—a kilometer is, if I recall my paleolinguistics, three-fifths of a mile—and the speedometers are all rigged accordingly so the drivers will think they're going two hundred and fifty. The cities are ridiculous, expensive, unsanitary, wasteful conglomerations of people who'd be better off and more productive if they were spread over the countryside.

"We need the rockets and trick speedometers and cities because, while you and your kind were being prudent and foresighted and not having children, the migrant workers, slum dwellers and tenant farmers were shiftlessly and short-sightedly having children—breeding, breeding. My God, how they bred!"

"Wait a minute," objected Barlow. "There were lots of people in our crowd who had two or three children."

"The attrition of accidents, illness, wars, and such took care of that. Your intelligence was bred out. It is gone. Children that should have been born never were. The just-average, they'll-get-along majority took over the population. The average IQ now is 45."

"But that's far in the future—"

"So are you," grunted the hawk-faced man sourly.

"But who are *you* people?"

"Just people—real people. Some generations ago the geneticists realized at last that nobody was going to pay any attention to what they said, so they abandoned words for deeds. Specifically, they formed and recruited for a closed corporation intended to maintain and improve the breed. We are their descendants, about three million of us. There are five billion of the others, so we are their slaves.

"During the past couple of years, I've designed a skyscraper, kept Billings Memorial Hospital here in Chicago running, headed off war with Mexico, and directed traffic at La Guardia Field in New York."

"I don't understand! Why don't you let them go to hell in their own way?"

The man grimaced. "We tried it once for three months. We holed up at the South Pole and waited. They didn't notice it. Some drafting-room people were missing; some chief nurses didn't show up; minor government people on the non-policy level couldn't be located. It didn't seem to matter.

"In a week there was hunger. In two weeks there were famine and plague; in three weeks war and anarchy. We called off the experiment; it took us most of the next generation to get things squared away again."

"But why *didn't* you let them kill each other off?"

"Five billion corpses mean about five hundred million tons of rotting flesh."

Barlow had another idea. "Why don't you sterilize them?"

"Two and one half billion operations is a lot of operations. Because they breed continuously, the job would never be done."

"I see. Like the marching Chinese!"

"Who the devil are they?"

"It was a—uh, paradox of my time. Somebody figured out that if all the Chinese in the world were to line up four abreast, I think it was, and start marching past a given point, they'd never stop because of the babies that would be born and grow up before they passed the point."

"That's right. Only instead of 'a given point,' make it 'the largest conceivable number of operating rooms that we could build and staff.' There could never be enough."

"Say!" said Barlow. "Those movies about babies—was that your propaganda?"

"It was. It doesn't seem to mean a thing to them. We have abandoned the idea of attempting propaganda contrary to a biological drive."

"So if you work *with* a biological drive?"

"I know of none which is consistent with inhibition of fertility."

Barlow's face went poker-blank, the result of years of careful discipline. "You don't, huh? You're the great brains, and you can't think of any?"

"Why, no," said the psychist innocently. "Can you?"

"That depends. I sold ten thousand acres of Siberian tundra—through a dummy firm, of course—after the partition of Russia. The buyers thought they were getting improved building lots on the outskirts of Kiev. I'd say that was a lot tougher than this job."

"How so?" asked the hawk-faced man.

"Those were normal, suspicious customers, and these are morons, born suckers. You just figure out a con they'll fall for; they won't know enough to do any smart checking."

The psychist and the hawk-faced man had also had training; they kept themselves from looking with sudden hope at each other.

"You seem to have something in mind," said the psychist.

Barlow's poker face went blanker still. "Maybe I have. I haven't heard any offer yet."

"There's the satisfaction of knowing that you've prevented Earth's resources from being so plundered," the hawk-faced man pointed out, "that the race will soon become extinct."

"I don't know that," Barlow said bluntly. "All I have is your word."

"If you really have a method, I don't think any price would be too great," the psychist offered.

"Money," said Barlow.

"All you want."

"More than you want," the hawk-faced man corrected.

"Prestige," added Barlow. "Plenty of publicity. My picture and my name in the papers and over TV every day, statues to me, parks and cities and streets and other things named after me. A whole chapter in the history books."

The psychist made a facial sign to the hawk-faced man that meant, "Oh, brother!"

The hawk-faced man signaled back, "Steady, boy!"

"It's not too much to ask," the psychist agreed.

Barlow, sensing a seller's market, said, "Power!"

"Power?" the hawk-faced man repeated puzzledly. "Your own hydro station or nuclear pile?"

"I mean a world dictatorship with me as dictator!"

"Well, now—" said the psychist but the hawk-faced man interrupted, "It would take a special emergency act of Congress but the situation warrants it. I think that can be guaranteed."

"Could you give us some indication of your plan?" the psychist asked.

"Ever hear of lemmings?"

"No."

"They are—were, I guess, since you haven't heard of them—little animals in Norway, and every few years they'd swarm to the coast and swim out to sea until they drowned. I figure on putting some lemming urge into the population."

"How?"

"I'll save that till I get the right signatures on the deal."

The hawk-faced man said, "I'd like to work with you on it, Barlow. My name's Ryan-Ngana." He put out his hand.

Barlow looked closely at the hand, then at the man's face. "Ryan what?"

"Ngana."

"That sounds like an African name."

"It is. My mother's father was a Watusi."

Barlow didn't take the hand. "I thought you looked pretty dark. I don't want to hurt your feelings, but I don't think I'd be at my best working with you. There must be somebody else just as well qualified, I'm sure."

The psychist made a facial sign to Ryan-Ngana that meant, "Steady *yourself*, boy!"

"Very well," Ryan-Ngana told Barlow. "We'll see what arrangement can be made."

"It's not that I'm prejudiced, you understand. Some of my best friends—"

"Mr. Barlow, don't give it another thought. Anybody who could pick on the lemming analogy is going to be useful to us."

And so he would, thought Ryan-Ngana, alone in the office after Tinny-Peete had taken Barlow up to the helicopter stage. So he would. Poprob had exhausted every rational attempt and the new Poprobattacklines would have to be irrational or sub-rational. This creature from the past with his lemming legends and his improved building lots would be a fountain of precious vicious self-interest.

Ryan-Ngana sighed and stretched. He had to go and run the San Francisco subway. Summoned early from the Pole to study Barlow, he'd left unfinished a nice little theorem. Between interruptions, he was slowly constructing an n-dimensional geometry whose foundations and superstructure owed no debt whatsoever to intuition.

Upstairs, waiting for a helicopter, Barlow was explaining to Tinny-Peete that he had nothing against Negroes, and Tinny-Peete wished he had some of Ryan-Ngana's imperturbability and humor for the ordeal.

The helicopter took them to International Airport, where, Tinny-Peete explained, Barlow would leave for the Pole.

The man from the past wasn't sure he'd like a dreary waste of ice and cold.

"It's all right," said the psychist. "A civilized layout. Warm, pleasant. You'll be able to work more efficiently there. All the facts at your fingertips, a good secretary—"

"I'll need a pretty big staff," said Barlow, who had learned from thousands of deals never to take the first offer.

"I meant a private, confidential one," said Tinny-Peete readily, "but you can have as many as you want. You'll naturally have top-primary-top priority if you really have a workable plan."

"Let's not forget this dictatorship angle," said Barlow.

He didn't know that the psychist would just as readily have promised him deification to get him happily on the "rocket" for the Pole. Tinny-Peete had no wish to be torn limb from limb; he knew very well that it would end that way if the population learned from this anachronism that there was a small elite which considered itself head, shoulders, trunk and groin above the rest. The fact that this assumption was perfectly true and the fact that the elite was condemned by its superiority to a life of the most grinding toil would not be considered; the difference would.

The psychist finally put Barlow aboard the "rocket" with some thirty people—real people—headed for the Pole.

Barlow was airsick all the way because of a post-hypnotic suggestion Tinny-Peete had planted in him. One idea was to make him as averse as possible to a return trip, and another idea was to spare the other passengers from his aggressive, talkative company.

Barlow, during the first day at the Pole, was reminded

of his first day in the army. It was the same now-where-the-hell-are-we-going-to-put-*you?* business until he took a firm line with them. Then instead of acting like supply sergeants they acted like hotel clerks.

It was a wonderful, wonderfully calculated buildup, and one that he failed to suspect. After all, in his time a visitor from the past would have been lionized.

At day's end he reclined in a snug underground billet with the 60 mile gales roaring yards overhead, and tried to put two and two together.

It was like old times, he thought—like a coup in real estate where you had the competition by the throat, like a 50-percent rent boost when you knew damned well there was no place for the tenants to move, like smiling when you read over the breakfast orange juice that the city council had decided to build a school on the ground you had acquired by a deal with the city council. And it was simple. He would just sell tundra building lots to eagerly suicidal lemmings, and that was absolutely all there was to solving The Problem that had these double-domes spinning.

They'd have to work out most of the details, naturally; but, what the hell, that was what subordinates were for. He'd need specialists in advertising, engineering, communications—did they know anything about hypnotism? That might be helpful. It not, there'd have to be a lot of bribery done, but he'd make sure—damned sure—there were unlimited funds.

Just selling building lots to lemmings . . .

He wished, as he fell asleep, that poor Verna could have been in on this. It was his biggest, most stupendous deal. Verna—that sharp shyster Sam Immerman must have swindled her. . . .

It began the next day with people coming to visit him. He knew the approach. They merely wanted to be helpful to their illustrious visitor from the past and would he help fill them in about his era, which unfortunately was somewhat obscure historically, and what did he think could be done about The Problem? He told them he was too old to be roped any more, and they wouldn't get any information out of him until he got a letter of intent from at least the Polar President, and a session of the Polar Congress empowered to make him dictator.

He got the letter and the session. He presented his program, was asked whether his conscience didn't revolt at its callousness, explained succinctly that a deal was a deal and anybody who wasn't smart enough to protect himself didn't deserve protection—*"Caveat emptor,"* he threw in for scholarship, and had to translate it to "Let the buyer beware." He didn't, he stated, give a damn about either the morons or their intelligent slaves; he'd told them his price and that was all he was interested in.

Would they meet it or wouldn't they?

The Polar President offered to resign in his favor, with certain temporary emergency powers that the Polar Congress would vote him if he thought them necessary. Barlow demanded the title of World Dictator, complete control of world finances, salary to be decided by himself, and the publicity campaign and historical writeup to begin at once.

"As for the emergency powers," he added, "they are neither to be temporary nor limited."

Somebody wanted the floor to discuss the matter, with the declared hope that perhaps Barlow would modify his demands.

"You've got the proposition," Barlow said. "I'm not knocking off even ten percent."

"But what if the Congress refuses, sir?" the President asked.

"Then you can stay up here at the Pole and try to work it out yourselves. I'll get what I want from the morons. A shrewd operator like me doesn't have to compromise; I haven't got a single competitor in this whole cockeyed moronic era."

Congress waived debate and voted by show of hands. Barlow won unanimously.

"You don't know how close you came to losing me,"

he said in his first official address to the joint Houses. "I'm not the boy to haggle; either I get what I ask or I go elsewhere. The first thing I want is to see designs for a new palace for me—nothing *un*ostentatious either —and your best painters and sculptors to start working on my portraits and statues. Meanwhile, I'll get my staff together."

He dismissed the Polar President and the Polar Congress, telling them that he'd let them know when the next meeting would be.

A week later, the program started with North America the first target.

Mrs. Garvy was resting after dinner before the ordeal of turning on the dishwasher. The TV, of course, was on and it said, "Oooh!"—long, shuddery and ecstatic, the cue for the *Parfum Assault Criminale* spot commercial. "Girls," said the announcer hoarsely, "do you want your man? It's easy to get him—easy as a trip to Venus."

"Huh?" said Mrs. Garvy.

"Wassamatter?" snorted her husband, starting out of a doze.

"Ja hear that?"

"Wha'?"

"He said 'easy like a trip to Venus.'"

"So?"

"Well, I thought ya couldn't get to Venus. I thought they just had that one rocket thing that crashed on the Moon."

"Aah, women don't keep up with the news," said Garvy righteously, subsiding again.

"Oh," said his wife uncertainly.

And the next day, on *Henry's Other Mistress*, there was a new character who had just breezed in: Buzz Rentshaw, Master Rocket Pilot of the Venus run. On *Henry's Other Mistress,* "the broadcast drama about you and your neighbors, *folksy* people, *ordinary* people, *real* people"! Mrs. Garvy listened with amazement over a cooling cup of coffee as Buzz made hay of her hazy convictions.

MONA: Darling, it's so good to see you again!

BUZZ: You don't know how I've missed you on that dreary Venus run.

SOUND: *Venetian blind run down; key turned in door lock.*

MONA: Was it *very* dull, dearest?

BUZZ: Let's not talk about my humdrum job, darling. Let's talk about us.

SOUND: *Creaking bed.*

Well, the program was back to normal at last. That evening Mrs. Garvy tried to ask again whether her husband was sure about those rockets, but he was dozing right through *Take It and Stick It,* so she watched the screen and forgot the puzzle.

She was still rocking with laughter at the gag line, "Would you buy it for a quarter?" when the commercial went on for the detergent powder she always faithfully loaded her dishwasher with on the first of every month.

The announcer displayed mountains of suds from a tiny piece of the stuff and coyly added: "Of course, Cleano don't lay around for you to pick up like the soap root on Venus, but it's pretty cheap and it's almost pretty near just as good. So for us plain folks who ain't lucky enough to live up there on Venus, Cleano is the real cleaning stuff!"

Then the chorus went into their "Cleano-is-the-stuff" jingle, but Mrs. Garvy didn't hear it. She was a stubborn woman, but it occurred to her that she was very sick indeed. She didn't want to worry her husband. The next day she quietly made an appointment with her family freud.

In the waiting room she picked up a fresh new copy of *Readers Pablum* and put it down with a faint palpitation. The lead article, according to the table of contents on the cover, was titled "The Most Memorable Venusian I Ever Met."

"The freud will see you now," said the nurse, and Mrs. Garvy tottered into his office.

His traditional glasses and whiskers were reassuring.

She choked out the ritual: "Freud, forgive me, for I have neuroses."

He chanted the antiphonal: "Tut, my dear girl, what seems to be the trouble?"

"I got like a hole in the head," she quavered. "I seem to forget all kinds of things. Things like everybody seems to know and I don't."

"Well, that happens to everybody occasionally, my dear. I suggest a vacation on Venus."

The freud stared, open-mouthed, at the empty chair. His nurse came in and demanded, "Hey, you see how she scrammed? What was the matter with *her?*"

He took off his glasses and whiskers meditatively. "You can search me. I told her she should maybe try a vacation on Venus." A momentary bafflement came into his face and he dug through his desk drawers until he found a copy of the four-color, profusely illustrated journal of his profession. It had come that morning and he had lip-read it, though looking mostly at the pictures. He leafed through to the article *Advantages of the Planet Venus in Rest Cures.*

"It's right there," he said.

The nurse looked. "It sure is," she agreed. "Why shouldn't it be?"

"The trouble with these here neurotics," decided the freud, "is that they all the time got to fight reality. Show in the next twitch."

He put on his glasses and whiskers again and forgot Mrs. Garvy and her strange behavior.

"Freud, forgive me, for I have neuroses."

"Tut, my dear girl, what seems to be the trouble?"

Like many cures of mental disorders, Mrs. Garvy's was achieved largely by self-treatment. She disciplined herself sternly out of the crazy notion that there had been only one rocket ship and that one a failure. She could join without wincing, eventually, in any conversation on the desirability of Venus as a place to retire, on its fabulous floral profusion. Finally she went to Venus.

All her friends were trying to book passage with the Evening Star Travel and Real Estate Corporation, but naturally the demand was crushing. She considered herself lucky to get a seat at last for the two-week summer cruise. The space ship took off from a place called Los Alamos, New Mexico. It looked just like all the spaceships on television and in the picture magazines, but was more comfortable than you would expect.

Mrs. Garvy was delighted with the fifty or so fellow-passengers assembled before takeoff. They were from all over the country, and she had a distinct impression that they were on the brainy side. The captain, a tall, hawk-faced, impressive fellow named Ryan-Something or other, welcomed them aboard and trusted that their trip would be a memorable one. He regretted that there would be nothing to see because, "due to the meteorite season," the ports would be dogged down. It was disappointing, yet reassuring that the line was taking no chances.

There was the expected momentary discomfort at take-off, and then two monotonous days of droning travel through space to be whiled away in the lounge at cards or craps. The landing was a routine bump and the voyagers were issued tablets to swallow to immunize them against any minor ailments. When the tablets took effect, the lock was opened and Venus was theirs.

It looked much like a tropical island on Earth, except for a blanket of cloud overhead. But it had a heady, other-wordly quality that was intoxicating and glamorous.

The ten days of the vacation were suffused with a hazy magic. The soap root, as advertised, was free and sudsy. The fruits, mostly tropical varieties transplanted from Earth, were delightful. The simple shelters provided by the travel company were more than adequate for the balmy days and nights.

It was with sincere regret that the voyagers filed again into the ship, and swallowed more tablets doled out to counteract and sterilize any Venus illnesses they might unwittingly communicate to Earth.

Vacationing was one thing. Power politics was another.

At the Pole, a small man was in a soundproof room, his face deathly pale and his body limp in a straight chair.

In the American Senate Chamber, Senator Hull-Mendoza (Synd., N. Cal.) was saying: "Mr. President and gentlemen, I would be remiss in my duty as a legislature if'n I didn't bring to the attention of the au-gust body I see here a perilous situation which is fraught with peril. As is well known to members of this au-gust body, the perfection of space flight has brought with it a situation I can only describe as fraught with peril. Mr. President and gentlemen, now that swift American rockets now traverse the trackless void of space between this planet and our nearest planetarial neighbor in space—and, gentlemen, I refer to Venus, the star of dawn, the brightest jewel in fair Vulcan's diadome—now, I say, I want to inquire what steps are being taken to colonize Venus with a vanguard of patriotic citizens like those minutemen of yore.

"Mr. President and gentlemen! There are in this world nations, envious nations—I do not name Mexico—who by fair means or foul may seek to wrest from Columbia's grasp the torch of freedom of space; nations whose low living standards and innate depravity give them an unfair advantage over the citizens of our fair republic.

"This is my program: I suggest that a city of more than 100,000 population be selected by lot. The citizens of the fortunate city are to be awarded choice lands on Venus free and clear, to have and to hold and convey to their descendants. And the national government shall provide free transportation to Venus for these citizens. And this program shall continue, city by city, until there has been deposited on Venus a sufficient vanguard of citizens to protect our manifest rights in that planet.

"Objections will be raised, for carping critics we have always with us. They will say there isn't enough steel. They will call it a cheap giveaway. I say there *is* enough steel for *one* city's population to be transferred to Venus, and that is all that is needed. For when the time comes for the second city to be transferred, the first, emptied city can be wrecked for the needed steel! And is it a give-away? Yes! It is the most glorious giveaway in the history of mankind! Mr. President and gentlemen, there is no time to waste—Venus must be American!"

Black-Kupperman, at the Pole, opened his eyes and said feebly, "The style was a little uneven. Do you think anybody'll notice?"

"You did fine, boy; just fine," Barlow reassured him.

Hull-Mendoza's bill became law.

Drafting machines at the South Pole were busy around the clock and the Pittsburgh steel mills spewed millions of plates into the Los Alamos spaceport of the Evening Star Travel and Real Estate Corporation. It was going to be Los Angeles, for logistic reasons, and the three most accomplished psychokineticists went to Washington and mingled in the crowd at the drawing to make certain that the Los Angeles capsule slithered into the fingers of the blindfolded Senator.

Los Angeles loved the idea and a forest of spaceships began to blossom in the desert. They weren't very good spaceships, but they didn't have to be.

A team at the Pole worked at Barlow's direction on a mail setup. There would have to be letters to and from Venus to keep the slightest taint of suspicion from arising. Luckily Barlow remembered that the problem had been solved once before—by Hitler. Relatives of persons incinerated in the furnaces of Lublin or Majdanek continued to get cheery postal cards.

The Los Angeles flight went off on schedule, under tremendous press, newsreel, and television coverage. The world cheered the gallant Angelenos who were setting off on their patriotic voyage to the land of milk and honey. The forest of spaceships thundered up, and up, and out of sight without untoward incident. Billions envied the Angelenos, cramped and on short rations though they were.

Wreckers from San Francisco, whose capsule came up second, moved immediately into the city of the angels for the scrap steel their own flight would require. Senator Hull-Mendoza's constituents could do no less.

The president of Mexico, hypnotically alarmed at this extension of *yanqui imperialismo* beyond the stratosphere, launched his own Venus-colony program.

Across the water it was England versus Ireland, France versus Germany, China versus Russia, India versus Indonesia. Ancient hatreds grew into the flames that were rocket ships assailing the air by hundreds daily.

Dear Ed, how are you? Sam and I are fine and hope you are fine. Is it nice up there like they say with food and close grone on trees? I drove by Springfield yesterday and it sure looked funny all the buildings down but of coarse it is worth it we have to keep the greasers in their place. Do you have any trouble with them on Venus? Drop me a line some time. Your loving sister, Alma.

Dear Alma, I am fine and hope you are fine. It is a fine place here fine climate and easy living. The doctor told me today that I seem to be ten years younger. He thinks there is something in the air here keeps people young. We do not have much trouble with the greasers here they keep to theirselves it is just a question of us outnumbering them and staking out the best places for the Americans. In South Bay I know a nice little island that I have been saving for you and Sam with lots of blanket trees and ham bushes. Hoping to see you and Sam soon, your loving brother, Ed.

Sam and Alma were on their way shortly.

Poprob got a dividend in every nation after the emigration had passed the halfway mark. The lonesome stay-at-homes were unable to bear the melancholy of a low population density; their conditioning had been to swarms of their kin. After that point it was possible to foist off the crudest stripped-down accommodations on would-be emigrants; they didn't care.

Black-Kupperman did a final job on President Hull-Mendoza, the last job that genius of hypnotics would ever do on any moron, important or otherwise.

Hull-Mendoza, panic-stricken by his presidency over an emptying nation, joined his constituents. The *Independence,* aboard which traveled the national government of America, was the most elaborate of all the spaceships—bigger, more comfortable, with a lounge that was handsome, though cramped, and cloakrooms for Senators and Representatives. It went, however, to the same place as the others and Black-Kupperman killed himself, leaving a note that stated he "couldn't live with my conscience."

The day after the American President departed, Barlow flew into a rage. Across his specially built desk were supposed to flow all Poprob high-level documents and this thing—this outrageous thing—called Poprob*term* apparently had got into the executive stage before he had even had a glimpse of it!

He buzzed for Rogge-Smith, his statistician. Rogge-Smith seemed to be at the bottom if it. Poprobterm seemed to be about first and second and third derivatives, whatever they were. Barlow had a deep distrust of anything more complex than what he called an "average."

While Rogge-Smith was still at the door, Barlow snapped, "What's the meaning of this? Why haven't I been consulted? How far have you people got and why have you been working on something I haven't authorized?"

"Didn't want to bother you, Chief," said Rogge-Smith. "It was really a technical matter, kind of a final cleanup. Want to come and see the work?"

Mollified, Barlow followed his statistician down the corridor.

"You still shouldn't have gone ahead without my okay," he grumbled. "Where the hell would you people have been without me?"

"That's right, Chief. We couldn't have swung it ourselves; our minds just don't work that way. And all that stuff you knew from Hitler—it wouldn't have occurred to us. Like poor Black-Kupperman."

They were in a fair-sized machine shop at the end of a slight upward incline. It was cold. Rogge-Smith pushed a button that started a motor, and a flood of arctic light poured in as the roof parted slowly. It showed a small spaceship with the door open.

Barlow gaped as Rogge-Smith took him by the elbow and his other boys appeared: Swenson-Swenson, the engineer; Tsutsugimushi-Duncan, his propellants man; Kalb-French, advertising.

"In you go, Chief," said Tsutsugimushi-Duncan. "This is Poprobterm."

"But I'm the World Dictator!"

"You bet, Chief. You'll be in history, all right—but this is necessary, I'm afraid."

The door was closed. Acceleration slammed Barlow cruelly to the metal floor. Something broke, and warm, wet stuff, salty tasting, ran from his mouth to his chin. Arctic sunlight through a port suddenly became a fierce lancet stabbing at his eyes; he was out of the atmosphere.

Lying twisted and broken under the acceleration, Barlow realized that some things had not changed, that Jack Ketch was never asked to dinner however many shillings you paid him to do your dirty work, that murder will out, that crime pays only temporarily.

The last thing he learned was that death is the end of pain.

Of course, there is one rather reliable solution for the population problem. The name of the game is War. War lovers might protest fairly that this well-established institution has had unjustified bad press, since it is known that war produces not only a commendable curtailment of population but also an impetus to technological innovation and a healthy spur to business.

The only problem, to be sure, is that in the event the war gets out of hand, the population curtailment may be excessive, the products of technology may no longer be relevant, and all in all, it may turn out to be—

A BAD DAY FOR SALES

Fritz Leiber

The big bright doors parted with a *whoosh* and Robie glided suavely onto Times Square. The crowd that had been watching the fifty-foot tall clothing-ad girl get dressed, or reading the latest news about the Hot Truce scrawl itself in yard-high script, hurried to look.

Robie was still a novelty. Robie was fun. For a little while yet he could steal the show.

But the attention did not make Robie proud. He had no more vanity than the pink plastic giantess, and she did not even flicker her blue mechanical eyes.

Robie radared the crowd, found that it surrounded him solidly, and stopped. With a calculated mysteriousness, he said nothing.

"Say, ma, he doesn't look like a robot at all. He looks sort of like a turtle."

Which was not completely inaccurate. The lower part of Robie's body was a metal hemisphere hemmed with sponge rubber and not quite touching the sidewalk. The upper was a metal box with black holes in it. The box could swivel and duck.

A chromium-bright hoopskirt with a turret on top.

"Reminds me too much of the Little Joe Baratanks," a

veteran of the Persian War muttered, and rapidly rolled himself away on wheels rather like Robie's.

His departure made it easier for some of those who knew about Robie to open a path in the crowd. Robie headed straight for the gap. The crowd whooped.

Robie glided very slowly down the path, deftly jogging aside whenever he got too close to ankles in skylon or sockassins. The rubber buffer on his hoopskirt was merely an added safeguard.

The boy who had called Robie a turtle jumped in the middle of the path and stood his ground, grinning foxily.

Robie stopped two feet short of him. The turret ducked. The crowd got quiet.

"Hello, youngster," Robie said in a voice that was smooth as that of a TV star, and was in fact a recording of one.

The boy stopped smiling. "Hello," he whispered.

"How old are you?" Robie asked.

"Nine. No, eight."

"That's nice," Robie observed. A metal arm shot down from his neck, stopped just short of the boy. The boy jerked back.

"For you," Robie said gently.

The boy gingerly took the red polly-lop from the neatly-fashioned blunt metal claws. A gray-haired woman whose son was a paraplegic hurried on.

After a suitable pause Robie continued, "And how about a nice refreshing drink of Poppy Pop to go with your polly-lop?" The boy lifted his eyes but didn't stop licking the candy. Robie wiggled his claws ever so slightly. "Just give me a quarter and within five seconds—"

A little girl wriggled out of the forest of legs. "Give me a polly-lop too, Robie," she demanded.

"Rita, come back here," a woman in the third rank of the crowd called angrily.

Robie scanned the newcomer gravely. His reference silhouettes were not good enough to let him distinguish the sex of children, so he merely repeated, "Hello, youngster."

"Rita!"

"Give me a polly-lop!"

Disregarding both remarks, for a good salesman is single-minded and does not waste bait, Robie said winningly, "I'll bet you read *Junior Space Killers*. Now I have here—"

"Uh-hhh, I'm a girl. *He* got a polly-lop."

At the word "girl" Robie broke off. Rather ponderously he said, "Then—" After another pause he continued, "I'll bet you read *Gee-Gee Jones, Space Stripper*. Now I have here the latest issue of that thrilling comic, not yet in the stationary vending machines. Just give me fifty cents and within five—"

"Please let me through. I'm her mother."

A young woman in the front rank drawled over her powder-sprayed shoulder, "I'll get her for you," and slithered out on six-inch platforms. "Run away, children," she said nonchalantly and lifting her arms behind her head, pirouetted slowly before Robie to show how much she did for her bolero half-jacket and her form-fitting slacks that melted into skylon just above the knees. The little girl glared at her. She ended the pirouette in profile.

At this age-level Robie's reference silhouettes permitted him to distinguish sex, though with occasional amusing and embarrassing miscalls. He whistled admiringly. The crowd cheered.

Someone remarked critically to his friend. "It would go better if he was built more like a real robot. You know, like a man."

The friend shook his head. "This way it's subtler."

No one in the crowd was watching the newscript overhead as it scribbled, "Ice Pack for Hot Truce? Vanadin hints Russ may yield on Pakistan."

Robie was saying, ". . . in the savage new glamor-tint we have christened Mars Blood, complete with spray applicator and fit-all fingerstalls that mask each finger completely except for the nail. Just give me five dollars—uncrumpled bills may be fed into the revolving rollers you see beside my arm—and within five seconds,—"

"No thanks, Robie," the young woman yawned.

"Remember," Robie persisted, "for three more weeks seductivising Mars Blood will be unobtainable from any other robot or human vendor."

"No thanks."

Robie scanned the crowd resourcefully. "Is there any gentleman here . . ." he began just as a woman elbowed her way through the front rank.

"I told you to come back!" she snarled at the little girl.

"But I didn't get my polly-lop!"

". . . who would care to . . ."

"Rita!"

"Robie cheated. Ow!"

Meanwhile the young woman in the half-bolero had scanned the nearby gentlemen on her own. Deciding that there was less than a fifty per cent chance of any of them accepting the proposition Robie seemed about to make, she took advantage of the scuffle to slither gracefully back into the ranks. Once again the path was clear before Robie.

He paused, however, for a brief recapitulation of the more magical properties of Mars Blood, including a telling phrase about "the passionate claws of a Martian sunrise."

But no one bought. It wasn't quite time yet. Soon enough silver coins would be clinking, bills going through the rollers faster than laundry, and five hundred people struggling for the privilege of having their money taken away from them by America's only genuine mobile sales-robot.

But now was too soon. There were still some tricks that Robie did free, and one certainly should enjoy those before starting the more expensive fun.

So Robie moved on until he reached the curb. The variation in level was instantly sensed by his under-scanners. He stopped. His head began to swivel. The crowd watched in eager silence. This was Robie's best trick.

Robie's head stopped swiveling. His scanners had found the traffic light. It was green. Robie edged forward. But then it turned red. Robie stopped again, still on the curb. The crowd softly *ahhed* its delight.

Oh, it was wonderful to be alive and watching Robie on such a wonderful day. Alive and amused in the fresh, weather-controlled air between the lines of bright skyscrapers with their winking windows and under a sky so blue you could almost call it dark.

(But way, way up, where the crowd could not see, the sky was darker still. Purple-dark, with stars showing. And in that purple-dark, a silver-green something, the color of a bud, plunged downward at better than three miles a second. The silver-green was a paint that foiled radar.)

Robie was saying, "While we wait for the light there's time for you youngsters to enjoy a nice refreshing Poppy Pop. Or for you adults—only those over five feet are eligible to buy—to enjoy an exciting Poppy Pop fizz. Just give me a quarter or—I'm licenced to dispense intoxicating liquors—in the case of adults one dollar and a quarter and within five seconds . . .

But that was not cutting it quite fine enough. Just three seconds later the silver-green bud bloomed above Manhattan into a globular orange flower. The skyscrapers grew brighter and brighter still, the brightness of the inside of the sun. The windows winked white fire.

The crowd around Robie bloomed too. Their clothes puffed into petals of flame. Their heads of hair were torches.

The orange flower grew, stem and blossom. The blast came. The winking windows shattered tier by tier, became black holes. The walls bent, rocked, cracked. A stony dandruff dribbled from their cornices. The flaming flowers on the sidewalk were all leveled at once. Robie was shoved ten feet. His metal hoopskirt dimpled, regained its shape.

The blast ended. The orange flower, grown vast, vanished overhead on its huge, magic beanstalk. It grew dark and very still. The cornice-dandruff pattered down. A few small fragments rebounded from the metal hoopskirt.

Robie made some small, uncertain movements, as if feeling for broken bones. He was hunting for the traffic light, but it no longer shone, red or green.

He slowly scanned a full circle. There was nothing anywhere to interest his reference silhouettes. Yet whenever he tried to move, his under-scanners warned him of low obstructions. It was very puzzling.

The silence was disturbed by moans and a crackling sound, faint at first as the scampering of rats.

A seared man, his charred clothes fuming where the blast had blown out the fire, rose from the curb. Robie scanned him.

"Good day, sir," Robie said. "Would you care for a smoke? A truly cool smoke? Now I have here a yet-unmarketed brand . . ."

But the customer had run away, screaming, and Robie never ran after customers, though he could follow them at a medium brisk roll. He worked his way along the curb where the man had sprawled, carefully keeping his distance from the low obstructions, some of which writhed now and then, forcing him to jog. Shortly he reached a fire hydrant. He scanned it. His electronic vision, though it still worked, had been somewhat blurred by the blast.

"Hello, youngster," Robie said. Then, after a long pause, "Cat got your tongue? Well, I've got a little present for you. A nice, lovely polly-lop." His metal arm snaked down.

"Take it, youngster," he said after another pause. "It's for you. Don't be afraid."

His attention was distracted by other customers, who began to rise up oddly here and there, twisting forms that confused his reference silhouettes and would not stay to be scanned properly. One cried, "Water," but no quarter clinked in Robie's claws when he caught the word and suggested, "How about a nice refreshing drink of Poppy Pop?"

The rat-crackling of the flames had become a jungle muttering. The blind windows began to wink fire again.

A little girl marched up, stepping neatly over arms and legs she did not look at. A white dress and the once taller bodies around her had shielded her from the brilliance and the blast. Her eyes were fixed on Robie. In them was the same imperious confidence, though none of the delight, with which she had watched him earlier.

"Help me, Robie," she said. "I want my mother."

"Hello, youngster," Robie said. "What would you like? Comics? Candy?"

"Where is she, Robie? Take me to her."

"Balloons? Would you like to watch me blow up a balloon?"

The little girl began to cry. The sound triggered off another of Robie's novelty circuits.

"Is something wrong?" he asked. "Are you in trouble? Are you lost?"

"Yes, Robie. Take me to my mother."

"Stay right here," Robie said reassuringly, "and don't be frightened. I will call a policeman." He whistled shrilly, twice.

Time passed. Robie whistled again. The windows flared and roared. The little girl begged, "Take me away, Robie," and jumped onto a little step in his hoopskirt.

"Give me a dime," Robie said. The little girl found one in her pocket and put it in his claws.

"Your weight," Robie said, "is fifty-four and one-half pounds, exactly."

"Have you seen my daughter, have you seen her?" a woman was crying somewhere. "I left her watching that thing while I stepped inside—Rita!"

"Robie helped me," the little girl was telling her moments later. "He knew I was lost. He even called a policeman, but he didn't come. He weighed me too. Didn't you, Robie?"

But Robie had gone off to peddle Poppy Pop to the members of a rescue squad which had just come around the corner, more robot-like than he in their fireproof clothing.

Well, now let's look at it another way. Suppose we don't wholly wipe ourselves out. Let's look at some of the possible futures that lie ahead in the joyous event that somehow we muddle through our food, population, and lethal pollution problems.

Let's examine, for example, some of the consequences of the motorcar. We know all about its propensity for pouring assorted toxins and stenches into the air, but do we really think as much as we ought to about its other anti-social traits? Are we ready to face up to such installations as—

STATION HR972

Kenneth Bulmer

Most mornings Bartram would see the crane driver from the auto repair station walk over to HR972 for coffee and a post mortem on the night's incidents and possibilities for the day. All the time the driver sat blockily in the rest area with his thick fingers cradling the plastic coffee cup, his head would be half-turned, like a bird eyeing a worm, listening on his earphone for the first notes of a call.

Libby, the torso technician for whose sake he walked the hundred extra yards for coffee, played it cool, daily less shy, daily more inclined to talk about her own handling of units and less to listen to his accounts of rapid crane manipulations.

The first time Bartram had said: "So long as you maintain your efficiency rating, Libby, I'm prepared to allow you to flirt between incidents." He'd quirked an eye at the fidgeting driver. "What Samuelson has to say about his crane driver being a clear hundred yards away from his cab is none of my affair."

Now he would pass them with a small friendly smile as he went up onto the roof of the station to take his morning observations.

"Morning, Chief," the night super, Cy Weiss, a small dark intense man with a woman's charm, would say as Bartram appeared. He'd go through the night's incidents in a kind of ritual pronouncement: "An easy one." "Bad." "Two fingers is all, didn't even have to bring her in." And so on, in a brief, capsulated edition of the night's news.

"Morning, Cy." Bartram waited until Weiss had left and he had been joined by Karl Grecos, the day super, and then he would cock his head toward the sky, ritually, and say, according to the state of the weather: "Big one today;" or, "Rain. Should slow things;" or, "Clouds clearing, we'll get them through this afternoon."

Grecos had the wide, flat shoulders of an athlete, fair luxuriant hair from his mother and a quizzical smile that seemed to ask imponderable questions. But his hands never shook when he held a scalpel. He owned to a fondness for oily food, and his waistline was beginning to advertise this.

They both leaned on the guardrail and looked out on the road.

The Road.

From here the limits of the ten-mile stretch for which Station HR972 was responsible lay on the one hand behind the swell of the hill and on the other lost in a gentle undulation of the land leading up to Sennocke Forest. The road lay across the countryside like a fat white worm. Transparent roofing arched across the twelve lanes, hanging in a cunning curve of convoluting strength, unbuttressed and unguyed, a free overarching sweep of plastic that membraned the artificial environment of the road from nature's anarchy without.

Occasionally through whims in the course of the road the northbound twelve lanes could be seen, a silvery-gray rotundity, beyond their own southbound highway. A brooding awareness of waiting sharpened movement on the road, so that the mechanics around the helicopters on the roof landing spots, the medics sitting checking their morning take-over logs in the ready area, the men carrying in supplies and others carting away the detritus of the night all moved as though imbued with that breath of waiting.

A few cars spun through the morning light, individual and widely separated on the road.

On this morning Bartram pushed at his sleeves and said: "I can smell it, Karl. Meteorology gave us twelve full hours of sunshine. No rain. We'll be busy."

"Yeah." Grecos breathed through his nose, hard. "Cy had it easy. That means—"

"The road," said Bartram. "Just look at it. It's an affront to nature, really—yet . . ."

"I always think," Grecos said, turning to lean on the parapet with his elbows angular, "It looks just like an extra-long pipe of spaghetti my kids like to draw out on the table."

Bartram laughed. "You mean before they add tomato sauce."

After a short splintery silence, Bartram added: "I meant tomato sauce, Karl."

"I know you did, Chief. Gets you all ways, the road."

A helicopter's rotors twanged around with a startling roar and then choked away into whickering gulps of air. The cars speeding like arterial blood cells along the road made little noise. Already the heat of the sun's reflections was activating anticondensation devices on the roof. Vents opened like anemones as thermocouples reacted.

Bartram pivoted the pedestal-mounted binoculars and sighted on the auto repair station a hundred yards north. Men over there were working about their copters and cranes.

"If Samuelson speaks to me about one of my staff luring one of his away—I'll be hard put to it not to be rude."

"Samuelson's all right, Chief. He's new on the road. He'll learn."

"If he doesn't he'll be back in a breaker's yard packaging cars into tin cans."

The gray-green plastic surface of the road reflected no highlights. Its semitactile tread hugged the cars to it as they sped imperiously past. Most of the cars so far this morning had selected the inner and center quads. The twelve lanes were divided into three groups of four lanes each, the inner subdivided for heavy trucks and articulateds, and lighter trucks and coaches. Checking the speed radar meters, Bartram saw only six cars traveling at over a hundred and fifty miles an hour, all on the outer two lanes of the center quad.

An automobile on the inner center quad swept past at ninety miles an hour.

"The fool!" said Bartram heatedly. Then the high, irritating wail of a police car tailing the laggard telescoped time, and the offending car increased its speed to conform to the law.

"That'll cost him a fat fine," said Grecos with satisfaction.

The police car cut down the off-staging ramp that swept around beneath the road and emerged again on the service road leading to HR972 and the auto repair station.

"It'll be Barney," said Bartram. "He'll have the feel of the road by now." That was part of the ritual too.

They went down in the elevator, talking quietly. Past the rest area, Bartram saw with a smirk that Libby's crane-driving beau had gone. The sound of coffee cups being washed swished steamily from the kitchen.

The ceremonial quality of those early morning actions, genuflecting through the build-up time of waiting, helped men and women to adjust off-road mentalities to the demands of the motorway. Barney, heavy, muscular, his black patrolman's uniform creasing sloppily from too much sitting in cars, puffed as he stood up, one hand grasping the car door. Bartram smiled.

"Morning, Barney. Big one today?"

"Yeah. That's for sure. Did you see that creepy-crawly horror? Ninety in the hundred-twenty-five, hundred-fifty lane!"

"You sireened him smartly."

"Sireened him! I'd like to put a boot in his guts!"

Walking with Barney back to the rest area for a coffee, Bartram said, "How's Tommy?"

At once Barney enthused. "He's doing just great! Law school suits him. He'll be a great man one day. One thing's for sure, I'll do anything to stop him being a cop on the road, so help me."

"He could do a lot worse." Bartram caught Grecos' eye and smiled; then they entered the station building; and, with the road out of vision, an unnatural relaxation took possession of them so that they spoke and moved with a louder, more flamboyant gesture.

Outside the road waited.

Grecos walked across to check the flow meters.

"Building up, chief," he called. "Better than ten a minute and rising."

"No worries yet."

"I heard tell they were talking about cutting down the distance intervals." Barney sloshed his coffee around watching the wave ripples. "They figured they could set the radars to half the distance. Pack more cars in a length that way."

"They're close enough as it is," Bartram said dourly.

"That's what we say. But they have to move traffic. Ten thousand cars want to hit the road—something has to give."

"Yeah. And we know what gives."

High atop the station, in every room, in the rest area, in the garages, on the helicopter spots, above the basins in the washrooms, the auto repair alarm shrilled. Hard on that strident call the alarm for HR972 chittered in harsh counterpoint.

Chairs crashed back. Coffee cups spilled. Feet hammered concrete. Helicopter vanes whirred into shining invisibility. The place emptied as though a time bomb set for *now* was found between everyone's legs.

Bartram's earphones said: "HR972. Grid six two eight. Center quad, two outer lanes."

That was one point two eight miles south of the station, set midway on its ten-mile stretch of road.

The helicopters rose buzzing. They slanted away steeply, low over the rounded continuous cylinder of the road, jets roaring. Early morning sunshine caught their white paint and dazzled from the red crosses.

Charlie, the ladder handler, crouched by the open trap in the floor of the chopper. His rough scarred hands grasped the controls, and wind tugged at his white coveralls. Bruce and Pete, the hook men, lay stomach down in front of him, their hands thrust deeply into the gloved remote-control equipment. Bartram glanced back. Everyone in the belly of his lead copter stood at stations, coveralled, helmeted, goggled, packs with their glaring red crosses strapped in regulation positions.

"Nice and smoothly now," he said over the intercom. "First today. Let's set the pattern."

The hook men moved their hands with gentle feeling motions. Below them at the end of the stinglike probes mechanical grapnels moved in unison. The copter pilot, Sally, a good flier, said, "Here we go. Hooks!"

Bruce and Pete struck, hooked the rings in the roof sections below, hoicked.

Like a bivalve forded open by a marlinspike the transparent roof panels opened upward and outwards. Charlie dropped his ladder clean through. It hit the gray-green plastic road beside a red sedan on its side, foam smothered, rear telescoped. Two roof panels further along the auto repair gang had their cranes down and were lifting the green roadster. It squealed like a trapped animal as metal tore. Police had sealed off the two outer lanes of the center quad, their furthest light and radar beacon four miles back.

Bartram turned on his back jets and dropped straight through the hole, boots together, hands on the controls, seeing the flaring jet stabbing below him. His control line sizzled down the ladder. He hit the road hard, staggered a pace, then snapped the link from the ladder and dived at the red saloon.

His team followed in order, moving smoothly about their work. He saw Libby, calm and unflurried; her jet cut as her feet touched down.

The auto repair gang had the yellow car and the late-model General Autos sedan, the last in this small, four-car pile up, hoisted away. Only the General Autos sedan could be recognized by make and year; the other cars were merely colored contortions of metal. The sweeping gang were already running their giant vacuum cleaners across the road, the broken shards of metal and glass, the bits of plastic and the odd items of personal belongings pinging as they whirled up into the bags.

"Hurry it up!" Bartram shouted over his phone. "The auto boys have nearly finished."

Team One had cut away the scarlet car's side. The team leader leaned in with his shears and cut away the driver's harness in four neat snips. The passengers sat cocooned in the airbags that had inflated around them in the moment of impact as transducers sensed the acceleration rate change. Swift stabbing jabs punctured the bags. Hands and grapnels took the passengers out. By this time the scarlet car, foam dripping, trailing metal and twisted strands of cabling, had been hoisted twenty feet above the road level.

The teams from HR972 worked either clinging to the car or treading air on their back jets.

The driver was hoisted away first. The harness had saved his life, and the absence of a dashboard and the deep padding over every projection had saved him from fatal injury. But his ribs were mangled, his pelvis splintered and flattened, his face congested. Libby took over with her assistant torso technicians, was already working on him as they floated up through the hole into the belly of the waiting copter.

"He'll do," she called down flatly.

The two woman passengers had been bruised from neck to knees. Calmly Bartram stripped their flowery dresses away, snipped and snapped at lacy underclothes, revealed white flesh turning green and blue as he watched. The team took over, cocooning the women, plastic compresses and ointments covering up in soothing balm as antishock injections turned brutal unconsciousness into controlled sleep. Bartram swung away.

Team Two was working on the green roadster, their white coveralled figures clustering around the car, strung under the roof like white moths around a green lamp.

Team Three had taken the auto-stretcher-bound driver of the General Autos sedan out, and he was already on his way up to the copter.

"Team Four!" called Bartram sharply. "What's the holdup?"

The yellow car had been concertinaed. Despite all the cunning guile of automobile manufacturers in transducer-actuated airbags, in padded safety within, in plastic-layered stretch glass, in box-girder construction, the yellow car looked like a cardboard carton that has been smacked between two fists. The road wheels had been taken away from where they had been scattered across the road. But the doors had not opened; their safety locks functioning still under the one hundred gravities stress at the moment of impact.

Team Four was trying to cut its way in.

Team Leader Steve said, breathlessly: "Jammed hard. Cutter flame too near driver. Going in from the roof."

"Well, get with it, Steve! Everyone else is away."

The other three cars had been emptied of casualties, the copters already whirring away back to HR972. Police were retrieving their radar and sight beacons, progressively pulling into the site of the incident. The four cars hung from the roof, and the auto repair gangs were beginning to take them out through the roof panels.

Police Super Metcalfe walked slowly up the white line marking the two outer lanes of the center quad. His face looked grave and calm, down tilted, the light catching the slant of his jaw and the white bristle of his eyebrows. He walked as a captain paces his bridge during a storm. Then he looked up with a sharp, decisive movement.

"All clear. You may open the lanes again."

His black car snarled alongside, and he stepped in and was whisked away. Sixty seconds later the first of the traffic whispered past the spot where the incident had occurred.

The road was open again.

All the time, traffic had been passing in a long blurred procession of speed on all the other ten lanes, unconcerned, hardly seeing, matter-of-fact.

Bartram angrily started to call Team Four.

Steve cut across. "Belaying cutting. Driver dead."

Bartram wiped his mouth with a tissue. "Well, you can't win them all."

They packed up and coptered back to the station.

The white buildings like shoe boxes below tilted as the copter swung for a landing, and Bartram's earphones said in the voice of the dispatcher: "Incident for HR972. Grid one nine five. Outer quad, three inner lanes."

"Up," said Bartram. Then: "Outer quad—that's always rough."

Grid position lay one point nine five miles from the beginning of their section as it emerged from Sennock Forest. Bartram looked ahead. "Twelve lanes of high-speed death," he said. "I must be feeling old."

This time they hit the road before the auto repair gangs had lifted all the cars. The outer quad was the high-speed quad. Two hundred, two hundred fifty miles an hour, strictly lane controlled. A pile-up could telescope a hundred cars, radar alarms locked to brakes or no damn radar alarms. Bartram sent support Teams Thirty through Forty to check the cars stopped, undamaged, in back of the incident.

"Look for internal bleeding, shock, cracked or bruised ribs, general buffeting." He cracked the whip. "You don't have to hit a car to damage yourself. Don't let any through until they've been checked."

Libby jetted past holding a girl with no legs, her aides with the plastic bags and the pumps hovering beneath.

The three lanes held a tangle of cars like a child's toy-car box at bedtime.

Libby's voice screamed, "You can't sew your damn legs until I've replaced the liver and pancreas!"

Gloria, the limb technician, screamed back: "Well hurry it up, Libby! The legs are out of deep freeze, and they won't wait all day!"

The swab-up boys were already squirting chemicals to clear off the blood from the road's neutral gray-green.

In the hospital box temporarily tethered from the roof Karl Grecos called down, his mike still worn beneath his surgeon's mask: "Chief! Unit's brain damaged too extensively. He'll never think normally—well, you know! Permission to check out—I've a waiting list—"

"Check him out, Karl."

Handlers sheeted out the stretcher, and another unit slid onto the table. Grecos trepanned and operated with an efficiency seldom matched on the road; but even he could not work miracles.

Gloria had begun attaching fresh legs to the girl, and Libby was deep within the belly of the girl's father, replacing kidneys that had been smashed like squashed oranges.

A handler triggered a pick-up truck across. Discarded legs and arms protruded like pencils from a glass. Bartram looked closer, said: "What's that head doing in there, Bill?"

"I had the okay on that from Mister Grecos, Chief. Clean decapitation off that roadster. Guy was driving with the top down. Took it off clean as a whistle."

"Check."

Cars were being hauled up to the roof out of the way to await their turn to be lifted through the access panels. The auto repair gangs were sweating it out today. Personnel from HR972, too, weren't sitting down on the job. Bartram chivvied and chased them. "You haven't begun the shift yet!"

"Can you hold that girl—that unit—on intravenous oxy till we hit the station?" Libby asked viciously.

"Just about." The nurse aide stepped up the flow.

"What's the problem, Libby?" asked Bartram, jetting across.

"All out of her size capacity lungs, chief. Why do these girls all have the same lung demands, I wonder?"

"Make a note to carry more spare lungs in that size bracket. I'll confirm in standing orders."

"Check."

Some of the choppers lifted off, their red crosses shining bravely against white paintwork. The auto repair gangs cleared their area. The police began to pull in their radar beacons. Police Super Metcalfe's car spun up, and he jumped out, ready to give the final word.

"Clear?" he asked Bartram.

"Clear. Didn't count the tally."

"Not too bad. Fifty cars—we think. Some of the pieces were rather small."

"Not as small as some of the bits we pick up."

Metcalfe grimaced. "You can keep your job, Bartram."

"If people intend to drive on the highways, then someone has to look out for them. What else should we do? Let them bleed to death by the roadside? Let them lose an arm or a leg or a liver and go through life without? When we have banks stuffed with human spare parts?"

"All right, Bartram. My job is to keep the road open. Your job is to repair the humans on the road. We work together."

"So long as we need roads then we'll be needed."

Metcalfe began his ceremonial walk down the white line.

"Until they design foolproof cars and foolproof roads, you mean."

"When they do."

"They will, one day."

"Speed the day, then."

Metcalfe waved his arms, shooing the last of the vacuum cleaners away. He signaled. His black car picked him up. Bartram jetted up to his copter. The road was open again.

Sixty seconds later traffic flowed past the site of the incident, traveling at two hundred, two hundred fifty miles an hour.

This time they made it back to the station. At Station HR972 a dynamic energy possessed them as kits were made up to strength, more spare arms and legs, kidneys, livers, jawbones, more plasma, more whole blood. More splints and bandages and vials of rare and costly drugs. More of everything to repair the human frame subjected to force it had not been designed to withstand, forces that would in another place and another time have killed irrevocably.

Down in the hospital medics were checking out units that had been processed, seeing them onto the ambulance service stretchers, making sure they brought back their own stretchers and skeletons—stores were touchy about unnecessary waste of materiel.

"There they go," Bartram said to Grecos, watching the ambulances pull away. They ground in low gear out up the service ramps and so out onto the road for conveyance to the city hospitals.

"Yeah," said Grecos. "The old pipeline."

"All patched up and smiling; they'll be out on the road again soon. Maybe we'll even have some of them through here again."

"Still and all, you have to *have* the road. I mean, roads are the lifeblood of our transportation system, aren't they?"

"Oh, sure," said Bartram, rubbing his jaw and remembering. "Sure."

"I mean—" Grecos looked his perplexity. "You can't legislate roads out of existence. I mean—they exist. They have to. How could our civilization exist, else?"

Bartram checked the flow meters. "Coming through better than fifty a minute now."

The alarms screamed. "Incident, HR972. Grid eight five six. Inner two lanes, center quad. Overspill to outer lane, inner quad."

"Hell!" said Grecos, running. "That'll be a coachload of kids. I can smell it."

Bartram snapped his transceiver over. "Additional juvenile supplies. Urgent. Get with it."

As they climbed into the copter, he said gently: "It's a quiet one today, Karl. Wait till tomorrow. Holiday. We'll be busy then."

The copter rose, the sun shining on the red crosses.

"Yeas. Busy. But I figure I'd rather be here than there." He jerked a thumb at the road.

Like a white worm devouring the world, the road thrummed on, uncaring.

One of the earliest prophesies of disaster in the science-fiction magazines was a story by the late David H. Keller, M.D., entitled "The Revolt of the Pedestrians." It was written in that heyday of the burgeoning motor car, the twenties. In Dr. Keller's imagination, the continued use of cars would so atrophy the human leg that before you knew it babies would be born with only vestigial stumps. (Ah, there, Lysenko, is that where you got it?)

Our newer writers see different sorts of division between our peoples, however. Even when the trigger is the automobile, the consequences, in their view, will be different, and maybe a good deal worse, as in—

X MARKS THE PEDWALK

Fritz Leiber

Based in material in Ch. 7, "First Clashes of the Wheeled and Footed Sects," of Vol. III of Burger's monumental *History of Traffic*, published by the Foundation for Twenty-Second-Century Studies.

The raggedy little old lady with the big shopping bag was in the exact center of the crosswalk when she became aware of the big black car bearing down on her.

Behind the thick bullet-proof glass, its seven occupants had a misty look, like men in a diving bell.

She saw there was no longer time to beat the car to either curb. Veering remorselessly, it would catch her in the gutter.

Useless to attempt a feint and double-back, such as any venturesome child executed a dozen times a day. Her reflexes were too slow.

Polite vacuous laughter came from the car's loudspeaker over the engine's mounting roar.

From her fellow pedestrians lining the curbs came a sigh of horror.

The little old lady dipped into her shopping bag and came up with a big blue-black automatic. She held it in both fists, riding the recoils like a rodeo cowboy on a bucking bronco.

Aiming at the base of the windshield, just as a big-game hunter aims at the vulnerable spine of a charging water buffalo over the horny armor of its lowered head, the little old lady squeezed off three shots before the car chewed her down.

From the right-hand curb a young woman in a wheel-chair shrieked an obscenity at the car's occupants.

Smythe-de Winter, the driver, wasn't happy. The little old lady's last shot had taken two members of his car pool. Bursting through the laminated glass, the steel-jacketed slug had traversed the neck of Phipps-McHeath and buried itself in the skull of Horvendile-Harker.

Braking viciously, Smythe-de Winter rammed the car over the right-hand curb. Pedestrians scattered into entries and narrow arcades, among them a youth bounding high on crutches.

But Smythe-de Winter got the girl in the wheelchair.

Then he drove rapidly out of the Slum Ring into the Suburbs, a shred of rattan swinging from the flange of his right fore mudguard for a trophy. Despite the two-for-two casualty list, he felt angry and depressed. The secure, predictable world around him seemed to be crumbling.

While his companions softly keened a dirge to Horvy and Phipps and quietly mopped up their blood, he frowned and shook his head.

"They oughtn't to let old ladies carry magnums," he murmured.

Witherspoon-Hobbs nodded agreement across the front-seat corpse. "They oughtn't to let 'em carry anything. God, how I hate Feet," he muttered, looking down at his shrunken legs. "Wheels forever!" he softly cheered.

The incident had immediate repercussions throughout the city. At the combined wake of the little old lady and the girl in the wheelchair, a fiery-tongued speaker inveighed against the White-Walled Fascists of Suburbia, telling to his hearers the fabled wonders of old Los Angeles, where pedestrians were sacrosanct, even outside crosswalks. He called for a hobnail march across the nearest lawn-bowling alleys and perambulator-traversed golf courses of the motorists.

At the Sunnyside Crematorium, to which the bodies of Phipps and Horvy had been conveyed, an equally impassioned and rather more grammatical orator reminded his listeners of the legendary justice of old Chicago, where pedestrians were forbidden to carry small arms and anyone with one foot off the sidewalk was fair prey. He broadly hinted that a holocaust, primed if necessary with a few tankfuls of gasoline, was the only cure for the Slums.

Bands of skinny youths came loping at dusk out of the Slum Ring into the innermost sections of the larger doughnut of the Suburbs, slashing defenseless tires, shooting expensive watchdogs, and scrawling filthy words on the pristine panels of matrons' runabouts which never ventured more than six blocks from home.

Simultaneously, squadrons of young suburban motorcycles and scooterites roared through the outermost precincts of the Slum Ring, harrying children off sidewalks, tossing stinkbombs through second-story tenement windows, and defacing hovelfronts with sprays of black paint.

Incidents—a thrown brick, a cut corner, monster tacks in the portico of the Auto Club—were even reported from the center of the city, traditionally neutral territory.

The Government hurriedly acted, suspending all traffic between the Center and the Suburbs and establishing a 24-hour curfew in the Slum Ring. Government agents moved only by centipede-car and pogo-hopper, to underline the point that they favored neither contending side.

The day of enforced non-movement for Feet and Wheels was spent in furtive vengeful preparations. Behind locked garage doors, machine guns that fired through the nose ornament were mounted under hoods, illegal scythe blades were welded to oversize hubcaps, and the stainless steel edges of flange fenders were honed to razor sharpness.

While nervous National Guardsmen hopped about the deserted sidewalks of the Slum Ring, grim-faced men and women wearing black armbands moved through the webwork of secret tunnels and hidden doors, distributing heavy-caliber small arms and spike-studded paving blocks, piling cobblestones on strategic rooftops, and sapping upward from the secret tunnels to create cartraps. Children got ready to soap intersections after dark. The Committee of Pedestrian Safety, sometimes known as Robespierre's Rats, prepared to release its two carefully hoarded antitank guns.

At nightfall, under the tireless urging of the Government, representatives of the Pedestrians and the Motorists met on a huge safety island at the boundary of the Slum Ring and the Suburbs.

Underlings began a noisy dispute as to whether Smythe-de Winter had failed to give a courtesy honk before charging, whether the little old lady had opened fire before the car had come within honking distance, how many wheels of Smythe-de's car had been on the sidewalk when he hit the girl in the wheelchair, and so on. After a little while the High Pedestrian and the Chief Motorist exchanged cautious winks and drew aside.

The red writhing of a hundred kerosene flares and the mystic yellow pulsing of a thousand firefly lamps mounted on yellow sawhorses ranged around the safety island illumined two tragic, strained faces.

"A word before we get down to business," the Chief Motorist whispered. "What's the current S.Q. of your adults?"

"Forty-one and dropping," the High Pedestrian replied, his eyes fearfully searching from side to side for eavesdroppers. "I can hardly get aides who are halfway *compos mentis*."

"Our own Sanity Quotient is thirty-seven," the Chief Motorist revealed. He shrugged helplessly. . . "The wheels inside my people's heads are slowing down. I do not think they will be speeded up in my lifetime."

"They say Government's only fifty-two," the other said with a matching shrug.

"Well, I suppose we must scrape out one more compromise," the one suggested hollowly, "though I must confess there are times when I think we're all the figments of a paranoid's dream."

Two hours of concentrated deliberations produced the new Wheel-Foot Articles of Agreement. Among other points, pedestrian handguns were limited to a slightly lower muzzle velocity and to .38 caliber and under, while motorists were required to give three honks at one block distance before charging a pedestrian in a crosswalk. Two wheels over the curb changed a traffic kill from third-degree manslaughter to petty homicide. Blind pedestrians were permitted to carry hand grenades.

Immediately the Government went to work. The new Wheel-Foot Articles were loudspeakered and posted. Detachments of police and psychiatric social hoppers centipedaled and pogoed through the Slum Ring, seizing outsize weapons and giving tranquilizing jet-injections to the unruly. Teams of hypnotherapists and mechanics scuttled from home to home in the Suburbs and from garage to garage, in-chanting a conformist serenity and stripping illegal armament from cars. On the advice of a rogue psychiatrist, who said it would channel off aggressions, a display of bullfighting was announced, but this had to be canceled when a strong protest was lodged by the Decency League, which had a large mixed Wheel-Foot membership.

At dawn, curfew was lifted in the Slum Ring and traffic reopened between the Suburbs and the Center. After a few uneasy moments it became apparent that the status quo had been restored.

Smythe-de Winter tooled his gleaming black machine along the Ring. A thick steel bolt with a large steel washer on either side neatly filled the hole the little old lady's slug had made in the windshield.

A brick bounced off the roof. Bullets pattered against the side windows.

Smythe-de ran a handkerchief around his neck under his collar and smiled.

A block ahead children were darting into the street, catcalling and thumbing their noses. Behind one of them limped a fat dog with a spiked collar.

Smythe-de suddenly gunned his motor. He didn't hit any of the children, but he got the dog.

A flashing light on the dash showed him the right front tire was losing pressure. Must have hit the collar as well! He thumbed the matching emergency-air button and the flashing stopped.

He turned toward Witherspoon-Hobbs and said with thoughtful satisfaction, "I like a normal orderly world, where you always have a little success, but not champagne heady; a little failure, but just enough to brace you."

Witherspoon-Hobbs was squinting at the next crosswalk. Its center was discolored by a brownish stain ribbon-tracked by tires.

"That's where you bagged the little old lady, Smythe-de," he remarked. "I'll say this for her now: she had spirit."

"Yes, that's where I bagged her," Smythe-de agreed flatly. He remembered wistfully the witchlike face growing rapidly larger, the jerking shoulders in black bombazine, the wild white-circled eyes. He suddenly found himself feeling that this was a very dull day.

As of this day and hour, our President has not succeeded in his campaign determination to Bring Us Together. There seems to be some question whether most of us want to be brought together; that is, we'd be perfectly well pleased to have all those other people try to be just like us, or if they can't manage that, at least to be what ever they can be that we find least offensive: But, there aren't a great many persons visible who want to change themselves in any way.

Still, there seems to be no question that civilization does not stand still, and if we do not find a way of coming closer together, we will surely find ourselves thrust further, and perhaps irrevocably far, apart. It even seems that this might be our last—

DAY OF TRUCE

Clifford D. Simak

I

The evening was quiet. There was no sign of the Punks. Silence lay heavily across the barren and eroded acres of the subdivision, and there was nothing moving—not even one of the roving and always troublesome dog packs.

It was too quiet, Max Hale decided.

There should have been some motion and some noise. It was as if everyone had taken cover against some known and coming violence—another raid perhaps. Although there was only one place against which a raid could possibly be aimed. Why should others care, Max wondered; why should they cower indoors, when they had long since surrendered?

Max stood upon the flat lookout-rooftop of the Crawford stronghold and watched the streets to north and west. It was by one of these that Mr. Crawford would be coming home. No one could guess which one, for he seldom used the same road. It was the only way one could cut down the likelihood of ambush or of barricade. Although ambush was less frequent now. There were fewer fences, fewer trees and shrubs; there was almost nothing behind which one could hide. In this barren area it called for real ingenuity to effect an ambuscade. But, Max reminded himself, no one had ever charged the Punks with lack of ingenuity.

Mr. Crawford had phoned that he would be late and Max was getting nervous. In another quarter hour, darkness would be closing in. It was bad business to be abroad in Oak Manor after dark had fallen. Or for that matter, in any of the subdivisions. For while Oak Manor might be a bit more vicious than some of the others of them, it still was typical.

He lifted his glasses again and swept the terrain slowly. There was no sign of patrols or hidden skulkers. There must be watchers somewhere, he knew. There were always watchers, alert to the slightest relaxation of the vigilance maintained at Crawford stronghold.

Street by street he studied the sorry houses, with their broken windowpanes and their peeling paint, still marked by the soap streaks and the gouges and the red-paint splashes inflicted years before. Here and there dead trees stood stark, denuded of their branches. Browned evergreens, long dead, stood rooted in the dusty yards—yards long since robbed of the grass that once had made them lawns.

And on the hilltop, up on Circle Drive, stood the ruins of Thompson stronghold, which had fallen almost five years before. There was no structure standing. It had been leveled stone by stone and board by board. Only the smashed and dying trees, only the twisted steel fence posts marked where it had been.

Now Crawford stronghold stood alone in Oak Manor. Max thought of it with a glow of pride and a surge of painful memory. It stood because of him, he thought, and he would keep it standing.

In this desert it was the last oasis, with its trees and grass, with its summerhouses and trellises, with the massive shrubbery and the wondrous sundial beside the patio, with its goldfish-and-lily pond and the splashing fountain.

"Max," said the walkie-talkie strapped across his chest.

"Yes, Mr. Crawford."

"Where are you located, Max?"

"Up on the lookout, sir."

"I'll come in on Seymour Drive," said Mr. Crawford's voice. "I'm about a mile beyond the hilltop. I'll be coming fast."

"The coast seems to be quite clear, sir."

"Good. But take no chances with the gates."

"I have the control box with me, sir. I can operate from here. I will keep a sharp lookout."

"Be seeing you," said Crawford.

Max picked up the remote-control box and waited for his returning master.

The car came over the hill and streaked down Seymour Drive, made its right-hand turn on Dawn, roared toward the gates.

When it was no more than a dozen feet away, Max pushed the button that unlocked the gates. The heavy bumper slammed into them and pushed them open. The buffers that ran along each side of the car held them aside as the machine rushed through. When the car had cleared them, heavy springs snapped them shut, and they were locked again.

Max slung the control-box strap over his shoulder and went along the rooftop catwalk to the ladder leading to the ground.

Mr. Crawford had put away the car and was closing the garage door as Max came around the corner of the house.

"It does seem quiet," said Mr. Crawford. "Much quieter, it would seem to me, than usual."

"I don't like it, sir. There is something brewing."

"Not very likely," said Mr. Crawford. "Not on the eve of Truce Day."

"I wouldn't put nothing past them dirty Punks," said Max.

"I quite agree," said Mr. Crawford, "but they'll be coming here tomorrow for their day of fun. We must treat them well for, after all, they're neighbors and it is a custom. I would hate to have you carried beyond the bounds of propriety by overzealousness."

"You know well and good," protested Max, "I would never do a thing. I am a fighter, sir, but I fight fair and honorable."

Mr. Crawford said, "I was thinking of the little gambit you had cooked up last year."

"It would not have hurt them, sir. Leastwise, not permanently. They might never have suspected. Just a drop or two of it in the fruit punch was all we would have needed. It wouldn't have taken effect until hours after they had left. Slow-acting stuff, it was."

"Even so," said Mr. Crawford sternly, "I am glad I found out in time. And I don't want a repeat performance, possibly more subtle, to be tried this year. I hope you understand me."

"Oh, certainly, sir," said Max. "You can rely upon it, sir."

"Well, good night, then. I'll see you in the morning."

It was all damn foolishness, thought Max—this business of a Day of Truce. It was an old holdover from the early days when some do-gooder had figured maybe there would be some benefit if the stronghold people and the Punks could meet under happy circumstance and spend a holiday together.

It worked, of course, but only for the day. For twenty-four hours there were no raids, no flaming arrows, no bombs across the fence. But at one second after midnight the feud took up again, as bitter and relentless as it had ever been.

It had been going on for years. Max had no illusions about how it all would end. Some day Crawford strong hold would fall, as had all the others in Oak Manor. But until that day, he pledged himself to do everything he could. He would never lower his guard nor relax his vigilance. Up to the very end, he would make them smart for every move they made.

He watched as Mr. Crawford opened the front door and went across the splash of light that flowed out from the hall. Then the door shut, and the house stood there, big and bleak and black, without a sliver of light showing anywhere. No light ever showed from the Crawford house. Well before the fall of night he always threw the lever on the big control board to slam steel shutters closed against all the windows in the place. Lighted windows made too good a nighttime target.

Now the raids always came at night. There had been a time when some had been made in daylight, but that was too chancy now. Year by year, the defenses had been built up, to a point where an attack in daylight was plain foolhardiness.

Max turned and went down the driveway to the gates. He drew on rubber gloves and with a small flashlight examined the locking mechanism. It was locked. It had never failed, but there might come a time it would. He never failed to check it once the gates had closed.

He stood beside the gates and listened. Everything was quiet, although he imagined he could hear the faint singing of the electric current running through the fence. But that, he knew, was impossible, for the current was silent.

He reached out with a gloved hand and stroked the fence. Eight feet high, he told himself, with a foot of barbed wire along the top of it, and every inch of it alive with the surging current.

And inside of it, a standby, auxiliary fence into which current could be introduced if the forward fence should fail.

A clicking sound came paddling down the driveway and Max turned from the gate.

"How you, boy," he said.

It was too dark for him to see the dog, but he could

hear it snuffling and snorting with pleasure at his recognition.

It came bumbling out of the darkness and pushed against his legs. He squatted down and put his arms about it. It kissed him sloppily.

"Where are the others, boy?" he asked, and it wriggled in its pleasure.

Great dogs, he thought. They loved the people in the stronghold almost to adoration, but had an utter hatred for every other person. They had been trained to have.

The rest of the pack, he knew, was aprowl about the yard, alert to every sound, keyed to every presence. No one could approach the fence without their knowing it. Any stranger who got across the fence they would rip to bits.

He stripped off the rubber gloves and put them in his pocket.

"Come on, boy," he said.

He turned off the driveway and proceeded across the yard—cautiously, for it was uneven footing. There was no inch of it that lay upon the level. It was cleverly designed so that any thrown grenade or Molotov cocktail would roll into a deep and narrow bomb trap.

There had been a time, he recalled, when there had been a lot of these things coming over the fence. There were fewer now, for it was a waste of effort. There had been a time, as well, when there had been flaming arrows, but these had tapered off since the house had been fireproofed.

He reached the side yard and stopped for a moment, listening, with the dog standing quietly at his side. A slight wind had come up, and the trees were rustling. He lifted his head and stared at the delicate darkness of them, outlined against the lighter sky.

Beautiful things, he thought. It was a pity there were not more of them. Once this area had been named Oak Manor for the stately trees that grew here. There, just ahead of him, was the last of them—a rugged old patriarch with its massive crown blotting out the early stars.

He looked at it with awe and appreciation—and with apprehension too. It was a menace. It was old and brittle and it should be taken down, for it leaned toward the fence and someday a windstorm might topple it across the wire. He should have mentioned it long ago to Mr. Crawford, but he knew the owner held this tree in a sentimental regard that matched his own. Perhaps it could be made safe by guywires to hold it against the wind, or at least to turn its fall away from the fence should it be broken or uprooted. Although it seemed a sacrilege to anchor it with guywires, an insult to an ancient monarch.

He moved on slowly, threading through the bomb traps, with the dog close at his heels, until he reached the patio, and here he stopped beside the sundial. He ran his hand across its rough stone surface and wondered why Mr. Crawford should set such a store by it. Perhaps because it was a link to the olden days before the Punks and raids. It was an old piece that had been brought from a monastery garden somewhere in France. That in itself, of course, would make it valuable. But perhaps Mr. Crawford saw in it another value, far beyond the fact that it was hundreds of years old and had come across the water.

Perhaps it had grown to symbolize for him the day now past when any man might have a sundial in his garden, when he might have trees and grass without fighting for them, when he might take conscious pride in the unfenced and unmolested land that lay about his house.

Bit by bit, through the running years, those rights had been eroded.

II

First it had been the little things—the casual, thoughtless trampling of the shrubbery by the playing small fry, the killing of the evergreens by the rampaging packs of happy dogs that ran with the playing small fry. For each boy, the parents said, must have himself a dog.

The people in the first place had moved from the jam-packed cities to live in what they fondly called the country, so that they could keep a dog or two and where their children would have fresh air and sunlight and room in which to run.

But too often this country was, in reality, no more than another city, with its houses cheek by jowl—each set on acre or half-acre lots, but still existing cheek by jowl.

Of course, a place to run. The children had. But no more than a place to run. There was nothing more to do. Run was all they could do—up and down the streets, back and forth across the lawns, up and down the driveways, leaving havoc in their trail. And in time the toddlers grew up, and in their teen-age years they still could only run. There was no place for them to go, nothing they might do. Their mothers foregathered every morning at the coffee klatches and their fathers sat each evening in the backyards, drinking beer. The family car could not be used because gasoline cost money and the mortgages were heavy and the taxes terrible and the other costs were high.

So to find an outlet for their energies, to work off their unrealized resentments against having nothing they could do, these older fry started out, for pure excitement only, on adventures in vandalism. There was a cutting of the backyard clotheslines, a chopping into bits of watering hoses left out overnight, a breaking and ripping up of the patios, ringing of the doorbells, smashing of the windows, streaking of the siding with a cake of soap, splashing with red paint.

Resentments had been manufactured to justify this vandalism, and now the resentments were given food to grow upon. Irate owners erected fences to keep out the children and the dogs, and this at once became an insult and a challenge.

And that first simple fence, Max told himself, had been the forerunner of the eight-foot barrier of electricity which formed the first line of defense in the Crawford stronghold. Likewise, those small-time soap-cake vandals, shrieking their delight at messing up a neighbor's house, had been the ancestors of the Punks.

He left the patio and went down the stretch of back-yard, past the goldfish-and-lily pond and the tinkling of the fountain, past the clump of weeping willows, and so out to the fence.

"Psst!" said a voice just across the fence.

"That you, Billy?"

"It's me," said Billy Warner.

"All right. Tell me what you have."

"Tomorrow is Truce Day and we'll be visiting—"

"I know all that," said Max.

"They're bringing in a time bomb."

"They can't do that," said Max, disgusted. "The cops will frisk them at the gates. They would spot it on them."

"It'll be all broken down. Each one will have a piece. Stony Stafford hands out the parts tonight. He has a crew that has been practicing for weeks to put a bomb together fast—even in the dark, if need be."

"Yeah," said Max, "I guess they could do it that way. And once they get it put together?"

"The sundial," Billy said. "Underneath the sundial."

"Well, thanks," said Max. "I am glad to know. It would break the boss' heart should something happen to the sundial."

"I figure," Billy said, "this might be worth a twenty."

"Yes," Max agreed. "Yes, I guess it would."

"If they ever knew I told, they'd take me out and kill me."

"They won't ever know," said Max. "I won't ever tell them."

He pulled his wallet from his pocket, turned on the flash, and found a pair of tens.

He folded the bills together, lengthwise, twice. Then he shoved them through an opening in the fence.

"Careful, there," he cautioned. "Do not touch the wire."

Beyond the fence he could see the faint white outline of the other's face. And a moment later, the hand that reached out carefully and grabbed the corner of the folded bills.

Max did not let loose of the money immediately. They stood, each of them, with their grip upon the bills.

"Billy," said Max, solemnly, "you would never kid me, would you? You would never sell me out. You would never feed me erroneous information."

"You know me, Max," said Billy. "I've played square with you. I'd never do a thing like that."

Max let go of the money and let the other have it.

"I am glad to hear you say that, Billy. Keep on playing square. For the day you don't, I'll come out of here and hunt you down and cut your throat myself."

But the informer did not answer. He was already moving off, out into the deeper darkness.

Max stood quietly, listening. The wind still blew in the leaves and the fountain kept on splashing, like gladsome silver bells.

"Hi, boy," Max said softly, but there was no snuffling answer. The dog had left him, was prowling with the others up and down the yard.

Max turned about and went up the yard toward the front again, completing his circuit of the house. As he rounded the corner of the garage, a police car was slowing to a halt before the gates.

He started down the drive, moving ponderously and deliberately.

"That you, Charley?" he called softly.

"Yes, Max," said Charley Pollard. "Is everything all right?"

"Right as rain," said Max.

He approached the gates and saw the bulky loom of the officer on the other side.

"Just dropping by," said Pollard. "The area is quiet tonight. We'll be coming by one of these days to inspect the place. It looks to me you're loaded."

"Not a thing illegal," Max declared. "All of it's defensive. That is still the rule."

"Yes, that is the rule," said Pollard, "but it seems to me that there are times you become a mite too enthusiastic. A full load in the fence, no doubt."

"Why, certainly," said Max. "Would you have it otherwise?"

"A kid grabs hold of it and he could be electrocuted, at full strength."

"Would you rather I had it set just to tickle them?"

"You're playing too rough, Max."

"I doubt it rather much," said Max. "I watched from here, five years ago, when they stormed Thompson stronghold. Did you happen to see that?"

"I wasn't here five years ago. My beat was Farview Acres."

"They took it apart," Max told him. "Stone by stone, brick by brick, timber by timber. They left nothing standing. They left nothing whole. They cut down all the trees and chopped them up. They uprooted all the shrubs. They hoed out all the flower beds. They made a desert of it. They reduced it to their level. And I'm not about to let it happen here, not if I can help it. A man has got the right to grow a tree and a patch of grass. If he wants a flower bed, he has a right to have a flower bed. You may not think so, but he's even got the right to keep other people out."

"Yes," said the officer, "all you say is true. But these are kids you are dealing with. There must be allowances. And this is a neighborhood. You folks and the others like you wouldn't have this trouble if you only tried to be a little neighborly."

"We don't dare be neighborly," said Max. "Not in a place like this. In Oak Manor, and in all the other manors and all the other acres and the other whatever-you-may-call-thems, neighborliness means that you let people overrun you. Neighborliness means you give up your right to live your life the way you want to live it. This kind of neighborliness is rooted way back in those days when the kids made a path across your lawn as a shortcut to the school bus and you couldn't say a thing for fear that they would sass you back and so create a scene. It started when your neighbor borrowed your lawn mower and forgot to bring it back and when you went to get it you found that he had broken it. But he pretended that he hadn't and for the sake of neighborliness, you didn't have the guts to tell him that he had and to demand that he pay the bill for the repairing of it."

"Well, maybe so," said Pollard, "but it's gotten out of hand. It has been carried too far. You folks have got too high and mighty."

"There's a simple answer to everything," Max told him stoutly. "Get the Punks to lay off us and we'll take down the fence and all the other stuff."

Pollard shook his head. "It has gone too far," he said. "There is nothing anyone can do."

He started to go back to the car, then turned back.

"I forgot," he said. "Tomorrow is your Truce Day. Myself and a couple of the other men will be here early in the morning."

Max didn't answer. He stood in the driveway and watched the car pull off down the street. Then he went up the driveway and around the house to the back door.

Nora had a place laid at the table for him and he sat down heavily, glad to be off his feet. By this time of the evening he was always tired. Not as young, he thought, as he once had been.

"You're late tonight," said the cook, bringing him the food. "Is everything all right?"

"I guess so. Everything is quiet. But we may have trouble tomorrow. They're bringing in a bomb."

"A bomb!" cried Nora. "What will you do about it? Call in the police, perhaps."

Max shook his head. "No, I can't do that. The police aren't on our side. They'd take the attitude we'd egged on the Punks until they had no choice but to bring in the bomb. We are on our own. And, besides, I must protect the lad who told me. If I didn't, the Punks would know and he'd be worthless to me then. He'd never get to know another thing. But knowing they are bringing something in, I can watch for it."

He still felt uneasy about it all, he realized. Not about the bomb itself, perhaps, but something else, something, that was connected with it. He wondered why he had this feeling. Knowing about the bomb, he all but had it made. All he'd have to do would be to locate it and dig it out from beneath the sundial.

He would have the time to do it. The day-long celebration would end at six in the evening and the Punks could not set the bomb to explode earlier than midnight. Any blast before midnight would be a violation of the truce.

He scooped fried potatoes from the dish onto his plate and speared a piece of meat. Nora poured his coffee and pulling out a chair, sat down opposite him.

"You aren't eating?" he asked.

"I ate early, Max."

He ate hungrily and hurriedly, for there still were things to do. She sat and watched him eat. The clock on the kitchen wall ticked loudly in the silence.

Finally she said: "It is getting somewhat grim, Max."

He nodded, his mouth full of food and unable to speak.

"I don't see," said the cook, "why the Crawfords want to stay here. There can't be much pleasure in it for them. They could move into the city and it would be safer there. There are the juvenile gangs, of course, but they mostly fight among themselves. They don't make life unbearable for all the other people."

"It's pride," said Max. "They won't give up. They won't let Oak Manor beat them. Mr. and Mrs. Crawford are quality. They have some steel in them."

"They couldn't sell the place, of course," said Nora. "There would be no one to buy it. But they don't need the money. They could just walk away from it."

"You misjudge them, Nora. The Crawfords in all their lives have never walked away from anything. They went through a lot to live here. Sending Johnny off to boarding school when he was a lad, since it wouldn't have been safe for him to go to school with the Punks out there. I don't suppose they like it. I don't see how they could. But they won't be driven out. They realize someone must stand up to all that trash out there, or else there's no hope."

Nora sighed. "I suppose you're right. But it is a shame. They could live so safe and comfortable and normal if they just moved to the city."

He finished eating and got up.

"It was a good meal, Nora," he said. "But then you always fix good meals."

"Ah, go on with you," said Nora.

He went into the basement and sat down before the shortwave set. Systematically, he started putting in his calls to the other strongholds. Wilson stronghold, over in Fair Hills, had had a little trouble early in the evening—a few stink bombs heaved across the fence—but it had quieted down. Jackson stronghold did not answer. While he was trying to get through to Smith stronghold in Harmony Settlement, Curtis stronghold in Lakeside Heights began calling him. Everything was quiet, John Hennessey, the Curtis custodian told him. It had been quiet for several days.

He stayed at the radio for an hour and by that time had talked with all the nearby strongholds. There had been scattered trouble here and there, but nothing of any consequence. Generally it was peaceful.

He sat and thought about the time bomb and there was still that nagging worry. There was something wrong, he knew, but he could not put his finger on it.

Getting up, he prowled the cavernous basement, checking the defense material—extra sections of fencing, piles of posts, pointed stakes, rolls of barb wire, heavy flexible wire mesh and all the other items for which some day there might be a need. Tucked into one corner, hidden, he found the stacked carboys of acid he had secretly cached away. Mr. Crawford would not approve, he knew, but if the chips ever should be down, and there was need to use those carboys, he might be glad to have them.

He climbed the stairs and went outside to prowl restlessly about the yard, still upset by that nagging something about the bomb he could not yet pin down.

The moon had risen. The yard was a place of interlaced light and shadow, but beyond the fence the desert acres that held the other houses lay flat and bare and plain, without a shadow on them except the shadows of the houses.

Two of the dogs came up and passed the time of night with him and then went off into the shrubbery.

He moved into the backyard and stood beside the sundial.

The wrongness still was there. Something about the sundial and the bomb—some piece of thinking that didn't run quite true.

He wondered how they knew that the destruction of the sundial would be a heavy blow to the owner of the stronghold. How could they possibly have known?

The answer seemed to be that they couldn't. They didn't. There was no way for them to know. And even if, in some manner, they had learned, a sundial most certainly would be a piddling thing to blow up when that single bomb could be used so much better somewhere else.

Stony Stafford, the leader of the Punks, was nobody's fool. He was a weasel—full of cunning, full of savvy. He'd not mess with any sundial when there was so much else that a bomb could do so much more effectively.

And as he stood there beside the sundial, Max knew where that bomb would go—knew where he would plant it were he in Stafford's place.

At the roots of that ancient oak which leaned toward the fence.

He stood and thought about it and knew that he was right.

Billy Warner, he wondered. Had Billy double-crossed him?

Very possibly he hadn't. Perhaps Stony Stafford might have suspected long ago that his gang harbored an informer and for that reason, had given out the story of the sundial rather than the oak tree. And that, of course, only to a select inner circle which would be personally involved with the placing of the bomb.

In such a case, he thought, Billy Warner had not done too badly.

Max turned around and went back to the house, walking heavily. He climbed the stairs to his attic room and went to bed. It had been, he thought just before he went to sleep, a fairly decent day.

III

The police showed up at eight o'clock. The carpenters came and put up the dance platform. The musicians appeared and began their tuning up. The caterers arrived and set up the tables, loading them with food and two huge punch bowls, standing by to serve.

Shortly after nine o'clock the Punks and their girls began to straggle in. The police frisked them at the gates and found no blackjacks, no brass knuckles, no bicycle chains on any one of them.

The band struck up. The Punks and their girls began to dance. They strolled through the yard and admired the flowers, without picking any of them. They sat on the grass and talked and laughed among themselves. They gathered at the overflowing boards and ate. They laughed and whooped and frolicked and everything was fine.

"You see?" Pollard said to Max. "There ain't nothing wrong with them. Give them a decent break and they're just a bunch of ordinary kids. A little hell in them, of course, but nothing really bad. It's your flaunting of this place in their very faces that makes them the way they are."

"Yeah," said Max.

He left Pollard and drifted down the yard, keeping as inconspicuous as he could. He wanted to watch the oak, but he knew he didn't dare to. He knew he had to keep away from it, should not even glance toward it. If he should scare them off, then God only knew where they would plant the bomb. He thought of being forced to hunt wildly for it after they were gone and shuddered at the thought.

There was no one near the bench at the back of the yard, near the flowering almond tree, and he stretched out on it. It wasn't particularly comfortable, but the day was warm and the air was drowsy. He dropped off to sleep.

When he woke he saw that a man was standing on the gravel path just beyond the bench.

He blinked hard and rubbed his eyes.

"Hello, Max," said Stony Stafford.

"You should be up there dancing, Stony."

"I was waiting for you to wake up," said Stony. "You are a heavy sleeper. I could of broke your neck."

Max sat up. He rubbed a hand across his face.

"Not on Truce Day, Stony. We all are friends on Truce Day."

Stony spat upon the gravel path.

"Some other day," he said.

"Look," said Max, "why don't you just run off and forget about it? You'll break your back if you try to crack this place. Pick up your marbles, Stony, and go find someone else who's not so rough to play with."

"Someday we'll make it," Stony said. "This place can't stand forever."

"You haven't got a chance," said Max.

"Maybe so," said Stony. "But I think we will. And before we do, there is just one thing I want you to know. You think nothing will happen to you even if we do. You think that all we'll do is just rip up the place, not harming anyone. But you're wrong, Max. We'll do it the way it is supposed to be with the Crawfords and with Nora. We won't hurt them none. But we'll get you, Max. Just because we can't carry knives or guns doesn't mean there aren't other ways. There'll be a stone fall on you or a timber hit you. Or maybe you'll stumble and fall into the fire. There are a lot of ways to do it and we plan to get you plenty."

"So," said Max, "you hate me. It makes me feel real bad."

"Two of my boys are dead," said Stony. "There are others who are crippled pretty bad."

"There wouldn't nothing happen to them, Stony, if you didn't send them up against the fence."

He looked up and saw the hatred that lay in Stony Stafford's eyes, but washing across the hatred was a gleam of triumph.

"Goodby, dead man," said Stony.

He turned and stalked away.

Max sat quietly on the bench, remembering that gleam of triumph in Stony Stafford's eyes. And that meant he had been right. Stony had something up his sleeve and it could be nothing else but the bomb beneath the oak.

The day wore on. In the afternoon, Max went up to the house and into the kitchen. Nora fixed him a sandwich, grumbling.

"Why don't you go out and eat off the tables?" she demanded. "There is plenty there."

"Just as soon keep out of their way," said Max. "I have to fight them all the rest of the year. I don't see why I should pal up with them today."

"What about the bomb?"

"Shhh," said Max. "I know where it is."

Nora stood looking out the window. "They don't look like bad kids," she said. "Why can't we make a peace of some sort with them?"

Max grunted. "It's gone too far," he said.

Pollard had been right, he thought. It was out of hand. Neither side could back down now.

The police could have put a stop to it to start with, many years ago, if they had cracked down on the vandals instead of adopting a kids-will-be-kids attitude and shrugging it all off as just an aggravated case of quarreling in the neighborhood. The parents could have stopped it by paying some attention to the kids, by giving them something that would have stopped their running wild. The community could have put a stop to it by providing some sort of recreational facilities.

But no one had put a stop to it. No one had even tried.

And now it had grown to be a way of life and it must be fought out to the bitter end.

Max had no illusions as to who would be the winner.

Six o'clock came and the Punks started drifting off. By six-thirty the last of them had gone. The musicians packed up their instruments and left. The caterers put away their dishes and scooped up the leftovers and the garbage and drove away. The carpenters came and got their lumber. Max went down to the gates and checked to see that they were locked.

"Not a bad day," said Pollard, speaking through the gates to Max. "They really aren't bad kids, if you'd just get to know them."

"I know them plenty now," said Max.

He watched the police car drive off, then turned back up the driveway.

He'd have to wait for a while, he knew, until the dusk could grow a little deeper, before he started looking for the bomb. There would be watchers outside the fence. It would be just as well if they didn't know that he had found it. It might serve a better purpose if they could be left to wonder if it might have been a dud. For one thing, it would shake their confidence. For another, it would protect young Billy Warner. And while Max could feel no admiration for the kid, Billy had been useful in the past and still might be useful in the future.

He went down to the patio and crawled through the masking shrubbery until he was only a short distance from the oak.

He waited there, watching the area out beyond the fence. There was as yet no sign of life out there. But they would be out there watching. He was sure of that.

The dusk grew deeper and he knew he could wait no longer. Creeping cautiously, he made his way to the oak.

Carefully, he brushed away the grass and leaves, face held close above the ground.

Halfway around the tree, he found it—the newly upturned earth, covered by a sprinkling of grass and leaves, and positioned neatly between two heavy roots.

He thrust his hand against the coolness of the dirt and his fingers touched the metal. Feeling it, he froze, then very slowly, very gently, pulled his hand away.

He sat back on his heels and drew in a measured breath.

The bomb was there, all right, just as he had suspected. But set above it, protecting it, was a contact bomb. Try to get the time bomb out and the contact bomb would be triggered off.

He brushed his hands together, wiping off the dirt.

There was, he knew, no way to get out the bombs. He had to let them stay. There was nothing he could do about it.

No wonder Stony's eyes had shown a gleam of triumph. For there was more involved than just a simple time bomb. This was a foolproof setup. There was nothing that could be done about it. If it had not been for the roots, Max thought, he might have taken a chance on working from one side and digging it all out. But with the heavy roots protecting it, that was impossible.

Stony might have known that he knew about it and then had gone ahead, working out a bomb set that no one would dare to mess around with.

It was exactly the sort of thing that would be up Stony's alley. More than likely, he was setting out there now, chuckling to himself.

Max stayed squatted, thinking.

He could string a line of mesh a few feet inside the tree, curving out to meet the auxiliary fence on either side. Juice could be fed into it and it might serve as a secondary defense. But it was not good insurance. A determined rush would carry it, for at best it would be flimsy. He'd not be able to install it as he should, working in the dark.

Or he could rig the tree with guywires to hold it off the

fence when it came crashing down. And that, he told himself, might be the thing to do.

He got up and went around the house, heading for the basement to look up some wire that might serve to hold the tree.

He remembered, as he walked past the short-wave set, that he should be sitting in on the regular evening check among the nearby strongholds. But it would have to wait tonight.

He walked on and then stopped suddenly as the thought came to him. He stood for a moment, undecided. then swung around and went back to the set.

He snapped on the power and turned it up.

He'd have to be careful what he said, he thought, for there was the chance the Punks might be monitoring the channels.

John Hennessey, custodian of the Curtis stronghold, came in a few seconds after Max had started calling.

"Something wrong, Max?"

"Nothing wrong, John. I was just wondering—do you remember telling me about those toys that you have?"

"Toys?"

"Yeah. The rattles."

He could hear the sound of Hennessey sucking in his breath.

Finally he said: "Oh, those. Yes, I still have them."

"How many would you say?"

"A hundred, probably. Maybe more than that."

"Could I borrow them?"

"Sure," said Hennessey. "Would you want them right away?"

"If you could," said Max.

"Okay. You'll pick them up?"

"I'm a little busy."

"Watch for me," said Hennessey. "I'll box them up and be there in an hour."

"Thanks, John," said Max.

Was it wrong? he wondered. Was it too much of a chance?

Perhaps he didn't have the right to take any chance at all.

But you couldn't sit forever, simply fending off the Punks. For if that was all you did, they'd keep on coming back. But hit back hard at them and they might get a bellyfull. You might end it once for all. The trouble was, he thought, you could strike back so seldom. You could never act except defensively, for if you took any other kind of action, the police were down on you like a ton of bricks.

He licked his lips.

It was seldom one had a chance like this—a chance to strike back lustily and still be legally defensive.

IV

He got up quickly and walked to the rear of the basement, where he found the heavy flexible mesh. He carried out three rolls of it and a loop of heavy wire to hang it on. He'd have to use some trees to stretch out the wire. He really should use some padding to protect the trees against abrasion by the wire, but he didn't have the time.

Working swiftly, he strung the wire, hung the mesh upon it, pegged the bottom of the mesh tight against the ground, tied the ends of it in with the auxiliary fence.

He was waiting at the gates when the truck pulled up. He used the control box to open the gates and the truck came through. Hennessey got out.

"Outside is swarming with Punks," he told Max. "What is going on?"

"I got troubles," said Max.

Hennessey went around to the back of the truck and lowered the tail gate. Three large boxes, with mesh insets, rested on the truck bed.

"They're in there?" asked Max.

Hennessey nodded. "I'll give you a hand with them."

Between them they lugged the boxes to the mesh curtain, rigged behind the oak.

"I left one place unpegged," said Max. "We can push the boxes under."

"I'll unlock the lids first," said Hennessey. "We can reach through with the pole and lift the lids if they are unlocked. Then use the pole again to tip the boxes over."

They slid the boxes underneath the curtain, one by one. Hennessey went back to the truck to get the pole. Max pegged down the gap.

"Can you give me a bit of light?" asked Hennessey. "I know the Punks are waiting out there. But probably they'd not notice just a squirt of it. They might think you were making just a regular inspection of the grounds."

Max flashed the light and Hennessey, working with the pole thrust through the mesh, flipped back the lids. Carefully, he tipped the boxes over. A dry slithering and frantic threshing sounds came out of the dark.

"They'll be nasty customers," said Hennessey. "They'll be stirred up and angry. They'll do a lot of circulating, trying to get settled for the night and that way, they'll get spread out. Most of them are big ones. Not many of the small kinds."

He put the pole over his shoulder and the two walked back to the truck.

Max put out his hand and the two men shook.

"Thanks a lot, John."

"Glad to do it, Max. Common cause, you know. Wish I could stay around . . ."

"You have a place of your own to watch."

They shook hands once again and Hennessey climbed into the cab.

"You better make it fast the first mile or so," said Max. "Our Punks may be laying for you. They might have recognized you."

"With the bumpers and the power I have," said Hennessey, "I can get through anything."

"And watch out for the cops. They'd raise hell if they knew we were helping back and forth."

"I'll keep an eye for them."

Max opened the gates and the truck backed out, straightened in the road and swiftly shot ahead.

Max listened until it was out of hearing, then checked to see that the gates were locked.

Back in the basement, he threw the switch that fed current into the auxiliary fence—and now into the mesh as well.

He sighed with some contentment and climbed the stairs out to the yard.

A sudden flash of light lit up the grounds. He spun swiftly around, then cursed softly at himself. It was only a bird hitting the fence in flight. It happened all the time. He was getting jittery, and there was no need of it. Everything was under control—reasonably so.

He climbed a piece of sloping ground and stood behind the oak. Staring into the darkness, it seemed to him that he could see shadowy forms out beyond the fence.

They were gathering out there and they would come swarming in as soon as the tree went down, smashing the fences. Undoubtedly they planned to use the tree as a bridge over the surging current that still would flow in the smashed-down fence.

Maybe it was taking too much of a chance, he thought. Maybe he should have used the guywires on the tree. That way there would have been no chance at all. But, likewise, there would have been no opportunity.

They might get through, he thought, but he'd almost bet against it.

He stood there, listening to the angry rustling of a hundred rattlesnakes, touchy and confused, in the area beyond the mesh.

The sound was a most satisfying thing.

He moved away, to be out of the line of blast when the bomb exploded, and waited for the Day of Truce to end.

It is in the cities that division shows itself most clearly and violently; and in the cities that the hope for reconciliation seems most empty.

Partly it is race, the poor blacks coming in and the well-off whites fleeing; partly it is economics, them as can afford it heading for the tax havens of the suburbs; partly it is dirt and crime and noise and aggravation.

Whatever it is, the lines are growing sharper between Fortress Suburbia and the latter-day Pictish marches of the cities, where the law cannot reach as you wander—

AMONG THE BAD BABOONS

Mack Reynolds

I

"One of these days you're going to pierce your eardrum doing that," Pamela Rozet said from the doorway.

"Uhhh?"

"That paintbrush. If you don't stop scratching the inside of your ear with it, you're going to hurt yourself. Didn't your mother ever tell you not to stick anything smaller than your elbow in your ear?"

Arthur Halleck took the end of the paintbrush in question out of his right ear and scowled dimly at it. He said, completely malapropos, "What in the name of the living Zoroaster ever happened to brushes? It was bad enough when they were making them out of nylon. What's this stuff? Anything to cheapen the product. The old masters used to paint with bristle brushes, or red sable hair. Have you ever been in a museum and looked real closely at an original Rembrandt, or even a Leonardo?"

"Yes," Pam said.

"Did you ever see any hair from their paint brushes?"

"I didn't look *that* close," she said.

"Well, you didn't. But take a look at some of Picasso's stuff, not to speak of mine. Hair, or other brush fiber, all through the paint." He tossed the offending brush to a

135

colorfully bespattered table. "I've been all over town. Into every art shop that survived in any shape at all. There's not a bristlebrush to be found."

"Possibly you can get some on the mainland, when you take this painting over."

"No," he growled disgustedly. "They don't make them any more. You can't ultra-mate the manufacture of decent bristle brushes. And anything you can't ultra-mate in the Ultra-welfare States goes down the drain."

He stepped back and stared gloomily at the painting on the easel.

"Is it finished?" she asked.

"Doesn't it *look* finished?" he demanded in irritation.

Pam came closer and looked and said patiently, "Long since I told you, Art, that I've never got beyond the impressionalists."

"Well, damn it, the Representational Abstract School is the nearest thing to the impressionalists for decades. Can't you see, confound it?"

"No."

"Well, look. It gives the same effect as the quick impression Van Gogh, Renoir, Degas and the rest demanded. You get a quick flash, and your immediate impression is that it's completely abstract, but then you realize that it's the ruin of the entrance to a subway station."

"I guess you do, at that," she said doubtfully.

He stared at the four-foot-square painting. "No wonder it's no good," he said. "Working with this quick-drying metallic acrylic paint on this ridiculous presdwood-duplicator board would have one of those Cro-Magnon cave painters climbing the wall."

"Aren't you going to have it duplicated and registered?"

"Of course. Sooner or later, I'm going to hit, Pam. Then it's you and me."

She looked at him, a shade of wistfulness in her overly tired face. She was a girl of averages, pleasantly so. Average height and weight and of an average prettiness, given her approximately thirty years of age. But there was a vulnerable something about her mouth that added. She was, and always had been, attractive to men who carried the dream, who were creative, ambitious.

"I thought it was already you and me, Art. That it had been for the past two years and more."

He said, a bit impatiently, "You know what I mean, Pam."

She went over to the window, avoiding the broken pane where it was patched with some old clothing, and rested her bottom on the ledge. She said, "Art, if we went back to the mainland and combined the income from our Inalienable Basic and added to that my royalties and your occasional sales, we'd be able to maintain a reasonably high standard of living. We'd also be in a position to make contacts, meet our own kind, associate with—."

"Associate with other charity cases," he broke in bitterly. "I've told you, Pam, I'll never become one more dependent on the Ultra-welfare State. I'll pay my own way in the world, or I'll go under. A man's *got* to be a man."

"You're not exactly paying your way right this minute, Arthur Halleck. We're scavengers, to use the politest term that comes to my tongue." Her tone was testy.

He shook his head. "Don't roach me, Pam. We don't take anything that belongs to anybody. If we didn't find it and use it, it'd slowly rot or rust away."

She said, slightly irritated herself now, "Look here, darling, you're not taking anything that belongs to anyone else either when you accept the dividends that accrue to your ten shares of Inalienable Basic."

"Those dividends don't grow on trees. Somebody does the work that produces them," he said stubbornly.

She was really impatient now. "Look, Art, the superabundance being produced under people's capitalism now is not the product of the comparative handful of workers and technicians who are required in industry and agriculture today. It's the product of the accumulated work of all mankind down through the ages. A million years ago some ancestor of yours and mine first used fire. The whole race has been doing it since. Five thousand years ago some slick over in the Near East first dreamed up the wheel. We've been using it ever since. Every generation comes up with something brand new to add to the accumulated pile of knowledge, know-how, art, science. This accumulated human know-how doesn't belong to anybody or to any group; it belongs to us all. At long last, as a result of it the human race has licked the problem of producing plenty for everyone. No one need go hungry any more, nor cold, nor unsheltered, nor uneducated, nor without proper medical care. This is the legacy our ancestors have left us. It belongs to all of us; as a matter of fact the ten shares of Inalienable Basic each citizen receives is a precious small slice of pie, if you ask me. Just enough to keep us lesser breeds from revolt."

"I still say it's charity," Art Halleck said stubbornly.

She brushed it off. "So what can you do about it? We didn't make this world and we're in no position to change its rules. Particularly over here. If we were on the mainland we might join the Futurists, or something."

He turned back to the painting on his easel and stared at it some more, saying over his shoulder, "I don't have to change the rules. Sooner or later, my work will hit, and I'll make my own way. You can still make your own way under People's Capitalism if you've got it on the ball. Those at the very top don't depend on Ultra-welfare State-issued Inalienable Basic."

"They sure don't," she said sourly. "They usually have inherited enough Variable Basic or private stock to keep them like gods all their lives. And as far as hitting sooner or later, it's obviously not sooner. How many of the last paintings sold?"

He looked at her. "Seven."

"Seventy dollars worth, eh? Just barely enough to duplicate and register this one. By the time you've paid your transport back and forth to Greater Washington and possibly bought a couple of paintbrushes or so, nothing left at all."

"One of these days I'll hit," he said stubbornly.

She gave up and turned and stared out the window in the direction of Washington Square.

II

She said finally, "Art, was it beautiful?"

He was busy cleaning his brushes now, grumbling about the speed with which his metallic-acrylic medium dried.

"Was what beautiful?"

"Manhattan—before."

"Oh. Well, no."

"You were born here, weren't you?"

"Up in the Bronx."

"Before the riots?"

"Ummm. I was just a kid, but come to think of it, I was already sketching, drawing." He snorted deprecation. "How many artists bother to learn to draw any more? It's like a writer never bothering to learn the alphabet."

"Why wasn't it beautiful?"

He gave up his unhappy viewing of his work and his brushes and came to stand next to her, an arm going unconsciously around her waist. He followed her line of vision down along MacDougal Street to the square where once scores of artist hopefuls had held their open-air shows.

He said thoughtfully, scowling, "It's an elastic word, 'beauty.' Means different things to different people. You can find beauty in just about anything—garbage dumps, battlefields, desert, just about anything. But largely, big cities don't lend themselves to beauty. Manhattan was probably a lovely setting back when the Indians were here, or even when the first small Dutch settlement was huddled down at this end of the island. But the way it was by the middle of the 20th century? No. I've never been out of North America to supposedly beautiful cities like Paris, Rome or Rio, but I have seen San Francisco. It had a certain amount of beauty—before the riots, of course."

"I understand they weren't so bad there."

"Bad enough. However, they've cleaned out some of

the ruins and resulted a pseudo-city there. It's hard to beat that Golden Gate setting."

They were silent for a moment, then she said, "How could it ever have happened, Art?"

He shrugged, and his words came slowly as he thought it out. "It could easily enough have been foreseen. A city like this had stopped making sense, Pam. The original reasons for cities—towns like Jericho began to be eight thousand years ago—had disappeared. Walled villages of farmers that could be defended against the nomads, trade centers built at crossroads, manufacturing centers, commercial centers. Putting walls around cities for defense stopped making sense. Modern transportation methods antiquated them as trade centers and manufacturing bases as industry was able to decentralize. Today, with communications what they are, even commercial centers are anachronisms. You can handle business from anywhere to anywhere."

"But what *happened?*"

"A lot of pressures. With the coming of automation and then ultra-mation, not only in manufacture but in agriculture, the undereducated farm laborers, the unemployables, the unplaceables flooded to the cities looking for jobs or in their absence, for relief, for free handouts. As their numbers grew, and with them ghettos and slums, the better-to-do city dwellers streamed out to suburbs. That meant a drop in tax income, and the city was faced with inadequate funds for slum clearance, education, police and firemen. Even things like garbage collection were inadequately financed. Which meant that still more of the better paid citizens left. Industry began to leave too, to get closer to sources of raw materials, and to areas where labor was cheaper. So taxes took another nose dive.

"Television played a major part. These slum dwellers could watch the typical TV program, which almost invariably portrayed the actors, and certainly the advertising actors, as living lives of plenty. Their apartments or homes were always beautiful and totally equipped, their clothes the latest of fashion, their food bountiful and of the best, their children healthy and handsome, the schools they attended ideal. Needless to say, the slum dwellers wanted these things. So some of the more aggressive made a few demonstrations—and were landed upon, to their further embitterment. Alarmed, more of the better elements left town for the suburbs, for New England, upstate New York, Jersey, Pennsylvania. Some of the more prosperous actually commuted to Florida, flying back and forth. More industry left town then, because of higher taxes and the higher insurance rates caused by the riots. So the city fathers brought in less income than ever, and there was less to spend on slum clearance, education, relief. So the riots grew in magnitude."

Art Halleck shrugged in distaste at the memory. "So it went, and finally we had the big one. And never really recovered from that. Oh, things continued for a while. But by this time, nobody who could possibly afford it was left living in places like Manhattan, Detroit, Chicago and so on. Nor any business that could possibly get out. So came another riot and another . . . and finally everybody left, including the police and firemen. That was the end."

"What happened to the slum element, the poverty stricken, the unadaptable?"

He looked down at her. "As a writer, I'd think you'd know at least as well as I."

"I wondered how you'd put it, in view of your feelings on the government issuing Inalienable Basic."

He said, slowly again, scowling and as if grudgingly, "I suppose it was in the cards. No alternative. At approximately the same time the cities were a confusion of riots and discontent, they issued Inalienable Basic to each citizen, thus guaranteeing womb to tomb security. Overnight, not even the poverty stricken wanted to remain in the big cities. It was cheaper to live elsewhere, not to speak of being more comfortable. So they streamed out like lemmings—or maybe rats. All except the handful of baboons, of course."

Pam shook her head and turned away from the view

of the street. "I sometimes wonder why they never came back."

"Who?"

"The police and all. Why didn't they reconstruct?"

"Why? Like I said, the original reason for cities was gone and the cost to rebuild was prohibitive. It wouldn't even be worthwhile trying to clean it up for farmland, or pasture, or whatever. Too much debris, too much sheer wreckage. Oh, some of the other towns have been reconstituted, at least partially. Denver and San Francisco. But largely, they've been just left, continuing to deteriorate as the years go by."

She looked at him.

"And with only a few scavengers, such as ourselves, left in the ruins. No electricity, no water, no sewage. Nothing."

He snorted, tired of the subject. "I wouldn't say exactly nothing. We don't do so badly. By the way, I should have something to eat before going down to Greater Washington."

"Caviar, turtle soup, roast pheasant, imported British plum pudding in brandy sauce, with a good French claret to wash it down."

"I'm tired of that damn caviar."

III

Mark Martino drifted in, as usual for lunch. He had four long-necked bottles in his arms. He also had an old-fashioned-looking six-shooter low on his right hip and an automatic pistol at belt level on his left. He looked surprisingly similar to that movie star of yesteryear Robert Taylor, but he wouldn't have known that.

"Hey, chum-pals," he said. "Get a load of this."

"What is it?" Pam said, looking up from the camp stove which sat on the electric range in the kitchen.

"It's a real *Bernkasteler Doktor und Bratenhofchen Trockenbeerenauslese.*"

"Oh great, now I know something I didn't know before."

"You, Pamela Rozet, are a peasant. This is the greatest of Riesling wines." He took one of the bottles and held it up and stared at the label and added, unhappily, "At least it once was; a Riesling shouldn't really age this long. Well, we'll see how it's held up."

"Where'd you find it?" Art said.

"You'd never think. In the cellar of that liquor store on the corner of West Third Street."

Art said, "I thought that joint had been looted bare years ago."

"Evidently so did everybody else," Mark said. "But this was down in the cellar, under a lot of crud that had evidently caved in back during the raids and riots. There was a whole case of this Riesling and some odd and ends of cordials. I covered it back over, but it won't do any good."

"Why not?" Pam said. "You don't have any gasoline over in your apartment, do you?"

"A couple of baboons spotted me coming out of the place with these. They'll root around till they've found it. You want me to go over and bring you a jerrycan?"

Pam said, "Please do. I'm just about out and haven't been able to find any for a week."

Art said, "Is that why you're all rodded up? The baboons?"

Mark, heading for the door, said, "Yeah. They were both strangers."

"Oh, hell," Art said. "We've been having it so easy here for months. You'd better tip off Julie and Tim."

"Already have," Mark said, leaving.

Art looked at Pam. "Maybe I'd better put off taking this painting down to the museum."

"Why?" she said wearily. "Baboons and hunters we've had before. Undoubtedly we'll have them again. Until—" she cut it off.

"Until what?"

"You know. Until one of these days, some baboon, or some hunter, kills one or both of us."

He didn't say anything.

Suddenly it came out in a rush.

"Arthur, we've *got* to get out of here. Arthur I'm afraid. I'm an awful coward."

He let the air out of his lungs and came erect from the kitchen chair upon which he had been sitting. He went over to the window and stared down.

Mark Martino came back with the can of gasoline.

"I don't know if this is white gas or not," he said.

Pam said, "It doesn't make any difference with this stove."

Mark said, "I ran into some butane in a sports section of a department store yesterday. Want it?"

"No, I suppose not. I threw the butane stove away. I'm used to this gasoline thing now. Not as hot, really, but we should be able to get gas for some time yet."

Mark said, "Well, even it's getting scarce. I haven't found a car with any in its tank for a coon's age." He looked from one of them to the other. "Did I interrupt a fight, or something?"

Pam said wearily, "No. No, not really."

Art said, "Pam wants to go back to the rat race."

She didn't say anything to that.

Mark said finally, "Well, why don't you? It doesn't make much sense, staying. We three and Julie and Tim are the only ones left in this neighborhood."

"Why don't you?" Art said. He wasn't arguing; his voice meant that he was actually curious.

Mark held up one of the green bottles he'd brought as his contribution toward the lunch. "You know what one of these would cost over on the mainland? That is, if you could find it at all."

"That couldn't be enough reason, even for a lush-head like you," Art said.

Mark thought about it. He said finally, ruefully, "I don't know. Wait a minute, I want to get something to read for you." He left again.

Pam said, "Why does anybody stay?"

Art knew he wasn't telling her anything she didn't know, but he said, "Some are criminals, fugitives from justice. Some are mental cases. Some, I suppose, are former immigrants, illegal entry immigrants without papers and not eligible to apply for their ten shares of Inalienable Basic if they went over to the mainland. We lump them all up and call them baboons. But the rest of us? Well, I suppose we're nonconformists, rebels against the Ultra-welfare State."

"That takes care of everybody but me," Pam said, checking the canned pheasant she'd been warming up.

"And you, then?" Art said. "Why are you here?"

"Because you are."

There could be no answer.

Mark Martino came in again, an age-yellowed paperback book in his hand. He was looking for a place.

"Listen to this," he said. "It's from a guy named Arthur C. Clarke. *Profiles of the Future,* written back in the sixties." He began reading. " 'Civilization cannot exist without new frontiers; it needs them both physically and spiritually. The physical need is obvious—new lands, new resources, new materials. The spiritual need is less apparent, but in the long run it is more important. We do not live by bread alone; we need adventure, variety, novelty, romance. As the psychologists have shown by their sensory deprivation experiments, a man goes swiftly mad if he is isolated in a silent, darkened room, cut off completely from the external world. What is true of individuals is also true of societies; they too can become insane without sufficient stimulus.' "

Mark tossed the book to the table. "I guess that's it. Whatever happened to the yen for adventure? A hundred years ago Americans were pushing West, fighting nature, fighting Indians, fighting each other over mines, cattle and land. When did the dividing line come—when we were willing to live vicarious adventure, watching make-believe heroes, Hollywood pretty boys, a good many of them queers, shoot up the Indians or kill by the scores the bad guys, the Nazis or commies, the Russians and Chinese. Why did we leave it to the Norwegians to crew the Kon-Tiki? and for the British and Sherpas to first scale Everest? We've become a bunch of gutless wonders, sitting in front of our Tri-Vision sets. The biggest frustration, the great tragedy of our current age is the new Central production ban on using cereals for beer or booze."

Art said sourly, "That won't be a frustration long. I understand that they came up with a new sort of combination tranquilizer and euphoric. Going to issue it so cheaply that it'll be nearly free. Non-habit-forming, supposedly no hangover, no bad effects. Keeps you perpetually happy, in a kind of perpetual daze. Even the children can have it. They call it Trank."

"What'll they think of next?" Mark marveled sarcastically. "Talk about bread and circuses. The Roman plutocracy never had it so good; they gave the proletariat a sadistic show and free wheat. But time marches on, and now we've got the credit from Inalienable Basic, twenty-four hour a day Tri-Vision teevee library, and music banks, and . . . what did you call it?"

"Trank," Art said. He looked at his friend strangely. "So you stay on here for the adventure. You with your big collection of guns. You with your prowling around the ruins looking for fancy booze and the like, hoping that the baboons or hunters will jump you. Hell, you're just a hunter yourself."

Mark was irritated and defensive. "I'm not a hunter. Maybe I like the adventure here, the chances you take just surviving, but I'm no hunter. I live here; this is my home. I defend myself. Maybe I even get my kicks out of getting into situations where I have to use my speed and my wits, but I never pick the fight, and I most certainly have never shot an unarmed baboon in the back the way these damned hunters will."

Pam began to set the food on the table. "Then what's the real reason for being here, Mark—aside from the adventure?"

IV

He pretended he had to think about it, even as he helped her put out the elaborate silverware Art had liberated from the ruins of Tiffany's years before.

He reached into a pocket and brought forth the durable plastic which was his Universal Credit Card. "I object to this being closer to me than my soul," he said. "My number, issued me at birth and from which I can never escape, even after death. A combination of what was once Social Security number, driver's license, bank account number, voter's registration, even telephone number and post office box number. It's everything. Regimentation carried to the ultimate. We thought the commies and Nazis had regimentation. Zoroaster! The computers know everything there is to know about me, from before I was born to long after I'm dead—they keep the records in their files forever. When my great-grandchildren want to have children, the computers will check back on good old Mark Martino for genetic purposes. Oh, swell. Talk about being a cog in a machine—hell, we're more nearly like identical grains of sand on a beach."

He held up his wrist to show his teevee phone. "Why I carry this, I don't know. I've always got it switched on Priority One, and there are only three persons on earth eligible to break in on me on Priority One. But look at this thing. With the coming of the satellite relays and international communications integrated, I can literally, and for practically no expense, talk to anybody on earth. Even if the poor cloddy is halfway up Mount Fuji in Japan. There's no escape. In the old days, the cost of phoning a friend, relative, business contact or whoever got on the prohibitive side when it was long distance, or especially international. Not now. For pennies you can talk to anyone in the world. But the trouble is, it works both ways—they can talk to you."

Art laughed. "I seldom wear my wristphone. And even the portable, in the next room, is always on Priority Two."

Mark growled, "That won't help you if it's a government bulletin or something. You're on tap, every minute of the day. How'd you like to be a Tri-Vision sex symbol or some other entertainment star? If one of them dared lower their priority to, say, five, they'd have a billion teevee phone calls come in within hours."

Pam said, "All right, all right, let's eat. Get the cork out of one of those bottles, Art, and let's sample the latest loot. So you're in revolt against modern society, Mark, so all right. At least you don't refuse to spend your dividends from your Inalienable Basic, the way Art does. And your royalties must accumulate so that when you make those sin trips of yours over to Nueva Las Vegas, or wherever, you must have quite a bit of credit on hand."

"Sin trips!" Mark protested, holding his right hand over his heart as though in injured innocence. "How can you say that? It's called research."

"Ha!" Art snorted.

"No jolly," Mark said. "I've got to keep up some touch. Have to know what they're listening to in the dives, both high and low. It's all very well to have two or three semi-classics in the music banks, but you've got to be continually turning out new stuff if you really want to hit the jackpot some day."

"Semi-classics," Art snorted. "I love Mother in the springtime; I love Mother in the fall."

Mark said reasonably, "It's what they want, Art. If you'd paint what they wanted, maybe you'd be selling better. Right now, they're going through a 1920's-1930's revival bit. Swell. I sit at my teevee phone and play over and over the so-called Hit Parade tunes, and over and over I listen to the old Bing Crosby and even Rudy Vallee tapes.

"And then pretty soon, just about when I'm ready to start tearing my hair out, something comes to me. I sit down to the piano. I beat it out. Sometimes the whole thing is done in an hour. Writing the lyrics is the hardest part."

Pam said interestedly, "Then what happens, Mark?"

"Well, there's various ways. If you're a second-rater, like me, your best bet is to get in touch with a slick to act as middleman, expediter or whatever you want to call him. He gets one of the stars, such as Truman Love . . ."

"Truman *Love,*" Art protested. "Is there really a singer with a name like that?"

"Of course. I tell you, Art, the mental caliber of the Tri-Vision and teevee fan is halving each year that goes by. They don't want to be bothered thinking even a tiny bit. A sloppy mopsy who likes to listen to sentimental slush about love can remember a name like Truman Love. It sticks with her. She knows very well, before she dials one of his songs, what it's going to be like. With a name like that, it couldn't be anything else."

"All right, all right, so the slick gets Truman Love to sing your song."

"Okay. We record it and pay the small amount involved in placing it in the music banks. If the slick is any good, he gets some publicity. One of the gossip commentators, one of the live comedians, that sort of thing. In the banks, it's filed under name of singer, name of song, type of song, band leader, name of band, name of each musician in the band, subject of song—such as love, mother, patriotism, children, that sort of thing—and finally, surprise, surprise, the writer or writers of the song."

"So," Art supplied, "whoever dials and plays it pays a small royalty."

"Very small," Mark said, nodding. "Differs for a single home teevee phone screen, or for, say, some live Tri-Vision show involving a band. If you're lucky, the song takes and maybe some more singers and bands want to record it. At any rate, you split the take four ways."

"Four ways?" Pam said. "You, the singer, the slick and who?"

"The recording company. They usually take one fourth too. They split their quarter between the company, the band leader and all members of the band."

Art shook his head. "By the time the drummer gets his slice, it must be pretty small potatoes."

"Not if it's played a few billion times," Mark said. "Besides, maybe I write a possible song once a month. He probably does a recording as often as once or twice a day. He might have literally thousands of tunes recorded, with his getting a tiny percentage of each."

"It's not as bad as newspapers," Pam said. "Reading a newspaper on your teevee phone will cost you ten cents. It has to be prorated among possibly a hundred journalists, columnists, editors and what have you. That means that on an average, each newspaperman involved gets possibly one mill, a tenth of a cent, per reading. Not even that, since the owners of the paper take their cut off the top."

Art said, shaking his head and digging into the pheasant, "What in the name of the holy living Zoroaster did they do before computers?"

"Well, they didn't handle it this way," Mark said. He looked at Art and changed the subject. "You're going down to Greater Washington this afternoon?"

"Yeah. I want to register this painting. I'll be back in a few hours. You'll keep an eye on Pam, won't you?"

"Of course. Uh . . . you have duplication and registration fee?"

Art looked at him, puzzled.

Mark said hurriedly, "I mean, without dipping into your dividends. I know you refuse to spend them."

Art went back to his food.

"Don't be so touchy," Mark said. "What I meant was, if you were a little short, you could always pay me back later."

Art said, "You know damn well I couldn't use your dollar credits to register my painting anyway. Nobody can spend your credits but you. Or do you want me to carry not only your credit card with me but your right thumb as well, for the print?"

Mark chuckled. "There are ways of getting around anything. I found some ancient coins in the wreckage of a numismatist's shop the other day. You could take them to Greater Washington, sell them, and have the amount credited to your account. Then use it."

"Thanks just the same," Art said tightly. "But I pay my own way, Mark. When I can't pay my own way by selling my paintings any longer, I'll give up my art and find some other kind of work."

"Well, it's more than I can say. I'm always in here sponging off you people."

Pam laughed at that. "Half the things we have here came from you. Why you're the one who found the bomb shelter, even."

The subject was safely changed. Mark said, "By the way, how's the bomb shelter holding out?"

"We're putting a sizable dent in it," Pam said. "I think I'm going to ask you boys to try and scout out some things not quite so exotic. A few cases of baked beans, corn, string beans and what have you. I'm beginning to get a permanent sour stomach from all this rich stuff. Which reminds me. I'm going to have to take a trip to the mainland, as soon as my dividends come in for next month, to load up on some fresh fruits and vegetables."

Mark said, "Why don't we make an expedition of it? Tim and Julie too. Both for the manpower to carry things and for protection."

Art said, "What time is it?"

Mark dialed his wristphone and said, "What time is it?"

A tinny voice responded, "When the bell sounds, it will be thirteen hours and thirteen minutes." A tiny bell sounded.

"Oh, oh," Art said. "I better get the damn painting wrapped and get going or I won't be back before dark."

"Listen," Pam said anxiously. "Don't you dare walk the streets that late. If you're held up, you stay in an auto-hotel on the mainland."

"I haven't enough dollar credit," he growled.

"You have lots of dollars in your credit balance."

"I mean my *own* credit."

She rolled her eyes upward. "You must be driving the

computers crazy with all that unspent credit you've accumulated. They probably can't figure out why, if you aren't using it currently, you don't buy Variable Basic stock, something to build up your portfolio and bring in more earnings."

"Earnings!" he snorted, coming to his feet and tossing his beautiful linen napkin—looted long months since from the wreckage of Macy's—to the table. "How can shares of stock, just sitting there, make any earnings? Only work earns anything."

V

Arthur Halleck, his wrapped painting clumsily under his arm, a sawed-off double-barrelled shotgun slung over his shoulders, peddled his bike up MacDougal to West Third Street and turned right. He peddled the five streets over to Broadway, expertly zigzagging in between the abandoned cars and trucks and debris. Broadway, being wider, was clearer. He turned left and tried to speed it up a bit.

It would have made more sense for them to have lived closer to the Grand Central vacuum-tube terminal, but they stubbornly hung on to staying in the Village. It was a matter of principle, in a way. The last of the artists, staying in the last of the art colonies. All five of them. He and Pam, Mark, Tim the poet and his girl Julie who long years ago had been a model.

However, the further uptown you got, the more hunters you ran into. They were too lazy to hike all the way down to Greenwich Village. Too lazy, and largely too timid. These empty streets, with all the windows, all the rooftops, all the doorways, any of which might shelter an armed baboon or even a fellow hunter, a bit on the trigger-happy side; these empty streets would give even a well armed, bullet-proof clothed hunter the willies.

He peddled up Broadway, keeping a weather eye peeled, right and left to Union Square. He was in more danger from a hunter—assuming there were any on the island today—than he was from a baboon. Most of the baboons that hung out in this area knew him, and there was more or less of a gentleman's agreement not to bother each other. There was no percentage in it, for that matter. They knew he wasn't worth jumping, that he didn't have anything worth risking a life for. Besides that, the shotgun over his shoulder was a great deterrent. There's something about a shotgun loaded with buckshot. Man in his time has evolved some exotic weapons for close-quarters combat, but there's something about a sawed-off shotgun. The bearer doesn't even have to be a good shot; in fact, he can be full of lead, his eyes beginning to go glazed, and still point it and pull the hair-trigger and accomplish one tremendous amount of revenge.

At Madison Square, he turned right and headed up Fifth. At the library, he left the bike for a moment, went inside through the side door which was still unblocked, and stashed his shotgun away in the place where he usually left it.

He was unarmed now, but it was only a couple of blocks. He peddled over to the Grand Central terminal and to where the police had their booth. There had been rumors that even this last vacuum-tube terminal on all Manhattan was going to be discontinued, but he doubted it. In spite of the supposed desertion of the whole island, there were still reasons for occasional visits—sometimes in considerable strength. Like last year when the delegation from Mexico City came up to mine the Metropolitan Museum of Fine Arts of its treasure of Aztec artifacts. They recovered quite a bit too, so he had heard. The looters earlier hadn't been interested in much except gold and obviously sophisticated art objects that were immediately saleable.

There were two police at the tube entry. He knew one of them slightly. He'd been here for a long time. He must have gone back to the old days, and Art Halleck wondered why he hadn't retired. His name was Williams, or something; or maybe it was William, though that almost invariably becomes Bill on the level at which they met.

They shook him down, the other cop being a little more thorough than Williams.

Williams said, "He's all right," but the other didn't pay much attention.

"Got a gun?" he said.

"No," Art said patiently.

The other snorted and continued to touch him where a man keeps a weapon.

"I said I didn't have a gun," Art said. "I know it's against the rules for me to carry a gun without a special permit, even in this town."

Williams said, "He's an old hand. He hides his gun a block or so away before he comes here."

The new guard said, "What's in the package?"

"A painting. I'm an artist."

The other snorted disbelief. "Let's see it."

Art's lips began to go white.

Williams said, "I've known him for a long time. He's a painter. Lives down in the Village."

The new guard said, "How do we know he hasn't scrounged some old master or something? Something that oughta be turned over to the national museum."

Art drew in his breath, and a muscle in his right cheek began to tic.

Williams said, "Look, Walt, if you want to open up his package, you can open up his package. However, if he had a Michelangelo in there, do you think he'd just amble up to us like this? Wouldn't he find himself a boat and ferry it over some dark night?"

Walt grumbled, "Well, if you say so. But it seems to me you take it awfully easy with these people."

"Like I said, I've known him a long time." To Art he said, soothingly, "How's that nice Miss Pamela?"

"She's all right," Art said. And then more graciously, "She's getting a lot of work done on her book. In a day or so, we'll be going over to get some fresh things."

The new guard named Walt, still miffed, said, "What'd

you mean *fresh* things? What do you eat, ordinarily? Looting's forbidden."

Art looked at him. "Ordinarily, we eat the stuff we still have left over in the kitchen cabinet and the refrigerator from before the time when the cops chickened out on the job and pulled off the island."

"Why you—"

"Okay, okay, you two," Williams said, getting between them. "Loosen up. You're both nice guys. Stop roaching each other. Walt McGivern, this is Art Halleck. If Walt's on this detail very long, he'll probably be seeing you from time to time, Art."

VI

Walt McGivern grunted something sourly and turned and walked off.

Art said, "What's roaching him?"

The older policeman said, "This isn't considered the most desirable detail around."

Art picked up his painting, preparatory to going on. "Then why do you stick it out, Williams?"

"Why do you?"

"I asked you first. But I can live here without paying rent, or practically anything else."

The police guard chuckled wryly. But then he drew in his breath and said, "I was born a few blocks from here, son." That wasn't quite enough, so he added, "I wasn't here during the few bad days. When I came back, the family was gone. I never found out how, or why, or where, or anything else. Hell, the whole neighborhood was gone."

"Sorry," Art said. "I shouldn't have asked."

"All right, son. The thing is, there aren't many folks left. In fact, practically none. I wish you and that nice Pamela girl would go on over to the mainland. However, as long as there are any decent people left at all, I kind of like to be here."

"The last of the neighborhood cops," Art muttered.

"What?"

"Nothing."

Art started off again, but at that moment two new comers emerged from the tube entry.

Art came to a halt and eyed them up and down deliberately as they approached the police booth.

He stared the first one full in the face and said, "You look like a couple of jokers out of a Tri-Vision show about hunters on Safari in Africa—you mopsy-monger."

The man's eyes bugged. "You . . . you can't talk to me that way, you . . . you cheap baboon!"

Art sneered at him. "I'm no baboon. Maybe the last of the bohemians, but I'm no baboon. I've got all my papers. I'm legal. There's no law against living on Manhattan—if you don't go around armed." He took in the other's automatic-recoiless rifle, and the heavy pistol at his waist, and then added, "You sonofabitch."

The newcomer turned quickly to Williams, who was inspecting the papers the two had handed him.

"Arrest this man!" he snapped.

Williams looked up, wide eyed. "What'd he do?"

"He slandered me. I demand you arrest him."

"I didn't hear him say anything," Williams said evenly.

The other newcomer came up. He was quieter, less lardy and less pompous than his companion, but he said to Art coldly. "Let me see your Uni-Credit Card."

"Go to hell, you mopsy-mongering hunter."

The other drew forth his own Uni-Credit Card and flashed it to Williams. "I want a complete police report on this man."

Walt McGivern came up. "What's going on?"

The second of the two hunters said coldly, "I'm Harry Kank, Inter-American Bureau of Investigation. Get me an immediate police report on this man."

Williams sighed and said, "Let me have your Universal Credit Card, Art." But then he amended that, looking defiantly at the newcomers. "I mean, Mr. Halleck."

Art's lips were white, but he reached into an inner

pocket and brought it forth. All five of them entered the police booth.

Williams put the card in the teevee phone slot and said, "Police record, please."

Within seconds a robot-like voice began, "Arthur Le-Roy Halleck. At age of sixteen arrested for participating in peace demonstration, without permit to parade. Released. At age of twenty arrested by traffic authorities for driving a floater manually while under the influence of alcohol. Suspended driver's license for one year. At age of twenty-five arrested for assault and battery. Charge dropped by victim. No further police record. Now believed to be living on the island of Manhattan, on MacDougal Street with Pamela Rozet, out of wedlock." The robot voice came to a halt, then said, "Are details required?"

Williams looked at the man who had named himself Harry Kank.

The Bureau of Investigation man said to Art, testily, "What was that assault and battery charge?"

Art said, "I slugged a man who made a snide remark about my paintings. He apologized later. Now he's a friend of mine. Want to get him on the phone?"

Kank glared at him, unspeaking for a moment. Then he snapped to Williams, "I suspect this man of being incompetent to handle his own affairs. Give me a credit check on him."

Williams opened his mouth, then closed it with a sigh. He said into the teevee phone, "Balance Check on this card."

Within seconds a robot voice said, "Ten shares, Inalienable Basic. No shares Variable Basic."

The two hunters snorted.

The robot voice went on, "Current cash credit, fourteen thousand four hundred and forty-five dollars and sixty-three cents."

The eyes of the two bugged.

Kank snapped, "Get that again. There must be some mistake."

Williams, also visibly taken aback, repeated his demand of the balance check on Art Halleck's account. It came out the same.

The Bureau of Investigation man's eyes were colder still, now. He said, "Where did you accumulate that much credit? Have you been looting here on the island and selling what you find to dealers on the mainland?"

Art said contemptuously. "Of that credit balance, I figure seventy-three dollars and some odd cents are mine. The rest belongs to the government of the United States of the Americas, as far as I'm concerned."

All were staring at him now.

Art said, "I haven't touched my dividends from my ten shares of Inalienable Basic for years. I don't want them. The seventy-three dollars is *mine*. It represents money I've taken in selling my paintings. If there was any way of giving the dividends back to the damn Ultra-welfare State, I would. But evidently there isn't. I can't even donate them to charity. There isn't any such thing any more—except the one big mopsy-mongering charity."

All four of them were still staring disbelief.

"You must be crazy," the first of the two hunters blurted.

But Kank came to a sudden decision and snapped at Williams, "If you're through with our papers, let me have them. As you'll note, we have permission to search various buildings in the Wall Street area for certain lost records. Do you have an armored floater available?"

"Well, yes sir."

"Very well, I'll requisition it." Harry Kank turned back to Art and stared at him. "Possibly we will see each other again . . . baboon."

"I'm not a baboon . . . hunter," Art sneered at him. "I see you know our terminology here on the island. Undoubtedly you have been here before. Undoubtedly with some similar trumped-up reason for prowling around, armed to the teeth. Maybe we *will* see each other again— you sonofabitch."

The high police official glared at him, but spun on his

heel and, with his plumper companion, followed after Walt McGivern.

Williams and Art stood there a moment, looking after them.

Williams said bitterly, "Some cop."

Art growled lowly, "Why can't something be done about those lousy funkers?"

Williams said, "You know as well as I do. There's no law in this city. Citizens who live here, or enter it, waive all legal protection. But anybody with pull can get special permission to come in armed, supposedly for some gobbledygook reason such as to search the library, or some museum, for something lost. Ha! Not one cloddy out of ten has any real legitimate reason. They come to thrill hunt. The ruined cities are the only place I know of in the world where you can legally shoot a man, woman or child and not even report it, if you don't want to bother. If you do bother, you report it as self-defense."

Walt McGivern was turning the armored police floater over to the two hunters.

Art said, in disgust still, "I better get going. Thanks, Williams."

Williams looked at him. "Thanks for what?"

Art headed for the entry to the vacuum-tube transport terminal.

VII

Back at the apartment house on MacDougal Street, Pam and Mark were still lingering over their coffee. In fact, in spite of the hour, Mark had gone to his own apartment and returned with a bottle of Napoleon brandy, the last of a case he had found in a ruined penthouse, some months ago.

They drank the coffee black and sipped at the cognac from enormous snifter glasses which had been liberated from Tiffany's at the same time as her silverware.

Pam looked distastefully at the remnants of their midday meal. "I'm getting awfully tired of this canned food," she said. "What is there about eating that makes you really prefer, not something like pressed duck under glass with orange sauce, but the kind of codfish gravy on toast that you used to eat in your poverty-stricken home as a kid?"

Mark chuckled, "Or some pasta, spaghetti or otherwise, such as your mother used to make herself. None of this store boughten stuff. And precious little to put over it save a bit of tomato sauce and when you were lucky, some grated cheese."

Pam said, "Whoever stocked that bomb shelter must have owned half of Fort Knox. He put in enough caviar and smoked salmon to last a regiment until any possible contamination from a nuclear bombing was gone. I never thought I'd get to the point where I got fed up with caviar."

Mark said laughingly, "I never even tasted it until after the city was abandoned. My first reaction was that it tasted like fish eggs."

She laughed at him. But then she said, "What in the world ever happened to cooking?"

He thought about it. "Like every other art, I suppose, or handicraft or skill for that matter. What cobbler could take pride in spending a few days on a pair of handmade shoes that had taken him half a lifetime in apprenticeship to learn to make when the potential customer could go down and buy a pair made in an automated factory that were *almost* as good and cost a fraction of what he had to charge? It was easier for the cobbler to go down to the factory and get a thirty-hour-a-week job. Or if none was available, to go on relief; or later, to live on his Inalienable Basic handout."

She frowned. "Well, that applies to the cobbler, but not ..."

"Not to an artist?" He grinned at her. Same thing. The idea of saving time, of devoting as much of your day to recreation, leisure, play, permeated our whole society. Cooking? A woman is considered mad to do such things as bake her own bread and pastry, cut up her own vegetables, learn how to trim her own meat. You saved so much *time* buying bakery bread, canned vegetables, frozen meat all neatly cut and packaged so that you never realized that it had once come off an animal. The fact that it simply didn't taste the same wasn't nearly as good and wasn't as nutrious either was allowed to go by the board. She saved time. What did she do with it? Sat and watched TV, or now, Tri-Vision. Supposedly she was being saved from drudgery, not art. But cooking is an art, and art takes time."

Pam was uncomfortable. She said, "Do you expect me to bake bread? I'm a writer. I don't want to spend eight hours a day cooking."

Mark Martino laughed. "Who am I to throw the first stone? You've heard some of the songs I write. They're a continual rehash of popular songs that were written and have been rewritten over and over for the better part of the past century."

"Why don't you try something more serious?"

"I have. Every clown wants to play Hamlet. Off and on I've been working on a light opera for nearly a year. It'll never be produced. People don't want even light opera today. It takes a bit of education to enjoy. Anybody can understand that perennial favorite I wrote, *I Love Mother in the Springtime*. It's not just musicians. Look at poetry, you who are a writer. In the old days a poet used to sweat turning out a sonnet, say. Very difficult form. Exactly fourteen lines, all of them hung together with rhyme, rhythm, meter, perfectly. It was too much work for the poet, so blank verse and then free verse came in. And then anarchy. The new poet never bothered to learn how to construct a sonnet, or to measure his lines in correct meter and to follow a rhythm system. He dashed off his inspired *poem* in a matter of a half hour and was surprised when after a few decades of this people stopped reading poetry."

He thought about it for a minute. "Same as in art. What happened to the painter who used to serve an apprenticeship of years learning the tools of his trade?

Our Art Halleck is the only painter I've even heard of for years who bothered to learn to draw. Too much work.''

"I suppose it permeates our whole society," Pam said, nodding. "Nobody takes pride in his work any more."

"How can you, under present circumstances? Take my original example, that cobbler. He made shoes, from beginning to end, and when the job was through he could look at them and say, 'There is the product of my efforts. I did a good job.' Put the same man in a factory turning out half a million pairs of shoes a day. His job, which he can handle dressed in a suit and wearing white shirt and tie, consists of staring at various dials and screens and occasionally throwing a switch, or checking a report. He never sees the leather; he never sees a pair of the completed product. How can he take pride in his work?"

She said slowly, "Well, in some fields the new system has its advantages. People's capitalism, I mean."

"Like, for instance?" he said skeptically.

"Well, I was interested earlier in your description of how a musical composer is rewarded for his efforts. In the long run, it's based on how his songs are received. I think it's even better for the free lance writer."

"It's basically the same, isn't it?"

"There are variations. For instance, in the old days a writer did, say, a novel. Good. When it was finished, he submitted it to a publishing house and an editor read it— at least, we hope he did. Possibly it never got to an editor. If the writer was an unknown, perhaps his novel was read, or quickly scanned, by a poorly paid reader who possibly didn't really have the qualifications to understand the book. All right, but suppose an editor did read it and liked it. By the way, many of these editors were frustrated writers who couldn't make the grade, but here they were in a position to accept or reject some hopeful's work. They hadn't made it but they were now in a position to criticize somebody else's writing. Anyway even after you got past the editor, that wasn't all. You might get a letter from him saying, 'I like it fine, but unfortunately this publishing house objects to protagonists being anarchists or matricides, or homosexuals, or whatever their various taboos might be."

Mark laughed sourly. "Well, it *was* their publishing company they could decide what they wanted to publish and what they didn't."

"Yes. That's my complaint. You see, we had freedom of the press. You could write anything you wanted. Getting it printed was another thing. You had to find some publishing company, or newspaper, or magazine, or whatever, who wanted to print it. If you couldn't locate one, then you still had the option of printing it yourself. Unfortunately, few writers had enough money to start their own publishing house or magazine."

"I see your point."

"Ummm. Today I write a book and take it to the nearest library and for a small amount of money I have it set up and registered in the national computer library files. It's registered by title, cross registered by author, subject, and whether it's fiction, non-fiction, juvenile, or whatever. Even the reviews are available to the potential reader. And reviewers and critics we shall always have with us."

"Amen. But suppose nobody wants to read it?"

"The same thing happens as happened before with writers. You don't make any money. But if somebody does want to read it, he pays a nominal sum to have it projected on his teevee phone screen library booster. If it becomes a best-seller, he makes a great deal. There might be holes in the system, but at least you aren't subject to the whims of editors and publishers. Anybody willing to sacrifice the comparatively small amount, about fifty dollars for the average length novel, can have his work presented to the public."

Mark said, "I'd think there'd be one hell of a large number of books each year."

"There are. But there's no limits to the number that the library banks can contain, after all. Another good thing is that every book ever printed remains in the banks—forever. Nothing ever goes out of print. It may go out of demand, practically everything does, sooner or later, but nothing goes out of print. The books I'm writing today will be available a thousand years from now, if anybody wanted to bother to read them."

Mark Martino said grudgingly, "I suppose the thing is that anybody can afford to go into the arts today. Whether anybody reads his books, buys his paintings, or listens to his music is another thing. That is still in the laps of the gods, as it always was. But at least you can make your fling."

"That's right," Pam sighed, coming to her feet. "I suppose I'd better throw these disposable plates out the window. A woman's work is never done."

Mark stood too. "I ate too much," he announced. "And that cognac didn't help any. I think I'll take a nap. Listen, Pam, if you decide to go out, bang on the door. I'll tag along, just for luck."

"Looking for adventure?" she said in deprecation.

He scowled at her. "I was laying that on a bit. It's not the only reason I stick around here on Manhattan, of course."

She was uncomfortable and stared down at the toe of her Etruscan revival sandal.

He said softly, "As you probably know, I'm really here for the same reason you are, Pamela."

She didn't say anything.

Mark said, "Art's a friend of mine. But if anything ever happens between you two . . ."

"Have a good nap, Mark."

VIII

Art Halleck went on down into the vacuum-tube terminal. He had to take a two-seater, since the larger carriers seldom came through this deserted spot. He stuck the painting in behind the seat and climbed in himself and brought the canopy over his head and dropped the pressurizer. He remembered the coordinates from the many times he had made the trip and dialed right through to the offices of the duplicator at the National Museum.

It might have been slightly cheaper if he had taken his two-seater to the pseudo-city of Princeton and from there taken a twenty-seater to Greater Washington. But that would have meant changing from two-seater to twenty-seater at Princeton, changing back again to a two-seater once he had arrived at the terminal in the capital. Too much time. He wanted to get back to Greenwich Village before dark. It was no good leaving Pam there alone, even though Mark was in the same building.

When the destination light flickered, he released the pressurizer and threw the canopy back and climbed out into the reception room of the Office of Duplication. He pulled the painting out from behind the seat and went to the reception desk. The door of the vacuum tube closed behind him.

He said into the reception screen, "Arthur Halleck requests immediate appointment to duplicate and register a painting."

The voice said, "Room 23. Mr. Ben MacFarlane."

Art knew MacFarlane. The other had handled Art's work before. He was a man who dabbled in painting himself, evidently not very successfully or he wouldn't have found it necessary to augment his dividends from his Inalienable Basic by holding down a job like this. Not that he wasn't lucky to have been able to get a job.

Art made his way down a corridor with which he was highly familiar, to Duplicating Room 23. There seemed to be no one else around, but, come to think of it, the last time he had been here he had spotted only one other artist hopeful. Only a few years ago you could have expected to see half a dozen or more. Evidently as time went by fewer and fewer would-be artists were trying to sell their stuff. He wondered vaguely if it was a matter of trying to make anything out of it. It did cost fifty dollars to duplicate and register just one painting. And fifty dollars was a sizable enough chunk to take out of anyone's credit balance if they had no more than their ten shares of Inalienable Basic to depend upon. Possibly a lot of painters these days were doing their work and then not bothering to show it or at most, showing it only to friends and neighbors. Or perhaps it was a matter of giving up painting completely and joining the ever increasing percentage of the population of the Ultra-welfare State in spending practically all free time staring into the Tri-Vision box.

It was a depressing trend of thought.

He activated the door screen, and shortly the door opened and he entered.

Ben MacFarlane was seated at his desk. He looked up and said, "Ah . . . Halleck, isn't it? Art Halleck."

Art said, "That's right. Hello, MacFarlane. How does it go?" He began unwrapping the painting.

"Slow, slow," the other said. He watched, only half interestedly as Art brought the painting forth. "Still doing that Representational-Abstract stuff, eh?"

"That's right," Art said.

"It's not selling," MacFarlane said.

"You're telling me." Art brought the painting over to him.

MacFarlane looked at it critically. "How did the last one go?"

"Sold seven so far," Art said.

"That's not too bad for a complete unknown."

"I've got three or four people who evidently collect me. Two down in Mexico, one in Hawaii and one in the Yukon, of all places. Sometimes you wonder what they're like, these people who have your things on their walls."

Ben MacFarlane stood and took up the painting. "You want to pay for this?"

"Sure," Art said. He brought his Uni-Credit Card from his inner pocket and put it in the desk slot and his thumbprint on the screen. MacFarlane touched a button and Art retrieved the card.

MacFarlane said, "I suppose you want to take the original back with you?"

"Of course."

The museum employee shrugged. "You'd be surprised how many don't. I suppose it's a matter of storage room in a mini-apartment. They come here and duplicate and register a painting and then tell us to throw the original away."

"Now that's pessimism," Art said. "Suppose you finally hit and these rich original collectors started wanting your works? Zoroaster, you'd kick yourself around the block."

MacFarlane, carrying the painting, left the room momentarily. When he returned, he handed the painting back to Art who began rewrapping it. MacFarlane settled back into his chair.

He said, "You still living in Greenwich Village?"

"That's right."

"You wouldn't know an old chum-pal of mine? Actually, I haven't seen him for ages. Fellow named Chuck Bellows."

Art looked up, scowling. "Tall guy with red hair?"

"That's right, Charles Bellows. Does old fashioned collages."

Art said, "He's dead."

"Dead! He can't be more than forty-five."

Art took a breath and said, "He had taken over a studio on Bleecker Street. Swanky place. A penthouse deal some millionaire must have originally owned. A friend of mine found him. Evidently it had been simple enough. Somebody must have knocked on the door and when he answered it, shot him."

"Zoroaster!"

"Yeah. Must have been what we call a baboon since the place was ransacked."

"Are there many of these uh baboons around?"

"No. Not many," Art said.

"I don't see why you stay, Halleck."

Art shook his head, even as he tied the string about the painting. "This is the third time today I've had to go into it," he said.

"I wasn't prying."

"I don't believe in taking charity," Art said. "And the way my things are selling, I couldn't make it on the mainland. In Greenwich Village I can make a go of it and continue painting. It's the most important thing in the world for me—my painting."

The other was only mildly surprised. Evidently, he had run into far-out ideas from artists before.

He said, "By the way, what kind of a price do you want set on this, Halleck?"

Art hesitated. He said, finally, "Five dollars."

MacFarlane shook his head. "I wouldn't if I were you."

"What do you mean?"

"It's a mistake a good many unarrived artists make. They think if they mark their prices down far enough, they'll sell. If I recall, you usually put a price of ten dollars on your things. If I were you, I'd make it twenty-five. There's still an element of snobbery in buying paintings, even though they are now available for practically nothing compared to the old days. Too many people, even among those with enough taste to want paintings on their walls, don't really know what they like. So they buy according to the current fad or according to the prestige of a painter. Something like in the old days, when people who had the money would buy a Picasso, not because they really understood or liked his work, but because he was a status symbol."

Art scowled at him, hesitating.

MacFarlane said, "I've been here a long time. In fact, since the duplicating process was first perfected. I even remember back to when people bought originals. But the perfection of duplicating paintings to such an extent that not even the artist can tell the difference between his original and the duplicates we can make literally by the millions made possibly the greatest change in the history of art."

"It sure did," Art said grimly. "And personally, I'm not sure I'm happy about it. For one thing, to make these perfect duplicates, I've got to paint on that damned presdwood-duplicator board, using nothing but metallic-acrylic paints. Frankly, I prefer canvas and oils."

MacFarlane chuckled sourly. "I'm afraid you'd be hard-put to find buyers for a canvas painting these days, Halleck. When a person wants to buy a painting today, he dials the art banks. There your paintings, along with those of every other artist who submits his work, are to be found listed by name of artist, name of school of painting, name of subject, name of principle involved, even cross listed under size of painting. He selects those that he feels he might be interested in and dials them. When he finds one he likes, he can order it. The artist decides the price. It's a system that works in this mass society of ours, Halleck. Everybody can afford paintings today. In the past only the fairly well to do could."

Art, almost ready to go, said sourly, "Okay, make the price ten dollars, as usual. I wonder if the average painter is any better off now than he was before. In the old days when you did sell a painting, you got possibly two or three hundred dollars for it. Today you get ten dollars and have to sell thirty duplicates of your original to earn the same amount."

"Yes, but there are potentially millions of buyers today. An artist who becomes only mildly known can boost his prices to, say, twenty-five or thirty-five dollars per painting, and if he sells a hundred thousand of them, he can put his returns into Variable Basic or some other investment and retire, if he wishes to retire. There has never been a period in history, Halleck, where the artist was so highly rewarded."

"*If* he hits," Art growled. "Well, wish me luck on this one, MacFarlane." He turned and headed for the door.

"That I do," MacFarlane said. "It's a tough racket, Halleck."

"It always has been," Art said. "It's just a matter of sticking it out until your time comes." The door opened before him.

IX

Pamela Rozet took up a heavy shopping bag and left the apartment, locking it behind her. She went to the stairway and mounted to the next floor. Mark Martino's door was open. He had probably left it that way so that he could hear any noises in the hall, just in case somebody came along while Art was gone.

She peered in the door.

Mark was stretched out on his comfort couch. There was an aged paperback book fallen to the floor by his side, and he was snoring slightly.

She hesitated. She hadn't liked the trend of their conversation an hour or so earlier. She had known that the other was in love with her and had been for a long time. A woman knows. However, he had never put it into words before, and she was sorry he had. She would just as well not continue the conversation, certainly not today.

She didn't awaken him. Instead, tiptoed away and went back to her own apartment. She hesitated momentarily, then went over to the weapons closet and got her twenty-two automatic rifle.

Both Art and Mark laughed about her favorite gun, pointing out that such a caliber wasn't heavy enough to dent a determined man. However, she claimed that at least she could hit something with this light gun, that it was easily carried, as opposed to something of heavier caliber, and that just carrying a gun was usually enough of a deterrent. You seldom really had to use it. In actuality, although she had never said so, she could not have used it on a fellow human being. It was simply not in her.

She carried the basket in her left hand, the rifle in her right, and headed out again.

Their apartment was on the fifth floor. The building was in good enough shape that they could have selected a place lower down and thus have eliminated considerable stair climbing; however, being this high gave a certain amount of defense. Baboons were inclined to be on the lazy side and, besides that, would make enough noise to give forewarning of their arrival.

The defense system was simple. Any friends coming up to visit, such as Julie and Tim, would give a shout before beginning to mount from the ground floor. If such a shout wasn't forthcoming, Art, Mark, or Pam would fire a couple of rounds at random into the ceiling above the stairwell. Invariably, that was answered by scurrying of feet below. Thus far, neither baboon nor hunter had dared continue to advance.

Down on the street, she carefully scanned the neighborhood before leaving the shelter of the doorway. She could see nothing living, save a ragtag cat a scurrying along.

She took up MacDougal, then turned left. Her destination was only a few blocks away.

The front of the house was so badly blasted that it would have been impossible to enter. Probably a gas main explosion, they had originally decided. It was a matter of going up a tiny alleyway clogged with debris and refuse to a small door leading to the basement and located improbably. Few would have considered prowling the alley.

She looked up and down again before entering the alley, then made her way quickly to the door and through. She took the flashlight from her basket and held it clumsily in the same hand in which she was carrying the twenty-two. She flicked it alive and started down the half-ruined stairs.

At the bottom, she turned left toward what would ordinarily have been assumed to be a furnace room. At the far side was a rack for wine bottles stretching all the way to the ceiling. The wine was long gone before Mark Martino had, through a sheer stroke of genius, found this treasure trove.

She threw the lever, cleverly hidden to one side, and the door began to grind protestingly. She pulled it toward her and directed the flashlight into the interior. It was as she had last seen it, not that she expected otherwise. Only Mark, Art and she knew about this retreat. They hadn't even told Tim and Julie.

Inside, she found one of the Coleman lanterns and lit it and leaned her gun against the wall.

The original owner had evidently expected a sizable

contingent to occupy this refuge if the bombs began to drop. He had probably had both a family and a staff of servants. And he had evidently expected the stay below ground to be a lengthy one. Aside from food and drink, there was a supply of oxygen in bottles, bottled water, several types of fuel, a variety of tools; formerly there had been quite a supply of weapons and ammunition, since plundered by Mark Martino.

She went over to the extensive storeroom and almost as though in a super-market, shuffled up and down the rows of canned, bottled and packaged foods, selecting an item here, another there.

She decided against taking a gallon of the drinking water. Too heavy to carry, what with the rifle and groceries. She could have Art come over tomorrow and get one. They preferred their drinking water to be bottled. For other use they depended upon a spring that had broken through a decaying wall in the subway tube right off the Washington Square entry.

Her basket was nearly full when a premonition touched her. She whirled.

Leaning in the doorway, grinning vacuously, was a hulking, bearded, dirt-befouled stranger. He was dressed in highly colorful sports clothing. The vicuna coat alone must have once been priced at several hundred dollars. However, it looked as though he had probably slept in it, and time and again.

Pam squealed fear and darted to where she had leaned her twenty-two. She pulled up abruptly.

The stranger grinned again. There was a slight trickle of spittle from the side of his mouth, incongruously reminding Pam Rozet of a stereotype Mississippi tobacco-chewing sharecropper.

"You looking for this, syrup?" he gurgled happily. He raised his left hand which held the twenty-two. His own weapon, an old military Garand M-1, was cradled under his right arm.

"I been watching you coming back to your house with this here big basket of yours all full of goodies for the past week. Never was able to follow you to where you went without you seeing me. And usual, one of your men was along. But today, just by luck, I saw you duck up that alley. Just by luck. Man, you really got it made here, eh? Wait'll my gang see this. Lush and all, eh? Man, lush is getting scarce on this here island."

Pam blurted, "Let me go. Please let me go. You can take all this . . ."

"Syrup, we sure will. But what's your hurry, syrup? You look like a nice clean mopsy. We will have a little fun, first off."

"Please let me go."

He grinned vacantly and took her little gun by the barrel and bashed it up against the cement wall, shattering stock and mechanism. He tossed the wreckage away to the floor.

He motioned over toward the steel cots, mattress-topped but now without blankets or pillows, since she and Art had taken these back to the apartment long since. "Now sit down a minute, and let's get kind of better acquainted. We're gonna get to be real good friends, syrup."

"No," she said, trembling uncontrollably. "Please let me go. Look, over there. All sorts of liquor. Even champagne. Or Scotch, if you like whisky. Very old Scotch."

His grin became sly, and he started toward her, shuffling his feet and spreading his hands out a little, as though to prevent her from attempting to slip past him. "The lush I can get later, syrup. I like nice clean girls."

Neither of them had seen the newcomer approach through the cellar door at the bottom of the steps.

The blast of gunfire caught her assailant in the back and stitched up from the base of his spine to the back of his head. He never lived to turn, simply pitched forward to her feet, gurgling momentarily, but then was still.

Behind him, a plumpish newcomer, dressed elaborately in what were obviously new hunting clothes and carrying a late model recoilless fully automatic rifle, pop-eyed down at the dead man.

"*Zo-ro-as-ter,*" he blurted.

Pam leaned back against the wall. "Oh, thank God," she said.

The newcomer brought his eyes up to her, taking in her trim suit, her well ordered hair, her general air of being.

He said, "How in the name of the world did you ever get into a place like this . . . Miss . . . ?"

Pam took a deep breath. "Rozet," she gaped. "Pamela Rozet. Oh . . . *thank* you."

He jabbed a finger in the direction of the fallen intruder. "That—that baboon . . . he could have killed you." His eyes took in her shattered light rifle, and then her clothing again. "You must be insane, coming to a place like this with no more than that little gun, and no bullet-proof clothes and—" He broke off in mid-sentence, and began to stare at her.

Pam took another deep breath and tried to control her shaking. "I'm a writer," she said. "I live here."

"Live here?" At first he didn't understand and looked about the bomb shelter. "You mean in this house? Up above? This is your family house; you still live here?"

She said, "No, not here. I live nearby with . . . with my husband. I . . . I write novels. He's an artist."

His eyes narrowed. "Live here?" he said.

She tried to straighten and collect herself. In a woman's gesture, she touched her hair. "That's right," she said.

"Why . . . why, you're nothing but a baboon yourself. You were looting."

Her face fell, and fear came to her eyes again.

She tried to continue talking. Explaining. How she and Art had had all their papers. How they were serious workers in the arts. But she could see the nakedness in his face. The words came out a stutter.

If she read him right, from his reaction to the killing of the baboon who had been about to attack her, this was his first time as a hunter, or at least, the first successful time. His first kill.

He brought the gun up slowly, deliberately and held it a little forward, as though showing it to her. He patted the stock. He caressed it, as though lovingly. A tongue, too small for his face, came out and licked his plump lower lip.

"You're a baboon yourself," he repeated, very softly, caressingly. "And there's no law protecting baboons, is there . . . dear? There's no law at all in the deserted cities. It's each man—and woman—for himself, isn't it? Before you're even allowed on the island, here, you have to waive all recourse to the police and the courts."

Her legs turned to water, and she sank to the floor and looked up at him numbly. "Please . . . don't hurt me . . ."

He held the gun out, as though to be sure she got a very good look at it—her messenger of eternity. "Of course, you've never hurt me, dear. And you never will . . . dear. Are you religious? Would you like to pray, or something . . . dear?"

She could feel her stomach churning. Her eyes wanted to roll up. She wanted desperately to faint.

There was a blast as though of dynamite in these confined quarters, and his features exploded forward in a gruesome mess. Part of the gore hit her skirt, but she didn't realize that until much later.

Mark Martino, putting his heavy six-shooter back into its holster, said from the doorway, "What is this, a massacre?"

But she was unconscious.

X

Later, she was semi-hysterical and couldn't get over it. Art said, "What in the hell happened?"

Mark Martino was pouring cognac into a kitchen tumbler. He had tried to get some down Pamela, but twice she had vomited it up. Now he was pouring for himself.

He said, "I dropped off into a nap after you left and I guess she didn't want to bother me. At any rate, when I woke she was gone. I took off after her. Evidently I barely made it. She must have been followed by a baboon . . ."

"Oh, damn," Art said.

"At any rate, when I got there the baboon was already dead. Evidently a hunter had followed him. I followed the hunter. It was like a parade. I finished the hunter. They were right there at the bomb shelter. We'll never be able to go back again. That hunter'll be found by his chum-pals. They never go around alone. There'll be at least one more."

Art said in disgust, "Couldn't you have dragged his body off somewhere else?"

"No," Mark said, in equal disgust, knocking back the brandy. "Pam had fainted. I had to get her out of there, and I didn't know how many baboons or how many hunters might be around. For all we know, that damn baboon was a part of a pack and the hunter might have had a dozen *sportsmen* friends."

"What'd he look like?" Art said, staring down dismally at Pam, stretched out on a couch, not knowing what to do in typical male helplessness.

"Kind of fat."

"There were only two of them," Art said. "I saw them at the tube. But he's probably some bigwig or other. The cloddy with him was some sort of police authority. He was able to commandeer a floater from Williams."

Mark poured some more cognac and offered the glass to Art who shook his head in refusal. He was disgusted.

"You'd better ditch that gun you used," he said. "They don't like hunters to get killed. They are almost invariably big shots. They'll probably come in here with a flock of cops and shake everybody down. Especially me. I had a run-in with these two at the tube entrance. But you're in the same building, and if they find that gun on you, the same caliber that killed him, they'll check it and you'll be in the soup."

"I already ditched it," Mark said. "I'm not stupid. Look, Art . . ." He set the bottle down on the table.

Art looked at him.

"You've got to get out of here," Mark said, throwing his glass into a corner, where it shattered. He turned and left the apartment.

When Pamela had gathered herself to the point of being coherent, Art was standing at the window, staring unseeingly down the street to Washington Square.

She came up behind him.

"Art."

He took a deep breath. "Yes."

"Art, forgive me. I'm a terrible coward."

He didn't say anything.

"Art, we've got to get out of here."

"Yes. I know."

Is the interface between city and suburb necessarily the battleground of tomorrow? Maybe not. Maybe our cities can find reasons for battling each other and wiping out all that lies between, as we use up our resources and forget what we wanted them for in the first place.

Attractive? Not very. It's harder to imagine even the worst-off city dweller of today envying—

THE LUCKIEST MAN IN DENV

C. M. Kornbluth

May's man Reuben, of the eighty-third level, Atomist, knew there was something wrong when the binoculars flashed and then went opaque. Inwardly he cursed, hoping that he had not committed himself to anything. Outwardly he was unperturbed. He handed the binoculars back to Rudolph's man Almon, of the eighty-ninth level, Maintainer, with a smile.

"They aren't very good," he said.

Almon put them to his own eyes, glanced over the parapet and swore mildly. "Blacker than the heart of a crazy Angel, eh? Never mind; here's another pair."

This pair was unremarkable. Through it, Reuben studied the thousand setbacks and penthouses of Denv that ranged themselves below. He was too worried to enjoy his first sight of the vista from the eighty-ninth level, but he let out a murmur of appreciation. Now to get away from this suddenly sinister fellow and try to puzzle it out.

"Could we—?" he asked cryptically, with a little upward jerk of his chin.

"It's better not to," Almon said hastily, taking the glasses from his hands. "What if somebody with stars happened to see, you know? How'd *you* like it if you saw some impudent fellow peering up at you?"

"He wouldn't dare!" said Reuben, pretending to be

179

stupid and indignant, and joined a moment later in Almon's sympathetic laughter.

"Never mind," said Almon. "We are young. Some day, who knows? Perhaps we shall look from the ninety-fifth level, or the hundredth."

Though Reuben knew that the Maintainer was no friend of his, the generous words sent blood hammering through his veins; ambition for a moment.

He pulled a long face and told Almon: "Let us hope so. Thank you for being my host. Now I must return to my quarters."

He left the windy parapet for the serene luxury of an eighty-ninth-level corridor and descended slow moving stairs through gradually less luxurious levels to his own Spartan floor. Selene was waiting, smiling, as he stepped off the stairs.

She was decked out nicely—too nicely. She wore a steely hued corselet and a touch of scent; her hair was dressed long. The combination appealed to him, and instantly he was on his guard. Why had she gone to the trouble of learning his tastes? What was she up to? After all, she was Griffin's woman.

"Coming *down?*" she asked, awed. "Where have you been?"

"The eighty-ninth, as a guest of that fellow Almon. The vista is immense."

"I've never been . . ." she murmured, and then said decisively: "You belong up there. And higher. Griffin laughs at me, but he's a fool. Last night in chamber we got to talking about you, I don't know how, and he finally became quite angry and said he didn't want to hear another word." She smiled wickedly. "I was revenged, though."

Blank-faced, he said: "You must be a good hand at revenge, Selene, and at stirring up the need for it."

The slight hardening of her smile meant that he had scored, and he hurried by with a rather formal salutation.

Burn him for an Angelo, but she was easy enough to take! The contrast of the metallic garment with her soft, white skin was disturbing, and her long hair suggested things. It was hard to think of her as scheming something or other; scheming Selene was displaced in his mind by Selene in chamber.

But what was she up to? Had she perhaps heard that he was to be elevated? Was Griffin going to be swooped on by the Maintainers? Was he to kill off Griffin so she could leech onto some rising third party? Was she perhaps merely giving her man a touch of the lash?

He wished gloomily that the binoculars-problem and the Selene problem had not come together. That trickster Almon had spoken of youth as though it were something for congratulation; he hated being young and stupid and unable to puzzle out the faulty binoculars and the warmth of Griffin's woman.

The attack alarm roared through the Spartan corridor. He ducked through the nearest door into a vacant bedroom and under the heavy steel table. Somebody else floundered under the table a moment later, and a third person tried to join them.

The firstcomer roared: "Get out and find your own shelter! I don't propose to be crowded out by you or to crowd you out either and see your ugly blood and brains if there's a hit. Go, now!"

"Forgive me, sir! At once, sir!" the latecomer wailed; and scrambled away as the alarm continued to roar.

Reuben gasped at the "sirs" and looked at his neighbor. It was May! Trapped, no doubt, on an inspection tour of the level.

"Sir," he said respectfully, "if you wish to be alone, I can find another room."

"You may stay with me for company. Are you one of mine?" There was power in the general's voice and on his craggy face.

"Yes, sir. May's man Reuben, of the eighty-third level, Atomist."

May surveyed him, and Reuben noted that there were

pouches of skin depending from cheekbones and the jaw line—dead-looking, coarse-pored skin.

"You're a well-made boy, Reuben. Do you have women?"

"Yes, sir," said Reuben hastily. "One after another— I *always* have women. I'm making up at this time to a charming thing called Selene. Well-rounded, yet firm, soft but supple, with long red hair and long white legs—"

"Spare me the details," muttered the general. "It takes all kinds. An Atomist, you said. That has a future, to be sure. I myself was a Controller long ago. The calling seems to have gone out of fashion—"

Abruptly the alarm stopped. The silence was hard to bear.

May swallowed and went on: "—for some reason or other. Why don't youngsters elect for Controller any more? Why didn't you, for instance?"

Reuben wished he could be saved by a direct hit. The binoculars, Selene, the raid, and now he was supposed to make intelligent conversation with a general.

"I really don't know, sir," he said miserably. "At the time there seemed to be very little difference—Controller, Atomist, Missiler, Maintainer. We have a saying, 'The buttons are different,' which usually ends any conversation on the subject."

"Indeed?" asked May distractedly. His face was thinly filmed with sweat. "Do you suppose Ellay intends to clobber us this time?" he asked almost hoarsely. "It's been some weeks since they made a maximum effort, hasn't it?"

"Four," said Reuben. "I remember because one of my best Servers was killed by a falling corridor roof—the only fatality and it had to happen to my team!"

He laughed nervously and realized that he was talking like a fool, but May seemed not to notice.

Far below them, there was a series of screaming whistles as the interceptors were loosed to begin their intricate, double basketwork wall of defense in a towering cylinder about Denv.

"Go on, Reuben," said May. "That was most interesting." His eyes were searching the underside of the steel table.

Reuben averted his own eyes from the frightened face, feeling some awe drain out of him. Under a table with a general! It didn't seem so strange now.

"Perhaps, sir, you can tell me what a puzzling thing, that happened this afternoon, means. A fellow—Rudolph's man Almon, of the eighty-ninth level—gave me a pair of binoculars that flashed in my eyes and then went opaque. Has your wide experience—"

May laughed hoarsely and said in a shaky voice: "That old trick! He was photographing your retinas for the blood-vessel pattern. One of Rudolph's men, eh. I'm glad you spoke to me; I'm old enough to spot a revival like that. Perhaps my good friend Rudolph plans—"

There was a thudding volley in the air and then a faint jar. One had got through, exploding, from the feel of it, far down at the foot of Denv.

The alarm roared again, in bursts that meant all clear; only one flight of missiles and that disposed of.

The Atomist and the general climbed out from under the table; May's secretary popped through the door. The general waved him out again and leaned heavily on the table, his arms quivering. Reuben hastily brought a chair.

"A glass of water," said May.

The Atomist brought it. He saw the general wash down what looked like a triple dose of xxx—green capsules which it was better to leave alone.

May said after a moment: "That's better. And don't look so shocked, youngster; you don't know the strain we're under. It's only a temporary measure which I shall discontinue as soon as things ease up a bit. I was saying that perhaps my good friend Rudolph plans to substitute one of his men for one of mine. Tell me, how long has this fellow Almon been a friend of yours?"

"He struck up an acquaintance with me only last week. I should have realized—"

"You certainly should have. One week. Time enough and more. By now you've been photographed, your fingerprints taken, your voice recorded and your gait studied without your knowledge. Only the retinascope is difficult, but one must risk it for a real double. Have you killed your man, Reuben?"

He nodded. It had been a silly brawl two years ago over precedence at the refectory; he disliked being reminded of it.

"Good," said May grimly. "The way these things are done, your double kills you in a secluded spot, disposes of your body and takes over your role. We shall reverse it. You will kill the double and take over *his* role."

The powerful, methodical voice ticked off possibilities and contingencies, measures, and countermeasures. Reuben absorbed them and felt his awe return. Perhaps May had not really been frightened under the table; perhaps it had been he reading his own terror in the general's face. May was actually talking to him of backgrounds and policies. "Up from the eighty-third level!" he swore to himself as the great names were uttered.

"My good friend Rudolph, of course, wants the five stars. You would not know this, but the man who wears the stars is now eighty years old and failing fast. I consider myself a likely candidate to replace him. So, evidently, must Rudolph. No doubt he plans to have your double perpetrate some horrible blunder on the eve of the election, and the discredit would reflect on me. Now what you and I must do—"

You and I—May's man Reuben and May—up from the eighty-third! Up from the bare corridors and cheerless bedrooms to marble halls and vaulted chambers! From the clatter of the crowded refectory to small and glowing restaurants where you had your own table and servant and where music came softly from the walls! Up from the scramble to win this woman or that, by wit or charm or the poor bribes you could afford, to the eminence from which you could calmly command your pick of the beauty of Denv! From the moiling intrigue of tripping your fellow Atomist and guarding against him tripping you to the heroic thrust and parry of generals!

Up from the eighty-third!

Then May dismissed him with a speech whose implications were deliriously exciting. "I need an able man and a young one, Reuben. Perhaps I've waited too long looking for him. If you do well in this touchy business, I'll consider you very seriously for an important task I have in mind."

Late that night, Selene came to his bedroom.

"I know you don't like me," she said pettishly, "but Griffin's such a fool and I wanted somebody to talk to. Do you mind? What was it like up there today? Did you see carpets? I wish I had a carpet."

He tried to think about carpets and not the exciting contrast of metallic cloth and flesh.

"I saw one through an open door," he remembered. "It looked odd, but I suppose a person gets used to them. Perhaps I didn't see a very good one. Aren't the good ones very thick?"

"Yes," she said. "Your feet sink into them. I wish I had a *good* carpet and four chairs and a small table as high as my knees to put things on and as many pillows as I wanted. Griffin's such a fool. Do you think I'll ever get those things? I've never caught the eye of a general. Am I pretty enough to get one, do you think?"

He said uneasily: "Of course you're a pretty thing, Selene. But carpets and chairs and pillows—" It made him uncomfortable, like the thought of peering up through binoculars from a parapet.

"I want them," she said unhappily. "I like you very much, but I want so many things and soon I'll be too old even for the eighty-third level, before I've been up higher, and I'll spend the rest of my life tending babies or cooking in the creche or the refectory."

She stopped abruptly, pulled herself together and gave him a smile that was somehow ghastly in the half-light.

"You bungler," he said, and she instantly looked at the

door with the smile frozen on her face. Reuben took a pistol from under his pillow and demanded, "When do you expect him?"

"What do you mean?" she asked shrilly. "Who are you talking about?"

"My double. Don't be a fool, Selene. May and I"— he savored it— "May and I know all about it. He warned me to beware of a diversion by a woman while the double slipped in and killed me. When do you expect him?"

"I really *do* like you," Selene sobbed. "But Almon promised to take me up there and I *knew* when I was where they'd see me that I'd meet somebody really important. I really do like you, but soon I'll be too old—"

"Selene, listen to me. Listen to me! You'll get your chance. Nobody but you and me will know that the substitution didn't succeed!"

"Then I'll be spying for you on Almon, won't I?" she asked in a choked voice. "All I wanted was a few nice things before I got too old. All right, I was supposed to be in your arms at 2350 hours."

It was 2349. Reuben sprang from bed and stood by the door, his pistol silenced and ready. At 2350 a naked man slipped swiftly into the room, heading for the bed as he raised a ten-centimeter poignard. He stopped in dismay when he realized that the bed was empty.

Reuben killed him with a bullet through the throat.

"But he doesn't look a bit like me," he said in bewilderment, closely examining the face. "Just in a general way."

Selene said dully: "Almon told me people always say that when they see their doubles. It's funny, isn't it? He looks just like you, really."

"How was my body to be disposed of?"

She produced a small flat box. "A shadow suit. You were to be left here and somebody would come tomorrow."

"We won't disappoint him." Reuben pulled the web of the shadow suit over his double and turned on the power. In the half-lit room, it was a perfect disappearance; by daylight it would be less perfect. "They'll ask why the body was shot instead of knifed. Tell them you shot me with the gun from under the pillow. Just say I heard the double come in and you were afraid there might have been a struggle."

She listlessly asked: "How do you know I won't betray you?"

"You won't, Selene." His voice bit. "You're *broken*."

She nodded vaguely, started to say something and then went out without saying it.

Reuben luxuriously stretched in his narrow bed. Later, his beds would be wider and softer, he thought. He drifted into sleep on a half-formed thought that some day he might vote with other generals on the man to wear the five stars—or even wear them himself, Master of Denv.

He slept healthily through the morning alarm and arrived late at his regular twentieth-level station. He saw his superior, May's man Oscar of the eighty-fifth level, Atomist, ostentatiously take his name. Let him!

Oscar assembled his crew for a grim announcement: "We are going to even the score, and perhaps a little better, with Ellay. At sunset there will be three flights of missiles from Deck One."

There was a joyous murmur and Reuben trotted off on his task.

All forenoon he was occupied with drawing plutonium slugs from hyper-suspicious storekeepers in the great rock-quarried vaults, and seeing them through countless audits and assays all the way to Weapons Assembly. Oscar supervised the scores there who assembled the curved slugs and the explosive lenses into sixty-kilogram warheads.

In mid-afternoon there was an incident. Reuben saw Oscar step aside for a moment to speak to a Maintainer whose guard fell on one of the Assembly Servers, and dragged him away as he pleaded innocence. He had been detected in sabotage. When the warheads were in and the Missilers seated, waiting at their boards, the two Atomists rode up to the eighty-third's refectory.

The news of a near-maximum effort was in the air; it was electric. Reuben heard on all sides in tones of self-congratulations; "We'll clobber them tonight!"

"That Server you caught," he said to Oscar. "What was he up to?"

His commander stared. "Are you trying to learn my job? Don't try it, I warn you. If my black marks against you aren't enough, I could always arrange for some fissionable material in your custody to go astray."

"No, no! I was just wondering why people do something like that."

Oscar sniffed doubtfully. "He's probably insane, like all the Angelos. I've heard the climate does it to them. You're not a Maintainer or a Controller. Why worry about it?"

"They'll brainburn him, I suppose?"

"I suppose. *Listen!*"

Deck One was firing. One, two, three, four, five, six. One, two, three, four, five, six. One, two, three, four, five, six.

People turned to one another and shook hands, laughed and slapped shoulders heartily. Eighteen missiles were racing through the stratosphere, soon to tumble on Ellay. With any luck, one or two would slip through the first wall of interceptors and blast close enough to smash windows and topple walls in the crazy city by the ocean. It would serve the lunatics right.

Five minutes later an exultant voice filled most of Denv.

"Recon missile report," it said. "Eighteen launched, eighteen perfect trajectories. Fifteen shot down by Ellay first-line interceptors; three shot down by Ellay second-line interceptors. Extensive blast damage observed in Griffith Park area of Ellay!"

There were cheers.

And eight Full Maintainers marched into the refectory silently, and marched out with Reuben.

He knew better than to struggle or ask futile questions. Any question you asked of a Maintainer was futile. But he goggled when they marched him onto an upward-bound stairway.

They rode past the eighty-ninth level and Reuben lost count, seeing only the marvels of the upper reaches of Denv. He saw carpets that ran the entire length of corridors, and intricate fountains, and mosaic walls, stained-glass windows, more wonders than he could recognize, things for which he had no name.

He was marched at last into a wood-paneled room with a great polished desk and a map behind it. He saw May, and another man who must have been a general—Rudolph?—but sitting at the desk was a frail old man who wore a circlet of stars on each khaki shoulder.

The old man said to Reuben: "You are an Ellay spy and saboteur."

Reuben looked at May. Did one speak directly to the man who wore the stars, even in reply to such an accusation?

"Answer him, Reuben," May said kindly.

"I am May's man Reuben, of the eighty-third level, an Atomist," he said.

"Explain," said the other general heavily, "if you can, why all eighteen of the warheads you procured today failed to fire."

"But they did!" grasped Reuben. "The Recon missile report said there was blast damage from the three that got through and it didn't say anything about the others failing to fire."

The other general suddenly looked sick and May looked even kindlier. The man who wore the stars turned inquiringly to the chief of the Maintainers, who nodded and said: "That was the Recon missile report, sir."

The general snapped: "What I said was that he would *attempt* to sabotage the attack. Evidently he failed. I also said he is a faulty double, somehow slipped with great ease into my good friend May's organization. You will find that his left thumb print is a clumsy forgery of the real Reuben's thumb print and that his hair has been artificially darkened."

The old man nodded at the chief of the Maintainers, who said: "We have his card, sir."

Reuben abruptly found himself being fingerprinted and deprived of some hair.

"The f.p.s. check, sir," one Maintainer said. "He's Reuben."

"Hair's natural, sir," said another.

The general began a rear-guard action: "My information about his hair seems to have been inaccurate. But the fingerprint means only that Ellay spies substituted his prints for Reuben's prints in the files—"

"Enough, sir," said the old man with the stars. "Dismissed. All of you. Rudolph, I am surprised. All of you, go."

Reuben found himself in a vast apartment with May, who was bubbling and chuckling uncontrollably, until he popped three of the green capsules into his mouth hurriedly.

"This means the eclipse for years of my good friend Rudolph," he crowed. "His game was to have your double sabotage the attack warheads and so make it appear that my organization is rotten with spies. The double must have been under post-hypnotic, primed to admit everything. Rudolph was so sure of himself that he made his accusations before the attack, the fool!"

He fumbled out the green capsules again.

"Sir," said Reuben, alarmed.

"Only temporary," May muttered, and swallowed a fourth. "But you're right. You leave them alone. There are big things to be done in your time, not in mine. I told you I needed a young man who could claw his way to the top. Rudolph's a fool. He doesn't need the capsules because he doesn't ask questions. Funny, I thought a coup like the double affair would hit me hard, but I don't feel a thing. It's not like the old days. I used to plan and plan, and when the trap went *snap* it was better than this stuff. But now I don't feel a thing."

He leaned forward from his chair; the pupils of his eyes were black bullets.

"Do you want to *work?*" he demanded. "Do you want your world stood on its head and your brains to crack and do the only worthwhile job there is to do? Answer me!"

"Sir, I am a loyal May's man. I want to obey your orders and use my ability to the full."

"Good enough," said the general. "You've got brains; you've got push. I'll do the spade work. I won't last long enough to push it through. You'll have to follow. Ever been outside of Denv?"

Reuben stiffened.

"I'm not accusing you of being a spy. It's really all right to go outside of Denv. I've been outside. There isn't much to see at first—a lot of ground pocked and torn up by shorts and overs from Ellay and us. Farther out, especially east, it's different. Grass, trees, flowers. Places where you could grow food.

"When I went outside, it troubled me. It made me ask questions. I wanted to know how we started. Yes—started. *It wasn't always like this.* Somebody built Denv. Am I getting the idea across to you? *It wasn't always like this!*

"Somebody set up the reactors to breed uranium and make plutonium. Somebody tooled us up for the missiles. Somebody wired the boards to control them. Somebody started the hydroponics tanks.

"I've dug through the archives. Maybe I found something. I saw mountains of strength reports, ration reports, supply reports, and yet I never got back to the beginning. I found a piece of paper and maybe I understood it and maybe I didn't. It was about the water of the Colorado River and who should get how much of it. How can you divide water in a river? But it could have been the start of Denv, Ellay, and the missile attacks."

The general shook his head, puzzled, and went on: "I don't see clearly what's ahead. I want to make peace between Denv and Ellay, but I don't know how to start or what it will be like. I think it must mean not firing, not even making any more weapons. Maybe it means that some of us, or a lot of us, will go out of Denv and live a different kind of life. That's why I've clawed my way up. That's why I need a young man who can claw with the best of them. Tell me what you think."

"I think," said Reuben measuredly, "it's magnificent—the salvation of Denv. I'll back you to my dying breath if you'll let me."

May smiled tiredly and leaned back in the chair as Reuben tiptoed out.

What luck, Reuben thought—what unbelievable luck to be at a fulcrum of history like this!

He searched the level for Rudolph's apartment and gained admission.

To the general, he said: "Sir, I have to report that your friend May is insane. He has just been raving to me, advocating the destruction of civilization as we know it, and urging me to follow in his footsteps. I pretended to agree—since I can be of greater service to you if I'm in May's confidence."

"So?" said Rudolph thoughtfully. "Tell me about the double. How did that go wrong?"

"The bunglers were Selene and Almon. Selene because she alarmed me instead of distracting me. Almon because he failed to recognize her incompetence."

"They shall be brainburned. That leaves an eighty-ninth-level vacancy in my organization, doesn't it?"

"You're very kind, sir, but I think I should remain a May's man—outwardly. If I earn any rewards, I can wait for them. I presume that May will be elected to wear the five stars. He won't live more than two years after that, at the rate he is taking drugs."

"We can shorten it," grinned Rudolph. "I have pharmacists who can see that his drugs are more than normal strength."

"That would be excellent, sir. When he is too enfeebled to discharge his duties, there may be an attempt to rake up the affair of the double to discredit you. I could then testify that I was your man all along and that May coerced me."

They put their heads together, the two saviors of civilization as they knew it, and conspired ingeniously long into the endless night.

A science fiction writer is never satisfied. If he thinks
of all the disasters that may befall the human race, he's
not content until he thinks of some of the possible
blessings—and realizes that they too may turn out to be
disasters. As for example—

THE MIDAS PLAGUE

Frederik Pohl

And so they were married.

The bride and groom made a beautiful couple, she in
her twenty-yard frill of immaculate white, he in his formal
gray ruffled blouse and pleated pantaloons.

It was a small wedding—the best he could afford. For
guests, they had only the immediate family and a few
close friends. And when the minister had performed the
ceremony, Morey Fry kissed his bride and they drove off
to the reception. There were twenty-eight limousines in
all (though it is true that twenty of them contained only
the caterer's robots) and three flower cars.

"Bless you both," said old man Elon sentimentally.
"You've got a fine girl in our Cherry, Morey." He blew
his nose on a ragged square of cambric.

The old folks behaved very well, Morey thought. At
the reception, surrounded by the enormous stacks of wedding gifts, they drank the champagne and ate a great many
of the tiny, delicious canapés. They listened politely to the
fifteen-piece orchestra, and Cherry's mother even danced
one dance with Morey for sentiment's sake, though it was
clear that dancing was far from the usual pattern of her
life. They tried as hard as they could to blend into the
gathering, but all the same, the two elderly figures in
severely simple and probably rented garments were dis-
mayingly conspicuous in the quarter-acre of tapestries and
tinkling fountains that was the main ballroom of Morey's
country home.

When it was time for the guests to go home and let the newlyweds begin their life together Cherry's father shook Morey by the hand and Cherry's mother kissed him. But as they drove away in their tiny runabout their faces were full of foreboding.

It was nothing against Morey as a person, of course. But poor people should not marry wealth.

Morey and Cherry loved each other, certainly. That helped. They told each other so, a dozen times an hour, all of the long hours they were together, for all of the first months of their marriage. Morey even took time off to go shopping with his bride, which endeared him to her enormously. They drove their shopping carts through the immense vaulted corridors of the supermarket, Morey checking off the items on the shopping list as Cherry picked out the goods. It was fun.

For a while.

Their first fight started in the supermarket, between Breakfast Foods and Floor Furnishings, just where the new Precious Stones department was being opened.

Morey called off from the list, "Diamond lavaliere, costume rings, earbobs."

Cherry said rebelliously, "Morey, I *have* a lavaliere. Please, dear!"

Morey folded back the pages of the list uncertainly. The lavaliere was on there, all right, and no alternative selection was shown.

"How about a bracelet?" he coaxed. "Look, they have some nice ruby ones there. See how beautifully they go with your hair, darling!" He beckoned a robot clerk, who bustled up and handed Cherry the bracelet tray. "Lovely," Morey exclaimed as Cherry slipped the largest of the lot on her wrist.

"And I don't have to have a lavaliere?" Cherry asked.

"Of course not." He peeked at the tag. "Same number of ration points exactly!" Since Cherry looked only dubious, not convinced, he said briskly, "And now we'd better be getting along to the shoe department. I've got to pick up some dancing pumps."

Cherry made no objection, neither then nor throughout the rest of their shopping tour. At the end, while they were sitting in the supermarket's ground-floor lounge waiting for the robot accountants to tote up their bill and the robot cashiers to stamp their ration books, Morey remembered to have the shipping department save out the bracelet.

"I don't want that sent with the other stuff, darling," he explained. "I want you to wear it right now. Honestly, I don't think I ever saw anything looking so *right* for you."

Cherry looked flustered and pleased. Morey was delighted with himself; it wasn't everybody who knew how to handle these little domestic problems just right!

He stayed self-satisfied all the way home, while Henry, their companion-robot, regaled them with funny stories of the factory in which it had been built and trained. Cherry wasn't used to Henry by a long shot, but it was hard not to like the robot. Jokes and funny stories when you needed amusement, sympathy when you were depressed, a never-failing supply of news and information on any subject you cared to name—Henry was easy enough to take. Cherry even made a special point of asking Henry to keep them company through dinner, and she laughed as thoroughly as Morey himself at its droll anecdotes.

But later, in the conservatory, when Henry had considerately left them alone, the laughter dried up.

Morey didn't notice. He was very conscientiously making the rounds: turning on the tri-D, selecting their after-dinner liqueurs, scanning the evening newspapers.

Cherry cleared her throat self-consciously, and Morey stopped what he was doing. "Dear," she said tentatively, "I'm feeling kind of restless tonight. Could we—I mean do you think we could just sort of stay home and—well, relax?"

Morey looked at her with a touch of concern. She lay back wearily, eyes half closed. "Are you feeling all right?" he asked.

"Perfectly. I just don't want to go out tonight, dear. I don't feel up to it."

He sat down and automatically lit a cigarette. "I see," he said. The tri-D was beginning a comedy show; he got up to turn it off, snapping on the tape-player. Muted strings filled the room.

"We had reservations at the club tonight," he reminded her.

Cherry shifted uncomfortably. "I know."

"And we have the opera tickets that I turned last week's in for. I hate to nag, darling, but we haven't used *any* of our opera tickets."

"We can see them right here on the tri-D," she said in a small voice.

"That has nothing to do with it, sweetheart. I—I didn't want to tell you about it, but Wainwright, down at the office, said something to me yesterday. He told me he would be at the circus last night and as much as said he'd be looking to see if we were there too. Well, we weren't there. Heaven knows what I'll tell him next week."

He waited for Cherry to answer, but she was silent.

He went on reasonably, "So if you *could* see your way clear to going out tonight—"

He stopped, slack-jawed. Cherry was crying, silently and in quantity.

"Darling!" he said inarticulately.

He hurried to her, but she fended him off. He stood helpless over her, watching her cry.

"Dear, what's the matter?" he asked.

She turned her head away.

Morey rocked back on his heels. It wasn't exactly the first time he'd seen Cherry cry—there had been that poignant scene when they Gave Each Other Up, realizing that their backgrounds were too far apart for happiness, before the realization that they *had* to have each other, no matter what. . . . But it was the first time her tears had made him feel guilty.

And he did feel guilty. He stood there staring at her.

Then he turned his back on her and walked over to the bar. He ignored the ready liqueurs and poured two stiff highballs, brought them back to her. He set one down beside her, took a long drink from the other.

In quite a different tone, he said, "Dear, what's the *matter?*"

No answer.

"Come on. What is it?"

She looked up at him and rubbed at her eyes. Almost sullenly, she said, "Sorry."

"I know you're sorry. Look, we love each other. Let's talk this thing out."

She picked up her drink and held it for a moment, before setting it down untasted. "What's the use, Morey?"

"Please. Let's try."

She shrugged.

He went on remorselessly, "You aren't happy, are you? And it's because of—well, all this." His gesture took in the richly furnished conservatory, the thick-piled carpet, the host of machines and contrivances for their comfort and entertainment that waited for their touch. By implication it took in twenty-six rooms, five cars, nine robots. Morey said, with an effort, "It isn't what you're used to, is it?"

"I can't help it," Cherry said. "Morey, you know I've tried. But back home—"

Dammit," he flared, "*this* is your home. You don't live with your father any more in that five-room cottage; you don't spend your evenings hoeing the garden or playing cards for matchsticks. You live here, with me, your husband! You knew what you were getting into. We talked all this out long before we were married—"

The words stopped, because words were useless. Cherry was crying again, but not silently.

Through her tears, she wailed: "Darling, I've tried. You don't *know* how I've tried! I've worn all those silly clothes and I've played all those silly games and I've gone out with you as much as I *possibly* could and—I've eaten all that terrible food until I'm actually getting fa-fa-fat! I thought I could stand it. But I just can't go on like this; I'm not used to it. I—I love you, Morey, but I'm going crazy, living like this. I can't help it, Morey—*I'm tired of being poor!*"

Eventually the tears dried up, and the quarrel healed, and the lovers kissed and made up. But Morey lay awake that night, listening to his wife's gentle breathing from the suite next to his own, staring into the darkness as tragically as any pauper before him had ever done.

Blessed are the poor, for they shall inherit the earth.

Blessed Morey, heir to more worldly goods than he could possibly consume.

Morey Fry, steeped in grinding poverty, had never gone hungry a day in his life, never lacked for anything his heart could desire in the way of food, or clothing, or a place to sleep. In Morey's world, no one lacked for these things; no one could.

Malthus was right—for a civilization without machines, automatic factories, hydroponics and food synthesis, nuclear breeder plants, ocean mining for metals and minerals . . .

And a vastly increasing supply of labor . . .

And architecture that rose high in the air and dug deep in the ground and floated far out on the water on piers and pontoons . . . architecture that could be poured one day and lived in the next . . .

And robots.

Above all, robots . . . robots to burrow and haul and smelt and fabricate, to build and farm and weave and sew.

What the land lacked in wealth, the sea was made to yield, and the laboratory invented the rest . . . and the factories became a pipeline of plenty, churning out enough to feed and clothe and house a dozen worlds.

Limitless discovery, infinite power in the atom, tireless labor of humanity and robots, mechanization that drove jungle and swamp and ice off the Earth, and put up office buildings and manufacturing centers and rocket ports in their place . . .

The pipeline of production spewed out riches that no

king in the time of Malthus could have known.

But a pipeline has two ends. The invention and power and labor pouring in at one end must somehow be drained out at the other . . .

Lucky Morey, blessed economic-consuming unit, drowning in the pipeline's flood, striving manfully to eat and drink and wear and wear out his share of the ceaseless tide of wealth.

Morey felt far from blessed, for the blessings of the poor are always best appreciated from afar.

Quotas worried his sleep until he awoke at eight o'clock the next morning, red-eyed and haggard, but inwardly resolved. He had reached a decision. He was starting a new life.

There was trouble in the morning mail. Under the letterhead of the National Ration Board, it said:

"We regret to advise you that the following items returned by you in connection with your August quotas as used and no longer serviceable have been inspected and found insufficiently worn." The list followed—a long one, Morey saw to his sick disappointment. "Credit is hereby disallowed for these and you are therefore given an additional consuming quota for the current month in the amount of four-hundred and thirty-five points, at least three-hundred and fifty points of which must be in the textile and home-furnishing categories."

Morey dashed the letter to the floor. The valet picked it up emotionlessly, creased it and set it on his desk.

It wasn't fair! All right, maybe the bathing trunks and beach umbrellas hadn't been *really* used very much—though how the devil, he asked himself bitterly, did you go about using up swimming gear when you didn't have time for such leisurely pursuits as swimming? But certainly the hiking slacks were used! He'd worn them for three whole days and part of a fourth; what did they expect him to do, go around in *rags?*

Morey looked belligerently at the coffee and toast that the valet-robot had brought in with the mail, and then steeled his resolve. Unfair or not, he had to play the game according to the rules. It was for Cherry, more than for himself, and the way to begin a new way of life was to begin it.

Morey was going to consume for two.

He told the valet-robot, "Take that stuff back. I want cream and sugar with the coffee—*lots* of cream and sugar. And besides the toast, scrambled eggs, fried potatoes, orange juice—no, make it half a grapefruit. *And* orange juice, come to think of it."

"Right away, sir," said the valet. "You won't be having breakfast at nine then, will you, sir?"

"I certainly will," said Morey virtuously. "Double portions!" As the robot was closing the door, he called after it, "Butter and marmalade with the toast!"

He went to the bath; he had a full schedule and no time to waste. In the shower, he carefully sprayed himself with lather three times. When he had rinsed the soap off, he went through the whole assortment of taps in order: three lotions, plain talcum, scented talcum and thirty seconds of ultra-violet. Then he lathered and rinsed again, and dried himself with a towel instead of using the hot-air drying jet. Most of the miscellaneous scents went down the drain with the rinse water, but if the Ration Board accused him of waste, he could claim he was experimenting. The effect, as a matter of fact, wasn't bad at all.

He stepped out, full of exuberance. Cherry was awake, staring in dismay at the tray the valet had brought. "Good morning, dear," she said faintly. "Ugh."

Morey kissed her and patted her hand. "Well!" he said, looking at the tray with a big, hollow smile. "Food!"

"Isn't that a *lot* for just the two of us?"

"Two of us?" repeated Morey masterfully. "Nonsense, my dear, I'm going to eat it all by myself!"

"Oh, Morey!" gasped Cherry, and the adoring look she gave him was enough to pay for a dozen such meals.

Which, he thought as he finished his morning exercises with the sparring-robot and sat down to his *real* breakfast, it just about had to be, day in and day out, for a long, long time.

Still, Morey had made up his mind. As he worked his way through the kippered herring, tea and crumpets, he ran over his plans with Henry. He swallowed a mouthful and said, "I want you to line up some appointments for me right away. Three hours a week in an exercise gym—pick one with lots of reducing equipment, Henry. I think I'm going to need it. And fittings for some new clothes—I've had these for weeks. And, let's see, doctor, dentist—say, Henry, don't I have a psychiatrist's date coming up?"

"Indeed you do, sir!" it said warmly. "This morning, in fact. I've already instructed the chauffeur and notified your office."

"Fine! Well, get started on the other things, Henry."

"Yes, sir," said Henry, and assumed the curious absent look of a robot talking on its TBR circuits—the "Talk Between Robots" radio—as it arranged the appointments for its master.

Morey finished his breakfast in silence, pleased with his own virtue, at peace with the world. It wasn't so hard to be a proper, industrious consumer if you *worked* at it, he reflected. It was only the malcontents, the ne'er-do-wells and the incompetents who simply could not adjust to the world around them. Well, he thought with distant pity, someone had to suffer; you couldn't break eggs without making an omelet. And his proper duty was not to be some sort of wild-eyed crank, challenging the social order and beating his breast about injustice, but to take care of his wife and his home.

It was too bad he couldn't really get right down to work on consuming today. But this was his one day a week to hold a *job*—four of the other six days were devoted to solid consuming—and besides, he had a group therapy session scheduled as well. His analysis, Morey told himself, would certainly take a sharp turn for the better, now that he had faced up to his problems.

Morey was immersed in a glow of self-righteousness as he kissed Cherry good-by (she had finally got up, all in a confusion of delight at the new regime) and walked out the door to his car. He hardly noticed the little man in enormous floppy hat and garishly ruffled trousers who was standing almost hidden in the shrubs.

"Hey, Mac." The man's voice was almost a whisper.

"Huh? Oh—what is it?"

The man looked around furtively. "Listen, friend," he said rapidly, "You look like an intelligent man who could use a little help. Times are tough; you help me, I'll help you. Want to make a deal on ration stamps? Six for one. One of yours for six of mine, the best deal you'll get anywhere in town. Naturally, my stamps aren't exactly the real McCoy, but they'll pass, friend, they'll pass—"

Morey blinked at him. "No!" he said violently, and pushed the man aside. Now it's racketeers, he thought bitterly. Slums and endless sordid preoccupation with rations weren't enough to inflict on Cherry; now the neighborhood was becoming a hangout for people on the shady side of the law. It was not, of course, the first time he had ever been approached by a counterfeit-ration-stamp hoodlum, but never at his own front door!

Morey thought briefly, as he climbed into his car, of calling the police. But certainly the man would be gone before they could get there; and after all, he had handled it pretty well as it was.

Of course, it would be nice to get six stamps for one.

But very far from nice if he got caught.

"Good morning, Mr. Fry," tinkled the robot receptionist. "Won't you go right in?" With a steel-tipped finger, it pointed to the door marked GROUP THERAPY.

Someday, Morey vowed to himself as he nodded and complied, he would be in a position to afford a private analyst of his own. Group therapy helped relieve the infinite stresses of modern living, and without it he might find himself as badly off as the hysterical mobs in the ration riots, or as dangerously anti-social as the counterfeiters. But it lacked the personal touch. It was, he thought, too public a performance of what should be a private affair, like trying to live a happy married life with an interfering, ever-present crowd of robots in the house—

Morey brought himself up in panic. How had *that* thought crept in? He was shaken visibly as he entered the room and greeted the group to which he was assigned.

There were eleven of them: four Freudians, two Reichians, two Jungians, a Gestalter, a shock therapist and the elderly and rather quiet Sullivanite. Even the members of the majority groups had their own individual differences in technique and creed, but despite four years with this particular group of analysts, Morey hadn't quite been able to keep them separate in his mind. Their names, though, he knew well enough.

"Morning, Doctors," he said. "What is it today?"

"Morning," said Semmelweiss morosely. "Today you come into the room for the first time looking as if something is really bothering you, and yet the schedule calls for psychodrama. Dr. Fairless," he appealed, "can't we change the schedule a little bit? Fry here is obviously under a strain; *that's* the time to start digging and see what he can find. We can do your psychodrama next time, can't we?"

Fairless shook his gracefully bald old head. "Sorry, Doctor. If it were up to me, of course—but you know the rules."

"Rules, rules," jeered Semmelweiss. "Ah, what's the use? Here's a patient in an acute anxiety state if I ever saw one—and believe me, I saw plenty—and we ignore it because the *rules* say ignore it. Is that professional? Is that how to cure a patient?"

Little Blaine said frostily, "If I may say so, Dr. Semmelweiss, there have been a great many cures made without the necessity of departing from the rules. I myself, in fact—"

"You yourself!" mimicked Semmelweiss. "You yourself never handled a patient alone in your life. When you going to get out of a group, Blaine?"

Blaine said furiously, "Dr. Fairless, I don't think I have

to stand for this sort of personal attack. Just because Semmelweiss has seniority and a couple of private patients one day a week, he thinks—"

"Gentlemen," said Fairless mildly. "Please, let's get on with the work. Mr. Fry has come to us for help, not to listen to us losing our tempers."

"Sorry," said Semmelweiss curtly. "All the same, I appeal from the arbitrary and mechanistic ruling of the chair."

Fairless inclined his head. "All in favor of the ruling of the chair? Nine, I count. That leaves only you opposed, Dr. Semmelweiss. We'll proceed with the psychodrama, if the recorder will read us the notes and comments of the last session."

The recorder, a pudgy, low-ranking youngster named Sprogue, flipped back the pages of his notebook and read in a chanting voice, "Session of twenty-fourth May, subject, Morey Fry; in attendance, Doctors Fairless, Bileck, Semmelweiss, Carrado, Weber—"

Fairless interrupted kindly, "Just the last page, if you please, Dr. Sprogue."

"Um—oh, yes. After a ten-minute recess for additional Rorschachs and an electro-encephalogram, the group convened and conducted rapid-fire word association. Results were tabulated and compared with standard deviation patterns, and it was determined that subject's major traumas derived from, respectively—"

Morey found his attention waning. Therapy was *good;* everybody knew that, but every once in a while he found it a little dull. If it weren't for therapy, though, there was no telling what might happen. Certainly, Morey told himself, he had been helped considerably—at least he hadn't set fire to his house and shrieked at the fire-robots, like Newell down the block when his eldest daughter divorced her husband and came back to live with him, bringing her ration quota along, of course. Morey hadn't even been *tempted* to do anything as outrageously, frighteningly immoral as *destroy* things or *waste* them—well, he admitted to himself honestly, perhaps a little tempted, once in a great while. But never anything important enough to worry about; he was sound, perfectly sound.

He looked up, startled. All the doctors were staring at him. "Mr. Fry," Fairless repeated, "will you take your place?"

"Certainly," Morey said hastily. "Uh—where?"

Semmelweiss guffawed. *"Told* you. Never mind, Morey; you didn't miss much. We're going to run through one of the big scenes in your life, the one you told us about last time. Remember? You were fourteen years old, you said. Christmas time. Your mother had made you a promise."

Morey swallowed. "I remember," he said unhappily. "Well, all right. Where do I stand?"

"Right here," said Fairless. "You're you; Carrado is your mother; I'm your father. Will the doctors not participating mind moving back? Fine. Now, Morey, here we are on Christmas morning. Merry Christmas, Morey!"

"Merry Christmas," Morey said half-heartedly. "Uh—Father dear, where's my—uh—my puppy that Mother promised me?"

"Puppy!" said Fairless heartily. "Your mother and I have something much better than a puppy for you. Just take a look under the tree there—it's a *robot!* Yes, Morey, your very own robot—a full-size thirty-eight-tube fully automatic companion robot for you! Go ahead, Morey, go right up and speak to it. Its name is Henry. Go on, boy."

Morey felt a sudden, incomprehensible tingle inside the bridge of his nose. He said shakily, "But I—I didn't *want* a robot."

"Of course you want a robot," Carrado interrupted. "Go on, child, play with your nice robot."

Morey said violently, "I *hate* robots!" He looked around him at the doctors, at the gray-paneled consulting room. He added defiantly, "You hear me, all of you? I *still* hate robots!"

There was a second's pause; then the questions began.

It was half an hour before the receptionist came in and announced that time was up.

In that half hour, Morey had got over his trembling and lost his wild, momentary passion, but he had remembered what for thirteen years he had forgotten.

He hated robots.

The surprising thing was not that young Morey had hated robots. It was that the Robot Riots, the ultimate violent outbreak of flesh against metal, the battle to the death between mankind and its machine heirs . . . never happened. A little boy hated robots, but the man he became worked with them hand in hand.

And yet, always and always before, the new worker, the competitor for the job, was at once and inevitably outside the law. The waves swelled in—the Irish, the Negroes, the Jews, the Italians. They were squeezed into their ghettoes, where they encysted, seethed and struck out, until the burgeoning generations became indistinguishable.

For the robots, that genetic relief was not in sight. And still the conflict never came. The feed-back circuits aimed the anti-aircraft guns and, reshaped and newly planned, found a place in a new sort of machine—together with a miraculous trail of cams and levers, and indestructible and potent power source and a hundred thousand parts and sub-assemblies.

And the first robot clanked off the bench.

Its mission was its own destruction; but from the scavenged wreck of its pilot body, a hundred better robots drew their inspiration. And the hundred went to work, and hundreds more, until there were millions upon untold millions.

And still the riots never happened.

For the robots came bearing a gift and the name of it was "Plenty."

And by the time the gift had shown its own unguessed ills, the time for a Robot Riot was past. Plenty is a habit-forming drug. You do not cut the dosage down. You kick it if you can; you stop the dose entirely. But the convulsions that follow may wreck the body once and for all.

The addict craves the grainy white powder; he doesn't hate it, or the runner who sells it to him. And if Morey as a little boy could hate the robot that had deprived him of his pup, Morey the man was perfectly aware that the robots were his servants and his friends.

But the little Morey inside the man—*he* had never been convinced.

Morey ordinarily looked forward to his work. The one day a week at which he *did* anything was a wonderful change from the dreary consume, consume, consume grind. He entered the bright-lit drafting room of the Bradmoor Amusements Company with a feeling of uplift.

But as he was changing from street garb to his drafting smock, Howland from Procurement came over with a knowing look. "Wainwright's been looking for you," Howland whispered. "Better get right in there."

Morey nervously thanked him and got. Wainwright's office was the size of a phone booth and as bare as Antarctic ice. Every time Morey saw it, he felt his insides churn with envy. Think of a desk with nothing on it but work surface—no calendar-clock, no twelve-color pen rack, no dictating machines!

He squeezed himself in and sat down while Wainwright finished a phone call. He mentally reviewed the possible reasons why Wainwright would want to talk to him in person instead of over the phone, or by dropping a word to him as he passed through the drafting room.

Very few of them were good.

Wainwright put down the phone and Morey straightened up. "You sent for me?" he asked.

Wainwright in a chubby world was aristocratically lean. As General Superintendent of the Design & Development Section of the Bradmoor Amusements Company, he ranked high in the upper section of the well-to-do. He rasped, "I certainly did. Fry, just what the hell do you think you're up to now?"

"I don't know what you m-mean, Mr. Wainwright," Morey stammered, crossing off the list of possible reasons for the interview all of the good ones.

Wainwright snorted. "I guess you don't. Not because you weren't told, but because you don't want to know. Think back a whole week. What did I have you on the carpet for then?"

Morey said sickly, "My ration book. Look, Mr. Wainwright, I know I'm running a little bit behind, but—"

"But nothing! How do you think it looks to the Committee, Fry? They got a complaint from the Ration Board about you. Naturally they passed it on to me. And naturally I'm going to pass it right along to you. The question is, what are you going to do about it? Good God, man, look at these figures—textiles, fifty-one per cent; food, sixty-seven per cent; amusements and entertainment, *thirty* per cent! You haven't come up to your ration in anything for months!"

Morey stared at the card miserably. "We—that is, my wife and I—just had a long talk about that last night, Mr. Wainwright. And, believe me, we're going to do better. We're going to buckle right down and get to work and—uh—do better," he finished weakly.

Wainwright nodded, and for the first time there was a note of sympathy in his voice. "Your wife. Judge Elon's daughter, isn't she? Good family. I've met the Judge many times." Then, gruffly: "Well, nevertheless, Fry, I'm warning you. I don't care how you straighten this out, but *don't let the Committee mention this to me again.*"

"No, sir."

"All right. Finished with the schematics on the new K-50?"

Morey brightened. "Just about, sir! I'm putting the first section on tape today. I'm very pleased with it, Mr. Wainwright, honestly I am. I've got more than eighteen thousand moving parts in it now, and that's without—"

"Good. Good." Wainwright glanced down at his desk. "Get back to it. And straighten out this other thing. You can do it, Fry. Consuming is everybody's duty. Just keep that in mind."

Howland followed Morey out of the drafting room, down to the spotless shops. "Bad time?" he inquired solicitously. Morey grunted. It was none of Howland's business.

Howland looked over his shoulder as he was setting up the programing panel. Morey studied the matrices silently, then got busy reading the summary tapes, checking them back against the schematics, setting up the instructions on the programing board. Howland kept quiet as Morey completed the setup and ran off a test tape. It checked perfectly; Morey stepped back to light a cigarette in celebration before pushing the *start* button.

Howland said, "Go on, run it. I can't go until you put it in the works."

Morey grinned and pushed the button. The board lighted up; within it, a tiny metronomic beep began to pulse. That was all. At the other end of the quarter-mile shed, Morey knew, the automatic sorters and conveyers were fingering through the copper reels and steel ingots, measuring hoppers of plastic powder and colors, setting up an intricate weaving path for the thousands of individual components that would make up Bradmoor's new K-50 Spin-a-Game. But from where they stood, in the elaborately muraled programing room, nothing showed. Bradmoor was an ultra-modernized plant; in the manufacturing end, even robots had been dispensed with in favor of machines that guided themselves.

Morey glanced at his watch and logged in the starting time while Howland quickly counter-checked Morey's raw-material flow program.

"Checks out," Howland said solemnly, slapping him on the back. "Calls for a celebration. Anyway, it's your first design, isn't it?"

"Yes. First all by myself, at any rate."

Howland was already fishing in his private locker for the bottle he кept against emergency needs. He poured with a flourish. "To Morey Fry," he said, "our most favorite designer, in whom we are much pleased."

Morey drank. It went down easily enough. Morey had conscientiously used his liquor rations for years, but he had never gone beyond the minimum, so that although liquor was no new experience to him, the single drink immediately warmed him. It warmed his mouth, his throat, the hollows of his chest; and it settled down with a warm glow inside him. Howland, exerting himself to be nice, complimented Morey fatuously on the design and poured another drink. Morey didn't utter any protest at all.

Howland drained his glass. "You may wonder," he said formally, "why I am so pleased with you, Morey Fry. I will tell you why this is."

Morey grinned. "Please do."

Howland nodded. "I will. It's because I am pleased with the world, Morey. My wife left me last night."

Morey was as shocked as only a recent bridegroom can be by the news of a crumbling marriage. "That's too ba— I mean is that a fact?"

"Yes, she left my beds and board and five robots, and I'm happy to see her go." He poured another drink for both of them. "Women. Can't live with them and can't live without them. First you sigh and pant and chase after 'em—you like poetry?" he demanded suddenly.

Morey said cautiously, "Some poetry."

Howland quoted: " 'How long, my love, shall I behold this wall between our gardens—yours the rose, and mine the swooning lily' Like it? I wrote it for Jocelyn— that's my wife—when we were first going together?"

"It's beautiful," said Morey.

"She wouldn't talk to me for two days." Howland drained his drink. "Lots of spirit, that girl. Anyway, I hunted her like a tiger. And then I caught her. *Wow!*"

Morey took a deep drink from his own glass. "What do you mean, *wow?*" he asked.

"*Wow.*" Howland pointed his finger at Morey. "*Wow,* that's what I mean. We got married and I took her home to the dive I was living in, and *wow* we had a kid, and *wow* I got in a little trouble with the Ration Board—nothing serious, of course, but there was a mixup—and *wow* fights.

"Everything was a fight," he explained. "She'd start with a little nagging, and naturally I'd say something or other back, and *bang* we were off. Budget, budget, budget; I hope to die if I ever hear the word 'budget' again. Morey, you're a married man; you know what it's like. Tell me the truth, weren't you just about ready to blow your top the first time you caught your wife cheating on the budget?"

"Cheating on the budget?" Morey was startled. "Cheating how?"

"Oh, lots of ways. Making your portions bigger than hers. Sneaking extra shirts for you on her clothing ration. You know."

"Damn it, I do *not* know!" cried Morey. "Cherry wouldn't do anything like that!"

Howland looked at him opaquely for a long second. "Of course not," he said at last. "Let's have another drink."

Ruffled, Morey held out his glass. Cherry wasn't the type of girl to *cheat*. Of course she wasn't. A fine, loving girl like her—a pretty girl, of a good family; she wouldn't know how to begin.

Howland was saying, in a sort of chant, "No more budget. No more fights. No more, 'Daddy never treated me like this.' No more nagging. No more extra rations for household allowance. No more—Morey, what do you say we go out and have a few drinks? I know a place where—"

"Sorry, Howland," Morey said. "I've got to get back to the office, you know."

Howland guffawed. He held out his wristwatch. As Morey, a little unsteadily, bent over it, it tinkled out the hour. It was a matter of minutes before the office closed for the day.

"Oh," said Morey. "I didn't realize—Well, anyway,

Howland, thanks, but I can't. My wife will be expecting me."

"She certainly will," Howland sniggered. "Won't catch *her* eating up your rations and hers tonight."

Morey said tightly, "Howland!"

"Oh, sorry, sorry." Howland waved an arm. "Don't mean to say anything against *your* wife, of course. Guess maybe Jocelyn soured me on women. But honest, Morey, you'd like this place. Name of Uncle Piggotty's, down in the Old Town. Crazy bunch hangs out there. You'd like them. Couple nights last week they had—I mean, you understand, Morey, I don't go there as often as all that, but I just happened to drop in and—"

Morey interrupted firmly. "Thank you, Howland. Must go home. Wife expects it. Decent of you to offer. Good night. Be seeing you."

He walked out, turned at the door to bow politely, and in turning back cracked the side of his face against the door jamb. A sort of pleasant numbness had taken possession of his entire skin surface, though, and it wasn't until he perceived Henry chattering at him sympathetically that he noticed a trickle of blood running down the side of his face.

"Mere flesh wound," he said with dignity. "Nothing to cause you *least* conshter—consternation, Henry. Now kindly shut your ugly face. Want to think."

And he slept in the car all the way home.

It was worse than a hangover. The name is "hold-over." You've had some drinks; you've started to sober up by catching a little sleep. Then you are required to be awake and to function. The consequent state has the worst features of hangover and intoxication; your head thumps and your mouth tastes like the floor of a bear pit, but you are nowhere near sober.

There is one cure. Morey said thickly, "Let's have a cocktail, dear."

Cherry was delighted to share a cocktail with him before dinner. Cherry, Morey thought lovingly, was a wonderful, wonderful, wonderful—

He found his head nodding in time to his thoughts, and the motion made him wince.

Cherry flew to his side and touched his temple. "Is it bothering you, darling?" she asked solicitously. "Where you ran into the door, I mean?"

Morey looked at her sharply, but her expression was open and adoring. He said bravely, "Just a little. Nothing to it, really."

The butler brought the cocktails and retired. Cherry lifted her glass. Morey raised his, caught a whiff of the liquor, and nearly dropped it. He bit down hard on his churning insides and forced himself to swallow.

He was surprised but grateful: It stayed down. In a moment, the curious phenomenon of warmth began to repeat itself. He swallowed the rest of the drink and held out his glass for a refill. He even tried a smile. Oddly enough, his face didn't fall off.

One more drink did it. Morey felt happy and relaxed, but by no means drunk. They went in to dinner in fine spirits. They chatted cheerfully with each other and Henry, and Morey found time to feel sentimentally sorry for poor Howland, who couldn't make a go of his marriage, when marriage was obviously such an easy relationship, so beneficial to both sides, so warm and relaxing—

Startled, he said, "What?"

Cherry repeated, "It's the cleverest scheme I ever heard of. Such a funny little man, dear. All kind of *nervous,* if you know what I mean. He kept looking at the door as if he was expecting someone, but of course that was silly. None of his friends would have come to *our* house to see him."

Morey said tensely, "Cherry, *please!* What was that you said about ration stamps?"

"But I told you, darling! It was just after you left this morning. This funny little man came to the door; the butler said he wouldn't give any name. Anyway, I talked to him. I thought he might be a neighbor, and I certainly would *never* be rude to any neighbor who might come to call, even if the neighborhood was—"

"The ration stamps!" Morey begged. "Did I hear you say he was peddling phony ration stamps?"

Cherry said uncertainly, "Well, I suppose that in a *way* they're phony. The way he explained it, they weren't the regular official kind. But it was four for one, dear—four of his stamps for one of ours. So I just took out our household book and steamed off a couple of weeks' stamps and—"

"How many?" Morey bellowed.

Cherry blinked. "About—about two weeks' quota," she said faintly. "Was that wrong, dear?"

Morey closed his eyes dizzily. "A couple of weeks' stamps," he repeated. "Four for one—you didn't even get the regular rate."

Cherry wailed, "How was I supposed to know? I never had anything like this when I was *home!* We didn't have food riots and slums and all these horrible robots and filthy little revolting men coming to the door!"

Morey stared at her woodenly. She was crying again, but it made no impression on the case-hardened armor that was suddenly thrown around his heart.

Henry made a tentative sound that, in a human, would have been a preparatory cough, but Morey froze him with a white-eyed look.

Morey said in a dreary monotone that barely penetrated the sound of Cherry's tears, "Let me tell you just what it was you did. Assuming, at best, that these stamps you got are at least average good counterfeits, and not so bad that the best thing to do with them is throw them away before we get caught with them in our possession, you have approximately a two-month supply of funny stamps. In case you didn't know it, those ration books are not merely ornamental. They have to be turned in every month to prove that we have completed our consuming quota for the month.

"When they are turned in, they are spot-checked. Every book is at least glanced at. A big chunk of them are gone over very carefully by the inspectors, and a certain percentage are tested by ultra-violet, infra-red, X-ray, radioisotopes, bleaches, fumes, paper chromatography and every other damned test known to Man." His voice was rising to an uneven crescendo. *"If* we are lucky enough to get away with using any of these stamps at all, we daren't—we simply *dare* not—use more than one or two counterfeits to every dozen or more real stamps.

"That means, Cherry, that what you bought is not a two-month supply, but maybe a two-*year* supply—and since, as you no doubt have never noticed, the things have expiration dates on them, there is probably no chance in the world that we can ever hope to use more than half of them." He was bellowing by the time he pushed back his chair and towered over her. "Moreover," he went on, "right *now,* right as of this *minute,* we have to make up the stamps you gave away, which means that at the very best we are going to be on double rations for two weeks or so.

"And that says nothing about the one feature of this whole grisly mess that you seem to have thought of least— namely that counterfeit stamps are against the *law!* I'm poor, Cherry; I live in a slum, and I know it; I've got a long way to go before I'm as rich or respected or powerful as your father, about whom I am beginning to get considerably tired of hearing. But poor as I may be, I can tell you *this* for sure: Up until now, at any rate, I have been *honest."*

Cherry's tears had stopped entirely and she was bowed white-faced and dry-eyed by the time Morey had finished. He had spent himself; there was no violence left in him.

He stared dismally at Cherry for a moment, then turned wordlessly and stamped out of the house.

Marriage! he thought as he left.

He walked for hours, blind to where he was going.

What brought him back to awareness was a sensation he had not felt in a dozen years. It was not, Morey abruptly realized, the dying traces of his hangover that made his stomach feel so queer. He was hungry—actually hungry.

He looked about him. He was in the Old Town, miles from home, jostled by crowds of lower-class people. The block he was on was as atrocious a slum as Morey had ever seen—Chinese pagodas stood next to rococo imitations of the chapels around Versailles; gingerbread marred every façade; no building was without its brilliant signs and flarelights.

He saw a blindingly overdecorated eating establishment called Billie's Budget Busy Bee and crossed the street toward it, dodging through the unending streams of traffic. It was a miserable excuse for a restaurant, but Morey was in no mood to care. He found a seat under a potted palm, as far from the tinkling fountains and robot string ensemble as he could manage, and ordered recklessly, paying no attention to the ration prices. As the waiter was gliding noiselessly away, Morey had a sickening realization: He'd come out without his ration book. He groaned out loud; it was too late to leave without causing a disturbance. But then, he thought rebelliously, what difference did one more unrationed meal make anyhow?

Food made him feel a little better. He finished the last of his *profiterole au chocolate,* not even leaving on the plate the uneaten one-third that tradition permitted, and paid his check. The robot cashier reached automatically for his ration book. Morey had a moment of grandeur as he said simply, "No ration stamps."

Robot cashiers are not equipped to display surprise, but this one tried. The man behind Morey in line audibly caught his breath, and less audibly mumbled something about *slummers.* Morey took it as a compliment and strode outside feeling almost in good humor.

Good enough to go home to Cherry? Morey thought seriously of it for a second; but he wasn't going to pretend he was wrong and certainly Cherry wasn't going to be willing to admit that *she* was at fault.

Besides, Morey told himself grimly, she was undoubtedly asleep. That was an annoying thing about Cherry at best: she never had any trouble getting to sleep. Didn't even use her quota of sleeping tablets, though Morey had spoken to her about it more than once. Of course, he reminded himself, he had been so polite and tactful about it, as befits a newlywed, that very likely she hadn't even understood that it was a complaint. Well, *that* would stop!

Man's man Morey Fry, wearing no collar ruff but his own, strode determinedly down the streets of the Old Town.

"Hey, Joe, want a good time?"

Morey took one unbelieving look. "You again!" he roared.

The little man stared at him in genuine surprise. Then a faint glimmer of recognition crossed his face. "Oh, yeah," he said. "This morning, huh?" He clucked commiseratingly. "Too bad you wouldn't deal with me. Your wife was a lot smarter. Of course, you got me a little sore, Jack, so naturally I had to raise the price a little bit."

"You skunk, you cheated my poor wife blind! You and I are going to the local station house and talk this over."

The little man pursed his lips. "We are, huh?"

Morey nodded vigorously. "Damn right! And let me tell you—" He stopped in the middle of a threat as a large hand cupped around his shoulder.

The equally large man who owned the hand said, in a mild and cultured voice, "Is this gentleman disturbing you, Sam?"

"Not so far," the little man conceded. "He might want to, though, so don't go away."

Morey wrenched his shoulder away. "Don't think you can strongarm me. I'm taking you to the police."

Sam shook his head unbelievingly. "You mean you're going to call the law in on this?"

"I certainly am!"

Sam sighed regretfully. "What do you think of that, Walter? Treating his wife like that. Such a nice lady too."

"What are you talking about?" Morey demanded, stung on a peculiarly sensitive spot.

"I'm talking about your wife," Sam explained. "Of course, I'm not married myself. But it seems to me that if I was, I wouldn't call the police when my wife was engaged in some kind of criminal activity or other. No, sir, I'd try to settle it myself. Tell you what," he advised, "why don't you talk this over with her? Make her see the error of—"

"Wait a minute," Morey interrupted. "You mean you'd involve my wife in this thing?"

The man spread his hands helplessly. "It's not me that would involve her, Buster," he said. "She already involved her own self. It takes two to make a crime, you know. I sell, maybe; I won't deny it. But after all, I can't sell unless somebody buys, can I?"

Morey stared at him glumly. He glanced in quick speculation at the large-sized Walter; but Walter was just as big as he'd remembered, so that took care of that. Violence was out; the police were out; that left no really attractive way of capitalizing on the good luck of running into the man again.

Sam said, "Well, I'm glad to see that's off your mind. Now, returning to my original question, Mac, how would you like a good time? You look like a smart fellow to me; you look like you'd be kind of interested in a place I happen to know of down the block."

Morey said bitterly, "So you're a dive-steerer too. A real talented man."

"I admit it," Sam agreed. "Stamp business is slow at night, in my experience. People have their minds more on a good time. And, believe me, a good time is what I can show 'em. Take this place I'm talking about, Uncle Piggotty's is the name of it, it's what I would call an unusual kind of place. Wouldn't you say so, Walter?"

"Oh, I agree with you entirely," Walter rumbled.

But Morey was hardly listening. He said, "Uncle Piggotty's, you say?"

"That's right," said Sam.

Morey frowned for a moment, digesting an idea. Uncle Piggotty's sounded like the place Howland had been talking about back at the plant; it might be interesting, at that.

While he was making up his mind, Sam slipped an arm through his on one side and Walter amiably wrapped a big hand around the other. Morey found himself walking.

"You'll like it," Sam promised comfortably. "No hard feelings about this morning, sport? Of course not. Once you get a look at Piggotty's, you'll get over your mad, anyhow. It's something special. I swear, on what they pay me for bringing in customers, I wouldn't do it unless I *believed* in it."

"Dance, Jack?" the hostess yelled over the noise at the bar. She stepped back, lifted her flounced skirts to ankle height and executed a tricky nine-step.

"My name is Morey," Morey yelled back. "And I don't want to dance, thanks."

The hostess shrugged, frowned meaningfully at Sam and danced away.

Sam flagged the bartender. "First round's on us," he explained to Morey. "Then we won't bother you any more. Unless you want us to, of course. Like the place?" Morey hesitated, but Sam didn't wait. "Fine place," he yelled, and picked up the drink the bartender left him. "See you around."

He and the big man were gone. Morey stared after them uncertainly, then gave it up. He was here, anyhow; might as well at least have a drink. He ordered and looked around.

Uncle Piggotty's was a third-rate dive disguised to look, in parts of it at least, like one of the exclusive upper-class country clubs. The bar, for instance, was treated to resemble the clean lines of nailed wood; but underneath the surface treatment, Morey could detect the intricate laminations of plyplastic. What at first glance appeared to be burlap hangings were in actuality elaborately textured synthetics. And all through the bar the motif was carried out.

A floor show of sorts was going on, but nobody seemed

to be paying much attention to it. Morey, straining briefly to hear the master of ceremonies, gathered that the wit was on a more than mildly vulgar level. There was a dispirited string of chorus beauties in long ruffled pantaloons and diaphanous tops; one of them, Morey was almost sure, was the hostess who had talked to him just a few moments before.

Next to him a man was declaiming to a middle-aged woman:

> Smote I the monstrous rock, yahoo!
> Smote I the turgid tube, Bully Boy!
> Smote I the cankered hill—

"Why, Morey!" he interrupted himself. "What are you doing here?"

He turned farther around and Morey recognized him. "Hello, Howland," he said. "I—uh—I happened to be free tonight, so I thought—"

Howland sniggered. "Well, guess your wife is more liberal than mine was. Order a drink, boy."

"Thanks, I've got one," said Morey.

The woman, with a tigerish look at Morey, said, "Don't stop, Everett. That was one of your most beautiful things."

"Oh, Morey's heard my poetry," Howland said. "Morey, I'd like you to meet a very lovely and talented young lady, Tanaquil Bigelow. Morey works in the office with me, Tan."

"Obviously," said Tanaquil Bigelow in a frozen voice, and Morey hastily withdrew the hand he had begun to put out.

The conversation stuck there, impaled, the woman cold, Howland relaxed and abstracted, Morey wondering if, after all, this had been such a good idea. He caught the eye-cell of the robot bartender and ordered a round of drinks for the three of them, politely putting them on Howland's ration book. By the time the drinks had come and Morey had just got around to deciding that it wasn't a very good idea, the woman had all of a sudden become thawed.

She said abruptly, "You look like the kind of man who thinks, Morey, and I like to talk to that kind of man. Frankly, Morey, I just don't have any patience at all with the stupid, stodgy men who just work in their offices all day and eat all their dinners every night, and gad about and consume like mad and where does it all get them anyhow? That's right; I can see you understand. Just one crazy rush of consume, consume from the day you're born *plop* to the day you're buried *pop!* And who's to blame if not the robots?"

Faintly, a tinge of worry began to appear on the surface of Howland's relaxed calm. "Tan," he chided, "Morey may not be very interested in politics."

Politics, Morey thought; well, at least that was a clue. He'd had the dizzying feeling, while the woman was talking, that he himself was the ball in the games machine he had designed for the shop earlier that day. Following the woman's conversation might, at that, give his next design some valuable pointers in swoops, curves, and obstacles.

He said, with more than half truth, "No, please go on, Miss Bigelow. I'm very much interested."

She smiled; then abruptly her face changed to a frightening scowl. Morey flinched, but evidently the scowl wasn't meant for him. "Robots!" she hissed. "Supposed to work for us, aren't they? Hah! We're their slaves, slaves for every moment of every miserable day of our lives. Slaves! Wouldn't you like to join us and be free, Morey?"

Morey took cover in his drink. He made an expressive gesture with his free hand—expressive of exactly what, he didn't truly know, for he was lost. But it seemed to satisfy the woman.

She said accusingly, "Did you know that more than three-quarters of the people in this country have had a nervous breakdown in the past five years and four months? That more than half of them are under the constant care of psychiatrists for psychosis—not just plain ordinary neurosis like my husband's got and Howland here has got and you've got, but psychosis. Like I've got. Did you know that? Did you know that forty percent of the population are essentially manic depressive, thirty-one percent are schizoid, thirty-eight percent have an assortment of other unfixed psychogenic disturbances, and twenty-four—"

"Hold it a minute, Tan," Howland interrupted critically. "You've got too many percents there. Start over again."

"Oh, the hell with it," the woman said moodily. "I wish my husband were here. He expresses it so much better than I do." She swallowed her drink. "Since you've wriggled off the hook," she said nastily to Morey, "how about setting up another round—on my ration book this time?"

Morey did; it was the simplest thing to do in his confusion. When that was gone, they had another on Howland's book.

As near as he could figure out, the woman, her husband and quite possibly Howland as well belonged to some kind of anti-robot group. Morey had heard of such things; they had a quasi-legal status, neither approved nor prohibited, but he had never come into contact with them before. Remembering the hatred he had so painfully relived at the psychodrama session, he thought anxiously that perhaps he belonged with them. But, question them though he might, he couldn't seem to get the principles of the organization firmly in mind.

The woman finally gave up trying to explain it, and went off to find her husband while Morey and Howland had another drink and listened to two drunks squabble over who bought the next round. They were at the Alphonse-Gaston stage of inebriation; they would regret it in the morning; for each was bending over backward to permit the other to pay the ration points. Morey wondered uneasily about his own points; Howland was certainly getting credit for a lot of Morey's drinking tonight. Served him right for forgetting his book, of course.

When the woman came back, it was with the large man Morey had encountered in the company of Sam, the counterfeiter, steerer and general man about Old Town.

"A remarkably small world, isn't it?" boomed Walter Bigelow, only slightly crushing Morey's hand in his. "Well, sir, my wife has told me how interested you are in the basic philosophical drives behind our movement, and I should like to discuss them further with you. To begin with, sir, have you considered the principle of Twoness?"

Morey said, "Why—"

"Very good," said Bigelow courteously. He cleared his throat and declaimed:

> *Han-headed Cathay saw it first,*
> *Bright as brightest solar burst;*
> *Whipped it into boy and girl,*
> *The blinding spiral-sliced swirl:*
> *Yang*
> *And Yin.*

He shrugged deprecatingly. "Just the first stanza," he said. "I don't know if you got much out of it."

"Well, no," Morey admitted.

"Second stanza," Bigelow said firmly:

> *Hegel saw it, saw it clear;*
> *Jackal Marx drew near, drew near;*
> *O'er his shoulder saw it plain,*
> *Turned it upside down again:*
> *Yang*
> *And Yin.*

There was an expectant pause. Morey said, "I—uh—"

"Wraps it all up, doesn't it?" Bigelow's wife demanded. "Oh, if only others could see it as clearly as you do! The robot peril *and* the robot savior. Starvation *and* surfeit. Always twoness, always!"

Bigelow patted Morey's shoulder. "The next stanza

makes it even clearer," he said. "It's really very clever—
I shouldn't say it, of course, but it's Howland's as much
as it's mine. He helped me with the verses." Morey darted
a glance at Howland, but Howland was carefully looking
away. "Third stanza," said Bigelow. "This is a hard one,
because it's long, so pay attention."

> Justice, tip your sightless scales;
> One pan rises, one pan falls.

"Howland," he interrupted himself, "are you *sure* about
that rhyme? I always trip over it. Well, anyway:

> Add to A and B grows less;
> A's B's partner, nonetheless.
> Next, the Twoness that there be
> In even electricity.
> Chart the current as it's found:
> Sine the hot lead; line the ground.
> The wild sine dances, soars, and falls,
> But only to figures the zero calls.
> Sine wave, scales, all things that be
> Share a reciprocity.
> Male and female, light and dark:
> Name the numbers of Noah's Ark!
> Yang
> And Yin!

"Dearest!" shrieked Bigelow's wife. "You've never
done it better!" There was a spatter of applause, and
Morey realized for the first time that half the bar had
stopped its noisy revel to listen to them. Bigelow was
evidently quite a well-known figure here.

Morey said weakly, "I've never heard anything like it."

He turned hesitantly to Howland, who promptly said,
"Drink! What we all need right now is a drink."

They had a drink on Bigelow's book.

Morey got Howland aside and asked him, "Look,
level with me. Are these people nuts?"

Howland showed pique. "No. Certainly not."

"Does that poem mean anything? Does this whole business of twoness mean anything?"

Howland shrugged. "If it means something to them, it means something. They're philosophers, Morey. They see deep into things. You don't know what a privilege it is for me to be allowed to associate with them."

They had another drink. On Howland's book, of course.

Morey eased Walter Bigelow over to a quiet spot. He said, "Leaving twoness out of it for the moment, what's this about the robots?"

Bigelow looked at him round-eyed. "Didn't you understand the poem?"

"Of course I did. But diagram it for me in simple terms so I can tell my wife."

Bigelow beamed. "It's about the dichotomy of robots," he explained. "Like the little salt mill that the boy wished for: it ground out salt and ground out salt and ground out salt. He had to have salt, but not *that* much salt. Whitehead explains it clearly—"

They had another drink on Bigelow's book.

Morey wavered over Tanaquil Bigelow. He said fuzzily, "Listen. Mrs. Walter Tanaquil Strongarm Bigelow. Listen."

She grinned smugly at him. "Brown hair," she said dreamily.

Morey shook his head vigorously. "Never mind hair," he ordered. "Never mind poem. Listen. In *pre-cise* and el-e-*men*-ta-ry terms, explain to me what is wrong with the world today."

"Not enough brown hair," she said promptly.

"Never mind hair!"

"All right," she said agreeably. "Too many robots. Too many robots make too much of everything."

"Ha! Got it!" Morey exclaimed triumphantly. "Get rid of robots!"

"Oh, no. No! No! No. We wouldn't eat. Everything is mechanized. Can't get rid of them, can't slow down production—slowing down is dying, stopping is quicker dying. Principle of twoness is the concept that clarifies all these—"

"No!" Morey said violently. "What should we *do?*"

"Do? I'll tell you what we should do, if that's what you want. I can tell you."

"Then tell me."

"What we should do is"—Tanaquil hiccupped with a look of refined consternation—"have another drink."

They had another drink. He gallantly let her pay, of course. She ungallantly argued with the bartender about the ration points due her.

Though not a two-fisted drinker, Morey tried. He really worked at it.

He paid the price, too. For some little time before his limbs stopped moving, his mind stopped functioning. Blackout. Almost a blackout, at any rate, for all he retained of the late evening was a kaleidoscope of people and places and things. Howland was there, drunk as a skunk, disgracefully drunk, Morey remembered thinking as he stared up at Howland from the floor. The Bigelows were there. His wife, Cherry, solicitous and amused, was there. And oddly enough, Henry was there.

It was very, very hard to reconstruct. Morey devoted a whole morning's hangover to the effort. It was *important* to reconstruct it, for some reason. But Morey couldn't even remember what the reason was; and finally he dismissed it, guessing that he had either solved the secret of twoness or whether Tanaquil Bigelow's remarkable figure was natural.

He did, however, know that the next morning he had waked in his own bed, with no recollection of getting there. No recollection of anything much, at least not of anything that fit into the proper chronological order or seemed to mesh with anything else, after the dozenth drink, when he and Howland, arms around each other's shoulders, composed a new verse on twoness and, plagia-

rizing an old marching tune, howled it across the boister-
ous barroom:

> *A twoness on the scene much later*
> *Rest in your refrigerator.*
> *Heat your house and insulate it.*
> *Next your food: Refrigerate it.*
> *Frost will damp your Freon coils,*
> *So flux in nichrome till it boils.*
> *See the picture? Heat in cold*
> *In heat in cold, the story's told!*
> *Giant-writ the sacred scrawl:*
> *Oh, the twoness of it all!*
> *Yang*
> *And Yin!*

It had, at any rate, seemed to mean something at the
time.

If alcohol opened Morey's eyes to the fact that there
was a twoness, perhaps alcohol was what he needed. For
there was.

Call it a dichotomy, if the word seems more couth. A
kind of two-pronged struggle, the struggle of two un-
wearying runners in an immortal race. There is the refrigerator inside the house. The cold air, the bubble of
heated air that is the house, the bubble of cooled air that
is the refrigerator, the momentary bubble of heated air
that defrosts it. Call the heat Yang, if you will. Call the
cold Yin. Yang overtakes Yin. Then Yin passes Yang.
Then Yang passes Yin. Then—

Give them other names. Call Yin a mouth; call Yang a
hand.

If the hand rests, the mouth will starve. If the mouth
stops, the hand will die. The hand, Yang, moves faster.

Yin may not lag behind.

Then call Yang a robot.

And remember that a pipeline has two ends.

Like any once-in-a-lifetime lush, Morey braced himself

for the consequences—and found startledly that there were none.

Cherry was a surprise to him. "You were so funny," she giggled. "And, honestly, so *romantic.*"

He shakily swallowed his breakfast coffee.

The office staff roared and slapped him on the back. "Howland tells us you're living high, boy!" they bellowed more or less in the same words. "Hey, listen to what Morey did—went on the town for the night of a lifetime *and didn't even bring his ration book along to cash in!*"

They thought it was a wonderful joke.

But, then, everything was going well. Cherry, it seemed, had reformed out of recognition. True, she still hated to go out in the evening and Morey never saw her forcing herself to gorge on unwanted food or play undesired games. But, moping into the pantry one afternoon, he found to his incredulous delight that they were well ahead of their ration quotas. In some items, in fact, they were *out*—a month's supply and more was gone ahead of schedule!

Nor was it the counterfeit stamps, for he had found them tucked behind a bain-marie and quietly burned them. He cast about for ways of complimenting her, but caution prevailed. She was sensitive on the subject; leave it be.

And virtue had its reward.

Wainwright called him in, all smiles. "Morey, great news! We've all appreciated your work here, and we've been able to show it in some more tangible way than compliments. I didn't want to say anything till it was definite, but—your status has been reviewed by Classification and the Ration Board. You're out of class Four Minor, Morey!"

Morey said tremulously, hardly daring to hope, "I'm a full Class Four?"

"Class Five, Morey. *Class Five!* When we do something, we do it right. We asked for a special waiver and got it—you've skipped a whole class." He added honestly, "Not that it was just our backing that did it, of course.

Your own recent splendid record of consumption helped a lot. I told you you could do it!"

Morey had to sit down. He missed the rest of what Wainwright had to say, but it couldn't have mattered. He escaped from the office, sidestepped the knot of fellow employees waiting to congratulate him, and got to a phone.

Cherry was as ecstatic and inarticulate as he. "Oh, darling!" was all she could say.

"And I couldn't have done it without you," he babbled, "Wainwright as much as said so himself. Said if it wasn't for the way we—well, *you* have been keeping up with the rations, it never would have got by the Board. I've been meaning to say something to you about that, dear, but I just haven't known how. But I do appreciate it. I— Hello?" There was a curious silence at the other end of the phone. "Hello?" he repeated worriedly.

Cherry's voice was intense and low. "Morey Fry, I think you're mean. I wish you hadn't spoiled the good news." And she hung up.

Morey stared slack-jawed at the phone.

Howland appeared behind him, chuckling. "Women," he said. "Never try to figure them. Anyway, congratulations, Morey."

"Thanks," Morey mumbled.

Howland coughed and said, "Uh—by the way, Morey, now that you're one of the big shots, so to speak, you won't—uh—feel obliged to—well, say anything to Wainwright, for instance, about anything I may have said while we—"

"Excuse me," Morey said, unhearing, and pushed past him. He thought wildly of calling Cherry back, of racing home to see just what he'd said that was wrong. Not that there was much doubt, of course. He'd touched her on her sore point.

Anyhow, his wristwatch was chiming a reminder of the fact that his psychiatric appointment for the week was coming up.

Morey sighed. The day gives and the day takes away. Blessed is the day that gives only good things.

If any.

The session went badly. Many of the sessions had been going badly, Morey decided; there had been more and more whispering in knots of doctors from which he was excluded, poking and probing in the dark instead of the precise psychic surgery he was used to. Something was wrong, he thought.

Something was. Semmelweiss confirmed it when he adjourned the group session. After the other doctors had left, he sat Morey down for a private talk. On his own time too—he didn't ask for his usual ration fee. That told Morey how important the problem was.

"Morey," said Semmelweiss, "you're holding back."

"I don't mean to, Doctor," Morey said earnestly.

"Who knows what you 'mean' to do? Part of you 'means' to. We've dug pretty deep, and we've found some important things. Now there's something I can't put my finger on. Exploring the mind, Morey, is like sending scouts through cannibal territory. You can't see the cannibals—until it's too late. But if you send a scout through the jungle and he doesn't show up on the other side, it's a fair assumption that something obstructed his way. In that case, we would label the obstruction 'cannibals.' In the case of the human mind, we label the obstruction a 'trauma.' What the trauma is, or what its effects on behavior will be, we have to find out, once we know that it's there."

Morey nodded. All of this was familiar; he couldn't see what Semmelweiss was driving at.

Semmelweiss sighed. "The trouble with healing traumas and penetrating psychic blocks and releasing inhibitions— the trouble with everything we psychiatrists do, in fact, is that we can't afford to do it too well. An inhibited man is under a strain. We try to relieve the strain. But if we succeed completely, leaving him with no inhibitions at all, we have an outlaw, Morey. Inhibitions are often socially necessary. Suppose, for instance, that an average man were not inhibited against blatant waste. It could happen, you know. Suppose that instead of consuming his ration quota in an orderly and responsible way, he did such things as set fire to his house and everything in it or dumped his food allotment in the river.

"When only a few individuals are doing it, we treat the individuals. But if it were done on a mass scale, Morey, it would be the end of society as we know it. Think of the whole collection of anti-social actions that you see in every paper. Man beats wife; wife turns into a harpy; junior smashes up windows; husband starts a black-market stamp racket. And every one of them traces to a basic weakness in the mind's defenses against the most important single anti-social phenomenon—failure to consume."

Morey flared, "That's not fair, Doctor! That was weeks ago! We've certainly been on the ball lately. I was just commended by the Board, in fact—"

The doctor said mildly, "Why so violent, Morey? I only made a general remark."

"It's just natural to resent being accused."

The doctor shrugged. "First, foremost, and above all, we do *not* accuse patients of things. We try to help you find things out." He lit his end-of-session cigarette. "Think about it, please. I'll see you next week."

Cherry was composed and unapproachable. She kissed him remotely when he came in. She said, "I called Mother and told her the good news. She and Dad promised to come over here to celebrate."

"Yeah," said Morey. "Darling, what did I say wrong on the phone?"

"They'll be here about six."

"Sure. But what did I say? Was it about the rations? If you're sensitive, I swear I'll never mention them again."

"I *am* sensitive, Morey."

He said despairingly, "I'm sorry. I just—"

He had a better idea. He kissed her.

Cherry was passive at first, but not for long. When he had finished kissing her, she pushed him away and actually giggled. "Let me get dressed for dinner."

"Certainly. Anyhow, I was just—"

She laid a finger on his lips.

He let her escape, and feeling much less tense, drifted into the library. The afternoon papers were waiting for him. Virtuously, he sat down and began going through them in order. Midway through the *World-Telegram-Sun-Post-and-News,* he rang for Henry.

Morey had read clear through to the drama section of the *Times-Herald-Tribune-Mirror* before the robot appeared. "Good evening," it said politely.

"What took you so long?" Morey demanded. "Where are all the robots?"

Robots do not stammer, but there was a distinct pause before Henry said, "Belowstairs, sir. Did you want them for something?"

"Well, no. I just haven't seen them around. Get me a drink."

It hesitated. "Scotch, sir?"

"Before dinner? Get me a Manhattan."

"We're all out of Vermouth, sir."

"All out? Would you mind telling me how?"

"It's all used up, sir."

"Now that's just ridiculous," Morey snapped. "We have never run out of liquor in our whole lives, and you know it. Good heavens, we just got our allotment in the other day, and I certainly—"

He checked himself. There was a sudden flicker of horror in his eyes as he stared at Henry.

"You certainly what, sir?" the robot prompted.

Morey swallowed. "Henry, did I—did I do something I shouldn't have?"

"I'm sure I wouldn't know, sir. It isn't up to me to say what you should and shouldn't do."

"Of course not," Morey agreed grayly.

He sat rigid, staring hopelessly into space, remembering. What he remembered was no pleasure to him at all.

"Henry," he said. "Come along, we're going below-stairs. Right now!"

It had been Tanaquil Bigelow's remark about the robots. *Too many robots—make too much of everything.*

That had implanted the idea; it germinated in Morey's home. More than a little drunk, less than ordinarily inhibited, he had found the problem clear and the answer obvious.

He stared around him in dismal worry. His own robots, following his own orders, given weeks before . . .

Henry said, "It's just what you *told* us to do, sir."

Morey groaned. He was watching a scene of unparalleled activity, and it sent shivers up and down his spine.

There was the butler-robot, hard at work, his copper face expressionless. Dressed in Morey's own sports knickers and golfing shoes, the robot solemnly hit a ball against the wall, picked it up, and teed it, hit it again, over and again, with Morey's own clubs. Until the ball wore ragged and was replaced; and the shafts of the clubs leaned out of true; and the close-stitched seams in the clothing began to stretch and abrade.

"My God!" said Morey hollowly.

There were the maid-robots, exquisitely dressed in Cherry's best, walking up and down in the delicate, slim shoes, sitting and rising and bending and turning. The cook-robots and the serving-robots were preparing dionysian meals.

Morey swallowed. "You—you've been doing this right along," he said to Henry. "That's why the quotas have been filled."

"Oh, yes, sir. Just as you told us."

Morey had to sit down. One of the serving-robots politely scurried over with a chair, brought from upstairs for their new chores.

Waste.

Morey tasted the word between his lips.

Waste.

You never wasted things. You *used* them. If necessary,

you drove yourself to the edge of breakdown to use them; you made every breath a burden and every hour a torment to use them, until through diligent consuming and/ or occupational merit, you were promoted to the next higher class, and were allowed to consume less frantically. But you didn't wantonly destroy or throw out. You *consumed*.

Morey thought fearfully: When the Board finds out about this . . .

Still, he reminded himself, the Board hadn't found out. It might take some time before they did, for humans, after all, never entered robot quarters. There was no law against it, not even a sacrosanct custom. But there was no reason to. When breaks occurred, which was infrequently, maintenance robots or repair squads came in and put them back in order. Usually the humans involved didn't even know it had happened, because the robots used their own TBR radio circuits and the process was next thing to automatic.

Morey said reprovingly, "Henry, you should have told —well, I mean reminded me about this."

"But, sir!" Henry protested. " 'Don't tell a living soul,' you said. You made it a direct order."

"Umph. Well, keep it that way. I—uh—I have to go back upstairs. Better get the rest of the robots started on dinner."

Morey left, not comfortably.

The dinner to celebrate Morey's promotion was difficult. Morey liked Cherry's parents. Old Elon, after the pre-marriage inquisition that father must inevitably give to daughter's suitor, had buckled right down to the job of adjustment. The old folks were good about not interfering, good about keeping their superior social status to themselves, good about helping out on the budget—at least once a week, they could be relied on to come over for a hearty meal, and Mrs. Elon had more than once remade some of Cherry's new dresses to fit herself, even to the extent of wearing all the high-point ornamentation.

And they had been wonderful about the wedding gifts, when Morey and their daughter got married. The most any member of Morey's family had been willing to take was a silver set or a few crystal table pieces. The Elons had come through with a dazzling promise to accept a car, a bird-bath for their garden and a complete set of living-room furniture! Of course, they could afford it—they had to consume so little that it wasn't much strain for them even to take gifts of that magnitude. But without their help, Morey knew, the first few months of matrimony would have been even tougher consuming than they were.

But on this particular night it was hard for Morey to like anyone. He responded with monosyllables; he barely grunted when Elon proposed a toast to his promotion and his brilliant future. He was preoccupied.

Rightly so. Morey, in his deepest, bravest searching, could find no clue in his memory as to just what the punishment might be for what he had done. But he had a sick certainty that trouble lay ahead.

Morey went over his problem so many times that an anesthesia set in. By the time dinner was ended and he and his father-in-law were in the den with their brandy, he was more or less functioning again.

Elon, for the first time since Morey had known him, offered him one of *his* cigars. "You're Grade Five—can afford to smoke somebody else's now, hey?"

"Yeah," Morey said glumly.

There was a moment of silence. Then Elon, as punctilious as any companion-robot, coughed and tried again. "Remember being peaked till I hit Grade Five," he reminisced meaningfully. "Consuming keeps a man on the go, all right. Things piled up at the law office, couldn't be taken care of while ration points piled up, too. And consuming comes first, of course—that's a citizen's prime duty. Mother and I had our share of grief over that, but a couple that wants to make a go of marriage and citizenship just pitches in and does the job, hey?"

Morey repressed a shudder and managed to nod.

"Best thing about upgrading," Elon went on, as if he had elicited a satisfactory answer, "don't have to spend so much time consuming, give more attention to work. Greatest luxury in the world, work. Wish I had as much stamina as you young fellows. Five days a week in court are about all I can manage. Hit six for a while; relaxed first time in my life, but my doctor made me cut down. Said we can't overdo pleasures. You'll be working two days a week now, hey?"

Morey produced another nod.

Elon drew deeply on his cigar, his eyes bright as they watched Morey. He was visibly puzzled, and Morey, even in his half-daze, could recognize the exact moment at which Elon drew the wrong inference. "Ah, everything okay with you and Cherry?" he asked diplomatically.

"Fine!" Morey exclaimed. "Couldn't be better!"

"Good, Good." Elon changed the subject with almost an audible wrench. "Speaking of court, had an interesting case the other day. Young fellow—year or two younger than you, I guess—came in with a Section Ninety-seven on him. Know what that is? Breaking and entering!"

"Breaking and entering," Morey repeated wonderingly, interested in spite of himself. "Breaking and entering what?"

"Houses. Old term; law's full of them. Originally applied to stealing things. Still does, I discovered."

"You mean he *stole* something?" Morey asked in bewilderment.

"Exactly! He *stole*. Strangest thing I ever came across. Talked it over with one of his bunch of lawyers later; new one on him, too. Seems this kid had a girl friend, nice kid but a little, you know, plump. She got interested in art."

"There's nothing wrong with that," Morey said.

"Nothing wrong with her, either. She didn't do anything. She didn't like him too much, though. Wouldn't marry him. Kid got to thinking about how he could get her to change her mind and—well, you know that big Mondrian in the Museum?"

"I've never been there," Morey said, somewhat embarrassed.

"Um. Ought to try it some day, boy. Anyway, comes closing time at the Museum the other day, this kid sneaks in. He steals the painting. That's right—*steals* it. Takes it to give to the girl."

Morey shook his head blankly. "I never heard of anything like that in my life."

"Not many have. Girl wouldn't take it, by the way. Got scared when he brought it to her. She must've tipped off the police, I guess. Somebody did. Took 'em three hours to find it, even when they knew it was hanging on a wall. Pretty poor kid. Forty-two room house."

"And there was a *law* against it?" Morey asked. "I mean it's like making a law against breathing."

"Certainly was. Old law, of course. Kid got set back two grades. Would have been more but, my God, he was only a Grade Three as it was."

"Yeah," said Morey, wetting his lips. "Say, Dad—"

"Um?"

Morey cleared his throat. "Uh—I wonder—I mean, what's the penalty, for instance, for things like—well, misusing rations or anything like that?"

Elon's eyebrows went high. "Misusing rations?"

"Say you had a liquor ration, it might be, and instead of drinking it, you—well, flushed it down the drain or something . . ."

His voice trailed off. Elon was frowning. He said, "Funny thing, seems I'm not as broadminded as I thought I was. For some reason, I don't find that amusing."

"Sorry," Morey croaked.

And he certainly was.

It might be dishonest, but it was doing him a lot of good, for days went by and no one seemed to have penetrated his secret. Cherry was happy. Wainwright found occasion after occasion to pat Morey's back. The wages of sin were turning out to be prosperity and happiness.

There was a bad moment when Morey came home to

find Cherry in the middle of supervising a team of packing robots; the new house, suitable to his higher grade, was ready, and they were expected to move in the next day. But Cherry hadn't been belowstairs, and Morey had his household robots clean up the evidences of what they had been doing before the packers got that far.

The new house was, by Morey's standards, pure luxury.

It was only fifteen rooms. Morey had shrewdly retained one more robot than was required for a Class Five, and had been allowed a compensating deduction in the size of his house.

The robot quarters were less secluded than in the old house, though, and that was a disadvantage. More than once Cherry had snuggled up to him in the delightful intimacy of their one bed in their single bedroom and said, with faint curiosity, "I wish they'd stop that noise." And Morey had promised to speak to Henry about it in the morning. But there was nothing he could say to Henry, of course, unless he ordered Henry to stop the tireless consuming through each of the day's twenty-four hours that kept them always ahead, but never quite far enough ahead, of the inexorable weekly increment of ration quotas.

But, though Cherry might once in a while have a moment's curiosity about what the robots were doing, she was not likely to be able to guess at the facts. Her upbringing was, for once, on Morey's side—she knew so little of the grind, grind, grind of consuming that was the lot of the lower classes that she scarcely noticed that there was less of it.

Morey almost, sometimes, relaxed.

He thought of many ingenious chores for robots, and the robots politely and emotionlessly obeyed.

Morey was a success.

It wasn't all gravy. There was a nervous moment for Morey when the quarterly survey report came in the mail. As the day for the Ration Board to check over the degree of wear on the turned-in discards came due, Morey began to sweat. The clothing and furniture and household goods the robots had consumed for him were very nearly in shreds. It had to look plausible, that was the big thing— no normal person would wear a hole completely through the knee of a pair of pants, as Henry had done with his dress suit before Morey stopped him. Would the Board question it?

Worse, was there something about the *way* the robots consumed the stuff that would give the whole show away? Some special wear point in the robot anatomy, for instance, that would rub a hole where no human's body could, or stretch a seam that should normally be under no strain at all?

It was worrisome. But the worry was needless. When the report of survey came, Morey let out a long-held breath. *Not a single item disallowed!*

Morey was a success—and so was his scheme!

To the successful man come the rewards of success. Morey arrived home one evening after a hard day's work at the office and was alarmed to find another car parked in his drive. It was a tiny two-seater, the sort affected by top officials and the very well-to-do.

Right then and there Morey learned the first half of the embezzler's lesson: anything different is dangerous. He came uneasily into his own home, fearful that some high officer of the Ration Board had come to ask questions.

But Cherry was glowing. "Mr. Porfirio is a newspaper feature writer and he wants to write you up for their 'Consumers of Distinction' page! Morey, I *couldn't* be more proud!"

"Thanks," said Morey glumly. "Hello."

Mr. Porfirio shook Morey's hand warmly. "I'm not exactly from a newspaper," he corrected. "Trans-video Press is what it is, actually. We're a news wire service; we supply forty-seven hundred papers with news and feature material. Every one of them," he added complacently, "on the required consumption list of Grades One through Six inclusive. We have a Sunday supplement self-help feature on consuming problems and we like to—well, give credit where credit is due. You've established an enviable record, Mr. Fry. We'd like to tell our readers about it."

"Um," said Morey. "Let's go in the drawing room."

"Oh, no!" Cherry said firmly. "I want to hear this. He's so modest, Mr. Porfirio, you'd really never know what kind of a man he is just to listen to him talk. Why, my goodness, I'm his wife and I swear *I* don't know how he does all the consuming he does. He simply—"

"Have a drink, Mr. Porfirio," Morey said, against all etiquette. "Rye? Scotch? Bourbon? Gin-and-tonic? Brandy Alexander? Dry Manha—I mean what would you like?" He became conscious that he was babbling like a fool.

"Anything," said the newsman. "Rye is fine. Now, Mr. Fry, I notice you've fixed up your place very attractively here and your wife says that your country home is just as nice. As soon as I came in, I said to myself, 'Beautiful home. Hardly a stick of furniture that isn't absolutely necessary. Might be a Grade Six or Seven.' And Mrs. Fry says the other place is even barer."

"She does, does she?" Morey challenged sharply. "Well, let me tell you, Mr. Porfirio, that every last scrap of my furniture allowance is accounted for! I don't know what you're getting at, but—"

"Oh, I certainly didn't mean to imply anything like *that!* I just want to get some information from you that I can pass on to our readers. You know, to sort of help them do as well as yourself. How *do* you do it?"

Morey swallowed. "We—uh—well, we just keep after it. Hard work, that's all."

Porfirio nodded admiringly. "Hard work," he repeated, and fished a triple-folded sheet of paper out of his pocket to make notes on. "Would you say," he went on, "that anyone could do well as you simply by devoting himself to it—setting a regular schedule, for example, and keeping to it very strictly?"

"Oh, yes," said Morey.

"In other words, it's only a matter of doing what you have to do every day?"

"That's it exactly. I handle the budget in my house—

more experience than my wife, you see—but no reason a woman can't do it."

"Budgeting," Porfirio recorded approvingly. "That's our policy, too."

The interview was not the terror it had seemed, not even when Porfirio tactfully called attention to Cherry's slim waistline ("So many housewives, Mrs. Fry, find it difficult to keep from being—well, a little plump") and Morey had to invent endless hours on the exercise machines, while Cherry looked faintly perplexed, but did not interrupt.

From the interview, however, Morey learned the second half of the embezzler's lesson. After Porfirio had gone, he leaped in and spoke more than a little firmly to Cherry. "That business of exercise, dear. We really have to start doing it. I don't know if you've noticed it, but you *are* beginning to get just a trifle heavier and we don't want that to happen, do we?"

In the following grim and unnecessary sessions on the mechanical horses, Morey had plenty of time to reflect on the lesson. Stolen treasures are less sweet than one would like, when one dare not enjoy them in the open.

But some of Morey's treasures were fairly earned.

The new Bradmoor K-50 Spin-a-Game, for instance, was his very own. His job was design and creation, and he was a fortunate man in that his efforts were permitted to be expended along the line of greatest social utility— namely, to increase consumption.

The Spin-a-Game was a well-nigh perfect machine for the purpose. "Brilliant," said Wainwright, beaming, when the pilot machine had been put through its first tests. "Guess they don't call me the Talent-picker for nothing. I knew you could do it, boy!"

Even Howland was lavish in his praise. He sat munching on a plate of petits-fours (he was still only a Grade Three) while the tests were going on, and when they were over, he said enthusiastically, "It's a beauty, Morey. That series-corrupter—sensational! Never saw a prettier piece of machinery."

Morey flushed gratefully.

Wainwright left, exuding praise, and Morey patted his pilot model affectionately and admired its polychrome gleam. The looks of the machine, as Wainwright had lectured many a time, were as important as its function: "You have to make them *want* to play it, boy! They won't play it if they don't *see* it!" And consequently the whole K series was distinguished by flashing rainbows of light, provocative strains of music, haunting scents that drifted into the nostrils of the passerby with compelling effect.

Morey had drawn heavily on all the old masterpieces of design—the one-arm bandit, the pinball machine, the juke box. You put your ration book in the hopper. You spun the wheels until you selected the game you wanted to play against the machine. You punched buttons or spun dials or, in any of 325 different ways, you pitted your human skill against the magnetic-taped skills of the machine.

And you lost. You had a chance to win, but the inexorable statistics of the machine's setting made sure that if you played long enough, you had to lose.

That is to say, if you risked a ten-point ration stamp—showing, perhaps, that you had consumed three six-course meals—your statistic return was eight points. You might hit the jackpot and get a thousand points back, and thus be exempt from a whole freezerful of steaks and joints and prepared vegetables; but it seldom happened. Most likely you lost and got nothing.

Got nothing, that is, in the way of your hazarded ration stamps. But the beauty of the machine, which was Morey's main contribution, was that, win or lose, you *always* found a pellet of vitamin-drenched, sugar-coated antibiotic hormone gum in the hopper. You played your game, won or lost your stake, popped your hormone gum into your mouth and played another. By the time that game was ended, the gum was used up, the coating dissolved; you discarded it and started another.

"That's what the man from the NRB liked," Howland told Morey confidentially. "He took a set of schematics back with him; they might install it on *all* new machines. Oh, you're the fair-haired boy, all right!"

It was the first Morey had heard about a man from the National Ration Board. It was good news. He excused himself and hurried to phone Cherry the story of his latest successes. He reached her at her mother's, where she was spending the evening, and she was properly impressed and affectionate. He came back to Howland in a glowing humor.

"Drink?" said Howland diffidently.

"Sure," said Morey. He could afford, he thought, to drink as much of Howland's liquor as he liked; poor guy, sunk in the consuming quicksands of Class Three. Only fair for somebody a little more successful to give him a hand once in a while.

And when Howland, learning that Cherry had left Morey a bachelor for the evening, proposed Uncle Piggotty's again, Morey hardly hesitated at all.

The Bigelows were delighted to see him. Morey wondered briefly if they *had* a home; certainly they didn't seem to spend much time in it.

It turned out they did, because when Morey indicated virtuously that he'd only stopped in at Piggotty's for a single drink before dinner, and Howland revealed that he was free for the evening, they captured Morey and bore him off to their house.

Tanaquil Bigelow was haughtily apologetic. "I don't suppose this is the kind of place Mr. Fry is used to," she observed to her husband, right across Morey, who was standing between them. "Still, we call it home."

Morey made an appropriately polite remark. Actually, the place nearly turned his stomach. It was an enormous glaringly new mansion, bigger even than Morey's former house, stuffed to bursting with bulging sofas and pianos and massive mahogany chairs and tri-D sets and bedrooms and drawing rooms and breakfast rooms and nurseries.

The nurseries were a shock to Morey; it had never occurred to him that the Bigelows had children. But they did and though the children were only five and eight, they were still up, under the care of a brace of robot nurse-maids, doggedly playing with their overstuffed animals and miniature trains.

"You don't know what a comfort Tony and Dick are," Tanaquil Bigelow told Morey. "They consume *so* much more than their rations. Walter says that every family ought to have at least two or three children to, you know, help out. Walter's so intelligent about these things, it's a pleasure to hear him talk. Have you heard his poem, Morey? The one he calls *The Twoness of*—"

Morey hastily admitted that he had. He reconciled himself to a glum evening. The Bigelows had been eccentric but fun back at Uncle Piggotty's. On their own ground, they seemed just as eccentric, but painfully dull.

They had a round of cocktails, and another, and then the Bigelows no longer seemed so dull. Dinner was ghastly, of course; Morey was nouveau-riche enough to be a snob about his relatively Spartan table. But he minded his manners and sampled, with grim concentration, each successive course of chunky protein and rich marinades. With the help of the endless succession of table wines and liqueurs, dinner ended without destroying his evening or his strained digestive system.

And afterward, they were a pleasant company in the Bigelow's ornate drawing room. Tanaquil Bigelow, in consultation with the children, checked over their ration books and came up with the announcement that they would have a brief recital by a pair of robot dancers, followed by string music by a robot quartet. Morey prepared himself for the worst, but found before the dancers were through that he was enjoying himself. Strange lesson for Morey: When you didn't *have* to watch them, the robot entertainers were fun!

"Good night, dears," Tanaquil Bigelow said firmly to the children when the dancers were done. The boys rebelled, naturally, but they went. It was only a matter of minutes, though, before one of them was back, clutching at Morey's sleeve with a pudgy hand.

Morey looked at the boy uneasily, having little experience with children. He said, "Uh—what is it, Tony?"

"Dick, you mean," the boy said. "Gimme your autograph." He poked an engraved pad and a vulgarly jeweled pencil at Morey.

Morey dazedly signed and the child ran off, Morey staring after him. Tanaquil Bigelow laughed and explained, "He saw your name in Porfirio's column. Dick *loves* Porfirio, reads him every day. He's such an intellectual kid, really. He'd always have his nose in a book if I didn't keep after him to play with his trains and watch tri-D."

"That was quite a nice write-up," Walter Bigelow commented—a little enviously, Morey thought. "Bet you make Consumer of the Year. I wish," he sighed, "that we could get a little ahead on the quotas the way you did. But it just never seems to work out. We eat and play and consume like crazy, and somehow at the end of the month we're always a little behind in something—everything keeps piling up—and then the Board sends us a warning, and they call me down and, first thing you know, I've got a couple of hundred added penalty points and we're worse off than before."

"Never you mind," Tanaquil replied staunchly. "Consuming isn't everything in life. You have your work."

Bigelow nodded judiciously and offered Morey another drink. Another drink, however, was not what Morey needed. He was sitting in a rosy glow, less of alcohol than of sheer contentment with the world.

He said suddenly, "Listen."

Bigelow looked up from his own drink. "Eh?"

"If I tell you something that's a *secret,* will you keep it that way?"

Bigelow rumbled, "Why, I guess so, Morey."

But his wife cut in sharply, "Certainly we will, Morey. Of course! What is it?" There was a gleam in her eye,

Morey noticed. It puzzled him, but he decided to ignore it.

He said, "About that write-up. I—I'm not such a hot-shot consumer, really, you know. In fact—" All of a sudden, everyone's eyes seemed to be on him. For a tortured moment, Morey wondered if he was doing the right thing. A secret that two people know is compromised, and a secret known to three people is no secret. Still—

"It's like this," he said firmly. "You remember what we were talking about at Uncle Piggotty's that night? Well, when I went home I went down to the robot quarters, and I—"

He went on from there.

Tanaquil Bigelow said triumphantly, "I *knew* it!"

Walter Bigelow gave his wife a mild, reproving look. He declared soberly. "You've done a big thing, Morey. A mighty big thing. God willing, you've pronounced the death sentence on our society as we know it. Future generations will revere the name of Morey Fry." He solemnly shook Morey's hand.

Morey said dazedly, "I *what?*"

Walter nodded. It was a valedictory. He turned to his wife. "Tanaquil, we'll have to call an emergency meeting."

"Of course, Walter," she said devotedly.

"And Morey will have to be there. Yes, you'll have to, Morey; no excuses. We want the Brotherhood to meet you. Right, Howland?"

Howland coughed uneasily. He nodded noncommittally and took another drink.

Morey demanded desperately, "What are you talking about? Howland, you tell me!"

Howland fiddled with his drink. "Well," he said, "it's like Tan was telling you that night. A few of us, well, politically mature persons have formed a little group. We—"

"*Little* group!" Tanaquil Bigelow said scornfully. "Howland, sometimes I wonder if you really catch the spirit of the thing at all! It's everybody, Morey, everybody in the world. Why, there are eighteen of us right here in Old Town! There are *scores more* all over the world! I knew you were up to something like this, Morey. I told Walter so the morning after we met you. I said, 'Walter, mark my words, that man Morey is up to something.' But I must say," she admitted worshipfully, "I didn't know it would have the *scope* of what you're proposing now! Imagine—a whole world of consumers, rising as one man, shouting the name of Morey Fry, fighting the Ration Board with the Board's own weapon—the robots. What poetic justice!"

Bigelow nodded enthusiastically. "Call Uncle Piggotty's, dear," he ordered. "See if you can round up a quorum right now! Meanwhile, Morey and I are going belowstairs. Let's go, Morey—let's get the new world started!"

Morey sat there open-mouthed. He closed it with a snap. "Bigelow," he whispered, "do you mean to say that you're going to spread this idea around through some kind of subversive organization?"

"Subversive?" Bigelow repeated stiffly. "My dear man, *all* creative minds are subversive, whether they operate singly or in such a group as the Brotherhood of Freemen. I scarcely like—"

"Never mind what you like," Morey insisted. "You're going to call a meeting of this Brotherhood and you want *me* to tell them what I just told you. Is that right?"

"Well—yes."

Morey got up. "I wish I could say it's been nice, but it hasn't. Good night!"

And he stormed out before they could stop him.

Out on the street, though, his resolution deserted him. He hailed a robot cab and ordered the driver to take him on the traditional time-killing ride through the park while he made up his mind.

The fact that he had left, of course, was not going to keep Bigelow from going through with his announced intention. Morey remembered, now, fragments of conversation from Bigelow and his wife at Uncle Piggotty's, and cursed himself. They had, it was perfectly true, said and hinted enough about politics and purposes to put him on his guard. All that nonsense about twoness had diverted him from what should have been perfectly clear: They were subversives indeed.

He glanced at his watch. Late, but not too late; Cherry would still be at her parents' home.

He leaned forward and gave the driver their address. It was like beginning the first of a hundred-shot series of injections: you know it's going to cure you, but it hurts just the same.

Morey said manfully: "And that's it, sir. I know I've been a fool. I'm willing to take the consequences."

Old Elon rubbed his jaw thoughtfully. "Um," he said.

Cherry and her mother had long passed the point where they could say anything at all; they were seated side by side on a couch across the room, listening with expressions of strain and incredulity.

Elon said abruptly, "Excuse me. Phone call to make." He left the room to make a brief call and returned. He said over his shoulder to his wife, "Coffee. We'll need it. Got a problem here."

Morey said, "Do you think—I mean what should I do?"

Elon shrugged, then, surprisingly, grinned. "What can you do?" he demanded cheerfully. "Done plenty already, I'd say. Drink some coffee. Call I made," he explained, "was to Jim, my law clerk. He'll be here in a minute. Get some dope from Jim, then we'll know better."

Cherry came over to Morey and sat beside him. All she said was, "Don't worry," but to Morey it conveyed all the meaning in the world. He returned the pressure of her hand with a feeling of deepest relief. Hell, he said to himself, why *should* I worry? Worst they can do to me is drop me a couple of grades, and what's so bad about that?

He grimaced involuntarily. He had remembered his

own early struggles as a Class One and what *was* so bad about that.

The law clerk arrived, a smallish robot with a battered stainless-steel hide and dull coppery features. Elon took the robot aside for a terse conversation before he came back to Morey.

"As I thought," he said in satisfaction. "No precedent. No laws prohibiting. Therefore no crime."

"Thank heaven!" Morey said in ecstatic relief.

Elon shook his head. "They'll probably give you a reconditioning and you can't expect to keep your Grade Five. Probably call it anti-social behavior. Is, isn't it?"

Dashed, Morey said, "Oh." He frowned briefly, then looked up. "All right, Dad, if I've got it coming to me, I'll take my medicine."

"Way to talk," Elon said approvingly. "Now go home. Get a good night's sleep. First thing in the morning, go to the Ration Board. Tell 'em the whole story, beginning to end. They'll be easy on you." Elon hesitated. "Well, fairly easy," he amended. "I hope."

The condemned man ate a hearty breakfast.

He had to. That morning, as Morey awoke, he had the sick certainty that he was going to be consuming triple rations for a long, long time to come.

He kissed Cherry good-by and took the long ride to the Ration Board in silence. He even left Henry behind.

At the Board, he stammered at a series of receptionist robots and was finally brought into the presence of a mildly supercilious young man named Hachette.

"My name," he started, "is Morey Fry. I—I've come to—talk over something I've been doing with—"

"Certainly, Mr. Fry," said Hachette. "I'll take you in to Mr. Newman right away."

"Don't you want to know what I did?" demanded Morey.

Hachette smiled. "What makes you think we don't know?" he said, and left.

That was Surprise Number One.

Newman explained it. He grinned at Morey and ruefully shook his head. "All the time we get this," he complained. "People just don't take the trouble to learn anything about the world around them. Son," he demanded, "what do you think a robot is?"

Morey said, "Huh?"

"I mean how do you think it operates? Do you think it's just a kind of a man with a tin skin and wire nerves?"

"Why, no. It's a machine, of course. It isn't *human*."

Newman beamed. "Fine!" he said. "It's a machine. It hasn't got flesh or blood or intestines—or a brain. Oh—" he held up a hand—"robots are *smart* enough. I don't mean that. But an electronic thinking machine, Mr. Fry, takes about as much space as the house you're living in. It has to. Robots don't carry brains around with them; brains are too heavy and much too bulky."

"Then how do they think?"

"With their brains, of course."

"But you just said—"

"I said they didn't *carry* them. Each robot is in constant radio communication with the Master Control on its TBR circuit—the 'Talk Between Robots' radio. Master Control gives the answer; the robot acts."

"I see," said Morey. "Well, that's very interesting but—"

"But you still don't see," said Newman. "Figure it out. If the robot gets information from Master Control, do you see that Master Control in return necessarily gets information from the robot?"

"Oh," said Morey. Then, louder, "Oh! You mean that all my robots have been—" The words wouldn't come.

Newman nodded in satisfaction. "Every bit of information of that sort comes to us as a matter of course. Why, Mr. Fry, if you hadn't come in today, we would have been sending for you within a very short time."

That was the second surprise. Morey bore up under it bravely. After all, it changed nothing, he reminded himself.

He said, "Well, be that as it may, sir, here I am. I

:ame in of my own free will. I've been using my robots to
:onsume my ration quotas—"

"Indeed you have," said Newman.

"—and I'm willing to sign a statement to that effect
any time you like. I don't know what the penalty is, but
I'll take it. I'm guilty; I admit my guilt."

Newman's eyes were wide. "Guilty?" he repeated.
"Penalty?"

Morey was startled. "Why, yes," he said. "I'm not
denying anything."

"Penalties," repeated Newman musingly. Then he began to laugh. He laughed, Morey thought, to considerable
excess; Morey saw nothing he could laugh at, himself, in
the situation. But the situation, Morey was forced to admit, was rapidly getting completely incomprehensible.

"Sorry," said Newman at last, wiping his eyes, "but I
couldn't help it. Penalties! Well, Mr. Fry, let me set your
mind at rest. I wouldn't worry about the penalties if I
were you. As soon as the reports began coming through
on what you had done with your robots, we naturally assigned a special team to keep observing you, and we for-
warded a report to the national headquarters. We made
certain—ah—recommendations in it and—well, to make
a long story short, the answers came back yesterday.

"Mr. Fry, the National Ration Board is delighted to
know of your contribution toward improving our distribution problem. Pending a further study, a tentative program has been adopted for setting up consuming-robot
units all over the country based on your scheme. Penalties? Mr. Fry, you're a *hero!*"

A hero has responsibilities. Morey's were quickly made
clear to him. He was allowed time for a brief reassuring
visit to Cherry, a triumphal tour of his old office, and then
he was rushed off to Washington to be quizzed. He found
the National Ration Board in a frenzy of work.

"The most important job we've ever done," one of the
high officers told him. "I wouldn't be surprised if it's the
last one we ever have! Yes, sir, we're trying to put our-

selves out of business for good and we don't want a single thing to go wrong."

"Anything I can do to help—" Morey began diffidently.

"You've done fine, Mr. Fry. Gave us just the push we've been needing. It was there all the time for us to see, but we were too close to the forest to see the trees, if you get what I mean. Look, I'm not much on rhetoric and this is the biggest step mankind has taken in centuries and I can't put it into words. Let me show you what we've been doing."

He and a delegation of other officials of the Ration Board and men whose names Morey had repeatedly seen in the newspapers took Morey on an inspection tour of the entire plant.

"It's a closed cycle, you see," he was told, as they looked over a chamber of industriously plodding consumer-robots working off a shipment of shoes. "Nothing is permanently lost. If you want a car, you get one of the newest and best. If not, your car gets driven by a robot until it's ready to be turned in and a new one gets built for next year. We don't lose the metals—they can be salvaged. All we lose is a little power and labor. And the Sun and the atom give us all the power we need, and the robots give us more labor than we can use. Same thing applies, of course, to all products."

"But what's in it for the robots?" Morey asked.

"I beg your pardon?" one of the biggest men in the country said uncomprehendingly.

Morey had a difficult moment. His analysis had conditioned him against waste and this decidedly was sheer destruction of goods, no matter how scientific the jargon might be.

"If the consumer is just using up things for the sake of using them up," he said doggedly, realizing the danger he was inviting, "we could use wear-and-tear machines instead of robots. After all why waste *them?*"

They looked at each other worriedly.

"But that's what *you* were doing," one pointed out with
a faint note of threat.

"Oh, no!" Morey quickly objected. "I built in satisfaction circuits—my training in design, you know. Adjustable circuits, of course."

"Satisfaction circuits?" he was asked. "Adjustable?"

"Well, sure. If the robot gets no satisfaction out of using up things—"

"Don't talk nonsense," growled the Ration Board official. "Robots aren't human. How do you make them
feel satisfaction? And adjustable satisfaction at that!"

Morey explained. It was a highly technical explanation,
involving the use of great sheets of paper and elaborate
diagrams. But there were trained men in the group and
they became even more excited than before.

"Beautiful!" one cried in scientific rapture. "Why, it
takes care of every possible moral, legal and psychological argument!"

"What does?" the Ration Board official demanded.
"How?"

"You tell him, Mr. Fry."

Morey tried and couldn't. But he could *show* how his
principle operated. The Ration Board lab was turned over
to him, complete with more assistants than he knew how
to give orders to, and they built satisfaction circuits for
a squad of robots working in a hat factory.

Then Morey gave his demonstration. The robots manufactured hats of all sorts. He adjusted the circuits at the
end of the day and the robots began trying on the hats,
squabbling over them, each coming away triumphantly
with a huge and diverse selection. Their metallic features
were incapable of showing pride or pleasure, but both
were evident in the way they wore their hats, their fierce
possessiveness . . . and their faster, neater, more intensive,
more *dedicated* work to produce a still greater quantity of
hats . . . which they also were allowed to own.

"You see?" an engineer exclaimed delightedly. "They
can be adjusted to *want* hats, to wear them lovingly, to

wear the hats to pieces. And not just for the sake of wearing them out—the hats are an incentive for them!"

"But how can we go on producing just hats and more hats?" the Ration Board man asked puzzledly. "Civilization does not live by hats alone."

"That," said Morey modestly, "is the beauty of it. Look."

He set the adjustment of the satisfaction circuit as porter-robots brought in skids of gloves. The hat-manufacturing robots fought over the gloves with the same mechanical passion as they had for hats.

"And that can apply to anything we—or the robots—produce," Morey added. "Everything from pins to yachts. But the point is that they get satisfaction from possession, and the craving can be regulated according to the glut in various industries, and the robots show their appreciation by working harder." He hesitated. "That's what I did for my servant-robots. It's a feedback, you see. Satisfaction leads to more work—and *better* work—and that means more goods, which they can be made to want, which means incentive to work, and so on, all around."

"Closed cycle," whispered the Ration Board man in awe. "A *real* closed cycle this time!"

And so the inexorable laws of supply and demand were irrevocably repealed. No longer was mankind hampered by inadequate supply or drowned by overproduction. What mankind needed was there. What the race did not require passed into the insatiable—and adjustable—robot maw. Nothing was wasted.

For a pipeline has two ends.

Morey was thanked, complimented, rewarded, given a ticker-tape parade through the city, and put on a plane back home. By that time, the Ration Board had liquidated itself.

Cherry met him at the airport. They jabbered excitedly at each other all the way to the house.

In their own living room, they finished the kiss they

had greeted each other with. At last Cherry broke away, laughing.

Morey said, "Did I tell you I'm through with Bradmoor? From now on I work for the Board as civilian consultant. *And,*" he added impressively, "starting right away, I'm a Class Eight!"

"My!" gasped Cherry, so worshipfully that Morey felt a twinge of conscience.

He said honestly, "Of course, if what they were saying in Washington is so, the classes aren't going to mean much pretty soon. Still, it's quite an honor."

"It certainly is," Cherry said staunchly. "Why, Dad's only a Class Eight himself and he's been a judge for I don't know *how* many years."

Morey pursed his lips. "We can't all be fortunate," he said generously. "Of course, the classes still will count for *something*—that is, a Class One will have so much to consume in a year; a Class Two will have a little less; and so on. But each person in each class will have robot help, you see, to do the actual consuming. The way it's going to be, special facsimile robots will—"

Cherry flagged him down. "I know, dear. Each family gets a robot duplicate of every person in the family."

"Oh," said Morey, slightly annoyed. "How did you know?"

"Ours came yesterday," she explained. "The man from the Board said we were the first in the area—because it was your idea, of course. They haven't even been activated yet. I've still got them in the Green Room. Want to see them?"

"Sure," said Morey buoyantly. He dashed ahead of Cherry to inspect the results of his own brainstorm. There they were, standing statue-still against the wall, waiting to be energized to begin their endless tasks.

"Yours is real pretty," Morey said gallantly. "But— say, is that thing supposed to look like me?" He inspected the chromium face of the man-robot disapprovingly.

"Only roughly, the man said." Cherry was right behind him. "Notice anything else?"

Morey leaned closer, inspecting the features of the facsimile robot at a close range. "Well, no," he said. "It's got a kind of a squint that I don't like, but—Oh, you mean *that!*" He bent over to examine a smaller robot, half hidden between the other pair. It was less than two feet high, big-headed, pudgy-limbed, thick-bellied. In fact, Morey thought wonderingly, it looked almost like—

"My God!" Morey spun around, staring wide eyed at his wife. "You mean—"

"I mean," said Cherry, blushing slightly.

Morey reached out to grab her in his arms.

"Darling!" he cried. "Why didn't you *tell* me?"

Did you ever have one of those days when the TV set goes on the blink, the electric company reports it's going to have to disconnect all the houses on your block overnight, the dishwasher breaks, the sewer people dig up your driveway, and your boss tells you that starting March 1st you are going to be replaced by an electronic machine?

If you did, did you ever think that one day your whole life might be like that?

NEW APPLES IN THE GARDEN

Kris Neville

Eddie Hibbs reported for work and was almost immediately called out on an emergency. It was the third morning in succession for emergencies.

This time a section of distribution cable had blown in West Los Angeles. Blown cable was routine, but each instance merited the attention of an assistant underground supervisor.

Eddie climbed down the manhole with the foreman of the maintenance crew. There were deep pull marks on the lead sheath above where the cable had blown.

"Where'd they get it?" he asked.

"It came in from a job on the East Side."

"Sloppy work," Eddie said. "Water got in the splice?"

"These new guys . . ." the foreman said.

Eddie fingered the pull marks. "I think she's about shot anyway. How much is like this?"

"A couple of hundred feet."

"All this bad?"

"Yep."

Eddie whistled. "About fifteen thousand dollars' worth. Well. Cut her back to here and make splices. Stand over them while they do it."

"I'll need two men for a week."

"I'll try to find them for you. Send through the paper."

"I can probably find maybe another thousand miles or so that's about this bad."

"Don't bother," Eddie said.

That was Eddie's productive work during the morning. With traffic and two sections of street torn up by the water people, he did not get back to his office until just before lunch. He listened to the Stock Market reports while he drove.

He learned that spiraling costs had retarded the modernization program of General Electronics and much of their present equipment was obsolete in terms of current price factors. He was also told to anticipate that declining sales would lead to declining production, thereby perpetuating an unfortunate cycle. And finally he was warned that General Electronics was an example of the pitfalls involved in investing in the so-called High-Growth stocks.

Eddie turned off the radio in the parking lot as the closing Dow-Jones report was starting.

During lunch, he succeeded in reading two articles in a six-week-old issue of *Electrical World,* the only one of the dozen technical journals he found time for now.

At 12:35 word filtered into the department that one of the maintenance crew, Ramon Lopez, had been killed. A forty-foot ladder broke while atop it Lopez was hosing down a pothead, and he was driven backward into the concrete pavement by the high-pressure water.

Eddie tried to identify the man. The name was distantly familiar but there was no face to go with it. Finally the face came. He smoked two cigarettes in succession. He stubbed the last one out angrily.

"That was a tough one," his supervisor, Forester, said, sitting on the side of Eddie's desk. Normally exuberant, he was left melancholy and distracted by the accident. "You know the guy?"

"To speak to."

"Good man."

"After I thought about it a little bit," Eddie said, "I

remembered he was transferring tomorrow. Something like this brings a man up short, doesn't it?"

"A hell of a shame. Just a hell of a shame."

They were silent for a minute.

"How was the market this morning?" Forester asked.

"Up again. I didn't catch the closing averages."

"I guess that makes a new high."

"Third straight day," Eddie said.

"Hell of a shame," Forester said.

"Yeah, Lopez was a nice guy."

"Well . . ." Forester's voice trailed off in embarrassment.

"Yeah, well . . ."

"I wanted to remind you about the budget meeting." Eddie glanced at his watch. "Hour and a half?"

"Yeah. You know, I feel like . . . never mind. What about the burial transformers, you get on it yet?"

"The ones we're running in the water mains for cooling? They're out of warranty. None of the local shops can rewind them until the manufacturer sends out a field engineer to set them up for the encapsulation process."

"How long is that going to take?" Forester asked.

"They tell me several months. Still doesn't leave us with anything. The plant says they've fixed the trouble, but between them and the rewind shop, they can buck it back and forth forever."

"I guess we'll have to go back to the pad-mounted type."

"People with the Gold Medallion Homes aren't going to like the pads by their barbecues."

Forester uncoiled a leg. "Draw up a memorandum on it, will you, Eddie?" He stood up. "That thing sure got me today. There's just entirely too many of these accidents. A ladder breaking. I don't know."

Eddie tried to find something intelligent to say. Finally he said, "It was a rough one, all right."

After Forester left, Eddie picked up, listlessly from the top of the stack one of the preliminary reports submitted for his approval.

The report dealt with three thousand capacitors purchased last year from an Eastern firm, now bankrupt. The capacitors were beginning to leak. Eddie called the electrical laboratory to see what progress was being made on the problem.

The supervisor refreshed his memory from the records. He reported: "I don't have any adhesive man to work on it. Purchasing has half a dozen suppliers lined up—but none have any test data. I don't know when we'll get the time. We're on a priority program checking out these new, low-cost terminations."

"Can't we certify the adhesive to some AIEE spec or something?" Eddie asked.

"I don't know of any for sealing capacitors, Eddie. Not on the maintenance end, at least."

"Maybe Purchasing can get a guarantee from one of the suppliers?"

"For the hundred dollars of compound that's involved? What good would that do us?"

Eddie thanked him and hung up. He signed the preliminary report.

He turned to the next one.

At 2:30 Forester came by and the two of them made their way between the jig-saw projections of maple and mahogany to the Conference Room.

Fourteen men were involved in the conference, all from operating departments. They shuffled in over a five minute period, found seats, lit cigarettes, talked and joked with one another.

When one of the assistants to the manager came in, they fell silent.

"Gentlemen," he said, "I think I'd better get right to the point today. The Construction Program in the Valley has now used up two bond issues. The voters aren't going to approve a third one."

He paused for effect then continued briskly: "I see by the morning's *Times* that the Mayor is appointing a watchdog commission. I guess you all saw it, too. The Department of Water and Power of the City of Los

Angeles is going to be badly—and I mean badly—in the red at the end of the fiscal year.

"We're in hot water.

"We do not seem to be getting through to the operating departments regarding the necessity for cost reduction. I have here last month's breakdown on the Bunker Hill substation 115 KV installation. Most of you have seen it already, I think. I had it sent around. Now—"

The analysis continued for some ten minutes to conclude with an explosion:

"We've got to impose a ten per cent across the board cut on operating expenses."

One of the listeners, more alert than the rest, asked, "That go for salaries?"

"For personnel making more than eight hundred dollars a month it does."

There was a moment of shocked silence.

"You can't make that stick," one of the supervisors said. "Half my best men will be out tomorrow looking for better offers—and finding them, too."

"I'm just passing on what I was told."

The men in the room shuffled and muttered under their breaths.

"O.K., that's the way they want it," one of the supervisors said.

"I've brought along the notices for the affected personnel. Please see they're distributed when you leave."

After the meeting, Forester walked with Eddie back to his desk.

"You be in tomorrow, Eddie?"

"I guess I will, Les. I really don't know, yet."

"I'd hate to lose you."

"It's going to make it pretty rough. A man's fixed expenses don't come down."

"I'll see what I can do for you; maybe upgrade the classification."

"Thanks, Les."

Back at his desk, Eddie looked at his watch. Nearly

time for the Safety Meeting. Lost-time injuries had been climbing for the last four months.

While waiting, he signed a sixty-three page preliminary report recommending a program for the orderly replacement of all transmission and distribution cable installed prior to 1946. It was estimated that the savings, in the long run, would total some quarter of a billion dollars. The initial expense, however, was astronomical.

After the Safety Meeting, Eddie prepared another memorandum indicating the acute need for a better training program and an increase in maintenance personnel. Shortage of qualified technicians was chronic.

At four twenty-five, the night supervisor phoned in to say he was having engine trouble with his new car and would be delayed until about six o'clock. Eddie agreed to wait for him.

Eddie dialed home to let his wife, Lois, know he would be late again. A modulated low-frequency note told him the home phone was out of order.

Ray Morely, one of the night-shift engineers, came in with coffee. "You still here, Eddie?"

"Yeah, until Wheeler makes it. His car's down."

"Market hit a new high."

"Yeah. I guess you heard about the meeting today?"

Ray sipped coffee. "Budget again? I missed the day crew. I got hung up in traffic and was a little late."

"A pay cut goes with it, this time."

"You're kidding?"

"Been by your desk yet?"

"No."

"I'm not kidding. Ten per cent for those making about eight hundred."

"Nobody's going to put up with that," Ray said. "We're in an engineering shortage. We've got ICBMs rusting in their silos all over the country because we can't afford the engineering maintenance—that's how bad it is. Everybody'll quit."

"I don't think they'll make it stick. Ramon Lopez,

one of the truck crew, was killed today hosing down a high-voltage pothead."

"No kidding?"

Eddie told him about the accident.

"That was a rough one to lose, wasn't it?"

The phone rang.

Ray said, "I'll get it."

He listened for a minute and hung up. "There's an outage in the Silver Lake Area. The brakes on a bus failed and took out an overhead section."

Eddie sat back. "No sense in you going. With work traffic on the surface streets until the freeway gets fixed, they won't get the truck there until 6:30 or so."

"Right." Ray drank coffee reflectively. "You going looking?"

"I'm an old-timer. I got a lot of seniority. How about you?"

"I got bills. It's going to cost me near a hundred a month—that's a steep bite."

"I still think they'll back off."

"They'll have to," Ray said. "If not right now, when the pressure gets on. You ask me, we've got them by the short hair." He settled into the chair. "I see it as an organic phenomenon. When society gets as complex as ours, it has to grow more and more engineers. But there's a feedback circuit in effect. The more engineers we grow, the more complex society becomes. Each new one creates the need for two more. I get a sort of feeling of—I don't know—vitality, I guess, when I walk into, say, an automated factory. All that machinery and all that electronic gear is like a single cell in a living organism—an organism that's growing every day, multiplying like bacteria. And it's always sick, and we're the doctors. That's job security. We're riding the wave of the future. I don't think they'll make a salary cut stick."

"I hope you're right," Eddie said.

Eddie checked out at 7:15, when the night supervisor

finally arrived. As he left the building, he noted that a
burglar alarm down the street had gone off; probably
because of a short circuit. The clanking set his nerves on
edge. Apprehensively he felt a rising wind against his
cheeks.

At home, he was greeted with a perfunctory kiss at the
door.

"Honey," Lois told him, "you took the checkbook, and
I didn't have any money."

"Something come up? I'm sorry."

"We're all out of milk. The milk man didn't come
today. Their homogenizing machinery broke down. I
phoned the dairy about nine; and then, of course, the
phone has been on the blink since about eleven or a
little before, so I couldn't ask you to bring some home."

"I kept trying to get you."

"I figured you had to work late again, when you
weren't here at six, and I knew you'd be here when
you got here."

Eddie sat down and she sat on the chair arm beside
him. "How did it go today?"

He started to tell her about the wage cut and Ramon
Lopez; but then he didn't want to talk about it. "So-so,"
he said. "There was an outage over in the Silver Lake
Area just before I left."

"Fixed yet?"

"I doubt it," he said. "Probably a couple of more
hours."

"Gee," she said, "when I think of all that meat in the
deep freezer . . ."

"I wouldn't stock so much," he said. "I really
wouldn't."

She twisted away from him. "Honey. I'm jittery. Something's . . . I don't know. In the air, I guess."

The wind rattled the windows.

While Lois was warming dinner, his son came in.

"Hi, Eddie."

"Hi, Larry."

"Eddie, when we gonna get the TV fixed?"

Eddie put down the newspaper. "We just don't have a hundred dollars or so right now." He searched for matches on the table by the chair. "Lois, oh, Lois, where're the matches?"

She came in. "They were all out Friday at the store, and I keep forgetting to lay in a supply. Use my lighter over there."

"About the TV—"

Lois was wiping her hands on the paper towel she had brought with her. "Replacement parts are hard to find for the older sets," she said. "Anyway. I read today Channel Three finally went off the air. That leaves only Two and Seven. And the programs aren't any good, now, are they? All those commercials and all?"

"They do use a lot of old stuff I've already seen," the son admitted, "but every once in a while there's something new."

"Let's talk about it some other time, Larry, O.K.?" Eddie said. "How's that? It's almost your bedtime. Studies done?"

"All but the Library report."

"Well, finish it, and—"

"I got to read the book down there. Two classes assigned it and they don't have the copies to let us check out. And I want to ask you about something, Eddie."

"Daddy's tired. His dinner's on. Come on, Eddie. I'll set it right now. And Larry, you've already eaten . . ."

After dinner, Eddie got back to the paper, the evening *Times*. It was down to eight pages, mostly advertising. There was a front-page editorial reluctantly announcing a price increase.

"They raise the price once more, and we'll just quit taking it," Lois said. "You read about the airplane crash in Florida? Wasn't that terrible? What do you think caused it?"

"Metal fatigue, probably," Eddie said. "It was a twenty-year-old jet."

"The company said it wasn't that at all."

"They always do," Eddie said.

"I don't guess the payroll check came today or you'd have mentioned it."

"Payroll's still all balled up. Somebody pressed a wrong button on the new machine and some fifty thousand un-coded cards got scattered all over the office."

"Oh, no! What do the poor people, who don't have bank accounts, do?"

"Just wait, like we wait."

"You had a bad day," Lois said. "I can tell."

"No . . ." Eddie said. "Not really, I guess."

"Still working on Saturday?"

"I guess so. Nothing was said. Maybe it'll get easier after the end of the month."

"You said it was all that new construction work in the Valley that's making you so shorthanded."

"That's part of it."

"They're not scheduled to finish until . . . when, sometime next year, isn't it?"

"The end of '81 right now."

"Eddie! Listen to me! I hardly ever see you any more. You're not going to have to put in all this overtime for the next two years!"

"Of course not," Eddie said. "Maybe after this month, that's all, and the work load will level off."

Larry, dressed for bed, came in. "Eddie?"

"Your father's tired."

"I want to ask him something."

"What is it, Larry?" Eddie asked.

"Eddie, you know the little culture I was running for science class? Something's wrong. Will you look at it?"

"Daddy's . . ."

"I'll look at it, Lois." Eddie accompanied his son to his son's room.

"What do you think is wrong, Dad?"

"Well, let's see . . . ."

"What is it?" Larry asked. "What made it stop growing?"

Eddie did not answer for a minute. Then: "You start with one or two . . . well, it's like this, Larry. I'm afraid it's dead. They grow exponentially. Figure out how much money you'd have at the end of a month if you started with just a penny and doubled your money every day. In just a little while, you'd have all the money in the world. Figure it out sometime. Things that grow exponentially, they just don't know when to quit. And your culture, here, it grew until the environment could no longer support it and all at once the food was eaten up and it died."

"I . . . see. . . . Something like that could just grow until it took over the whole world, couldn't it?"

Again Eddie was silent for a moment. Then he rumpled his son's hair. "That's science fiction, Larry."

Later, while they were listening to FM, there was a news break reporting a fire out of control in South Los Angeles.

"That's near Becky's, I'll bet," she said. "I better phone."

The phone was still out of order.

"I sure feel cut off without a phone."

After an interlude of music, Lois said, "Larry wants to be an engineer, now. I guess after what you said, maybe that's a pretty good thing."

Eddie looked up from his cigarette. "Why this all of a sudden?"

"One of his teachers told him what you said—there's a growing engineering shortage."

"I thought he wanted to be an astronaut."

"You know Larry. That was last week. His teacher said we're not going to start up the space program again. It's too expensive. We just don't have the technical manpower and materials to spare."

"We are in . . . But these kids, young kids they're turning out—they aren't getting the education today. And if anything, I sometimes think it almost makes our jobs even worse, correcting their mistakes. I sometimes wonder where it's all going to stop."

There was more news from the fire front.

Fire fighters were having a very difficult time. Two water mains had broken and the pressure was dropping. The fire was reported to have been caused by the explosion of a gas main. Rising winds did not promise to abate until dawn.

"I sure wish I could get through to Beck," Lois said. "Oh, I guess I told you, did I? Her sister has hypoglycemia, they found out. That's why she's been tired all the time."

"Never heard of it."

"Low blood sugar. It's caused by an overactive gland on the pancreas. And treatment is just the opposite of what you'd think, too. I'll bet you'd never guess. If you increase the amount of sugar in the diet, the gland becomes just that much more active to get rid of it and the hypoglycemia gets worse. It's what I'll bet you engineers call a feedback. Isn't that what you call it? Well . . . the way doctors treat it is to *reduce* the amount of sugar you eat. And after a little bit, the pancreas gets back its normal function, and the patient gets well. I told you you'd never guess!"

After a long time, Eddie said, very softly, "Oh."

Just after midnight, they went to bed.

"I've been . . ." Lois began and then stopped. "I don't know. Jumpy. The market was up again today. Another all-time high. Do you think there'll be another Crash? Like 'way back in 1929."

She could feel him lying tense beside her in the darkness. "No," he said slowly, "I don't think so. I don't think there'll be a Crash."

In spite of the warmth of the room, she could not

suppress an involuntary shudder whose cause was nameless. Suddenly, she did not want to ask any more questions.

The wind was rattling the windows.

Well, all right, you say, but I've heard all these warnings before. Fairfield Osborn was yacking about this
stuff a quarter of a century ago, and somebody else
fifty years before him, and if you come right down to it,
probably Cain slew Abel because he got tired of hearing him grouse about how things had gone downhill
since the Garden of Eden. And we're still alive, aren't
we?

Sure we are, friend. But think of this: sooner or later
the world will end. At that time, the one generation
then alive will turn out to be correct in its prophecies
of doom.

How do you know this isn't the one? How do you
know that *this* isn't—

THE YEAR OF THE JACKPOT

Robert A. Heinlein

I

At first Potiphar Breen did not notice the girl who was
undressing.

She was standing at a bus stop only ten feet away. He
was indoors, but that would not have kept him from
noticing; he was seated in a drugstore booth adjacent to
the bus stop; there was nothing between Potiphar and
the young lady but plate glass and an occasional pedestrian.

Nevertheless he did not look up when she began to
peel. Propped up in front of him was a Los Angeles
Times; beside it, still unopened, were the *Herald-Express*
and the *Daily News.* He was scanning the newspaper
carefully, but the headline stories got only a passing
glance.

He noted the maximum and minimum temperatures in
Brownsville, Texas, and entered them in a neat black
notebook. He did the same with the closing prices of

three blue chips and two dogs on the New York Exchange, as well as the total number of shares.

He then began a rapid sifting of minor news stories, from time to time entering briefs of them in his little book.

The items he recorded seemed randomly unrelated—among them were a publicity release in which Miss National Cottage Cheese Week announced that she intended to marry and have twelve children by a man who could prove that he had been a lifelong vegetarian, a circumstantial but wildly unlikely Flying Saucer report, and a call for prayers for rain throughout Southern California.

Potiphar had just written down the names and addresses of three residents of Watts, California, who had been miraculously healed at a tent meeting of the God-is-All First Truth Brethren by the Reverend Dickie Bottomley, the eight-year-old evangelist, and was preparing to tackle the *Herald-Express,* when he glanced over his reading glasses and saw the amateur ecdysiast on the street corner outside.

He stood up, placed his glasses in their case, folded the newspapers and put them carefully in his right coat pocket, counted out the exact amount of his check and added fifteen per cent. He then took his raincoat from a hook, placed it over his arm, and went outside.

By now the girl was practically down to the buff. It seemed to Potiphar Breen that she had quite a lot of buff, yet she had not pulled much of a house. The corner newsboy had stopped hawking his disasters and was grinning at her, and a mixed pair of transvestites who were apparently waiting for the bus had their eyes on her. None of the passers-by stopped. They glanced at her, and then, with the self-conscious indifference to the unusual of the true Southern Californian, they went on their various ways.

The transvestites were frankly staring. The male member of the team wore a frilly feminine blouse, but his skirt was a conservative Scottish kilt. His female companion wore a business suit and Homburg hat; she stared with lively interest.

As Breen approached, the girl hung a scrap of nylon on the bus stop bench, then reached for her shoes. A police officer, looking hot and unhappy, crossed with the lights and came up to them.

"Okay," he said in a tired voice, "that'll be all, lady. Get them duds back on and clear out of here."

The female transvestite took a cigar out of her mouth. "Just what business is it of yours, officer?" she asked.

The cop turned to her. "Keep out of this!" He ran his eyes over her getup, and that of her companion. "I ought to run both of you in, too."

The transvestite raised her eyebrows. "Arrest us for being clothed, arrest her for not being. I think I'm going to like this." She turned to the girl, who was standing still and saying nothing, as if she were puzzled by what was going on. "I'm a lawyer, dear." She pulled a card from her vest pocket. "If this uniformed Neanderthal persists in annoying you, I'll be delighted to handle him."

The man in kilts said, "Grace! Please!"

She shook him off. "Quiet, Norman. This *is* our business." She went on to the policeman, "Well? Call the wagon. In the meantime, my client will answer no questions."

The official looked unhappy enough to cry, and his face was getting dangerously red. Breen quietly stepped forward and slipped his raincoat around the shoulders of the girl.

She looked startled and spoke for the first time. "Uh—thanks." She pulled the coat about her, cape fashion.

The female attorney glanced at Breen then back to the cop. "Well, officer? Ready to arrest us?"

He shoved his face close to hers. "I ain't going to give you the satisfaction!" He sighed and added, "Thanks, Mr. Breen. You know this lady?"

"I'll take care of her. You can forget it, Kawonski."

"I sure hope so. If she's with you, I'll do just that. But get her out of here, Mr. Breen—please!"

The lawyer interrupted. "Just a moment. You're interfering with my client."

Kawonski said, "Shut up, you! You heard Mr. Breen —she's with him. Right, Mr. Breen?"

"Well—yes. I'm a friend. I'll take care of her."

The transvestite said suspiciously. "I didn't hear *her* say that."

Her companion said, "Grace! There's our bus."

"And I didn't hear her say she was your client," the cop retorted. "You look like a—" his words were drowned out by the bus brakes—"and besides that, if you don't climb on that bus and get off my territory, I'll . . . I'll . . ."

"You'll what?"

"Grace! We'll miss our bus."

"Just a moment, Norman. Dear, is this man really a friend of yours? Are you with him?"

The girl looked uncertainly at Breen, then said in a low voice, "Uh, yes. He is. I am."

"Well . . ." The lawyer's companion pulled at her arm. She shoved her card into Breen's hand and got on the bus. It pulled away.

Breen pocketed the card.

Kawonski wiped his forehead. "Why did you do it, lady?" he said peevishly.

The girl looked puzzled. "I—I don't know."

"You hear that, Mr. Breen? That's what they all say. And if you pull 'em in, there's six more the next day. The Chief said—" He sighed. "The Chief said—well, if I had arrested her like that female shyster wanted me to, I'd be out at a Hundred and Ninety-sixth and Ploughed Ground tomorrow morning, thinking about retirement. So get her out of here, will you?"

The girl said, "But—"

"No 'buts', lady. Just be glad a real gentleman like Mr. Breen is willing to help you." He gathered up her clothes, handed them to her. When she reached for them, she again exposed an uncustomary amount of skin. Kawonski hastily gave the clothing to Breen instead, who crowded them into his coat pockets.

She let Breen lead her to where his car was parked, got in and tucked the raincoat around her so that she was rather more dressed than a girl usually is. She looked at him.

She saw a medium-sized and undistinguished man who was slipping down the wrong side of thirty-five and looked older. His eyes had that mild and slightly naked look of the habitual spectacles-wearer who is not at the moment with glasses. His hair was gray at the temples and thin on top. His herringbone suit, black shoes, white shirt, and neat tie smacked more of the East than of California.

He saw a face which he classified as "pretty" and "wholesome" rather than "beautiful" and "glamorous." It was topped by a healthy mop of light brown hair. He set her age at twenty-five, give or take eighteen months. He smiled gently, climbed in without speaking and started his car.

He turned up Doheny Drive and east on Sunset. Near La Cienega, he slowed down. "Feeling better?"

"Uh, I guess so Mr.—Breen?"

"Call me Potiphar. What's your name? Don't tell me if you don't want to."

"Me? I'm—I'm Meade Barstow."

"Thank you, Meade. Where do you want to go? Home?"

"I suppose so. Oh, my, no. I can't go home like *this*." She clutched the coat tightly to her.

"Parents?"

"No. My landlady. She'd be shocked to death."

"Where, then?"

She thought. "Maybe we could stop at a filling station and I could sneak into the ladies' room."

"Maybe. See here, Meade—my house is six blocks from here and has a garage entrance. You could get inside without being seen."

She stared. "You don't *look* like a wolf!"

"Oh, but I am! The worst sort." He whistled and gnashed his teeth. "See? But Wednesday is my day off."

She looked at him and dimpled. "Oh, well! I'd rather wrestle with you than with Mrs. Megeath. Let's go."

He turned up into the hills. His bachelor diggings were one of the many little frame houses clinging like fungus to the brown slopes of the Santa Monica Mountains. The garage was notched into this hill; the house sat on it.

He drove in, cut the ignition, and led her up a teetery inside stairway into the living room.

"In there," he said, pointing. "Help yourself." He pulled her clothes out of his coat pockets and handed them to her.

She blushed and took them, disappeared into his bedroom. He heard her turn the key in the lock. He settled down in his easy chair, took out his notebook, and started with the *Herald-Express*.

He was finishing the *Daily News* and had added several notes to his collection when she came out. Her hair was neatly rolled; her face was restored; she had brushed most of the wrinkles out of her skirt. Her sweater was neither too tight nor deep cut, but it was pleasantly filled. She reminded him of well water and farm breakfasts.

He took his raincoat from her, hung it up, and said, "Sit down, Meade."

She said uncertainly, "I had better go."

"If you must, but I had hoped to talk with you."

"Well—" She sat down on the edge of his couch and looked around. The room was small, but as neat as his necktie and as clean as his collar. The fireplace was swept; the floor was bare and polished. Books crowded bookshelves in every possible space. One corner was filled by an elderly flat-top desk; the papers on it were neatly in order. Near it, on its own stand, was a small electric calculator. To her right, French windows gave out on a tiny porch over the garage. Beyond it she could see the sprawling city, where a few neon signs were already blinking.

She sat back a little. "This is a nice room—Potiphar. It looks like you."

"I take that as a compliment. Thank you." She did not answer; he went on, "Would you like a drink?"

"Oh, would I!" She shivered. "I guess I've got the jitters."

He stood up. "Not surprising. What'll it be?"

She took Scotch and water, no ice; he was a Bourbon-and-gingerale man. She soaked up half her highball in silence, then put it down, squared her shoulders and said, "Potiphar?"

"Yes, Meade?"

"Look, if you brought me here to make a pass, I wish you'd go ahead and make it. It won't do you a bit of good, but it makes me nervous to wait."

He said nothing and did not change his expression.

She went on uneasily, "Not that I'd blame you for trying—under the circumstances. And I *am* grateful. But . . . well, it's just that I don't—"

He came over and took both her hands. "I haven't the slightest thought of making a pass at you. Nor need you feel grateful. I butted in because I was interested in your case."

"My *case?* Are you a doctor? A psychiatrist?"

He shook his head. "I'm a mathematician. A statistician, to be precise."

"Huh? I don't get it."

"Don't worry about it. But I would like to ask some questions. May I?"

"Oh, sure! Of course! I owe you that much—and then some."

"You owe me nothing. Want your drink sweetened?"

She gulped the balance and handed him her glass, then followed him out into the kitchen. He did an exact job of measuring and gave it back.

"Now tell me why you took your clothes off," he said.

She frowned. "I don't know. I *don't* know. I don't *know*. I guess I just went crazy." She added, round-eyed,

"But I don't feel crazy. Could I go off my rocker and not know it?"

"You're not crazy . . . not more so than the rest of us," he amended. "Tell me, where did you see someone else do this?"

"Huh? I never have."

"Where did you read about it?"

"But I haven't. Wait a minute—those people up in Canada. Dooka-somethings."

"Doukhobors. That's all? No bareskin swimming parties? No strip poker?"

She shook her head. "No. You may not believe it, but I was the kind of a little girl who undressed under her nightie." She colored and added, "I still do—unless I remember to tell myself it's silly."

"I believe it. No news stories?"

"No. Yes, there was! About two weeks ago, I think it was. Some girl in a theater—in the audience, I mean. But I thought it was just publicity. You know the stunts they pull here."

He shook his head. "It wasn't. February 3rd, the Grand Theater, Mrs. Alvin Copley. Charges dismissed."

"How did *you* know?"

"Excuse me." He went to his desk, dialed the City News Bureau. "Alf? This is Pot Breen. They still sitting on that story? . . . Yes, the Gypsy Rose file. Any new ones today?"

He waited. Meade thought that she could make out swearing.

"Take it easy, Alf—this hot weather can't last forever. Nine, eh? Well, add another—Santa Monica Boulevard, late this afternoon. No arrest." He added, "Nope, nobody got her name. A middle-aged woman with a cast in one eye. I happened to see it . . . who, me? Why would I want to get mixed up? But it's rounding into a very, very interesting picture."

He put the phone down.

Meade said, "Cast in one eye, indeed!"

"Shall I call him back and give him your name?"

"Oh, no!"

"Very well. Now, Meade, we seemed to have located the point of contagion in your case—Mrs. Copley. What I'd like to know next is how you felt, what you were thinking about, when you did it."

She was frowning intently. "Wait a minute, Potiphar. Do I understand that *nine other girls* have pulled the stunt I pulled?"

"Oh, no. Nine others *today*. You are—" he paused briefly— "the three hundred and nineteenth case in Los Angeles County since the first of the year. I don't have figures on the rest of the country, but the suggestion to clamp down on the stories came from the eastern news services when the papers here put our first cases on the wire. That proves that it's a problem elsewhere, too."

"You mean that women all over the country are peeling off their clothes in public? Why, how shocking!"

He said nothing. She blushed again and insisted, "Well, it *is* shocking, even if it was me, this time."

"No, Meade. One case is shocking; over three hundred makes it scientifically interesting. That's why I want to know how it felt. Tell me about it."

"But—all right, I'll try. I told you I don't know why I did it; I still don't. I—"

"You remember it?"

"Oh, yes! I remember getting up off the bench and pulling up my sweater. I remember unzipping my skirt. I remember thinking I would have to hurry because I could see my bus stopped two blocks down the street. I remember how *good* it felt when I finally—" She paused and looked puzzled. "But I still don't know why."

"What were you thinking about just before you stood up?"

"I don't remember."

"Visualize the street. What was passing by? Where were your hands? Were your legs crossed or uncrossed? Was there anybody near you? What were you thinking about?"

"Nobody was on the bench with me. I had my hands

in my lap. Those characters in the mixed-up clothes we
standing nearby, but I wasn't paying attention. I wasr
thinking much except that my feet hurt and I wanted
get home—and how unbearably hot and sultry the weatl
er was. Then—" her eyes became distant—"suddenly
knew what I had to do, and it was very urgent that
do it. So I stood up and I—and I—" Her voice becan
shrill.

"Take it easy!" he said sharply. "Don't do it again

"Huh? Why, Mr. Breen! I wouldn't do anything lil
that."

"Of course not. Then what happened after you u
dressed?"

"Why, you put your raincoat around me and you kno
the rest." She faced him. "Say Potiphar, what were yc
doing with a raincoat? It hasn't rained in weeks. This
the driest, hottest rainy season in years."

"In sixty-eight years, to be exact."

"Sixty—"

"I carry a raincoat anyhow. Just a notion of mine, b
I feel that when it does rain, it's going to rain awfull
hard." He added, "Forty days and forty nights, maybe.

She decided that he was being humorous and laughe

He went on, "Can you remember how you got th
idea of undressing?"

She swirled her glass and thought. "I simply don
know."

He nodded. "That's what I expected."

"I don't understand—unless you think I'm crazy. D
you?"

"No. I think you had to do it and could not help it an
don't know why and can't know why."

"But you know." She said it accusingly.

"Maybe. At least I have some figures. Ever take an
interest in statistics, Meade?"

She shook her head. "Figures confuse me. Never min
statistics—I want to know why I did what I did!"

He looked at her very soberly. "I think we're lem
mings, Meade."

She looked puzzled, then horrified. "You mean those little furry mouselike creatures? The ones that—"

"Yes. The ones that periodically make a death migration, until millions, hundreds of millions of them drown themselves in the sea. Ask a lemming why he does it. If you could get him to slow up his rush toward death, even money says he would rationalize his answer as well as any college graduate. But he does it because he has to—and so do we."

"That's a horrid idea, Potiphar."

"Maybe. Come here, Meade. I'll show you figures that confuse me, too." He went to his desk and opened a drawer, took out a packet of cards. "Here's one. Two weeks ago, a man sues an entire state legislature for alienation of his wife's affection—and the judge lets the suit be tried. Or this one—a patent application for a device to lay the globe over on its side and warm up the arctic regions. Patent denied, but the inventor took in over three hundred thousand dollars in down payments on North Pole real estate before the postal authorities stepped in. Now he's fighting the case and it looks as if he might win. And here—prominent bishop proposes applied courses in the so-called facts of life in high schools."

He put the card away hastily. "Here's a dilly—a bill introduced in the Alabama lower house to repeal the laws of atomic energy. Not the present statutes, but the natural laws concerning nuclear physics; the wording makes that plain." He shrugged. "How silly can you get?"

"They're crazy."

"No, Meade. One like that might be crazy; a lot of them becomes a lemming death march. No, don't object— I've plotted them on a curve. The last time we had anything like this was the so-called Era of Wonderful Nonsense. But this one is much worse." He delved into a lower drawer, hauled out a graph. "The amplitude is more than twice as great and we haven't reached peak. What the peak will be, I don't dare guess—three separate rhythms, reinforcing."

She peered at the curves. "You mean that the lad with

the arctic real estate deal is somewhere on this line?"

"He adds to it. And back here on the last crest are the flagpole sitters and the goldfish swallowers and the Ponzi hoax and the marathon dancers and the man who pushed a peanut up Pikes Peak with his nose. You're on the new crest—or you will be when I add you in."

She made a face. "I don't like it."

"Neither do I. But it's as clear as a bank statement. This year the human race is letting down its hair, flipping its lip with a finger, and saying, 'Wubba, wubba, wubba.' "

She shivered. "Do you suppose I could have another drink? Then I'll go."

"I have a better idea. I owe you a dinner for answering questions. Pick a place and we'll have a cocktail before."

She chewed her lip. "You don't owe me anything. And I don't feel up to facing a restaurant crowd. I might—I might—"

"No, you wouldn't," he said sharply. "It doesn't hit twice."

"You're sure? Anyhow, I don't want to face a crowd." She glanced at his kitchen door. "Have you anything to eat in there? I can cook."

"Um, breakfast things. And there's a pound of ground top round in the freezer compartment and some rolls. I sometimes make hamburgers when I don't want to go out."

She headed for the kitchen. "Drunk or sober, fully dressed or—or naked, I can cook. You'll see."

He did see. Open-faced sandwiches with the meat married to toasted buns and the flavor garnished rather than suppressed by scraped Bermuda onion and thin-sliced dill, a salad made from things she had scrounged out of his refrigerator, potatoes crisp but not vulcanized. They ate it on the tiny balcony, sopping it down with cold beer.

He sighed and wiped his mouth. "Yes, Meade, you can cook."

"Some day I'll arrive with proper materials and pay you
ack. Then I'll prove it."

"You've already proved it. Nevertheless, I accept. But
 tell you three times—which makes it true, of course—
at you owe me nothing."

"No? If you hadn't been a Boy Scout, I'd be in jail."
Breen shook his head. "The police have orders to keep
 quiet at all costs—to keep it from growing. You saw
at. And, my dear, you weren't a person to me at the
me. I didn't even see your face."

"You saw plenty else!"

"Truthfully, I didn't look. You were just a—a statis-
ic."

She toyed with her knife and said puzzled, "I'm not
ure, but I think I've just been insulted. In all the twenty-
ive years that I've fought men off, more or less success-
ully, I've been called a lot of names—but a 'statistic?'
Vhy, I ought to take your slide rule and beat you to
eath with it."

"My dear young lady—"

"I'm not a lady, that's for sure. But I'm *not* a statistic,
either."

"My dear Meade, then. I wanted to tell you, before you
did anything hasty, that in college I wrestled varsity mid-
dleweight."

She grinned and dimpled. "That's more the talk a girl
ikes to hear. I was beginning to be afraid you had been
ssembled in an adding machine factory. Potty, you're
eally a dear."

"If that is a diminutive of my given name, I like it. But
f it refers to my waistline, I definitely resent it."

She reached across and patted his stomach. "I like your
vaist line; lean and hungry men are difficult. If I were
cooking for you regularly, I'd really pad it."

"Is that a proposal?"

"Let it lie, let it lie. Potty, do you really think the whole
country is losing its buttons?"

He sobered at once. "It's worse than that."

"Huh?"

"Come inside. I'll show you."

They gathered up dishes and dumped them in the sink,
Breen talking all the while.

"As a kid, I was fascinated by numbers. Numbers are
pretty things, and they combine in such interesting con-
figurations. I took my degree in math, of course, and got
a job as a junior actuary with Midwestern Mutual—the
insurance outfit. That was fun. No way on Earth to tell
when a particular man is going to die, but an absolute
certainty that so many men of a certain age group would
die before a certain date. The curves were so lovely—
and they always worked out. Always. You didn't have to
know *why;* you could predict with dead certainty and
never know why. The equations worked; the curves were
right.

"I was interested in astronomy, too; it was the one
science where individual figures worked out neatly, completely, and accurately, down to the last decimal point
that the instruments were good for. Compared with astronomy, the other sciences were mere carpentry and
kitchen chemistry.

"I found there were nooks and crannies in astronomy
where individual numbers won't do, where you have to
go over to statistics, and I became even more interested. I
joined the Variable Star Association and I might have
gone into astronomy professionally, instead of what I'm
in now—business consultation—if I hadn't gotten interested in something else."

" 'Business consultation?' " repeated Meade. "Income
tax work?"

"Oh, no. That's too elementary. I'm the numbers boy
for a firm of industrial engineers. I can tell a rancher
exactly how many of his Hereford bull calves will be
sterile. Or I can tell a motion picture producer how much
rain insurance to carry on location. Or maybe how big a
company in a particular line must be to carry its own
risk in industrial accidents. And I'm right. I'm always
right."

"Wait a minute. Seems to me a big company would *have* to have insurance."

"Contrariwise. A really big corporation begins to resemble a statistical universe."

"Huh?"

"Never mind. I got interested in something else—cycles. Cycles are everything, Meade. And everywhere. The tides. The seasons. Wars. Love. Everybody knows that in the spring the young man's fancy lightly turns to what the girls never stopped thinking about, but did you know that it runs in an eighteen-year-plus cycle as well? And that a girl born at the wrong swing of the curve doesn't stand nearly as good a chance as her older or younger sister?"

"Is *that* why I'm still a doddering old maid?"

"You're twenty-five?" He pondered. "Maybe, but your chances are improving again; the curve is swinging up. Anyhow, remember you are just one statistic; the curve applies to the group. Some girls get married every year."

"Don't call me a statistic," she repeated firmly.

"Sorry. And marriages match up with acreage planted to wheat, with wheat cresting ahead. You could almost say that planting wheat makes people get married."

"Sounds silly."

"It *is* silly. The whole notion of cause-and-effect is probably superstition. But the same cycle shows a peak in house building right after a peak in marriages."

"Now that makes sense."

"Does it? How many newlyweds do you know who can afford to build a house? You might as well blame it on wheat acreage. We don't know *why;* it just *is.*"

"Sun spots, maybe?"

"You can correlate sunspots with stock prices, or Columbia River salmon, or women's skirts. And you are just as much justified in blaming short skirts for sunspots as you are in blaming sunspots for salmon. We don't know. But the curves go on just the same."

"But there has to be some *reason* behind it."

"Does there? That's mere assumption. A fact has no

'why.' There it stands, self-demonstrating. Why did you take your clothes off today?"

She frowned. "That's not fair."

"Maybe not. But I want to show you why I'm worried."

He went into the bedroom, came out with a large roll of tracing paper.

"We'll spread it on the floor. Here they are, all of them. The 54-year cycle—see the Civil War there? See how it matches in? The eighteen-and-one-third-year cycle, the 9-plus cycle, the 41-month shorty, the three rhythms of Sunspots—everything, all combined in one grand chart: Mississippi River floods, fur catches in Canada, stock market prices, marriages, epidemics, freight-car loadings, bank clearings, locust plagues, divorces, tree growth, wars, rainfall, Earth magnetism, building construction, patents applied for, murders—you name it; I've got it there."

She stared at the bewildering array of wavy lines. "But Potty, what does it mean?"

"It means that these things all happen, in regular rhythm, whether we like it or not. It means that when skirts are due to go up, all the stylists in Paris can't make 'em go down. It means that when prices are going down, all the controls and supports and government planning can't make 'em go up." He pointed to a curve. "Take a look at the grocery ads. Then turn to the financial page and read how the Big Brains try to double-talk their way out of it. It means that when an epidemic is due, it happens, despite all the public health efforts. It means we're lemmings."

She pulled her lip. "I don't like it. 'I am the master of my fate,' and so forth. I've got free will, Potty. I know I have—I can feel it."

"I imagine every little neutron in an atom bomb feels the same way. He can go *spung!* or he can sit still, just as he pleases. But statistical mechanics work out all the same and the bomb goes off—which is what I'm leading up to. See anything odd there, Meade?"

She studied the chart, trying not to let the curving lines confuse her.

"They sort of bunch up over at the right end."

"You're dern tootin' they do! See that dotted vertical line? That's right now—and things are bad enough. But take a look at that solid vertical; that's about six months from now—and that's when we get it. Look at the cycles —the long ones, the short ones, all of them. Every single last one of them reaches either a trough or a crest exactly on—or almost on—that line."

"That's bad?"

"What do you think. Three of the big ones troughed back in 1929 and the depression almost ruined us . . . even with the big 54-year cycle supporting things. Now we've got the big one troughing—and the few crests are not things that help. I mean to say, tent caterpillars and influenza don't do us any good. Meade, if statistics mean anything, this tired old planet hasn't seen a trend like this since Eve went into the apple business. I'm scared."

She searched his face. "Potty, you're not simply having fun with me? You know I can't check up on you."

"I wish to heaven I were. No, Meade, I can't fool about numbers; I wouldn't know how. This is it. —The Year of the Jackpot."

Meade was very silent as he drove her home. When they approached West Los Angeles, she said, "Potty?"

"Yes, Meade?"

"What do we *do* about it?"

"What do you do about a hurricane? You pull in your ears. What can you do about an atom bomb? You try to outguess it, not be there when it goes off. What else can you do?"

"Oh." She was silent for a few moments, then added, "Potty, will you tell me which way to jump?"

"Huh? Oh, sure! If I can figure it out."

He took her to her door, turned to go.

She said, "Potty!"

He faced her. "Yes, Meade?"

She grabbed his head, shook it—then kissed him fiercely on the mouth. "There, is that just a statistic?"

"Uh, no."

"It had better not be," she said dangerously. "Potty, I think I'm going to have to change your curve."

II

RUSSIANS REJECT UN NOTE
MISSOURI FLOOD DAMAGE EXCEEDS RECORD
MISSISSIPPI MESSIAH DEFIES COURT
NUDIST CONVENTION STORMS BAILEY'S BEACH
BRITISH-IRAN TALKS STILL DEADLOCKED
FASTER-THAN-LIGHT WEAPON PROMISED
TYPHOON DOUBLING BACK ON MANILA
MARRIAGE SOLEMNIZED ON FLOOR OF HUDSON

New York, 13 July—In a specially constructed diving suit built for two, Merydith Smithe, café society headline girl, and Prince Augie Schleswieg of New York and the Riviera were united today by Bishop Dalton in a service televised with the aid of the Navy's ultra-new—

As the Year of the Jackpot progressed, Breen took melancholy pleasure in adding to the data which proved that the curve was sagging as predicted. The undeclared World War continued its bloody, blundering way at half a dozen spots around a tortured globe. Breen did not chart it; the headlines were there for anyone to read. He concentrated on the odd facts in the other pages of the papers, facts which, taken singly, meant nothing, but taken together showed a disastrous trend.

He listed stock market prices, rainfall, wheat futures, but the "silly season" items were what fascinated him. To be sure, some humans were always doing silly things—but at what point had prime damfoolishness become commonplace? When, for example, had the zombie-like professional models become accepted ideals of American womanhood? What were the gradations between National Cancer Week and National Athlete's Foot Week? On what day had the American people finally taken leave of horse sense?

Take transvestism. Male-and-female dress customs were arbitrary, but they had seemed to be deeply rooted in the culture. When did the breakdown start? With Marlene Dietrich's tailored suits? By the late nineteen-forties, there was no "male" article of clothing that a woman could not wear in public—but when had men started to slip over the line? Should he count the psychological cripples who had made the word "drag" a by-word in Greenwich Village and Hollywood long before this outbreak? Or were they "wild shots" not belonging on the curve? Did it start with some unknown normal man attending a masquerade and there discovering that skirts actually were more comfortable and practical than trousers? Or had it started with the resurgence of Scottish nationalism reflected in the wearing of kilts by many Scottish-Americans?

Ask a lemming to state his motives! The outcome was in front of him, a news story. Transvestism by draft dodgers had at last resulted in a mass arrest in Chicago which was to have ended in a giant joint trial—only to have the deputy prosecutor show up in a pinafore and defy the judge to submit to an examination to determine the judge's true sex. The judge suffered a stroke and died and the trial was postponed—postponed forever, in Breen's opinion; he doubted that this particular blue law would ever again be enforced.

Or the laws about indecent exposure, for that matter. The attempt to limit the Gypsy Rose syndrome by ignoring it had taken the starch out of enforcement. Now here was a report about the All Souls Community Church of Springfield; the pastor had reinstituted ceremonial nudity. Probably the first time this thousand years, Breen thought, aside from some screwball cults in Los Angeles. The reverend gentleman claimed that the ceremony was identical with the "dance of the high priestess" in the ancient temple of Karnak.

Could be, but Breen had private information that the "priestess" had been working the burlesque and nightclub circuit before her present engagement. In any case, the holy leader was packing them in and had not been arrested.

Two weeks later a hundred and nine churches in thirty-three states offered equivalent attractions. Breen entered them on his curves.

This queasy oddity seemed to him to have no relation to the startling rise in the dissident evangelical cults throughout the country. These churches were sincere, earnest, and poor—but growing, ever since the War. Now they were multiplying like yeast.

It seemed a statistical cinch that the United States was about to become godstruck again. He correlated it with Transcendentalism and the trek of the Latter Day Saints. Hmm, yes, it fitted. And the curve was pushing toward a crest.

Billions in war bonds were now falling due; wartime marriages were reflected in the swollen peak of the Los Angeles school population. The Colorado River was at a record low, and the towers in Lake Mead stood high out of the water. But the Angelenos committed communal suicide by watering lawns as usual. The Metropolitan Water District commissioners tried to stop it. It fell between the stools of the police powers of fifty "sovereign" cities. The taps remained open, trickling away the life blood of the desert paradise.

The four regular party conventions—Dixiecrats, Regular Republicans, the Regular Regular Republicans, and the Democrats—attracted scant attention, because the Know-Nothings had not yet met. The fact that the "American Rally," as the Know-Nothings preferred to be called, claimed not to be a party but an educational society did not detract from their strength. But what was their strength? Their beginnings had been so obscure that Breen had had to go back and dig into the files, yet he had been approached twice this very week to join them, right inside his own office—once by his boss, once by the janitor.

He hadn't been able to chart the Know-Nothings. They gave him chills in his spine. He kept column-inches on them, found that their publicity was shrinking while their numbers were obviously zooming.

Krakatoa blew up on July 18th. It provided the first important trans-pacific TV-cast. Its effect on sunsets, on solar constant, on mean temperature, and on rainfall would not be felt until later in the year.

The San Andreas fault, its stresses unrelieved since the Long Beach disaster of 1933, continued to build up imbalance—an unhealed wound running the full length of the West Coast.

Pelee and Etna erupted. Mauna Loa was still quiet.

Flying Saucers seemed to be landing daily in every state. Nobody had exhibited one on the ground—or had the Department of Defense sat on them? Breen was unsatisfied with the off-the-record reports he had been able to get; the alcoholic content of some of them had been high. But the sea serpent on Ventura Beach was real; he had seen it. The troglodyte in Tennessee he was not in a position to verify.

Thirty-one domestic air crashes the last week in July . . . was it sabotage, or was it a sagging curve on a chart? And that neopolio epidemic that skipped from Seattle to New York? Time for a big epidemic? Breen's chart said it was. But how about bacteriological warfare? Could a chart *know* that a Slav biochemist would perfect an efficient virus-and-vector at the right time?

Nonsense!

But the curves, if they meant anything at all, included "free will"; they averaged in all the individual "wills" of a statistical universe—and came out as a smooth function. Every morning, three million "free wills" flowed toward the center of the New York megalopolis; every evening, they flowed out again—all by "free will" and on a smooth and predictable curve.

Ask a lemming! Ask *all* the lemmings, dead and alive. Let them take a vote on it!

Breen tossed his notebook aside and phoned Meade. "Is this my favorite statistic?"

"Potty! I was thinking about you."

"Naturally. This is your night off."

"Yes, but another reason, too. Potiphar, have you ever taken a look at the Great Pyramid?"

"I haven't even been to Niagara Falls. I'm looking for a rich woman, so I can travel."

"I'll let you know when I get my first million, but—"

"That's the first time you've proposed to me this week."

"Shut up. Have you ever looked into the prophecies they found inside the pyramid?"

"Look, Meade, that's in the same class with astrology— strictly for the squirrels. Grow up."

"Yes, of course. But, Potty, I thought you were interested in anything odd. This is odd."

"Oh. Sorry. If it's 'silly season' stuff, let's see it."

"All right. Am I cooking for you tonight?"

"It's Wednesday, isn't it?"

"How soon will you get here?"

He glanced at his watch. "Pick you up in eleven minutes." He felt his whiskers. "No, twelve and a half."

"I'll be ready. Mrs. Megeath says these regular dates mean that you're going to marry me."

"Pay no attention to her. She's just a statistic and I'm a wild datum."

"Oh well, I've got two hundred and forty-seven dollars toward that million. 'By!"

Meade's prize to show him was the usual Rosicrucian come-on, elaborately printed, and including a photograph (retouched, he was sure) of the much disputed line on the corridor wall which was alleged to prophesy, by its various discontinuities, the entire future. This one had an unusual time scale, but the major events were all marked on it—the fall of Rome, the Norman Invasion, the Discovery of America, Napoleon, the World Wars.

What made it interesting was that it suddenly stopped —now.

"What about it, Potty?"

"I guess the stonecutter got tired. Or got fired. Or they

hired a new head priest with new ideas." He tucked it into his desk. "Thanks. I'll think about how to list it."

But he got it out again, applied dividers and a magnifying glass.

"It says here," he announced, "that the end comes late in August—unless that's a fly speck."

"Morning or afternoon? I have to know how to dress."

"Shoes will be worn. All God's chilluns got shoes." He put it away.

She was silent for a moment, then said, "Potty, isn't it about time to jump?"

"Huh? Girl, don't let *that* thing affect you! That's 'silly season' stuff."

"Yes. But take a look at *your* chart."

Nevertheless, he took the next afternoon off, spent it in the reference room of the main library, confirmed his opinion of soothsayers. Nostradamus was pretentiously silly; Mother Shippey was worse. In any of them you could find whatever you looked for.

He did find one item in Nostradamus that he liked: "The Oriental shall come forth from his seat . . . he shall pass through the sky, through the waters and the snow, and he shall strike each one with his weapon."

That sounded like what the Department of Defense expected the commies to try to do to the Western Allies.

But it was also a description of every invasion that had come out of the "heartland" in the memory of mankind.

Nuts!

When he got home, he found himself taking down his father's Bible and turning to Revelations. He could not find anything he could understand, but he got fascinated by the recurring use of precise numbers. Presently he thumbed through the Book.

His eye lit on: "Boast not thyself of tomorrow; for thou knowest not what a day may bring forth."

He put the Book away, feeling humbled, but not cheered.

The rains started the next morning.

The Master Plumbers elected Miss Star Morning "Miss Sanitary Engineering" on the same day that the mortician designated her as "The Body I Would Like Best to Prepare," and her option was dropped by Fragrant Features.

Congress voted $1.37 to compensate Thomas Jefferson Meeks for losses incurred while an emergency postman for the Christmas rush of 1936, approved the appointment of five lieutenant generals and one ambassador and adjourned in less than eight minutes.

The fire extinguishers in the midwest orphanage turned out to be filled with nothing but air.

The chancellor of the leading football institution sponsored a fund to send peace messages and vitamins to the Politburo.

The stock market slumped nineteen points and the tickers ran two hours late.

Wichita, Kansas, remained flooded while Phoenix, Arizona, cut off drinking water to areas outside city limits.

And Potiphar Breen found that he had left his raincoat at Meade Barstow's rooming house.

He phoned her landlady, but Mrs. Megeath turned him over to Meade.

"What are you doing home on a Friday?" he demanded.

"The theater manager laid me off. Now you'll have to marry me."

"You can't afford me. Meade—seriously, baby, what happened?"

"I was ready to leave the dump anyway. For the last six weeks the popcorn machine has been carrying the place. Today I sat through *The Lana Turner Story* twice. Nothing to do."

"I'll be along."

"Eleven minutes?"

"It's raining. Twenty—with luck."

It was more nearly sixty. Santa Monica Boulevard was a navigable stream; Sunset Boulevard was a subway jam. When he tried to ford the streams leading to Mrs. Megeath's house, he found that changing tires with the wheel wedged against a storm drain presented problems.

"Potty!" she exclaimed when he squished in. "You look like a drowned rat."

He found himself suddenly wrapped in a blanket robe belonging to the late Mr. Megeath and sipping hot cocoa while Mrs. Megeath dried his clothing in the kitchen.

"Meade, I'm 'at liberty' too."

"Huh? You quit your job?"

"Not exactly. Old Man Wiley and I have been having differences of opinion about my answers for months—too much 'Jackpot factor' in the figures I give him to turn over to clients. Not that I call it that, but he has felt that I was unduly pessimistic."

"But you were right!"

"Since when has being right endeared a man to his boss? But that wasn't why he fired me; it was just the excuse. He wants a man willing to back up the Know-Nothing program with scientific double-talk and I wouldn't join." He went to the window. "It's raining harder."

"But the Know-Nothings haven't got any program."

"I know that."

"Potty, you should have joined. It doesn't mean anything. I joined three months ago."

"The hell you did!"

She shrugged. "You pay your dollar and you turn up for two meetings and they leave you alone. It kept my job for another three months. What of it?"

"Well, I'm sorry you did it; that's all. Forget it. Meade, the water is over the curbs out there."

"You had better stay here overnight."

"Mmm . . . I don't like to leave *Entropy* parked out in this stuff all night. Meade?"

"Yes, Potty?"

"We're both out of jobs. How would you like to duck north into the Mojave and find a dry spot?"

"I'd love it. But look, Potty, is this a proposal or just a proposition?"

"Don't pull that 'either-or' stuff on me. It's just a suggestion for a vacation. Do you want to take a chaperone?"

"No."

"Then pack a bag."

"Right away. But pack a bag *how?* Are you trying to tell me it's *time to jump?*"

He faced her, then looked back at the window.

"I don't know," he said slowly, "but this rain might go on quite a while. Don't take anything you don't have to have—but don't leave anything behind you can't get along without."

He repossessed his clothing from Mrs. Megeath while Meade was upstairs. She came down dressed in slacks and carrying two large bags; under one arm was a battered and rakish teddy bear.

"This is Winnie," she said.

"Winnie the Pooh?"

"No, Winnie Churchill. When I feel bad, he promises me blood, sweat, and tears; then I feel better. You did say to bring anything I couldn't do without, didn't you?" She looked at him anxiously.

"Right."

He took the bags. Mrs. Megeath had seemed satisfied with his explanation that they were going to visit his (mythical) aunt in Bakersfield before looking for jobs. Nevertheless, she embarrassed him by kissing him good-by and telling him to "take care of my little girl."

Santa Monica Boulevard was blocked off from use. While stalled in traffic in Beverly Hills, he fiddled with the car radio, getting squawks and crackling noises, then finally one station nearby: "—in effect," a harsh, high, staccato voice was saying, "the Kremlin has given us till sundown to get out of town. This is your New York reporter, who thinks that in days like these every American must personally keep his powder dry. And now for a word from—"

Breen switched it off and glanced at her face. "Don't worry," he said. "They've been talking that way for years."

"You think they are bluffing?"

"I didn't say that, I said, 'Don't worry.'"

But his own packing, with her help, was clearly on a "survival-kit" basis—canned goods, all his warm clothing, a sporting rifle he had not fired in over two years, a first-aid kit and the contents of his medicine chest. He dumped the stuff from his desk into a carton, shoved it into the back seat along with cans and books and coats, and covered the plunder with all the blankets in the house. They went back up the rickety stairs for a last check.

"Potty, where's your chart?"

"Rolled up on the back-seat shelf. I guess that's all—hey, wait a minute!" He went to a shelf over his desk and began taking down small, sober-looking magazines. "I dern near left behind my file *of The Western Astronomer* and the *Proceedings of the Variable Star Association.*"

"Why take them?"

"I must be nearly a year behind on both of them. Now maybe I'll have time to read."

"Hmm . . . Potty, watching you read professional journals is not my notion of a vacation."

"Quiet, woman! You took Winnie; I take these."

She shut up and helped him. He cast a longing eye at his electric calculator, but decided it was too much like the White Knight's mousetrap. He could get by with his slide rule.

As the car splashed out into the street, she said, "Potty, how are you fixed for cash?"

"Huh? Okay, I guess."

"I mean, leaving while the banks are closed and everything." She held up her purse. "Here's my bank. It isn't much, but we can use it."

He smiled and patted her knee. "Good gal! I'm sitting on my bank; I started turning everything to cash about the first of the year."

"Oh. I closed out my bank account right after we met."

"You did? You must have taken my maunderings seriously."

"I always take you seriously."

Mint Canyon was a five-mile-an-hour nightmare, with visibility limited to the tail lights of the truck ahead. When they stopped for coffee at Halfway, they confirmed what seemed evident: Cajon Pass was closed and long-haul traffic for Route 66 was being detoured through the secondary pass.

At long, long last they reached the Victorville cutoff and lost some of the traffic—a good thing, because the windshield wiper on his side had quit working and they were driving by the committee system.

Just short of Lancaster, she said suddenly, "Potty, is this buggy equipped with a snorkel?"

"Nope."

"Then we had better stop. I see a light off the road."

The light was an auto court. Meade settled the matter of economy versus convention by signing the book herself; they were placed in one cabin. He saw that it had twin beds and let the matter ride. Meade went to bed with her teddy bear without even asking to be kissed good night. It was already gray, wet dawn.

They got up in the late afternoon and decided to stay over one more night, then push north toward Bakersfield. A high-pressure area was alleged to be moving south, crowding the warm, wet mass that smothered Southern California. They wanted to get into it. Breen had the wiper repaired and bought two new tires to replace his ruined spare, added some camping items to his cargo, and bought for Meade a .32 automatic, a lady's social-purpose gun.

"What's this for?" she wanted to know.

"Well, you're carrying quite a bit of cash."

"Oh. I thought maybe I was to use it to fight you off."

"Now, Meade—"

"Never mind. Thanks, Potty."

They had finished supper and were packing the car with their afternoon's purchases when the quake struck. Five inches of rain in twenty-four hours, more than three billion tons of mass suddenly loaded on a fault already overstrained, all cut loose in one subsonic, stomach-twisting rumble.

Meade sat down on the wet ground very suddenly; Breen stayed upright by dancing like a log-roller. When the ground quieted down somewhat, thirty seconds later, he helped her up.

"You all right?"

"My slacks are soaked." She added pettishly, "But, Potty, it never quakes in wet weather. *Never*. You said so yourself."

"Keep quiet, can't you?" He opened the car door and switched on the radio, waited impatiently for it to warm up.

"—your Sunshine Station in Riverside, California. Keep tuned to this station for the latest developments. As of now it is impossible to tell the size of this disaster. The Colorado River aqueduct is broken; nothing is known of the extent of the damage nor how long it will take to repair it. So far as we know, the Owens River Valley aqueduct may be intact, but all persons in the Los Angeles area are advised to conserve water. My personal advice is to stick your washtubs out into this rain.

"I now read from the standard disaster instructions, quote: 'Boil all water. Remain quietly in your homes and do not panic. Stay off the highways. Cooperate with the police and render—' Joe! Catch that phone! '—render aid where neccessary. Do not use the telephone except for—' Flash! An unconfirmed report from Long Beach states that the Wilmington and San Pedro waterfront is under five feet of water. I repeat, this is unconfirmed. Here's a message from the commanding general, March Field: 'Official, all military personnel will report—' "

Breen switched it off. "Get in the car."

He stopped in the town, managed to buy six five-gallon tins and a jeep tank. He filled them with gasoline and packed them with blankets in the back seat, topping off the mess with a dozen cans of oil. Then they started rolling.

"What are we doing, Potiphar?"

"I want to get west of the valley highway."

"Any particular place west?"

"I think so. We'll see. You work the radio, but keep an eye on the road, too. That gas back there makes me nervous."

Through the town of Mojave and northwest on 466 into the Tehachapi Mountains—

Reception was poor in the pass, but what Meade could pick up confirmed the first impression—worse than the quake of '06, worse than San Francisco, Managua, and Long Beach lumped together.

When they got down out of the mountains, the weather was clearing locally; a few stars appeared. Breen swung left off the highway and ducked south of Bakersfield by the county road, reached the Route 99 super-highway just south of Greenfield. It was, as he had feared, already jammed with refugees. He was forced to go along with the flow for a couple of miles before he could cut west at Greenfield toward Taft. They stopped on the western outskirts of the town and ate at an all-night joint.

They were about to climb back into the car when there was suddenly "sunrise" due south. The rosy light swelled almost instantaneously, filled the sky, and died. Where it had been, a red-and-purple pillar of cloud was spreading to a mushroom top.

Breen stared at it, glanced at his watch, then said harshly, "Get in the car."

"Potty! That was—"

"That used to be Los Angeles. Get in the car!"

He drove silently for several minutes. Meade seemed to be in a state of shock, unable to speak. When the sound reached them, he again glanced at his watch.

"Six minutes and nineteen seconds. That's about right."

"Potty, *we should have brought Mrs. Megeath.*"

"How was I to know?" he said angrily. "Anyhow, you can't transplant an old tree. If she got it, she never knew it."

"Oh, I hope so!"

"We're going to have all we can do to take care of ourselves. Take the flashlight and check the map. I want to turn north at Taft and over toward the coast."

"Yes, Potiphar."

She quieted down and did as she was told. The radio gave nothing, not even the Riverside station; the whole broadcast range was covered by a curious static, like rain on a window.

He slowed down as they approached Taft, let her spot the turn north onto the state road, and turned into it. Almost at once a figure jumped out into the road in front of them, waved his arms violently. Breen tromped on the brake.

The man came up on the left side of the car, rapped on the window. Breen ran the glass down. Then he stared stupidly at the gun in the man's left hand.

"Out of the car," the stranger said sharply. "I've got to have it."

Meade reached across Breen, stuck her little lady's gun in the man's face and pulled the trigger. Breen could feel the flash on his own face, never noticed the report. The man looked puzzled, with a neat, not-yet-bloody hole in his upper lip—then slowly sagged away from the car.

"Drive on!" Meade said in a high voice.

Breen caught his breath. "But you—"

"Drive on! *Get rolling!*"

They followed the state road through Los Padres National Forest, stopping once to fill the tank from their cans. They turned off onto a dirt road. Meade kept trying the radio, got San Francisco once, but it was too jammed with static to read. Then she got Salt Lake City, faint but clear;

"—since there are no reports of anything passing our radar screen, the Kansas City bomb must be assumed to have been planted rather than delivered. This is a tentative theory, but—"

They passed into a deep cut and lost the rest.

When the squawk box again came to life, it was a crisp new voice: "Air Defense Command, coming to you over the combined networks. The rumor that Los Angeles has been hit by an atom bomb is totally unfounded. It is true that the Western metropolis has suffered a severe earthquake shock, but that is all. Government officials and the Red Cross are on the spot to care for the victims, but—and I repeat—there has *been no atomic bombing*. So relax and stay in your homes. Such wild rumors can damage the United States quite as much as enemy bombs. Stay off the highways and listen for—"

Breen snapped it off. "Somebody," he said bitterly, "has again decided that 'Mama knows best.' They won't tell us any bad news."

"Potiphar," Meade said sharply, "that was an atom bomb, wasn't it?"

"It was. And now we don't know whether it was just Los Angeles—and Kansas City—or every big city in the country. All we know is that they are lying to us."

He concentrated on driving. The road was very bad.

As it began to get light, she said, "Potty, do you know where we're going? Are we just keeping out of cities?"

"I think I know. If I'm not lost." He stared around them. "Nope, it's all right. See that hill up forward with the triple gendarmes on its profile?"

"Gendarmes?"

"Big rock pillars. That's a sure landmark. I'm looking for a private road now. It leads to a hunting lodge belonging to two of my friends—an old ranch house actually, but as a ranch it didn't pay."

"They won't mind us using it?"

He shrugged. "If they show up, we'll ask them. *If* they show up. They lived in Los Angeles."

The private road had once been a poor grade of wagon trail; now it was almost impassable. But they finally topped a hogback from which they could see almost to the Pacific, then dropped down into a sheltered bowl where the cabin was.

"All out, girl. End of the line."

Meade sighed. "It looks heavenly."

"Think you can rustle breakfast while I unload? There's probably wood in the shed. Or can you manage a wood range?"

"Just try me."

Two hours later Breen was standing on the hogback, smoking a cigarette and staring off down to the west. He wondered if that was a mushroom cloud up San Francisco way. Probably his imagination, he decided, in view if the distance. Certainly there was nothing to be seen to the south.

Meade came out of the cabin. "Potty!"

"Up here."

She joined him, took his hand and smiled, then snitched his cigarette and took a deep drag. She exhaled it and said, "I know it's sinful of me, but I feel more peaceful than I have in months."

"I know."

"Did you see the canned goods in that pantry? We could pull through a hard winter here."

"We might have to."

"I suppose. I wish we had a cow."

"What would you do with a cow?"

"I used to milk four of them before I caught the school bus, every morning. I can butcher a hog, too."

"I'll try to find you a hog."

"You do and I'll manage to smoke it." She yawned. "I'm suddenly terribly sleepy."

"So am I. And small wonder."

"Let's go to bed."

"Uh, yes. Meade?"

"Yes, Potty?"

"We may be here quite a while. You know that, don't you?"

"Yes, Potty."

"In fact, it might be smart to stay put until those curves all start turning up again. They should, you know."

"Yes. I had figured that out."

He hesitated, then went on, "Meade, will you marry me?"

"Yes." She moved up to him.

After a time he pushed her gently away and said, "My dear, my very dear—uh—we could drive down and find a minister in some little town."

She looked at him steadily. "That wouldn't be very bright, would it? I mean, nobody knows we're here and that's the way we want it. Besides, your car might not make it back up that road."

"No, it wouldn't be very bright. But I want to do the right thing."

"It's all right, Potty. It's all *right*."

"Well, then . . . kneel down here with me. We'll say them together."

"Yes, Potiphar." She knelt and he took her hand. He closed his eyes and prayed wordlessly.

When he opened them he said, "What's the matter?"

"The gravel hurts my knees."

"We'll stand up, then."

"No. Look, Potty, why don't we just go in the house and say them there?"

"Huh? Hell's bells, woman, we might forget to say them entirely. Now repeat after me: I, Potiphar, take thee, Meade—"

III

OFFICIAL: STATIONS WITHIN RANGE RELAY TWICE. EXECUTIVE BULLETIN NUMBER NINE—ROAD LAWS PREVIOUSLY PUBLISHED HAVE BEEN IGNORED IN MANY INSTANCES. PATROLS ARE ORDERED TO SHOOT WITHOUT WARNING AND PROVOST MARSHALS ARE DIRECTED TO USE DEATH PENALTY FOR UNAUTHORIZED POSSESSION OF GASOLINE. BIOLOGICAL WARFARE AND RADIATION QUARANTINE REGULATIONS PREVIOUSLY ISSUED WILL BE RIGIDLY ENFORCED. LONG LIVE THE UNITED STATES! HARLEY J. NEAL, LIEUTENANT GENERAL, ACTING CHIEF OF GOVERNMENT. ALL STATIONS RELAY TWICE.

THIS IS THE FREE RADIO AMERICA RELAY NETWORK. PASS

THIS ALONG, BOYS! GOVERNOR BRADLEY WAS SWORN IN TODAY AS PRESIDENT BY ACTING CHIEF JUSTICE ROBERTS UNDER THE RULE-OF-SUCCESSION. THE PRESIDENT NAMED THOMAS DEWEY AS SECRETARY OF STATE AND PAUL DOUGLAS AS SECRETARY OF DEFENSE. HIS SECOND OFFICIAL ACT WAS TO STRIP THE RENEGADE NEAL OF RANK AND TO DIRECT HIS ARREST BY ANY CITIZEN OR OFFICIAL. MORE LATER. PASS THE WORD ALONG.

HELLO, CQ, CQ, CQ. THIS IS W5KMR, FREEPORT. QRR, QRR! ANYBODY READ ME? ANYBODY? WE'RE DYING LIKE FLIES DOWN HERE. WHAT'S HAPPENED? STARTS WITH FEVER AND A BURNING THIRST, BUT YOU CAN'T SWALLOW. WE NEED HELP. ANYBODY READ ME? HELLO, CQ 75, CQ 75 THIS IS W5 KING MIKE ROGER CALLING QRR AND CQ 75, BY FOR SOMEBODY . . . ANYBODY!

THIS IS THE LORD'S TIME, SPONSORED BY SWAN'S ELIXIR, THE TONIC THAT MAKES WAITING FOR THE KINGDOM OF GOD WORTHWHILE. YOU ARE ABOUT TO HEAR A MESSAGE OF CHEER FROM JUDGE BROOMFIELD, ANOINTED VICAR OF THE KINGDOM ON EARTH. BUT FIRST A BULLETIN——SEND YOUR CONTRIBUTIONS TO MESSIAH, CLINT, TEXAS. DON'T TRY TO MAIL THEM——SEND THEM BY A KINGDOM MESSENGER OR BY SOME PILGRIM JOURNEYING THIS WAY. AND NOW THE TABERNACLE CHOIR FOLLOWED BY THE VOICE OF THE VICAR ON EARTH——

——THE FIRST SYMPTOM IS LITTLE RED SPOTS IN THE ARMPITS. THEY ITCH. PUT PATIENTS TO BED AT ONCE AND KEEP 'EM COVERED UP WARM. THEN GO SCRUB YOURSELF AND WEAR A MASK, WE DON'T KNOW YET HOW YOU CATCH IT. PASS IT ALONG, ED.

——NO NEW LANDINGS REPORTED ANYWHERE ON THIS CONTINENT. THE FEW PARATROOPERS WHO ESCAPED THE ORIGINAL SLAUGHTER ARE THOUGHT TO BE HIDING OUT IN THE POCONOS. SHOOT——BUT BE CAREFUL; IT MIGHT BE TESSIE. OFF AND CLEAR. UNTIL NOON TOMORROW——

The statistical curves were turning up again. There was no longer doubt in Breen's mind about that. It might not even be necessary to stay up here in the Sierra Madres through the winter, though he rather thought they would. It would be silly to be mowed down by the tail of a dying epidemic, or be shot by a nervous vigilante, when a few months' wait would take care of everything.

He was headed out to the hogback to wait for sunset and do an hour's reading. He glanced at his car as he passed it, thinking that he would like to try the radio. He suppressed the yen; two-thirds of his reserve gasoline was gone already just from keeping the battery charged for the radio—and here it was only December. He really ought to cut it down to twice a week. But it meant a lot to catch the noon bulletin of Free America and then twiddle the dial a few minutes to see what else he could pick up.

But for the past three days Free America had not been on the air—solar static maybe, or perhaps just a power failure. But that rumor that President Brandley had been assassinated—it hadn't come from the Free radio and it hadn't been denied by them, either, which was a good sign.

Still, it worried him.

And that other story that lost Atlantis had pushed up during the quake period and that the Azores were now a little continent—almost certainly a hangover of the "silly season"—but it would be nice to hear a followup.

Rather sheepishly, he let his feet carry him to the car. It wasn't fair to listen when Meade wasn't around. He warmed it up, slowly spun the dial, once around and back. Not a peep at full gain; nothing but a terrible amount of static.

Served him right.

He climbed the hogback, sat down on the bench he had dragged up there—their "memorial bench," sacred to the memory of the time Meade had bruised her knees on the gravel—sat down and sighed. His lean belly was stuffed with venison and corn fritters; he lacked only tobacco to make him completely happy.

The evening cloud colors were spectacularly beautiful, and the weather was extremely balmy for December; both, he thought, caused by volcanic dust, with perhaps an assist from atom bombs.

Surprising how fast things went to pieces when they started to skid! And surprising how quickly they were going back together, judging by the signs. A curve reaches through and then starts right back up.

World War III was the shortest big war on record—forty cities gone, counting Moscow and the other slave cities as well as the American ones—and then *whoosh!* neither side fit to fight.

Of course, the fact that both sides had thrown their Sunday punch over the North Pole through the most freakish arctic weather since Peary invented the place had a lot to do with it, he supposed.

It was amazing that any of the Russian paratroop transport had gotten through at all.

Breen sighed and pulled a copy of *The Western Astronomer* out of his pocket. Where was he? Oh, yes, *"Some Notes on the Stability of G-Type Stars with Especial Reference to Sol,"* by Dynkowski, Lenin Institute, translated by Heinrich Ley, F. R. A. S.

Good boy, Ski—sound mathematician. Very clever application of harmonic series and tightly reasoned.

Breen started to thumb for his place when he noticed a footnote that he missed. Dynkowski's own name carried down to it: "This monograph was denounced by *Pravda* as 'romantic reactionaryism' shortly after it was published. Professor Dynkowski has been unreported since and must be presumed to be liquidated."

The poor geek! Well, he probably would have been atomized by now anyway, along with the goons who did him in. He wondered if the army really had gotten all the Russki paratroopers. He had killed his own quota; if he hadn't gotten that doe within a quarter-mile of the cabin and headed right back, Meade would have had a bad time. He had shot them in the back and buried them beyond the woodpile.

He settled down to some solid pleasure. Dynkowski was a treat. Of course, it was old stuff that a G-type star, such as the Sun, was potentially unstable; a G-O star could explode, slide right off the Russell diagram, and end up as a white dwarf. But no one before Dynkowski had defined the exact conditions for such a catastrophe, nor had anyone else devised mathematical means of diagnosing the instability and describing its progress.

He looked up to rest his eyes from the fine print and saw that the Sun was obscured by a thin low cloud—one of those unusual conditions where the filtering effect is just right to permit a man to view the Sun clearly with the naked eye. Probably volcanic dust in the air, he decided, acting almost like smoked glass.

He looked again. Either he had spots before his eyes or that was one fancy big Sunspot. He had heard of being able to see them with the naked eye, but it had never happened to him.

He longed for a telescope.

He blinked. Yep, it was still there, about three o'clock. A *big* spot—no wonder the car radio sounded like a Hitler speech.

He turned back and continued on to the end of the article, being anxious to finish before the light failed.

At first his mood was sheerest intellectual pleasure at the man's tight mathematical reasoning. A three percent imbalance in the solar constant—yes, that was standard stuff; the Sun would nova with that much change. But Dynkowski went further. By means of a novel mathematical operator which he had dubbed "yokes," he bracketed the period in a star's history when this could happen and tied it down with secondary, tertiary, and quaternary yokes, showing exactly the time of highest probability.

Beautiful! Dynkowski even assigned dates to the extreme limit of his primary yoke, as a good statistician should.

But, as Breen went back and reviewed the equations,

his mood changed from intellectual to personal. Dynkowski was not talking about just any G-O star. In the latter part, he meant old Sol himself, Breen's personal Sun—the big boy out there with the oversize freckle on his face.

That was one hell of a big freckle! It was a hole you could chuck Jupiter into and not make a splash. He could see it very clearly now.

Everybody talks about "when the stars grow old and the Sun grows cold," but it's an impersonal concept, like one's own death.

Breen started thinking about it very personally. How long would it take, from the instant the imbalance was triggered until the expanding wave front engulfed Earth? The mechanics couldn't be solved without a calculation, even though they were implicit in the equations in front of him. Half an hour, for a horseback guess, from incitement until the Earth went *phutt!*

It hit him with gentle melancholy. No more? Never again? Colorado on a cool morning . . . the Boston Post Road with autumn wood smoke tanging the air . . . Bucks County bursting with color in the spring. The wet smells of the Fulton Fish Market—no, that was gone already. Coffee at the *Morning Call.* No more wild strawberries on a hillside in Jersey, hot and sweet as lips. Dawn in the South Pacific with the light airs cool velvet under your shirt and never a sound but the chuckling of the water against the sides of the old rust bucket—what was her name? That was a long time ago—the S. S. *Mary Brewster.*

No more Moon if the Earth was gone. Stars, but no one to gaze at them.

He looked back at the dates bracketing Dynkowski's probability yoke.

"Thine alabaster cities gleam, undimmed by—"

He suddenly felt the need for Meade and stood up.

She was coming out to meet him. "Hello, Potty! Safe to come in now—I've finished the dishes."

"I should help."

"You do the man's work; I'll do the woman's work. That's fair." She shaded her eyes. "What a sunset! We ought to have volcanoes blowing their tops every year."

"Sit down and we'll watch it."

She sat beside him.

"Notice the Sunspot? You can see it with your naked eye."

She stared. "Is that a Sunspot? It looks as if somebody had taken a bite out of it."

He squinted his eyes at it again. Damned if it didn't look bigger!

Meade shivered. "I'm chilly. Put your arm around me."

He did so with his free arm, continuing to hold hands with the other.

It *was* bigger. The spot was growing.

What good is the race of man? Monkeys, he thought; monkeys with a touch of poetry in them, cluttering and wasting a second-string planet near a third-string star. But sometimes they finish in style.

She snuggled to him. "Keep me warm."

"It will be warmer soon—I mean I'll keep you warm."

"Dear Potty." She looked up. "Potty, something funny is happening to the sunset."

"No, darling—to the Sun."

He glanced down at the journal, still open beside him. He did not need to add up the two dates and divide by two to reach the answer. Instead, he clutched fiercely at her hand, knowing with an unexpected and overpowering burst of sorrow that this was THE END.